Thomas Keneally

Thomas Keneally began his writing career in 1964 and has published twenty-five novels since. They include *Schindler's Ark*, which won the Booker Prize in 1982 and was subsequently made into the film *Schindler's List*, and *The Chant of Jimmie Blacksmith*, *Confederates* and *Gossip from the Forest*, each of which was shortlisted for the Booker Prize. His most recent novels are *The Office of Innocence*, *The Tyrant's Novel* and *The Widow and Her Hero*. He has also written several works of non-fiction, including his boyhood memoir *Homebush Boy*, *The Commonwealth of Thieves* and *Searching for Schindler*. He is married with two daughters and lives in Sydney.

ALSO BY THOMAS KENEALLY

Fiction

The Place at Whitton
The Fear
Bring Larks and Heroes
Three Cheers for the Paraclete
The Survivor
A Dutiful Daughter
The Chant of Jimmie Blacksmith
Blood Red, Sister Rose
Gossip from the Forest
Season in Purgatory
A Victim of the Aurora
Passenger
Confederates
The Cut-rate Kingdom
Schindler's Ark
A Family Madness
The Playmaker
Towards Asmara
By the Line
Flying Hero Class
Woman of the Inner Sea
Jacko
A River Town
Bettany's Book
The Office of Innocence
The Tyrant's Novel
The Widow and Her Hero

Non-fiction

Outback
The Place Where Souls Are Born
Now and in Time to Be: Ireland and the Irish
Memoirs from a Young Republic
Homebush Boy: A Memoir
The Great Shame
The Commonwealth of Thieves
Searching for Schindler

For Children

Ned Kelly and the City of Bees
Roos in Shoes

The People's Train

THOMAS KENEALLY

SCEPTRE

First published in Australia in 2009 by Vintage
An imprint of Random House Australia Pty Ltd

First published in Great Britain in 2009 by Sceptre
An imprint of Hodder & Stoughton
An Hachette UK company

1

A CIP catalogue record for this title is available from the British Library

Hardback ISBN 978 0 340 95185 9
Trade Paperback ISBN 978 0 340 98054 5

Printed and bound in the UK by CPI Mackays, Chatham ME5 8TD

Hodder & Stoughton policy is to use papers that are natural, renewable and recyclable products and made from wood grown in sustainable forests. The logging and manufacturing processes are expected to conform to the environmental regulations of the country of origin.

Hodder & Stoughton Ltd
338 Euston Road
London NW1 3BH

www.hodder.co.uk

To Judith

Part One

My Exile and Wanderings

By F. A. (Artem) Samsurov

(Late Hero of the Soviet Revolution)

Translated into English from the 2nd Russian edition,

Moscow, Progress Publishing, 1953

1

When I first came to Brisbane in the year 1911, I wrote often to my sister Zhenya Trofimova, as I had not done during my escape or while Suvarov and I were surviving in Shanghai. That I had not written earlier was not due to lack of affection, but to the fact I was so unsettled. But now I felt that for a time I had reached the end of journeying. I dedicate these pages, which were written in exile, to her.

Trofimov, my brother-in-law, was at that stage a Donetz coal miner, a noble soul and a reader, who – although I did not know it at the time – had recently been overcome by gases and dust clouds in the Verkhneye No. 3 mine. When they first opened those workings, the priest came down the shaft with holy water and incantations. But no blessing would prove equal to the unholy atmosphere of the mine.

I move ahead too fast. Exile is my story, not black lung.

I was amazed at first arrival in the city by the fact that even the poor did not eat horsemeat. Yes, they ate rabbits, of which there are too many. Did that mean it was a working man's paradise already, without a revolution? Well . . . the men in the railway camp near Warwick, where I had worked early in my Australian experience, did not think so. The system remained the system. There were men I knew who fed their children a slice of bread and lard four evenings a week. Yet I remembered intelligent Russians who – having never been there – declared that Australia was a working man's paradise. But the reality, even in a new country, was that the old world had been imported there in one lump.

However, this was a good place for a tired old prisoner to rest in the sun and between battles. Brisbane ran up a hill in a bow of river and sat without any fuss under the humid sky. And Russia had come there. I went along to a meeting of the Association of Russian Emigrants on the south side of the river, Stanley Street. There were Russians of all shades there, vague liberals, Mensheviks, disappointed Agrarian Socialists (who once lived with peasants but found them mean and wanting), Revolutionary Socialists, anarchists and Wobblies. And also people who just wanted to take a rest from the tsar. The association was run by decent people, including an engineer, Rybukov. Old Rybukov had begun as a tally-clerk at Cannon Hill meatworks but, though always suffering bad asthma, was a figure of authority now that he had a good job as an engineer in the tramways.

My old friend from Shanghai, big lean A. I. 'Grisha' Suvarov was there, still a beanpole with freckles. Once he had walked two days from a place named Stanthorpe, through the bush to visit me at the railway camp. But now he had a job at the Cannon Hill meatworks and he had boasted he could get me a job too, as he did – lugging carcases of sheep and beef onto ships. The meatworks and the wharves were heavily Russian, apart from the Australians – there must have been two-fifths Russians there. After my sometimes exhausting adventures, I felt I needed to labour hard – the more carcases I hoisted the more my brain revived.

In any case, the trouble with this Association of Russian Emigrants was that, apart from wheezy old Rybukov, they seemed to be on a brain holiday too. They showed no consciousness and were purely social and charitable. They went on nature hikes to Mount Coot-tha and so on. I hated to see an organisation so wasted and wanted to make it into something more useful and active. The usual hikes and chess would be all very creditable if our political minds were engaged as well. But it was not so. As Suvarov said correctly, we needed a

Russian league, one that looked after newcomers better, was not too scared or comfortable to greet them, and was a union of Russian workers as well. We needed a newspaper too, a political one, not a social flimsy. Where we could get Cyrillic type from in this city I just didn't know. But at least Rybukov had got hold of the association's constitution and was writing a new one.

After we'd discussed it, we all turned up – all we recent Russian arrivals – to the association's next meeting. In the extra business, after the old committee had decided on a Russian folk concert at the Buranda Hall – to which Australian trade unionists were to be invited and asked to contribute a silver coin to a Russian famine fund – I rose to move that all places on the committee be declared vacant, and that a new committee be elected that night and immediately present a new constitution to the membership, allowing them an hour to read and approve it. So the new Souz Russkikh Emigrantov came into existence, and I was elected president. I felt invigorated. I was just at the stage again – after my long escape and pilgrimage – to become active.

At the next meeting of the *souz,* I moved that we produce a political and social newspaper every two weeks. The old music teacher, Chernikov, who had been president of the association for ten years, was appalled by the idea of politics.

But we have never had any trouble from the authorities, Chernikov said, his voice trembling. You don't understand, he said. This is not a country for political philosophy.

I could hear Rybukov, in his alpaca suit, wheeze angrily. The climate here is bad for his breathing – it is humid and full of vivid flowering plants. One encounter with a frangipani, with its dolorous, opium-like scent, or a walk under a flowering jacaranda, can threaten Rybukov's health as the cold of Manchuria never did.

Chernikov went on, The police took an interest in us in the past, but when they discovered we were more a social body, they were happy to leave us alone. Look now, I was a *narodnik* when it was very dangerous to be. I knew the men of the Second First of June – we published a paper together. So it's not as if I haven't done my bit.

Rybukov kept wheezing angrily. I suppose you were hanged, he suggested. With Generalov and Ulyanov.

These were the names of men who had tried to kill Tsar Alexander.

It was important to soothe people who agreed with Chernikov, since we needed their support too. I was willing to edit the news-sheet, to get it printed and published, and put my name to it. I wanted a good relationship with the government too, but that does not mean we could not discuss ideas. We could give the paper a pleasant, unprovocative name. I suggested *Ekho Avstralii*. The old committee were half-consoled by that name.

As for setting the type, there was a Russian compositor who worked for a Polish printing company in Ernest Street. The owner already printed invitations to the union's (formerly association's) events. I said I would employ the compositor – I hoped on a voluntary basis. I would find a printing press – in the hope of having the sum needed to pay for it voted by the committee – and I would do the printing, distributing and posting of the thing.

And the enthusiasm of Rubinov, the tramways man, and of my friend Suvarov, a fellow member of the Australian Workers Union, clinched it. Both offered to contribute articles, as I knew they were dying to do. The motion was carried with excitement by the young men on the floor, and a frown from old Chernikov and his mates. It was further moved that some articles should be in Russian and some – social events, job advice for émigrés, that sort of thing – in English.

They have a saying at the abattoirs that busy people race around like blue-arsed flies. I was a blue-arsed fly in the next two weeks. It might have been easier to give ourselves a few months to get the first edition out, but that would have driven me mad with a sense that this great sunny place was howling for voices and I was not providing them.

I ran into problems. The Polish printer in Ernest Street was not an internationalist and told me he had no Cyrillic script and had come to Australia to get away from Cossacks and Russians. And the Russian alphabet, it seemed. Then I discovered that to begin a newspaper in Queensland you had to deposit a five-hundred-pound bond with the attorney-general of the state. So much for the freedom of the press in the sunny workers' paradise of Australia! I had received from my membership a budget of one hundred and fifty pounds and did not intend to go back to them for more. Besides, with five hundred pounds, we could do so much for the cane-cutters who came to Brisbane for Christmas, or we could create a Russian library.

I sent away to Melbourne for Cyrillic script and I was allowed to rent an old, stand-up, Boston-style hand-operated printing press for ten shillings a week from the People's Printery (the printery used by the Trades and Labour Hall). Our rented press and its printing frames had been rendered obsolete by newer, automatic machines, but when Suvarov and I and a few others dismantled ours in the lane behind the People's Printery, loaded it onto a dray and took it to the Stefanovs', where I'd rented a room for the press, I felt the old subversive exhilaration. I wanted our first edition of *Ekho* to be out by the time the Russian workers came in from the bush for the Russian Christmas, which came twelve days after the Western one, on 7 January.

It was pleasant to have a reason to write again. It was pleasant to ask my friends for material. My lanky friend Suvarov was self-taught but a genuine thinker. He had already written a piece on the shortcomings and sentimentalities of agrarian socialism, which saw the peasant commune, despite all its narrow-mindedness, cheating, lust for land and money-lending, as the structure out of which a revolution could be made. Suvarov and I, being peasants, we knew how crazy the whole thing was – as bad as Tolstoy's idea that by wearing a smock and helping bring in the harvest he was chasing more than a sentimental fantasy. Rybukov was in fact translating Suvarov's piece into English for the weekly *Brisbane Worker*, but now I wished to set it in Russian.

Altogether, our little group of comrades would make some noise in the great Australian torpor.

2

It did not take much attendance at Australian Workers Union meetings and general events at Trades Hall for my friend Suvarov to sense there was a strike coming, and that it would grow out of the Queensland Tramways depot. Although the strike would look only to improvements in the always hard-up life of workers who would utter grievances about wages, health and compensation for injury, it was to be welcomed just the same. Every strike was an education and got us closer to the day when the great truth would break on the workers, and they'd no longer ask for crumbs but for the whole table. The more strikes, the more of an education in the futility and pain of wringing from bosses the right to wear a badge, the right to better hours and overtime pay. But this one was to be an education for Suvarov and me too, in how things worked in Queensland.

One of the triggers of this strike was a fellow named Joseph Freeman Bender, manager of the Brisbane Tramways, which belonged in turn to the great General Electric company of the United States. Mr Bender grew up in industrial Pittsburgh and had no time for unions, and had told the *Brisbane Telegraph* so. He was determined to keep union members out of his tramway sheds. Rybukov, who worked on a special project of some kind in Bender's engineering department, said at dinner at Adler's one night that he would come out with the strikers and to hell with Bender. That night his coughing woke us like artillery.

Kelly, our hulking, red-headed friend from the Australian Labour Federation, went to talk to Mr Bender about peaceably unionising the sheds, but the chat became bitter, and Bender told Kelly that in Pittsburgh men like him were regularly and properly shot dead by the forces of good order – that trainloads of troopers and Pinkerton men were brought in to do that job. I wish you a happy birthday too, said Kelly.

A nice man, Mr Bender, said Kelly ultimately; a credit to American civilisation and, of course, a good Freemason, but purely for business reasons.

In Russia the intelligentsia used the lodges to plot an end to the tsarist system, but overthrowing monarchs was not on Bender's slate.

I said to Kelly, He speaks of arms. We should have arms too!

Kelly threw up his hands. You've got to be kidding, Tom!

Kelly is a genial man who grew up in poverty, son of a waterside worker. He likes to drink, and he and his executive, called 'the Reds' by the respectable papers who have never seen a real Red, do half their organisational work and stumble on their best ideas at the Trades Hall Hotel.

I told him just a little – only a little – about Kharkov back in late 1905, the siege of the engineering workshop. The shelling and so on.

That could never happen here, he said. Though . . . some years back the squatters talked of Nordenfeldt guns to be used on shearers . . . No, that couldn't happen now. And anyhow, you didn't win the fight back there, where you came from. Did you?

Not yet, I told him. But it was a war. The Cossacks had the best of carbines and cannons and their horses to trample people. Are the Queensland police any less in power?

I told him that on the way home each day I passed the barracks in Roma Street where officers harangued the militia boys. One day an officer was caning a boy in front of the others. It looked pretty much like a tsarist situation to me, I said.

Chocos, he said.

I beg your pardon?

Chocolate soldiers, Tom. Chocolate officers like to throw their weight around.

I suggested that at the very least we could post armed workers on the upper floors or roofs of buildings to protect fleeing strikers if the police charged a march.

You're having me on, said Kelly. Look, we just don't do that sort of stuff here.

What about this Eureka Stockade of yours?

It was a different situation. That's sixty years back. Look, we'll do okay here with moral force. But for God's sake don't mention guns. The police will go crazy. Bloody hell!

The second figure of the triangle at one of whose points Mr Bender sat was the premier of the state, Digby Denham, another union-hater who might fall to Thomas Joseph Ryan at the next election, and the third was Police Commissioner Urquhart, who had killed hundreds of natives in the north of the state at a place named Kaldoon and was so proud of it that he left the bones as a public lesson. He would now have liked to make a similar set of marvels with the bones of militants.

At the Trades Hall Hotel, one of Kelly's men would always say, Thought you bloody Russians could drink, as they held their icy schooners and I stood with my seven-ounce glass of lemonade, which I barely sipped because it was too sugared, in the British manner. Didn't think you were a bloody wowser, Tom.

They would tell stories about Mr Joseph Freeman Bender, who was admired for extending the tracks out to Toowong. It wasn't an accident that they ran by his fine house, Endrim, in Woodstock Road. But then he did not deign to travel to his office in ordinary trams with the common people. He possessed his own personal tram, named 'the Palace', which picked him up in the mornings on the way through Auchenflower to town, and then collected sundry cronies, business giants, lawyers, Supreme Court judges and even politicians. Even when empty, the Palace ran back and forth to his home every ten to fifteen minutes during the day, and every twenty minutes during the evening. The Palace was fitted with a bar and a piano and armchairs and sofas.

One of Kelly's so-called Reds said, I'd like to see what a plug of dynamite might do to this palace on wheels. Let's see how that works one bloody morning when Digby Denham's chatting away on the sofa with Chief Justice bloody Cooper.

Justice Cooper was quick to charge trade unionists with contempt, and Kelly himself had served a month in Boggo Road jail for the sake of the dignity of Mr Cooper's court.

It was clear from the amount of time given to the subject of Mr Bender and his friends in the saloon bar of the Trades Hall Hotel that Kelly and the Trades Hall apparatus would dearly love to attack capital by way of the managing director of Brisbane Tramways.

Despite the heat in that end-of-year period, we would stage a series of lectures too. I would lecture on Marxist theory, my friend Grisha Suvarov on the strike he organised in Vyborg in 1907, and Professor Klushin on the war of 1905. An American Russian named Beladov would speak on American anarcho-syndicalism – otherwise known as the Wobblies. So when they came to town, an intellectual feast awaited our brothers from the Ipswich railways sheds, the Darling Downs camps, the dairy farms of the coast north of Brisbane, and the cane fields of Rockhampton.

Kelly, in the meantime, proved no respecter of religious festivals. We had affiliated the Russian Emigrants Union with Trades Hall, and now Kelly called a meeting there on the night of western Christmas, the Australians following the Gregorian calendar as in their northern European places of origin. Not that there had been much ceremony in our boarding house, except that organised by our two Polish boarders. Little Mrs Adler was Jewish and the rest of us were saving our celebrations and strong liquors for 7 January. In fact, this sweltering Christmas-night meeting was tactically brilliant of Kelly, for the next day's newspapers would have room only for cricket and horse races.

3

That night I arrived early to the Trades Hall, a fine sturdy stone building. Many of my fellow Adler house residents were with me, as was the engineer Rybukov, who had moved by now to his own house in Roma Street. You wouldn't have guessed my friends and I were refugees from northern winters. Each of us brought his own climate of sodden tropic air in with him, our own musk of very Australian sweat.

I found Kelly at the back of the hall, wearing a dented homburg, and congratulated him on his stratagem.

Yes, he said, and there won't be one of them here who isn't a bit fired up. The shortcomings of their Christmas tables, eh? And the threadbare presents they were forced to give to kids. They'll be ready for a big step, all right. And with any luck, two-thirds of them will be pissed!

Then he told me the Trades Hall pub was letting anyone with a union badge in the back door. He'd squared it with his cousin, who was a cop in the licensing division.

You'll speak from the floor tonight, won't you, Tom? he asked me.

In my bad English?

But the idea excited me, and I agreed.

The world over, there is nothing quite like men and women

suffused with the same fraternal discontent filling a hall. Fifteen minutes before the meeting was to begin, men furrowed by labour and women aged too early by harsh tasks were looking for spaces around the wall, the men concentrating earnestly on rolling their own reed-thin cigarettes. And yet it was often a false exhilaration that hung over such events, I knew. Besides, the old question remained: did these men and women want a new world, or would an extra ten shillings in their pay packet settle all their discontents? I thought I already knew the answer to that one.

As president of the Russian Emigrants Union, I had a seat in the second row. The women in the room were a minority but I found myself seated next to two of them, an older woman and a younger who might have been her daughter. Looking at their British countenances, I felt a stab of insignificance. How could I influence a meeting with poor English and when allocated a seat in the second row? A man from the Waterside Workers, Billy Foster of the Tramways Union, Burkitt of the Seaman's Union, Pongrass of the Australian Workers Union with all its shearers and farmhands, and Ryan, the man who desired to become premier – they had the front-row seats and sat secure with their ideas and their control of language.

The two women to my right were engaged in lively conversation with each other. They seemed to think themselves in no way inferior to the executive of the Australian Workers Union or to any other potentates. The older woman, beside me, was grey-haired, quite aged in fact, but she talked with a lot of animation. Her enthusiasm was unblunted by years. The younger woman beyond her was brown-haired beneath her straw bonnet and looked untouched by the heat in white blouse, floral jacket and lemon skirt. The older woman's hair was tightly bunched, and her little hat was tethered with hatpins, but the younger's brown hair fell free. She was animated too. Even sitting she looked tall, with a broad, full-lipped face. She could have been a St Petersburg intellectual – she had that look of having been refined by thought. But she also seemed mature, un-maidenly. No coy pretension to her. Such are the glories that lie on the north bank of the Brisbane River, I thought, in Auchenflower or Kelvin Grove!

There was so much chatter in the hall, and they seemed to tolerate that beery, cheap-tobacco air so well, that I felt confident enough to speak to these women, and, when there was a lull in their conversation, turned to the older one.

Excuse me, madam, I said. May I introduce myself? I am Artem – Tom – Samsurov of the Russian Emigrants Union.

She said in a reedy voice that she was very pleased to meet me. Her name was Mrs Amelia something or other – it was only later that I learned her surname was spelled *Pethick*. I am present here, said this small elderly lady, as president of the Typists and Secretarial Services Union.

I had not heard of such an entity.

I believed, she went on to explain, that young women were not properly protected by the Clerks' Union. We are a group who have special problems of working conditions and dignity. I hope you are more understanding than some of our Australian brothers, Mr Samsurov.

I said I hoped I was too. Perhaps I said it a little loudly, in the silly hope that the woman on the other side of Mrs Pethick would hear.

And the young lady here, I said. She is your lieutenant?

Amelia Pethick laughed very pleasantly.

Oh no! This young woman is nobody's lieutenant, Mr Samsurov.

For the first time the brown-haired one took notice of me. She half-smiled in a puzzled way, not having heard the beginning of my conversation with Mrs Pethick.

Mrs Mockridge, said the little old woman, would you care to meet Mr Tom or Artem Samsurov of the Russians? Mr Samsurov, this is Mrs Hope Mockridge.

The long-faced, brown-haired young woman smiled broadly. She was very beautiful in a classic way.

How interesting, she said. What brought you Russians here? The tsar I know about, and his cruel secret police. And Cossacks and all the rest of it.

I grinned back. Cossacks and gendarmes and the Okhrana had something to do with it, I admitted.

Okhrana?

The tsar's secret police, I explained.

You obviously escaped Stolypin's necktie, Mr Samsurov? Hope Mockridge observed, waving a large straw hat she held on her knee.

I wished to tell them the reason I had not worn that infamous tsarist minister's noose or necktie was because I had been in prison when Stolypin was at his work. But how could I say so to people I had just met, in a crowded hall a world away? What did they know of the Nikolayevski, and what did they know of Siberia? So I chose to laugh.

Hope Mockridge said, That was a mad question, wasn't it? None of my business. But how interesting that there are Russians in Brisbane! And in the cane fields too, I hear.

Yes, I told her. There are nearly five hundred of us.

One question I can ask without seeming stupid, she said. Did you come to us by way of Western Europe or the East?

By Shanghai, I told her.

That is amazing, she said seriously. I've never been to Shanghai, I'm sad to say. Really fascinating.

An eager girl with a pinched face appeared at the end of our row and called to Hope Mockridge, who got up and went to embrace her. The old woman, Amelia Pethick, told me, Hope is fascinated by the Russians. Can't speak a word of the language, of course. Neither can I. But . . . well, I think the whole world pities you for your tsar.

But may I ask you, what is Mrs Mockridge's reason for being here?

She needs no reason, Mr Tom. She is a lawyer and works with the attorney-general's department, but sometimes represents us all by special leave. She is a good friend to many of us and gives her advice to Trades Hall for free.

Mrs Hope Mockridge finished her discussion with the pinched-face girl at the end of the row and returned to us. In the word of the priests: Alleluia! She took up our conversation by asking me whether I thought the foreign concessions in Shanghai should be got rid of. I told her I hoped the concessions wouldn't vanish just yet, because there were good boarding houses for émigrés in Little Vienna, among the Austrian Jews, and in some parts of the French quarter – havens for fleeing enemies of the tsar. The Chinese would throw off the imperial powers in the end, I said.

Most union people in Australia don't have much time for the Chinese, she confided. They fear them for their cheap labour – likely to undercut wages, you see. And their opium, of course.

Now the speeches started. Kelly called on various union leaders to speak, and plump T. J. Ryan, in a good suit and with the chicken fat of Christmas on his handsome jowls, spoke as a Labor Party man, promising the normal improvements. For a start, his favourite promise about meat. The working man cannot afford to feed his children meat! he said. This in Australia, where meat is abundant! But the pastoralists (the big landowners were always referred to by this term, *pastoralists*) kept the price of meat artificially high. Not only would a Labor government support unionism in the workplace, but the new state meat shops . . .

An overwhelming number in the hall were enthusiastic about this promise.

The local Wobblies man – in the English-speaking world they called the International Workers of the World *Wobblies* – spoke now. He was thin and sour, and hoped that the Australian workers as a whole could embrace the benefit of the one great union yet unformed. The problem – the bosses' rejection and punishment of unionism from the tramways to the waterfront to the cane fields of the north to the furthest railway siding of the west – could be solved by solidarity, fraternity and the experience of all unions not only acting as one but becoming one. Then, there would be no need of any government. Mr Ryan made us offers, said the Wobbly, and bid on the health of our children, as if we have a stake in the society and as if governments could deliver us the paradise. But we don't need him, we can take what is ours. Ryan, he said, reminded him of the old ditty:

I've read my Bible ten times through,
And Jesus justifies me,

The man who does not vote for me,
By Christ, he crucifies me.

The Wobblies in the audience took up the refrain, singing:

So bump me into parliament,
Bounce me any way,
Bang me into parliament
The next election day!

They finished with hoots, followed by cheers and a great deal of clapping, and Mrs Amelia Pethick and Mrs Hope Mockridge laughed indulgently.

I had no idea the Wobblies were so strong up here, said Mrs Pethick.

Billy Foster of the Tramways addressed a more practical issue when he got up. Would the big guns, he asked – the Australian Workers Union, the Australian Labour Federation – would they support his men if they wore their union badges to work at Bender's depots?

The crowd was willing to speak for all. There were lusty cries of Yes, yes!

The brush-headed Irish leader of the Railways Union spoke. As an old railway man myself, I paid attention. He was willing to close down the railways from Ingham in the north to Toowoomba in the west. The Waterside Workers man spoke and promised he would close down the wharves, and Pongrass of the Australian Workers Union promised everything from closing down shearing to leaving the bourgeoisie without beer and bread.

Soon after, Kelly got up and held out his hands to quiet the audience. We have here tonight, he told them, a man who has had experience of general strikes more recent than the last one here. He has been involved in leading them in Russia against the barbarous tsarist regime. Tom Samsurov of the Waterside Workers and the Russian Emigrants Union is here in the hall. Tom, come up here and advise us on the practicalities.

I admit I do not flee a rostrum – even one from which I need to speak in a foreign tongue – from the vanity of believing I have something to tell people. My experience was first of all of a populace that had armed itself against Cossacks, as the workers in Kharkov did in the early winter of 1905, when the Japanese were finishing off humiliating our army and navy. The populace armed themselves? Not quite. There was a particular party financer, a skilful party bullion raider and bank robber, who made it possible for us to buy rifles from corrupt sergeants in weapons depots and so arm our people.

As I stood up I could feel the keen attention of Mrs Hope Mockridge – Mrs Pethick had said Russia fascinated her, but I had a suspicion her interest came more from Russian novels than from Marx, that to her I was a Russian gentleman out of a Turgenev novel, instead of the literate Gorki-style peasant I was. Yet as Kelly continued to gesture me to the platform, my thoughts about Mrs Mockridge's interest remained unworthy and stupid but powerful. I faced the steamy, smoky air, and the furrowed but fresh faces of hope.

Facing a foreign crowd you get a sense of how shaky your grasp of their language is. I had had that experience trying to speak in French in the Russian School in Paris. You could persuade a mirror you were eloquent. A crowd was a different matter. I said, I ask your pardon for my English so bad. They laughed, and some whistled. If your leadership find, I continued, that you wish to support a general strike, then we must all be solid, like one hand.

I made a fist.

We must look for and after each other like brothers and sisters. And how is that done? We must have a strike committee over all. Our strike committee must be our government for the time being. We must look to it for everything we expect – it must deliver us bread, medicine, arms and money-support.

I deliberately mentioned arms but quickly glossed over it. I don't think most of them heard me. It had also occurred to me that, in spite of what I'd said to Kelly in the pub, if we marched, the Queensland police, heavy-handed as they might be, probably did not have quite the same habit of charging into marchers with carbines and sabres as the Cossacks did, and certainly didn't have artillery.

And we must have a strike newspaper, I went on, to inform our members which businesses are with us, and which will supply the strikers with food and other goods. The unions must also spend money on helping the strikers and their families. Now, not all such strikes work in the near future. Some do, but they have not worked fully yet for my native country. But over a long run they have a powerful effect and bring closer the day when the workers will decide their own wages, in justice, and not as a favour from capital. Then we would have more justice than 'a few bob rise', 'a few more bob in the kick'.

At least that was what I intended to say, and I hope it came out more or less accurately. My talk about *the day when the workers will decide their own wages* wasn't quite in accord with Kelly's ideas, but in a room so full of goodwill and yearning, people will cheer anything that sounds approximately right to them.

I descended to sit beside Mrs Pethick. She took my wrist with her lace-gloved little hand.

Wonderful. You spoke about total overthrow as my late husband used to. None of these Kellys and Ryans do that.

Billy Foster then renewed his question. If Bender sacked men for wearing Tramways Union badges, were we sure we would stick with these men and support them in spirit and with any resources of cash and food we could get together? Again, a fury of yelling from the hall.

And let us not forget, he said, the wise advice of our Russian brother. We must be like one fist.

Again there seemed to be universal support for this, from the Wobblies, who liked the word one – one big union that ruled the earth from pole to pole – and from the sculpted smile of Mrs Hope Mockridge. But Brisbane had not had a general strike for twenty years. It was one thing to sign on to occupy foreign ground, but being on it was another thing again. As always on hearing these proposals of action, men and women thought they were listening to glad tidings of the achievement of earthly paradise.

I could have told them of Kharkov and the railway and textile and engineering workers I talked to in those days, six years back. All remembered the great drought and famine of their childhoods, and their mothers baking the bitter famine bread of rye husks and bark, nettles and moss. Some of them even mentioned it in speeches from the floor. The joined fervour they felt, hearing what had begun happening that summer in Moscow and St Petersburg, and therefore what could yet happen in Kharkov, redeemed those bitter half-toxic crumbs they'd eaten in childhood and made them meaningful or even holy. But what they were hearing from our committee were proposals not only of justice but of woe and weeping. For in the meantime, rabbles of Black Hundreds, mobs armed by the gendarmes (as – with our love for all things French – we called the police), went around the streets looking to murder unionists like them, along with Jews, students and anyone with ideas like ours.

Ah well, back to Brisbane. After I had said good evening to Mrs Pethick and Mrs Mockridge, I joined the members of our *souz* outside and, not being a drinking man, walked home with Suvarov, who was occasionally a drinker but had gin and vodka waiting for him at Adler's.

Well, Artem, he said to me, twisting his long reddish features in that peculiar long-lipped smile of his, one does what one can in a distant place.

4

In early January, as planned on Christmas night, Billy Foster's Tramways members turned up for work at the depots wearing their union badges and, on the orders of Joseph Freeman Bender, they were immediately dismissed. The sacked men then marched to Brisbane Trades Hall, the House of Kelly as some called it. The word went round the meatworks and wharves, where I was lugging carcases from the meatworks to the refrigerated holds of ships. We immediately stopped work and walked into town. A tremendous number of men and women had turned up to be addressed by Kelly in his sweat-stained homburg.

Kelly suggested that the meeting pass a motion to empower the leadership of unions to attend the city offices of Joseph Freeman Bender and protest the dismissals face to face. The motion was pushed into the heavens by a roar of affirmation. If you think that in talking like that I retain a certain cynicism, it was out of the suspicion that I needed to save some of my breath for the ultimate, coming porridge, the true overthrow which would occur in some indefinite future.

When Kelly read out the forty-three names of the delegation to confront Mr Bender, mine was among the others. So, I noticed, was Hope Mockridge's, and towards the bottom of the list, close to where my own name lay, was that of the ancient, sturdy Amelia Pethick.

It had been announced in the press, in a notice paid for by Mrs Hope Mockridge, that this union delegation intended to seek a meeting with Mr Bender, and so he could now hardly back out, with the half of the city he usually spoke to telling him to put the delegation in its place, and the half he never spoke to telling him to give way.

The next afternoon there were press photographers ready to take pictures as we assembled in front of the marble gates of the offices of Brisbane Tramways in Adelaide Street. On the pavement with Kelly was a well-dressed couple, the man wiry-haired and studious-looking, the woman pale and slightly freckled under a large straw hat and a parasol, her long neck extended as if she was sniffing peril. She had a pencil in her hand and a notebook, which she kept writing in.

Kelly introduced me. Warwick O'Sullivan, president of the Australian Socialist Party, and his frowning wife, Olive.

Tom is what they call a Bolshevik. You ought to listen to these Russians. They've got more brands of socialism than a lolly shop.

Would you mind spelling your name, sir? asked Olive O'Sullivan.

I did so, and she wrote it in her notebook.

No, she said, apart from *Tom Samsurov*, could you spell your Russian name?

I did so. A-r-t-e-m – but pronounced *Artyom*, I explained. She made a note of it.

They reckon in Melbourne, said O'Sullivan, that Brisbane is the Zurich of the Southern Hemisphere. All the best socialists are here because the state is so backward. *Vide* Russia!

The O'Sullivans had come up from Melbourne to observe the corroboree, Kelly said. Warwick O'Sullivan wrung my hand with a warmth that remained in my memory of him. He said something very few Australians ever said.

I've read about you fellows. So which faction do you belong to?

Bolsheviki, I told him. A group inside the Social Democratic Party. Since 1903, that is.

Yes, said O'Sullivan. I was reading the great Julius Martov though. *The Lesson of the Events in Russia*. He doesn't like your group, does he?

A man from Melbourne who read Martov? This was something.

He belongs to the other faction, I explained. In their way, the differences are very wide.

Well you know, I think they're right, those people, O'Sullivan confessed. Being a social improver won't bring the socialist state in the end. I mean, as Olive says, we can work through the unions, but only to bring about the solidarity that will bring the whole rotten edifice down.

And it must come down, Olive murmured, making a note. Her accent was less raw than O'Sullivan's, and I thought theirs might be the sort of alliance often seen among radicals the world over, between a self-educated worker and some lawyer's or doctor's carefully reared daughter.

At Kelly's signal we moved inside the Brisbane Tramways building. It had a lift, but we took the stairs to the third floor so that our solidarity wasn't broken up into little groups. As a creaky gentleman, I stayed behind to help Amelia of the Typists and Secretarial Services Union.

Are you sure you don't want to take the lift? I asked her.

Not at all, said Amelia, with a tight smile. I am my association militant, and so I must take the stairs like the others!

On the third floor the leaders of our brethren found the main office door locked. It was a deliberate humiliation, to keep us there, the sweat from our stair-climbing going dry on us. Kelly knocked a number of times and called to whoever was inside that we had an appointment with Mr Bender.

That brought no response. We're not going away, Mr Bender, cried Kelly, and don't forget the gentlemen of the press are observing this.

Still nothing happened. Hope Mockridge in a brown jacket and a hat with flowers stepped up and began hammering on the door.

This is Hope, Freeman, you idiotic man! If you don't open this door at once, we'll begin singing and we won't go away and you'll look like a coward.

She listened for movement. Then she turned to the rest of us.

Very well, she said. Now, like a churchwoman leading a hymn, she began with 'Workers of the World, Awaken!' She sang in a fine contralto, joined more roughly by the rest of us. It was an International Workers of the World song, a song of the Wobblies. But I wasn't going to argue the difference between the sentiments of syndicalists like them and Marxists like me that afternoon.

Workers of the world, awaken!
Break your chains, demand your rights.
All the wealth you make is taken
By exploiting parasites.
Shall you kneel in deep submission
From your cradles to your graves?

We were really belting it out. Kelly the Irish tenor, O'Sullivan the baritone, Hope Mockridge the contralto, and many of the others stuck creakily between registers.

Is the height of your ambition
To be good and willing slaves?
Arise, ye prisoners of starvation!
Fight for your emancipation;
Arise, ye slaves of every nation.
In one union grand!
Our little ones for bread are crying . . .

And now the door opened. There was a woman of about thirty-five standing there, flushed in the face.

I'm sorry, miss, said Hope Mockridge. They always send the workers out against the workers.

The delegation on the stairs laughed.

The woman said, Could you all come into the waiting room, please? Mr Bender will be with you in a second.

We crowded in, and the flushed woman returned to her seat behind a desk and buried her head in a journal. Beyond frosted glass beside her desk we could hear the chatter of typewriters. A door from the inner office opened and there, without intermediaries or lieutenants, was Mr Bender. He was a tall man, and he did not look happy. Immediately Hope Mockridge spoke to him.

What game are you up to, Freeman? This won't do you any good.

I wouldn't have expected to see you here, Mrs Mockridge. With the rabble.

No one could laugh as quickly as Mrs Mockridge if she wanted to.

With the *rabble*? she asked. Oh, you were always a master of the language.

Why are you a traitor to your kind? asked Bender, angry and stupid enough to concentrate his chagrin on this one vocal woman. What does your husband think of this?

I didn't ask him. But you're quite right – class traitor I am! But, Freeman, surely you are here to deal with our forty-three union representatives. Shall we leave *my* chastising to private moments?

And who should I speak to? asked Mr Bender.

Kelly said, I'm here. Charlie Kelly. The Trades and Labour Council.

Bender turned his gaze on Kelly as if he had not known of his existence until now. Clearly he saw Kelly not as the spokesman for the desires and aspirations of workers, but as some sort of accidental opportunist who had found himself a niche. Both readings were correct in a sense, but Bender faced nothing but defeat playing according to the second of these versions.

Kelly exhorted him to accept unionism and union representation within his depots and workshops. A unionised worker was a happier worker, he said. A happy worker was a productive worker. The entire unionised workforce of Queensland, said Kelly, wanted the tramway unionised as well and brought into the twentieth century, and the unions of Queensland would bring on a general strike if Mr Bender did not permit it. Mr Bender's own business associates would not be happy at such a prospect.

It was gratifying to me as a jumped-up peasant and railway worker to discover that management are as uniformly foolish as we would like to depict them – just as owned by their narrow interest as the poor are by their hunger.

Mr Bender said, I am on record as being opposed to unionism on principle. And on principle, I will not let it operate within my workshops and depots.

Without unionism, Kelly asked, how are your men to ask for better conditions?

Man to man, said Mr Bender. Face to face.

You mean slave to master, Mr Bender?

You paint the picture any way you like.

Some men groaned. Amelia Pethick had recovered her breath and found her voice. She called in a fluting manner, Your relationship to your workers is too unequal, Mr Bender. It's a machine against flesh. You know that.

More slumming ladies, Mrs Pethick, said Bender.

It was a further mistake of his to attack an old favourite of the crowd's.

Shame, Freeman, shame! said the tigress Hope Mockridge.

Kelly remained sturdy amid all this. Despised by Bender but not taking a backward step.

So you are sure you want this, Mr Bender? he asked.

You will find, said Bender, that the premier of this splendid state is already swearing in special constables to deal with your scum. Do you know why I oppose unions? Do you really want to know? I'll tell you. Because they strangle new creation, that's why. I have in my employ an engineer who has devised a wonder of the age, a single-line train he calls a monorail. This is happening here, in Brisbane – yes, in dreamy old Brisbane. This tram or train or whatever you call it runs on a single rail!

I thought, That engineer is Rybukov.

How am I, asked Bender, full of just rage, to find the funds to build such a system, the first in the world, if I am to be bled white by unions? I won't find them, and the world will be the poorer. *You* will be the poorer. I ask you to desist and back off and respect the spirit of invention.

You can have both, you bastard, one of our delegates called. Pull something out of your own bloody pocket to build your own fucking railway.

Please, leave my office, Bender cried out, or I shall call the police.

Then, said Kelly, it's on for young and old.

Let it be, said Bender.

We filed out again, my role among the revolutionaries of Queensland being to help Mrs Pethick back down the steps. I felt I had known that strong old woman a long time. But forthright Mrs Mockridge seemed a more remote figure than that.

5

We all marched back to Trades Hall and were put to work on the same huge floor. Hope Mockridge worked frantically, speaking to businesses on the telephone, persuading them to give discounts to union members, and calling journalists she knew on the *Brisbane Telegraph*, all of them secretly sympathetic but wary for the sake of their jobs. Mrs Pethick clattered out letters of great length with an ease that spoke well of her ageing knuckles. She had brought some of her union girls in to do work for us.

Suvarov and I took a job no one else seemed to want. From the crowd of strikers milling outside, Rybukov, Suvarov and I recruited three hundred solid men to supervise the marches and keep order when the strike began. I called on men I knew from the railway workshops, from the meatworks, and men from the tramways who were friends of Rybukov – who seemed, for an ailing man, to know every muscular fellow in the state of Queensland. These marshals were to keep order – Kelly was big on that – but also to be a vanguard, and if necessary to protect their fellows from police batons and from arrest.

My and Suvarov's three hundred constables, once I'd got them together, were suddenly not really mine or Suvarov's to command – I worked hand in hand with a compact, wiry, and apparently nervous fellow named Riley, an official of the Clerks' Union who had previously been a sergeant of the Queensland police. Kelly gave the final control to him because Australians did not like to take orders from anyone too foreign. I did not mind so much, since Riley consulted me on everything. Riley was emphatic that our constables were to prevent looting and disorder, because that's what the press and the government would like to see. But he and I were still arguing the matter of what they should do if directly attacked by mounted police. It was difficult to form a phalanx against horses and swinging clubs.

Should we put our marshals on horseback? I asked.

Where would we get that many mounts from? asked Riley, making the point that if we gathered the sort of back paddock horse some workers had for the kids to ride to school, in a crush and a panic they could do as much harm to the strikers as the police might.

As I gathered the list of marshals together the idea came to me of asking my two comrades, Pethick and Mockridge, to join me at the Samarkand Café in Merrivale Street for Russian tea. They were curious about Russia, and I had a warm regard for both of them. (I admit I found Hope Mockridge enchanting in a way normal to a man, a way it was best to own up to rather than permit to turn morbid.)

I approached Amelia Pethick and issued my invitation. Amelia smiled and said she would be dependent on Hope for escort but that she would be very interested to taste authentic Russian tea. I then chased down the frenetic Hope Mockridge, who was visiting Trades Hall during her lunch break from her other role as a lawyer in the attorney-general's office. She stopped work, and she stopped frowning too, and said yes, she would be pleased to accompany Mrs Pethick. We were now forswearing the trams, but she was sure she could get one of the men who were lending their services as drivers to take them over to South Brisbane.

On the day, I finished my day's work on the docks and washed myself at the pump at Mrs Adler's back garden and hurried to the

Samarkand to await the arrival of the two women. The owners of the teashop were half-Russian, half-Tartar and came from the city after which the teahouse was named. I chatted to the husband and wife as the daughter made sweet cakes in the kitchen out the back, occasionally coming out to join in the conversation herself. A number of the older members of the Russian Emigrants Union, not all of them admirers of mine, were already ensconced at tables reading year-old Russian newspapers. I went to my own table with a Sydney paper that had been shipped up the coast, and read a dreary piece on land taxes. My hands, unaware that I was supposed to be a grown revolutionary, were sweaty enough to pick up ink stains from the newsprint.

When the door opened, Hope Mockridge entered on her own. She was the type of political woman I had seen before and had an attraction to – elegant without having to concentrate on it, or without it having to be the point. Such women frowned greatly but always had a solid income behind them. Mrs Mockridge held her purse in front of her, as to shield herself from Russian strangeness in the middle of South Brisbane, but she also carried the half-smile of a child who expected to have wonders revealed to her.

The old committee members of the *souz* watched like stunned fish, mouths agape, as she passed. She was an exotic bird in the Samarkand Café. They closed their mouths and bent to hiss at each other. As if I had put their beloved old association in further peril still by inviting Australians to tea.

Is Mrs Pethick coming separately? I asked her.

She sends her sincerest apologies, Mrs Mockridge told me. She is exhausted by her work. But she said she would be grateful to be asked in the future.

I moved a chair out to seat Mrs Mockridge.

I understand, I told her.

She also said that she didn't think I needed a chaperone. Do I, Mr Samsurov?

I guarantee your safety, madam. I sat down.

She looked me in the eye. That is a guarantee I trust, she said.

Kelly would never forgive me if I did anything to destroy your faith in the working class, I said.

Dear God, she said. At the end all you care about is the opinion of other men. You are a man of your own mind, aren't you?

I told her I wouldn't give myself such high praise.

Are you married, Tom? she asked. In Russia?

I told her no. I have not had the time, I said. But you are married, Mrs Mockridge.

My husband is a very distinguished lawyer, she said, with a trace of mockery. He is . . . he's not well. Certainly not all the time.

I had already spoken to Kelly about this, and knew that her husband was what they called a silk, a King's Counsel, but that he was a dipsomaniac who had been – until a recent reform – advanced enough in that disease that people had begun to avoid using him, even though his position in society was still very high, the Mockridges being one of those old pastoralist families of Queensland whose mental habits and view of the world might not have been so far from that of Russian nobles.

On the subject of marriage, I asked Hope Mockridge, have you seen the O'Sullivans? They are such a devoted couple.

In fact, they reminded me of my old friends and mentors Vladimir Ilich and Krupskaya, with Krupskaya as the inexhaustible recorder and transcriber of a great mind.

Don't you think, asked Hope, that she's perhaps too devoted?

So, a wife can be too devoted?

She can be if she doesn't have room to look around on her own behalf. And even breathe for herself.

The daughter of the house set the teapot on top of the samovar and laid a plate of sweet cakes on the table. Next she brought a bowl of honey and another of apricot jam. I asked Mrs Hope Mockridge whether she would have honey or jam in her tea, and when she said honey, I spooned some into our sturdy glass tumblers. The daughter took the teapot, poured into it a small concentrate of tea from the samovar, then opened the lower tap to pour water into our pot. This – to me – ordinary process fascinated Hope Mockridge.

Why doesn't she just pour it straight from the top tap? she asked when the girl had gone.

She'd be arrested for murder, I said. There's a *zavarka*, an essence of tea, in the samovar. It seeps through the water, but if it's too highly concentrated it will take your breath away and give you hallucinations, or even a heart attack.

I don't believe it, she said, smiling.

Prisoners, I said, real prisoners in Russia, drink the *zavarka* in the hope they'll die.

A person can suicide with tea? asked Hope Mockridge, laughing, but willing to be convinced. Then she frowned. It must be so terrible what the tsar's police do to prisoners!

Taste the tea. You will find it delightful.

She tasted it, and claimed she found it to be first class.

You must think me a prize idiot, she said then. I am perhaps too fascinated by Russia. It comes from reading *War and Peace* when a person is just seventeen. The most marvellous book to read during a long summer on a Queensland sheep station.

Tolstoy is sentimental about peasants, I told her. He could afford to be. He had enough of them working for him.

Yes, but he worked *with* them, didn't he? He wore peasant clothing.

I admitted that was so. It was a well-meaning question on her part. Russia was very hard to explain to someone on a humid afternoon in Queensland. Even to a woman so interested in it. When I was a child, my mother's family still mocked the young city people who had come to the villages before I was born, thinking that the peasant commune was a union of humble people who had renounced their egoism – the commune a sort of model locomotive that would take all Russians straight from agricultural life to a socialist republic.

The Russian peasants Tolstoy worked with will never make a revolution on their own, I told Mrs Mockridge. They will stand up occasionally if their crops or cattle are taken, and face the Cossack cavalry, but they will always lose and go back to God and vodka and prayers for the tsar. They dream of seizing the earth but have no scheme at all to overthrow the things that have made the earth a misery.

I told her about Mikhail Romas, a nobleman, who was what could be called an Agrarian Socialist – that is, one who believed the revolution would come from the countryside. He took with him into the world of the peasants his twenty-year-old protégé, Maxim Gorki, the future author – indeed, my favourite author of all. They tried to set up peasant cooperatives – Romas trying and trying far more than Gorki. Endlessly, against discouragement, even when the local money-lenders put dynamite in his firewood, he tried. Gorki was a peasant like me, and he knew as Romas didn't what he and his friend were really up against. Whereas people like Romas, those young 'go-to-the-people' radicals, didn't understand that the peasant hated all outsiders for a start. People like Romas did not comprehend the truth about men like my grandfather, a humorous but vicious old goat who had his own capitalist desires – to buy timber land, to acquire a mill, to burn elegant kerosene lamps in his house. And some of his friends, grasping old village shop-owners who wanted to keep prices high and looked upon the young university students with their bourgeois guilt and their talk of the Christian nature of cooperatives with disbelief.

You are hard on the peasants, she said.

Well, I am one. Forgive me, but the idea that people can become ennobled by misery is a very bourgeois one.

And hence the sort of notion I have is false? she asked me with a smile. Oh dear, I do have a great deal to learn.

Please, I said, you can't be expected to understand all the complications. You know far more than most about the whole sorry mess.

I called for the girl to come and refill Hope's cup, and urged her to try the cakes.

She took one. I dare not have too many, she told me. My mother and aunts are all very plump. And I am very vain. It's disgraceful. Why should a woman care how she looks? But for some reason I do.

Because the world is pleased to see beauty, I told her, prickling with sudden internal heat. It's no small thing to enliven the world with beauty.

Well, she said, Australian men don't generally speak as well as that of women. If we're lucky, we might be complimented by comparison to stud cattle or merino sheep.

In Russia too. I regret you might be less preferred than a draught-horse.

She smiled. You seem so sure of what you know, Tom, whereas we are all over the place with our ideas.

We have had the help of great thinkers, I told her. Kelly is a wonderful fellow but no one would say a great thinker.

It's a long time since a general strike has been contemplated, she told me. If I were a believer I would pray for its success.

I did not dare say yet that sometimes the point was to lose. That losing could be winning. Instead, I asked her about her family.

Hers was in its way a characteristic Queensland tale. Queensland had been a British penal outpost before it was named to honour Britain's Queen Victoria. When it became its own self-governing region, as it now was under a federal constitution, its size was three times that of the Ukraine. Into the downs country west of Brisbane had come pastoralists, great ranchers who settled on 'stations' of thousands upon thousands of acres, and then reached further and further out into fringes of stone and desert, looking for pasture. Her grandfather, she said, was one of the pastoralists whom Kelly and his ilk denounced. He came from Northern Ireland, she told me, and I had already sentimentally decided that Hope Mockridge's looks were classically Celtic. He was one of the men who had tried to destroy the Shearers' Union twenty years before, and had brought in troops and Gatling guns.

But he was also a kindly old fellow, she went on, and he loved me, the fact that I had a bit of spirit. But you see, the kindliest of men always *do* combine to protect their interests. It's almost not their fault, even if it's unjust. But it's what humans do. You can't expect capital not to behave like capital, or property like property. Decent men, affectionate men – they all behave badly under the wrong system, a system of land grabs and land hunger. On the good side, he treated shearers well – he didn't feed them on offal and off-cuts like some pastoralists. But like Bender, he hated the idea of them banding together to get more out of him. Wasn't he being generous enough already? That was what he always asked. He certainly thought he was. He said to me once, They'd take my land if they could. He had a strong sense of what socialism is, and talked about it more and more as he got older. I think he made me interested in it too, and that was an outcome he wouldn't have liked. And yet, men like him . . . their story will, I'm sure, not be without interest at some future date.

For the moment, I admitted, I believe your grandfather has little to fear. At least for twenty more years . . .

Twenty more years? she asked. I'll be a woman of fifty-two.

A woman unburdened by age, I said, as gallantly as I could.

Apart from that she was not very interested in talking much further about her family. They were scandalised that she should wilfully insist on studying law – they were frightened about bad influences at the University of Queensland, and indeed she had been attracted to the Socialist Students Club.

I came here to look into your past, not mine, she told me then, with her wonderful smile of new-world frankness. One didn't find a smile like that in St Petersburg. So frank, so unabashed, and so commanding.

The next day a general meeting at Trades Hall voted formally to begin the general strike, and our strike committee went into full operation. There was to be a march from the Trades Hall eastwards to Fortitude Valley. Jolly Tom Ryan argued that a clause concerning the peaceable intentions of the trade unions should be placed at the head of the strike statement. No harm done. Whether a march was to be peaceful depended on the police and the special constables and, to be honest, whether the Wobblies set a fire or whether the Irish broke the windows of Irish-Need-Not-Apply stores in Brunswick and Wickham streets. Likewise the generality of men must be prevented from attacking Chinese businesses on the suspicion that Bender might break the strike with Chinese drivers and conductors.

The wife of Mr Riley, my co-marshal, had got hold of some red material and made a sash for each of our men, including Suvarov and me. Early in the morning we met our three hundred under the thin shade of the gum trees in the park across from the Trades Hall. How different from the grimy locomotive shops of Kharkov it was! Riley was uneasy about telling the men to put themselves between any police baton and the bulk of marchers. We decided we would have on either side of the vanguard of the march twenty of our marshals marching in a straight line, well spaced but obvious. If the police charged they would be ready to move in front of the first-row dignitaries and absorb the impact. We put together a Praetorian guard of forty or so men. They had a thankless job, but Riley was cheerful and said 'the big fellers' were ready for it. A further two hundred and twenty of our men were to line the route of the march, while the final forty were to bring up the rear, to help people escape and to protect them if things went extremely badly.

Before we moved out Riley wanted to know did I want to speak, but I said, No, you speak. You're an Irishman and I'm a stranger. When the time came, and Riley's strong voice was heard through a megaphone, men to whom tobacco was a short commodity stamped out their cigarettes the better to listen to him.

He did a good job. Our marchers all have different ideas in their heads, he said. Your job is to keep them marching for one thing – unionism's right to enter the Queensland workplace. We're not here to fight old quarrels. Our quarrel is to do with the capitalist, and the fact he can't permit unionism into his head. Now the publican of the Trades Hall Hotel has declared the bar open to men who can produce a union card. I'd just point out that you must have a good head to do your job today. If you walk off pissed, you disgrace the sash my wife made you. Moderation in all things, gentlemen.

Some of our constables moved away, delighted as workers often were at a rumour of free alcohol. I'm glad I don't have time for the stuff, I told Suvarov, who was standing by in his red sash.

The procession moved off at eleven. By that hour there were twenty-five thousand marchers, and fifty thousand spectators along the streets, an army untrained but full of potential. The lines were fifteen or so abreast and the procession two miles long. The front row comprised Tom Ryan, wearing a red rosette, and other Labor parliamentarians, with Warwick O'Sullivan and his wife at the left side of the line. Near the vanguard, in the second or third row, was a battalion of young women led by the magnificent Mrs Amelia Pethick in a straw hat. Wives and children of workers had decorated their family mongrels with bands of red ribbon, and owners of small shops dependent on the earnings of workers cheered us on our way. There were red ribbons tied to telegraph poles and even some of the drays waiting for us to pass through intersections were decorated with red bunting. The office girls from the company of lawyers who did the Trades Hall work waved to us from their upstairs windows. Walter O'Sullivan began to sing in a raw tenor, and others joined in, ragged singing in this ragged nation:

Arise, ye starvelings from your slumbers,
Arise, ye prisoners of want,
For reason in revolt now thunders
And at last ends the age of cant.
So, comrades
Come rally
And the last fight let us face . . .

Soon the procession passed occasional detachments of police, to whom the strikers called to join the march, some of our red-sashed marshals waving to this policeman or that.

On open ground at Fortitude Valley the thousands came to a stop and Kelly came forward and made a speech through a megaphone, announcing the strike and applauding the good order with which the march had taken place. He told us again about the causes and provocations that created the strike. Then, becoming practical, he explained that the committee would issue coupons that would be honoured by certain stores, a list of which had been printed and would be prominently displayed and distributed. There would be a daily bulletin. The bulletin would inform men and women of marches, for, said Kelly, repeating my own thought, we have become an army. Indeed, railway men and miners at Ipswich, and fourteen thousand cane-cutters, rail workers and miners in the far north of the huge province, had stopped work in support of us.

Tommy Ryan formally declared the support of the Labor Party for the strike. He and the other Labor men of course used the general discontent to urge everyone to vote for their party, as if doing that would bring about the promised age. It must have been politeness on the part of Kelly and other Queenslanders not to ask why the Labor prime minister of Australia, Andrew Fisher down in Melbourne, had failed to produce a working man's paradise in either of his two prime ministerships, even though he made much of the fact that he had started at the coalface in Scotland at the age of ten. Tom Ryan pointed to Fisher's recent law to create a people's bank, the Commonwealth Bank, as if it were yet another step on the path to heaven. Fisher himself was a Queenslander by immigration, had been a miner at Gympie, and Kelly hoped for practical favours from him. If the workers were attacked by the police, surely Fisher would offer Australian troops to keep the peace.

From my position behind the vanguard of our men I noticed that Commissioner Urquhart's police cavalry, the Queensland Cossacks, had gathered up ahead of us and on our flanks and were looking on. To me, they didn't seem too troubled by the thought of federal troops.

But that first march was allowed to go off well. Even the daily press praised the good order of the marchers, though it understated the numbers involved. Police permission was sought for smaller processions on the following days. It was interesting, this business of seeking permission, and Urquhart's lieutenant, Deputy Commissioner Geoffrey Cahill, gave permission – perhaps because the press had suggested it was better to have us marching than looting like some gang of Russian revolutionaries!

6

It was at the end of the second day of the strike that the strike committee met at Trades Hall, and I saw Hope and Amelia once more. The weather was torrid and Amelia looked exhausted. I thought that in the wake of our successful march I could take the Samarkand option again. I made my way to her after the meeting and said, Come with me now, Mrs Pethick. I will find a car to take us to South Brisbane and I'll make you better with Russian tea.

She said, Oh, that would be nice! But ask Hope too. For I need a chaperone, you know.

There were a few trams running, crewed clumsily by special constables, but Amelia Pethick's principles would not permit her to catch them. We did find a man from the Clerks' Union to drive us to the Samarkand. We invited him in with us, but he told us he'd rather park in the shade of a nearby banyan tree and sleep – despite the falling pods and the bird droppings, he said.

Once we were seated in the teahouse, Amelia drank thirstily of the tea.

Oh, you have revived me, Mr Samsurov, I was ready to wilt. You know, I have been here in Brisbane since I was twenty-eight years old but have never got used to this terrible heat. My late husband had no problems with it. He was a muscular man, like you.

And she went straight from this reflection about heat, as if she remembered similar descriptions of Russian heat mirages from novels, to raise a question about my country, the one everyone seemed to raise first.

Surely your tsar cannot last much longer?

I'm afraid the liberals and the gentry have grown fond of him again. The ordinary people they used to admire have proved too unwashed to be good company.

Yes, said Amelia, most bourgeois people are so delicate in the nostril. But I married a stevedore, so I know about sweat.

For a second, I could see a passionate young woman behind the older and sturdy one – running away with her lover from London to the colonies.

I explained that in 1905 and even later there had been a lot of fighting in the streets and glass was broken, and the liberal press, initially sympathetic to the strikers, now began to lay the blame entirely at their door. I did not go on to explain that where opinion did not work to blacken the rebels, the army brought in the artillery, as in engineering shed No. 5 at Kharkov, where I was flattened to the floor by a shell burst and woke to find someone's entire naked leg seeping by my cheek, like one of the carcases I later toted at the Brisbane meatworks.

I am sure, said Amelia, that our beloved premier, Mr Digby Denham, would follow if possible the same principles as your tsar, because power, like water the world over, always finds the same level.

Hope mentioned that her husband, who knew Mr Denham, said there would be militia corps sent out to deal with us.

Chocolate soldiers and little chocolate gods! said Amelia. How easy it is to buy people with the smallest morsel of authority.

A Trades Council car was waiting for us outside, but Amelia decided not to get into the machine. I don't need a ride from here, Hope. Let Tom walk me back home over the bridge. It's a lovely evening.

Hope argued and argued with her but Amelia would not be moved and said she was thoroughly revived. Amelia and I set off down the street and up onto the bridge footway. The evening had turned cool and windy; women crossing towards us from the direction of the city were hanging onto their hats.

I am sorry you must escort an old lady, Tom, Amelia told me, her own hat turned down against the strong, cleansing wind.

I told her I was honoured.

Hope would rather be here. You would probably rather she was. That's normal.

I told her, I don't quite understand Mrs Mockridge. I don't understand her motives or her class.

Oh, her class is nothing to her. You are not confused by me and I'm the daughter of a baronet.

I looked at her. The wind cut at her fine features.

Yes, and married a socialist stevedore and would do it again. Certainly. Again. I have had a wonderful life here, she said. And it is not over. But I miss my husband. He was a man of true courage, true force. We lived like a pair of gardeners in our little cottage, as happy as Roman philosophers. And we believed this was the crucial age. When everything would be broken and re-made, as we had broken and re-made everything in our marriage.

I stared at her like a rural oaf. She had been happy in a way I found it hard to be. I had never quite got the two things together, the revolutionary self and what one might call, inaccurately maybe, the soul – the place where the trembling spirit lives.

Amelia said, Hope is married to a powerful man, Mr Samsurov, here in Queensland. A man of powerful connections. His friends blame him for not keeping his wife 'under control'. May I say this straight out, Tom, without any shadow play? She is an innocent. You can see that by the way she grills you about Russia, surely? I wanted to tell you that. She married an older man when he was very charming and amused by her radicalism, as if her opinions were a dew that would soon evaporate. They didn't. Now she has been quite ill at times . . . I'm babbling . . . She has been quite ill. She stays with her husband because that's what's done. But she might equally run off with a revolutionary because that's also what's done. You understand.

She looked at me again as wavelets came cresting up the river. I wanted to tell you. I didn't want you to misread her. If you were thinking of . . . well, of some socialist romance, it shouldn't happen, Tom. She's not well enough. I tell you for your own good.

I said I understood.

I feel like a foolish old woman, she said.

And we did not talk much on the second half of our walk. I thought there was no escaping the reality. With women, the intimate and the political were all one thing. I had learned that from my fine mother.

7

Even more people came to Brisbane, attracted by our strike. In the Trades Hall Hotel one day, Kelly introduced me to a small red-headed man of about my own age named Paddy Dykes who had come all the way from the far-off silver and iron-ore fields of Broken Hill in New South Wales.

You're the first Russian I've met, he told me, raising up his wrinkled face. We don't have many Russians in Broken Hill.

I noticed that like me he drank lemonade.

Paddy's a journalist, Kelly told me.

I wouldn't put it so high as that, said the little man. I'm writing pieces though. The *Australian Worker.* It really wants to know what's happening up here. I'll be at Friday's march.

Strangely, he said it as if he was guaranteeing my safety. I liked him at once, this rugged little gnome from the Australian desert, though I could not foresee how closely we would in time be bound.

But our application for a march on the first Friday of February 1912 was refused by Police Commissioner Urquhart and his lieutenant, Cahill. Riley and I got together again with our marshals. Some of the Labor men had absented themselves – citing their respect for law and order. Just the same, most of our marshals and fifteen thousand unionists arrived at Market Square and rallied in good order. Amelia's young women were still with us in numbers and made sure the other unionists saw them by getting to Market Square early in the day and waiting there with their banners, patient despite the heat and humidity. Directed by the marshals, we moved off and weaved among the city buildings into Market Street. Ahead was a line of unmounted police. I thought at once, The cavalry will come from the flanks, just as in Russia.

In front of us an inspector began reading the riot act as we marched towards him. The police now stepped forward to meet our front line, where, among others, Walter O'Sullivan and his recording angel of a wife were again marching. At first our people pushed forward, absorbing blows as the police wielded their batons. I was with our sashed marshals near the head of the procession and could hear men and women calling to the troopers, the Queensland Cossacks, with their splendid mounts and pipe-clayed helmets who now rode in, Join us, mates! Come on, workers, join your cobbers. Mounted troopers were waiting in ambush in Ann Street. Voices pleaded with them too, because once removed from their saddles and pipe-clayed leather, they too had little enough to go home to. I saw Mrs O'Sullivan advancing blindly while still writing, her head tucked in towards her husband's shoulder.

Special constables, sworn-in gentlemen, were waiting on foot behind the cavalry and also advanced now from the riverside of Ann Street, delighted to be licensed to teach the trade unions a lesson. The chief charge of the mounted police came from Eagle Street and was led against the front of the procession and its leading flanks by Deputy Commissioner Cahill on his bay horse. As he spurred forward I could hear him bellow, Give it to them, boys! Into them!

When the charging horse and foot police and special constables found the ranks of the unionists at front too dense, they moved onto the pavement and down our flanks. I could feel the heat of horseflesh bearing down. Special constables also swarmed onto the footpaths on either side of Market Street, pursuing spectators and even the wives of workers, bludgeoning them with batons. I saw one special beating an old man, a mere onlooker. They were more vicious than the true police; they were fighting for their world order.

I found myself face to face with three real enough professional policemen, batons in hand.

Please, I said. Gentlemen, I am one of the chief marshals to keep order. Please let me speak to the commissioner.

Somehow I was not surprised when all three said to me such things as Fuck you for a foreign troublemaker, and began laying into me. I raised my hands but started to lose my footing. As I went to the ground with a whack on the temple, I had a sepia vision, like a sickly photograph, of troopers wading in among Amelia's typists. Amelia, a little old stick of a woman, lunged at Deputy Commissioner Cahill, running her hatpin through his upper leg and withdrawing it. A policeman grabbed her wrist from behind, another wrapped his arms around her frail waist and lifted her off her feet. Rising again, with bile in my mouth, I tried to go to Amelia. But I could not see her. All was chaos and our marchers were teeming back through Market Square, looking for safety in the streets behind it. Then there was Paddy Dykes the silver miner. Take my arm, Tom, he yelled. I was happy to do so.

Supporting me, the silver miner was also surrounded. I ought to tell you I am writing for the *Australian Worker* newspaper, he informed the police. I am a journalist.

They actually paused to listen to this little bantam. A special constable moved in to swipe him with a baton. But he cried, Do you want to be named and shamed in the press? I have your number.

Even though that was not the truth, the baton-wielder backed off. He had extraordinary authority, this little red-headed fellow from Broken Hill.

More constables arrived and dragged me away from Paddy to an area where horse-drawn wagons waited to convey us to magistrates. Inside the dark wagon were Suvarov and also Rybukov. My head throbbed and I heard my voice from a distance as I told Rybukov he should not have marched. The others compared bruises and cursed the special constables as prize bastards.

Beneath the main police station, I now had my first experience of an Australian holding cell, but it was not an extended stay. We were taken upstairs in groups to appear before a bench of three magistrates.

Some of my marshals were in my group. The magistrates looking down on us had a severity in their faces they had probably got too jaded to use against burglars and vagrants, their normal diet.

I was astonished to see Hope appear in a wig and a black robe. She was wonderful to see, and angelic beside the magistrates.

The chief magistrate called on her in a tight voice. You represent these men, Mrs Mockridge?

She said she did. She began our defence. Hardly any of the marchers knew that permission had not been given for the march, she argued. Even the organisers did not know, since the commissioner's refusal had come so late. These men, said Hope (how well named she was), these men marched in innocent good order, unaware of the denial of a licence for the procession.

In the gallery, with other men of the press, Paddy Dykes sat recording events for the *Australian Worker.*

I indicated to Hope in sign language that I wanted to speak for my marshals. She frowned, then told their worships that one of the defendants, an emigrant unfamiliar with Queensland law, wanted to make a statement. The magistrates turned their gaze my way. I said that I was one of the leaders of the strike marshals whose job it was to keep order on the march. If it had been left to us, order there would have been, imposed by men the strikers respected. As it was, the sudden baton charge gave us no time to tell the marchers to withdraw.

Thank you, said the magistrate in a voice empty of gratitude.

We were fined ten pounds each and threatened with jail at our next offence.

Rybukov, Suvarov and I were held back for a special talking to by the chief magistrate. The sovereign state of Queensland was kind enough to welcome energetic immigrants, we were told, but not rioters of foreign anarchist backgrounds.

This upset Rybukov very much and caused him to wheeze aloud at the magistrate, We are not anarchists. Anarchists are children.

★

I would find out the next morning that an array of charges were levelled at Amelia Pethick when she was brought into court on her own as an especial offender, charged with causing grievous bodily harm to Deputy Commissioner Geoffrey Cahill and the damage of a police horse.

A policeman produced in court the bloodied hatpin he had found on the ground near the affray. Hope, who was defending her, asked the bench whether it was credible that a woman of the scale of Mrs Pethick posed a threat to a big man like Cahill, especially if he sat atop a police mare. And yet Commissioner Cahill wanted us to believe that this woman of five feet two inches had been able to reach the Commissioner's upper thigh with a hatpin! Perhaps, she suggested, Mr Cahill should enter the court on his seventeen-hands mare and we could find out whether Mrs Pethick could reach his stirrups, let alone his thigh.

In the court people laughed, but the magistrates did not. Amelia confused things by saying she had been charged down, and that she was ashamed of her actions since she intended only to wound Cahill, her assailant, not the poor brute who carried him.

She was remanded for trial and bail was set at one hundred pounds, which the Trades Hall officials meanly decided she should meet herself and out of her Typists and Secretarial Services Union's fees. (It was Hope Mockridge, in fact, who put up the money.)

Premier Digby Denham praised the firm but just action of the police and declared *respectable Queensland* had rejected us. Hope's husband Mr Mockridge KC now chose, like much of Brisbane's bourgeoisie, to be alienated from the strikers by the events of Baton Friday, as we would call it. Hope wondered why blows delivered by the police, together with the resistance of the most inoffensive of strikers, Amelia Pethick, had suddenly made the strikers unworthy and dangerous to society.

I found out later from Hope that something like this discourse took place:

Mr Mockridge emerged from his study the Sunday following the march and asked his wife where she was going on the Sabbath. A good roast was cooking downstairs, he told her.

I'll be at Trades Hall most of the day, she told him.

There is work to do on a Sunday? I thought that the point of a strike was no work.

Hope asked her husband, You wouldn't be free for some *pro bono* work, would you, Edgar?

If your people had had a permit to march, I would make myself available.

The permit system is unjust. Some judge, with the right nudging, might overthrow it in favour of freedom of assembly. Freedom of assembly subject to a permit is not freedom.

Mr Mockridge returned to his study. Things had happened between them which would have made it too painful for him to be angry or to prohibit. But before closing the door he noted that Bender was keeping his personal special tram going.

Tomorrow, he said, I intend to ride on Freeman's Palace special. I have told him as much.

So he made his public stand for the opposition, with the clear hope that she would quit the strikers or else suffer an intensified shame among her own kind of people. So, for principle, he was willing to make the surmised rift in his marriage more public still.

8

At the Sunday meeting of the strike committee, I noticed how pale Hope looked. She was worried, she said, for Amelia, who was resting at home from her warrior deeds of Friday. The question now was whether we should march again, in protest against the necessity for police permits. Kelly proposed that marches be suspended for some days but that one be considered for the following Friday, one week after Baton Friday. The membership could vote to decide what we should do – whether to defy the specials and the police one more time. Kelly declared that the prospect of another such march would bring out the resolve in the membership engaged in the strike.

It will mean bugger all, said Billy Foster of the Tramways Union. He seemed quite dejected.

Kelly said that on Monday he would call on Prime Minister Fisher, the Scottish miner from Queensland, to send his troops to protect us. Some of the Labor Party men argued against it, saying that whichever way Fisher jumped it would be used to embarrass him. But there weren't as many notables of the Labor Party there that day – with one eye on the ballot box, they had read the Saturday papers and decided that the strike was no longer popular. And they could, after all, plead that it was the Sabbath.

Pongrass of the AWU, a big man, told us, I don't know how I can keep up my members' enthusiasm without marches.

We'll have to march! the cry came back from some at the long table on the stage where we sat.

There was a Wobbly there who said mournfully that sometimes the only action left was direct action.

Suvarov shook his head. We had direct action in Russia, he said, and all it did was give Stolypin and de Witt a chance to choke us further and shell the factory suburbs of Moscow. For direct action – in the Wobbly tongue – usually meant explosives.

Hope agreed with Suvarov. Let me tell you all, gentlemen, she said, that Sir Digby Denham and Freeman Bender would be very pleased if one cane truck from the north was dynamited . . . that would be a real birthday present to them. A march, on the other hand, by peaceful unionists – they fear that the most.

To sustain us in our discussions, we fetched black tea from a large and battered enamel pot at the end of the room, and then we sat around sipping it and talking particularly on the topic of cash for strikers' families, and whether or not to march. Others of our membership were blunting their doubts with cut-rate beer at the Trades Hall Hotel. I noticed Paddy Dykes, drawing on his tea at the back of the room and taking many notes, though his method of writing didn't seem as demented as Olive O'Sullivan's. I had seen him earlier, talking earnestly and jotting in a little notebook.

G'day, Tom, he called. I've telegraphed the editor about you. Would you like to write something on Russia for us?

It was an attractive idea; the *Australian Worker* was fervently read and passed round on the eastern coast of the southern continent. You could help me with my English if I did so? I asked.

No problem. Not that I'm any great stylist. I came on the pen by accident.

It would be an honour, I told Paddy earnestly.

It emerged the next day that Premier Digby Denham had also asked the prime minister for federal troops. It was true that the prime minister was in an impossible position of the political variety. Fisher could last in his post as long as he nodded to the unions while winking at the powers of capital. There was even the risk now that he might send his troops to support the Queensland police. In the end Fisher sent us a donation of thirty pounds but also sent telegrams denying either side troops.

Later in the week it was announced in the *Truth* by a gossip writer masquerading as a political one that Mr Mockridge KC had been catching Joseph Freeman Bender's private tram car to his offices near the law courts, in contrast to his wife's actions. Who will triumph in this connubial struggle? the writer asked. But Hope still turned up to Trades Hall before work and after, and during her lunch period, and sat talking to Amelia, now back to her best but still facing charges.

When I ran into Walter O'Sullivan at Trades Hall, he asked me to question my march marshals. In the melee of the police charge, had anyone picked up his wife's notebook? She had dropped it as her husband wisely shuttled her up a laneway to escape the batons, and it had been full of notes very precious to her. I promised to ask.

O'Sullivan shook his locks and said, It upsets her so much. She feels she has an incomplete record. Women are differently built from us. Sometimes they are defeated by small matters, yet then they survive the ones that tip us off kilter. The notebook means a lot to Olive.

Our initial decision to march again that Friday was rejected by a Tuesday night meeting. There had been an incident. The day before some strikers' children had hurled stones at Mr Bender's tram, the Palace, and might have put a dent in one of its panels. They had been chased and some of them taken into custody, and nobody wanted them beaten by officers of the law because of what we might do that Friday. But even those of us who believed in a final salutary defeat arising from the ashes did not want the strike to fall apart so early. Men were now talking of looting, Billy Foster warned me. He was against another march.

When they talk of looting they're really talking about going back to work, he said. Looting isn't natural to them; they're just mouthing off.

The *Truth*, that awful piece of gutter journalism we all nonetheless read, carried a cartoon that weekend of Hope as a dirt-faced urchin hurling rocks at a tram that carried her eminent husband. But yet again she was all day at Trades Hall, writing material for the strike bulletin, discussing legal representation in subcommittees.

Then, on Wednesday, a telegram came. The Commonwealth Arbitration Court would hear the tramworkers' case. Waved off by men with banners, Kelly and other Trades Hall delegates caught a steamer to Melbourne to appear before the court. Freeman Bender caught the same ship but travelled in greater luxury. Workers lined the shore and cheered Kelly and his gang down the broad reaches of the estuary. An arbitration court seemed a remarkable thing even to me, a cynic about any state other than a workers' one. It certainly glimmered like a miraculous icon in the imagination of the Queenslanders. Justice Higgins of the court had established the *basic* or *foundational* wage so that men and women could live *in frugal comfort*. He was a hero to the unions, though I did ask Hope whether *frugal* and *comfort* didn't contradict each other.

Ah, she acknowledged, that's the question, isn't it, Tom?

The intimacy of the first name always returned me, in ways I tried to hide, to my peasant callowness, which I hoped she couldn't see.

She seemed to have been revived by the news. She had met Justice Higgins and said he came from the same Ulster background as her grandparents, yet he'd adopted as his founding principles neither self-interest nor *Das Kapital* but – strangely for a Protestant – Pope Leo XIII's encyclical, *Rerum Novarum,* which concerned itself – oddly for a priestly document – with social justice.

Anticipation of Higgins's decision, and an inexact knowledge of the Arbitration Act, kept the unions excited for ten days. It was harsh weather in Brisbane, with violent thunderstorms sweeping up over the mangrove flats of Moreton Bay far too late every afternoon to save the populace from blistering days.

The news was published in the paper before Kelly and his people got back home. Mr Higgins decided that unionists were entitled to wear their badges, and declared that the company should not dismiss its tramway men for such a reason. But he did not have the power to *make* Mr Bender take the men back – he 'enjoined him' to do so. When this news broke I called in at the strike bulletin office, where I encountered the little fellow Paddy Dykes.

He asked me, You okay from when the cops whaled into you?

I said I was much better than if he hadn't been there. Then, Tell me, what does *enjoin* mean?

He screwed up his face in a way that made me cherish his conscientiousness.

You know Christ's Sermon on the Mount? he asked.

Yes.

Blessed are the meek – all that?

Yes.

That's *enjoining*. It is – I have to tell you – so much piss and wind. It's a prayer, and we all know how hopeless that is.

He held up the latest stencilled strike bulletin, which declared: *Justice Higgins stands up for strikers!*

That's the way they choose to see it.

The steam ferry brought the delegates in from their ship to the wharf near the Customs House. But when Kelly and his team went to see Bender and Digby Denham, they found that neither of them was interested. Bender was not bound to take the tramways men back. He would not answer to Judge Higgins's enjoining.

We meatworkers of the Australian Workers Union were not nearly finished, however. I had by now almost forgotten my earlier and quite correct Bolshevik scepticism about the strike. It was no more than human to wish that our fraternity would prevail or at least put up a genuine struggle.

9

At table at Adler's boarding house, I was occasionally teased by my fellow lodgers, particularly Suvarov, about my sipping tea with a lady such as Hope Mockridge.

Suvarov, set on mischief, had sparkling eyes and a delighted, long-lipped smile. Sometimes in his life, of course, mischief sought him out more readily than he ever sought it. Klebhanov from the Tramways Union looked wearier these days, but he liked to laugh too. With the scarring of his face from a beating during the 1902 strike in St Petersburg, he was in a position to say, We are not all unmarked Russian princes like Artem Samsurov.

I am a man who carries dead sheep for a living, into the cold store. For shipping to feed the industrial masses of Britain. Do you call that a prince?

Suvarov often asked, But how did you get away with your beautiful unmarked face, Artem, long as the Caspian, broad as the Azov? Are you a true Bolshevik? Has no servant of the state ever landed a blow on you?

On the day they opened cannon fire on the railway engineering shop in Kharkov, there were plenty of ruined faces. But I did not like to say so. Klebhanov of the Tramways was the rare sort of fellow who liked to recount what had befallen him, and I let him. Tales of

Butyrka Prison and exile. Suvarov, on the other hand, though a joker, kept pretty silent about the catastrophes that had brought about his scars.

At Trades Hall, Hope Mockridge was another person looking tired. Violet patches like the world's bruises showed beneath her eyes. Amelia was to appear in court the following week, and it seemed to weigh more on Hope than it did on the old woman.

By charging Amelia with malicious damage to a police horse and aggravated assault upon the deputy commissioner himself, Cahill attracted some opprobrium from the cartoonists of the popular press. But that did not stop a number of businesses who had offered discounted clothes and groceries to strikers from removing themselves from our list. Rybukov gave up his lease on his house and returned to Adler's. He said to me soon after, The tsar would love these Queenslanders. They're more obedient than Russians.

I wanted very much to go and talk to Hope and reassure her, and tell her that her splendid face and her splendid mind were above all the sniping of the newspapers, but I knew that I did not understand half of what was weighing on her, that I had no grounds to present myself as a comforter.

Then the Director of Public Prosecutions announced one morning that evidence against Amelia Pethick and others, held in his office – including police documents, a record of interview, and seized possessions (among them a bloodied hatpin) – had gone missing. The director said he suspected malfeasance. The more irreverent afternoon paper, which sold well among the working class, suggested that the documents may indeed have been taken by the police, embarrassed for Deputy Commissioner Cahill's sake lest the trial rallied support for the frail Amelia Pethick, or required him to show his punctured thigh or, as rumour had it, arse. In any case, the prosecution could not proceed until the documents were retrieved.

It occurred even to me that the Director of Public Prosecutions was part of the attorney-general's department and shared the same premises in splendid George Street, near the top of the hill on which the Queensland parliament building stood. And Hope Mockridge worked in the attorney-general's department, and might have removed the file. Hence the violet streaks beneath her eyes.

Within a few days the press had raised the same surmise, though very carefully, fearful that the Mockridges or Hope herself might sue for slander. At Trades Hall I noticed Olive O'Sullivan back in womanhood's bloom and writing in her notebooks. I congratulated O'Sullivan on her revived spirits and he said, Yes, it was wonderful. Along with Amanda's hatpin, Olive's notebook had also been rescued from the care of the public prosecutor and had been returned to Olive at the O'Sullivans' boarding house by messenger.

As happy as Olive was, Amelia had a somewhat less optimistic tale to tell that evening. A lot of her girls were under pressure from their parents to leave the strike.

Their mothers, said Amelia, ask them who will want to marry a girl who takes such an undue part in a strike?

Well, I said, would they want to marry a man who didn't like women to stand up?

You don't need to convince me, she sighed. But now there's the witch-hunt at the attorney-general's. They're going to make a scapegoat of the poor girl.

Hope?

Yes, this strike has caused nothing but misery for her. Samsurov, come, let's take her away to an early tea at my place in Peel Street. If no one will drive us, we can walk.

It was agreed, and I was pleased that tea was seen as the cure-all here as in Russia. But I wondered why Amelia, who'd warned me off Hope the week before, wanted to put us together at the same tea table again.

In the end Hope herself offered to drive us there in her car. She was brisk that afternoon and seemed restored to her old form. All she had said to me when I first met Amelia and herself behind Trades Hall was, Very well then, Tom, we're going!

To get the thing started I was requested to crank the engine over as she sat at the wheel. The machine thundered with a sudden smell of oil and we had the breeze coming straight at us when we swung down

Ann Street, up Roma and past North Quay. During our progress there was quite a degree of what I would call speculation on the streets of Brisbane – people gawped at us, as Hope, her flimsy scarf flying, took us to the great bend in the Brisbane River and off the main road to Milton and into Amelia's tranquil street.

It is to be noted that climate caused Queenslanders to build their houses on stilts, free of flood water and so as to allow wind to circulate both over the ceiling and under the floor. This was a clever arrangement, I thought. But one needed to ascend steps to reach the front verandah and the door. The three of us did so at Amelia's house, leaving the car, near-silent, its cooling parts ticking like a clock, under a tree. Amelia opened her front door without a key – an aspect of Australia that I couldn't help admiring. I was reminded of the remoter villages of Russia, where most people couldn't afford locks. The air inside the house was thick and smelled of some spice Amelia had been careful to put in place to fight some of the indignities of the climate.

Amelia went to the kitchen to prepare things, insisting that it was her kitchen and she would not tolerate Hope or myself in it. I suddenly found it hard to start a conversation with Hope. I knew I was in the classic and well-worn stages of sentimental love, a delusional sickness. The marriage of souls I respected best in the world was that of my sister to Trofimov the miner. It was a marriage of equals. Or if not, it was Trofimov himself who was the unequal partner, stricken with his miner's chest. And I thought too of the comradely marriage between Vladimir Ilich, our party leader, and his wife Krupskaya, which I had not observed directly. By contrast the state I was in was the same despicable one that led in the end to such glories as premature age for women, wife-beating, squalor, and a million domestic meannesses. If a man is a Marxist, he is meant to have the attitudes of a monk. There is meant to be no false romance in his life, no doomed and morbid loves as in Tolstoy. Fraternity and utility are the virtues of his existence. When I went to the railways in Perm, I felt I fulfilled my utility there. I found enough belief and hope to sustain me – like a Christian pilgrim of ancient days – in the long escape from the Aldan to Nikolayevsk-on-the-Amur.

Yet my pilgrim composure was – for the moment – gone. I knew it was better for a man to react sensibly to desire without dressing it up in the tatty and theatrical clothes of deathless adoration. Yet I was tempted to spout to Hope about devotion.

From where we sat, Hope and I could see on Amelia's mantelpiece and occasional tables photos of a younger Amelia and her husband, the English socialist stevedore who had brought her to Australia.

Ah, I said, it is very nice and cool in here.

As she threw her head back to let the cooler air at her throat I studied the wonderful lines of Hope's face. They were of the kind, I thought, that men would prefer to remain stationary, a head placed on a pedestal, a painting, an object for viewing. She would not consent to such a role, of course, this woman who had stood up for us with such coolness and wit in the magistrates' courtroom, this counsellor wise and skilled and ironic.

Suddenly she said, We are not going to win this.

No. But winning will be holding out, I told her. People should get used to holding out if they want to win in the end. By enduring they learn, for example, to understand the way the press works, the way most bourgeois support falls away . . . how the strikers take the blame for their own hopes. Learning that is no small thing; it is a sort of victory.

She lowered her head, made a doubtful mouth, and did not seem too cheered by my argument.

But do you really, really, Tom, foresee the end you want? I mean, the true end? The golden age?

Oh yes, I told her. These things are hard to believe in until they come about. But the slaves were freed, the serfs were freed. And capital will fall.

She shifted her head to one side. She didn't have a taste for waiting that afternoon.

Well, I tried to comfort her, some things happen suddenly. At a . . . at a gulp.

A gulp?

She laughed at my choice of word. I blushed, as red-faced as some provincial bank clerk. Where we sat, the silence grew, and then dear Amelia arrived with a tray of tea and teacups and put it on her dining table. Both Mrs Mockridge and I stood and bent to the tray, anxious to be helpful in setting things out on the table. I was happy to be at this work. When the tray was clear – milk, sugar, teapot, cups and saucers, ornamental spoons and sugar – Amelia chirped with joy and returned to the kitchen to get what she called *the comestibles*. These turned out to be cucumber sandwiches and a hearty English-style fruitcake, bleeding a fruity sap in the humid air. I saw a great cherry glisten in the midst of the dark cake. Opulence, I thought.

Amelia darted to a cupboard for one last errand and brought forth a decanter of sherry and another of what looked like whisky. She also placed three dainty if minuscule wineglass-shaped vessels for us to take our choice of the liquors.

Amelia said, Not as exciting as the Samarkand Café, Tom, but we rough Queenslanders do our best.

With tongs, Amelia put two sandwiches on my plate and a healthy slice of fruitcake. Oh, she then said, scraping her chair backwards rapidly. I meant also to fetch my atlas. If you don't mind, Tom – if it involves no personal pain to you, of course – Hope and I would dearly love you to point out where you come from in Russia.

It won't cause me any pain, I assured her, laughing and partly lying as well.

She excused herself and vanished again from the room.

When she was gone, Hope laughed, a first full-throated laugh.

She blames me for being curious about Russia. But she's the one who's curious. Mind you, she knows Russian history . . .

Amelia was back with the large volume, which looked heavy enough to snap her thin wrists. Please, she said, pour yourself some whisky, Tom.

I nearly did so, to celebrate the headiness of this teatime with Hope, but all my training went against it. The men who drank were the ones most often caught, most often subverted.

Thank you, Mrs Pethick . . . Amelia. But I am not a drinker.

Admirable, said Amelia. You, Hope?

Hope was already pouring herself a tumbler, as frankly as a man would.

Amelia was leafing through the enormous atlas.

Mr Samsurov . . . Tom . . . while I was making tea, did my young friend Hope say anything to you about my prosecution file?

No, I said. But whoever took it did a brave thing.

Or perhaps the public prosecutor is simply inefficient, Hope suggested.

I hope you didn't do it, my dear, Amelia told Hope, because it was too great a risk. And anyhow, I was rather looking forward to pleading guilty to the impaling of Deputy Commissioner Cahill with a hatpin. I am a soldier at heart. She laughed at her own idea.

Then whoever took the file, said Hope, has really spoiled your fun, haven't they, Amelia?

They rather have, Amelia agreed, and winked at me, but did not sit until she'd opened the page to a splendid map of Russia. She placed it in front of me. My finger strayed along the north-eastern Ukrainian–Russian border, and I read the transliterated names of rivers and towns. I found the place.

I was born here, I told them, near the Ukrainian border. My village was near this place, Yelets. Yes, Glebovo. There. Well, I'm surprised we are important enough for an atlas of the world! My mother was Ukrainian but of Russian stock. My mother's family were part of the plantation of Russian people in Ukraine.

A garden of people, I thought. Some of them nettles and weeds, but like many such plants, tall – that couldn't be denied. It was a long time since I'd spoken the name of Glebovo.

But I kept on prattling away. I think my temperament is like my mother's and grandmother's, I announced. I remembered for a second Maxim Gorki's love for his grandmother.

My father was a decent fellow, I told them. But music and drink consoled him for the state of the world.

I paused. Then on I went. Pulling the clots of information up out of a deep vein.

It is black soil around there, I told them. Like some of the Darling Downs.

All at once I was captured by an image of my young parents, riding in a cart to the Yelets monastery, to the Church of the Assumption, to have their wedding blessed. It was a blessing that left them poorer. I was born at the right time, though, a time when the new system of schooling had arrived. Without my letters, I'm sure I could have been the biggest drunk, the worst brute.

In case they imagined a perfect place, I went on, Sadly, the air is full of the smell of tanneries down by the river. Later, the technical school I went to was here, see. Ekaterinoslav. South of Kharkov. Then the technical university. In Moscow.

I noticed that Moscow lay like a gem of red and black in the map's middle. If I was for the moment vainglorious in my reminiscences in front of Hope and Amelia, a stab of the old anguish came back soon enough. Uncertainty, a savage grandfather. Arrest.

Amelia coughed as if she understood. Astonishing what a map can conjure up, she said. Old places and old feelings.

Before I gave the atlas back to Amelia, I looked eastward and let my finger stray to Perm and all the railways intersecting there in the foothills of the Urals, and the railway crossing over the mountains and away, now a single isolated black line across reaches of birch forest and taiga to exile on the Aldan and Zeya rivers, where I began my interminable walk out to the railway at Blagoveshchensk near Manchuria, and then on to the Pacific shore. I felt a strange, crusty weariness overcome me again – I had forgotten that during my Brisbane time. Jail can bring about a kind of mental exhaustion. Then escape acts as a stimulant but is hard on the spirit as well. I could name three members of the Russian Workers Union who did not recover from the walk out of Siberia. One was a Socialist Revolutionary who hanged himself from a hardwood beam in Toowong. Another was a hopeless drunk sometimes seen raving on street corners in Brisbane. The third, Menschkin, was arrested in Brisbane for stealing from shops – kleptomania. The police overlooked his crime and now everyone knew he reported to them weekly on the activities of Queensland's Russians.

Kleptomania is, of course, a prison habit, especially for poor prisoners who lack anyone to bring them hampers. Even a *katorznik*, a political prisoner, would pick up anything he could. And once you had eaten a cockroach to allay hunger, once you had felt a toxic envy for a man whose cockroach seemed larger than yours, you were spoiled for polite shopping.

I turned the pages looking for Vladivostok, Sakhalin, Eastern China.

My eye lit on Shanghai.

I said, Do you know Suvarov of the Australian Workers Union?

Neither of them did.

Grisha. He was my good friend in Shanghai. In the end, it was easy to get ashore and lose ourselves – yes, even though we weren't Chinese. Everyone thought you were a sailor on shore leave. It was in fact a little like Queensland was until a few months back. The immigration agent up here was a dear old German named Schwartz who liked socialists and didn't like the tsar. And he knew that in Queensland cane needed cutting and railways needed building. So he was not a severe gatekeeper of the Commonwealth of Australia.

I am not sure why I made these confessions to the women. When I looked at their faces, I saw they did not know what to ask me next, or whether they'd probed too far. I said, So here I am in Brisbane. Is this not enough?

Suddenly I wanted to get away from the map of Russia. I closed the book.

Amelia remarked, As an educated man, Tom, you must resent being required to labour?

No, I told her. I need to labour. Possibly in a difficult climate. It leaves my mind free.

Curious, said Amelia. My husband used to say that.

Nonetheless, and without rancour against the late Mr Pethick, I wondered if he had ever had his anus violated by a revolver barrel. What could be done with the men who had committed such things, should the revolution come? What school could they be sent to for redemption? Which brought me back to the subject of destroyed souls.

I was just thinking about a man named Menschkin, I told the women. He marches with us, but I'm afraid he then goes to the tsarist consul, McDonald, and to the police.

That's horrible, said Hope. What can you do to stop him?

It might be best not to stop him, I said. Rather fill his head with information that proves groundless. As an agent provocateur he's hilarious. Even the police must know he has a comic aspect.

In what sense is he *hilarious*? asked Amelia.

Once he hung around a Russian Emigrants Union meeting telling us how to make mercury bombs in pots of lard. Men who exhort us to make bombs are always working for the tsar. Or for the Police Commissioner of Queensland.

How does one make a bomb? Hope asked. Out of *lard*, you say?

Incendiaries are made of lard and phosphate. Or explosives of mercury and lard. I'm not sure of the details because I'm not of anarchist bent.

I would have thought nothing could match dynamite, murmured Hope.

I turned to my tea and drank it quickly.

You poor man, Amelia said. I've upset you with the atlas, haven't I? I am sorry.

I held a hand up, denying it.

Amelia murmured, No, you have clearly been through a lot, Tom. Yet many of the leaders of your movement live in exile in comparative comfort. Does that ever concern you?

They've all been through the mill themselves, I told her. One way or another. Plekhanov, that great old man, and Struve and Martov and Vladimir Ilich Lenin. They've all suffered. As a child, Vladmir Ilich saw his brother Alexander hanged. His education was interrupted by exile and bannings from universities. Now he's entitled to some time to write.

I saw Hope shiver in the humid air. I reached a hand out, though it did not touch her. Are you well?

I hear what you're telling us, she said, but I sense that there's a great deal more behind it.

I shrugged.

You mention anarchists so scathingly, Tom. I remember reading a piece – in the *London Illustrated News*, I believe – about a young woman on New Year's Eve, sitting by a window in a Russian city and looking out at a snow-covered road. The provincial governor was due to travel down it, and she had a bomb in a tin box inside a fine handbag she had bought just for this event. Buying a handbag for such a thing . . . Anyhow, while she sat waiting there was a knock on her door and it was a group of Russian children, children in masks, who threw millet seeds at the house and wanted to be paid for doing it.

Yes, I said. It brings good luck.

So she got them to stay, this young woman, and made them tea. And then she saw the governor's cavalry escort riding past, and told them to leave. She walked out into the street with her bomb, noticed a friend, a man who also carried a bomb. When the governor's carriage drew near, her friend threw his bomb under the carriage, but it stuck in snow and did not explode. So she threw hers. And it killed the governor, and she went to prison . . . An anarchist, you see. And so brave.

Would you want to bomb people in Brisbane? I asked.

No. But it's the level of conviction that interests me.

Yet, I insisted, surely you don't envy the naivety of people who believe the world can be changed by one bomb thrown into a particular carriage. Or even by twenty bombs thrown into twenty particular carriages.

Well no, she conceded, almost with an air of disappointment. But I wondered . . . Say I had taken your prosecution file, Amelia – which I deny, anyhow . . . What could happen to me in Russia, Tom? Imprisonment?

If you had done it, or maybe if you hadn't, you would certainly be jailed or exiled.

Maybe to our station in the Darling Downs, said Hope to lighten the mood.

Something like that. Or maybe to the distant north. Cooktown, say.

Even so, we get off lightly here, don't we?

She definitely wanted to believe that.

So say I was that person, the one who took Amelia's file. With all the embarrassment surrounding the issue, I might lose my job. But after a while I could begin practising at the bar, you see. I could perhaps find work with the Arbitration Court in Melbourne. Melbourne winters are harsh by Queensland standards, but the point is, there would be no Siberia for me.

She smiled at me – what I thought of as an Australian smile. It was something alien, unreserved, open. And there might have been some pride there, in the ploy she had pulled off – if indeed it had been her.

Amelia said, It sounds as if the hypothetical *you*, Hope, is disappointed not to be more severely punished.

And so it did.

Amelia turned to me. But Artem, tell me, you speak as if you're subject to the orders of your party. That you go wherever they say.

I entered into the spirit of the occasion. I would show off as I believed Hope was doing.

I'll tell you of a case of obedience, I said. A friend of mine . . . Slatkin . . . has been a loyal member of the party for a decade or more. He's worked with secret strike committees. He recruited strikers from among disloyal or disgruntled soldiers of the tsar. The party is his life. He has a good intellect, and he's very amusing.

He had also occasionally been a bank robber, but I did not tell them that.

Ah, said Amelia, an ideal fellow.

The leader of our faction, Vladimir Ilich, who is a great intellectual, has a high opinion of my friend. Vladimir Ilich had another friend named Nikolai Stürmer, the owner – by inheritance from an uncle – of a massive engineering company. Soon young Nikolai, who was a supporter of our party despite being a capitalist, died tragically of tuberculosis and left his money and his plant to the two Stürmer women, his sisters. Vladimir Ilich asked my friend Slatkin and another of our agents to approach the sisters, charm them, marry them, and secure their wealth for the party. So my friend did approach Daria, one of the sisters, with his condolences, and won her over – she had not met too many fellows like him: earthy and humorous, yet well read. They married and the support Nikolai Stürmer had given the party was continued by his sister and Slatkin. The happy couple remitted many thousands if not millions of roubles to the party through its Swiss bank.

Oh my God, said Amelia, shaking her head. That *is* obedience!

And distasteful, said Hope. Are you asking why we don't feel outrage at the lady bomber, but feel distaste for this?

Amelia shook her head. Surely you're teasing us, Tom. Surely this did not happen.

No, Mrs Pethick, I assure you it did. And everyone is happy. The party has funds and is able to stand by its principles and finance its efforts. And my friend was very happy, the last time I heard. And so was his wife. No one was damaged, yet everyone who knows the story says, How shocking!

The two women looked at each other. Then Amelia said, No one can really approve of that story, Tom. Can they? But it is correct of you to shake up our comfortable assumptions.

I'm sorry, Mrs Pethick . . . I'm just making the point. I didn't want to offend you.

No, said Amelia. Not in the least.

No, Hope agreed.

I was willing now to play the contrite male who has gone too far, told the wrong story in the presence of ladies. At least it might stop them quizzing me about Russia all the time.

But your friend's motives, said Hope. They were so cold, so planned.

And so effectual, Hope, Amelia reminded her.

We drank the dregs of tea.

I can drive you home, Tom, Hope offered.

No, there is no need.

We thanked Amelia, and I walked with Hope to open the car door and then crank the engine. As she was about to get into the car, she stopped. She had come to a sudden decision – I didn't know what it was, and the idea that something new was to be said excited me. We were both standing, either side of Hope's car door, in the infinite possibility of the moment.

She said, I wanted to tell you, perhaps out of vanity . . . I stole Amelia's prosecution file and put it in the stove in our kitchen when the Irish maid was out. I saved Olive Sullivan's notebook and left it on a table at Trades Hall.

I smiled. I always knew you did it, Hope, I assured her. So . . . what *will* happen to you?

I'll resign from the public service with a show of great chagrin over their implication that I might have done it.

I laughed with her.

And then I will take a holiday for a few months, and then I'll apply to the Queensland bar for admission. The vote may be split but I shall be admitted. I told you inside that there's no great danger for me.

Well, great danger isn't necessary. It doesn't ennoble the soul.

Because what she had given me was a precious thing – I couldn't imagine her telling that to her husband straight out – I responded in kind.

I will entrust something to you too, I said. As a gift. I am not going back to my boarding house now. I am going to another house belonging to the Stefanovs, in Merrivale Street. I have rented a room there.

You have left your old boarding house?

No. The truth is that I have rented a room to house a printing press. I have a compositor to do the setting. He begins on Monday. The first edition of the *Australian Ekho* will be printed there behind drawn curtains.

She said, almost at once, I may have time on my hands soon. Could I come and help you in any way?

It would be a waste of your talent, dear Mrs Mockridge.

But it was of course the offer I was fishing for.

You said that prison made you want simple, physical work. I could benefit from some simple work too. Folding and stacking a Russian newspaper sounds very attractive for the moment.

She and I were complicit from then. We knew that we would

be something like plotters in the shadow of the rickety old printing press. It was beyond believing, though, that we would in the end add the weight of desire to the Stefanovs' floorboards or the narrow single bed, little more than a cot, with which the room was furnished. It served only a mundane purpose: I would sometimes lie down and spend the night there after finishing my work in the small hours.

10

One morning, as Freeman Bender's ornate tram – the Palace – moved up Milton Road towards the city, a man wearing a mask of black, the anarchist colour, and presumed to be of the Chicago faction, the dominant Wobbly faction in Australia, emerged from behind a lamppost on the corner of Cribb Street and threw a bomb made out of a large jam tin at one of the tram's windows. As the bomb exploded, the driver brought the tram to a halt and it did not leave the tracks. Because of the strengthened and wire-meshed windows of the tram, some of the blast was deflected back across the street, where, said witnesses, it knocked the anarchist on his arse, after which the masked man was seen running down Cribb Street before darting into a lane and vanishing.

The explosion had come as an utter surprise to those inside the tram, and had done them some damage. Commissioner Urquhart received cuts to his forehead from flying glass, the Supreme Court's Justice Cooper suffered facial wounds from glass and was bruised by a flying occasional table. Mr Mockridge KC, seated with his back to the window, suffered deep neck and scalp wounds from the glass and a broken arm.

These minor injuries of Brisbane worthies were mourned in the daily papers with a reverence appropriate to the wounds of Christ. Of course, they brought Hope and her husband back into the public eye, and, most importantly, they served as proof even to the strikers that the strike had gone too far and that now nothing further could be hoped for. Here – went the argument – was the fundamental havoc that lay behind a supposedly peaceful plea for better wages! Australians liked order, and dynamite was disorder and outside the scope of their desires.

I wondered had the troublemaker Menschkin done it to discredit the strikers, but decided that, if so, it would have been designed to do far less damage to the fathers of the city than it had.

Within a day or two of the dynamite outrage, Hope Mockridge resigned from the attorney-general's department. For days we did not see her at Trades Hall. Perhaps she was nursing her husband, who had been sent home from hospital. Whether worse things happened in Russia or not, I wanted to hear from her. Had the government forced her out of our company with threats?

I had, in the meantime, asked Walter O'Sullivan to speak to the *souz* one evening. In company with Suvarov and Paddy Dykes, whom we'd met by accident along the way and who intended to report on O'Sullivan's speech, I neared Buranda Hall very early.

Mr Dykes, said Suvarov, tell me: are you a miner who writes for newspapers or a newspaperman who used to be a miner?

Paddy thought about it.

A newspaperman who used to be a miner is the answer, I think – but not the best man at either, I'm sad to say. You see, I went to this meeting in Sydney once and saw Billy Hughes speak. Now, there's a man no more educated than me. And throw into that, if you like, a face like a green prawn. And he has a Welsh voice and adenoids. But when he spoke . . . Here was a bloke who used to repair umbrellas for a living. I thought, well, anything's possible. He's attorney-general of the Commonwealth of Australia. A bloke no more educated than me! And he makes a law for a bank for ordinary people. And I decided, Paddy, you can get off your backside and do more. I began writing for the *Worker*. I was still a miner. But now . . .

Now you're a journalist, I told him.

I bloody hope so, he said.

Artem, Suvarov said as we walked up to the hall, a wooden structure set in its own patch of high grass, look out the back!

There was a dray at the rear of the hall, and a man in shirtsleeves was hauling cases between it and the back door. The three of us advanced up the side of the hall, listening to the clatter as the dray-driver shifted his crates through an open door into the small room at the back of the hall. Then Menschkin emerged, looking happier than I'd seen him lately.

Ah, he said, going pale. Mr Samsurov and Mr Suvarov.

He did not bother to refer to Paddy Dykes.

Suvarov's carroty hair seemed to blaze in the evening air. He stepped up to Menschkin and asked what he was doing.

I am delivering . . . Someone ordered . . .

Then he simply ran. He was faster than anyone would think. Suvarov chased him for a while but then obviously wondered what good catching him would do, given Menschkin's protection from the Queensland police.

We went into the back room, where crates of beer bottles with no labels on them were stacked high. Sly grog, said Paddy at once. The bastard!

Illegal liquor. Menschkin's demented plan was to leave it here, out of sight, and then the police could raid, find it and close the hall and the *souz* down. Paddy and I looked at each other, and began laughing at Menschkin's childlike plans. He was going to a crazy amount of effort to please his masters. Suvarov, Paddy and I loaded the dray again with the unlabelled beer, and led its horse by the halter two hundred yards or so down the street, where we unhitched the horse and left the animal grazing in the lush pavement grass, and the beer standing in the dray, waiting for any adventurous passer-by to sample it.

O'Sullivan and his wife arrived early to look over the platform and to practise elocution – something that Olive supervised. Eeh, aah, ooh, said O'Sullivan, stretching his jaw muscles. I began to wonder had I made a mistake. But when the crowd arrived and he started to speak there was no doubting his seriousness, nor even his philosophic affinity with Vladimir Ilich. What does Australia need? he asked. And what the world? Does it need a gang of part-time social democrats whose chief task is to prove to their betters that they are responsible people, good managers of the public purse? Where will that ever get us? The Australian Socialist Party is based on the proposition of overthrowing – to defeat capitalism, not to finesse it; to undermine it rather than dance with it. In this task, said O'Sullivan, we do not welcome dilettantes. We plan to be the party to whom people turn when they have become aware that the earth belongs to those who labour *on* it, and the factory belongs to those who labour *in* it. At this stage we do not seek votes. We seek activists.

By the end of the meeting, I had been impressed sufficiently to take an entry form and join his ASP.

Olive approached me, notepad in hand. I know we have met before, she said, but would you mind writing your name out here? In roman script?

I did so. I saw Suvarov joining too. We were now members of an antipodean echo of Vladimir Ilich's organisation.

Across the city men began to return to work at the meatworks and the waterfront and railways. But Mr Freeman Bender would not take the tramway strikers back. So much for the mercy of Justice Higgins! The Trades Hall declared the strike had ended with a moral victory, and so I returned to work as well, since there is no sense in being a strike force of one.

The good news was that the first edition of *Australian Ekho*, eight pages in length, had been printed, distributed and posted. A typical letter from readers came from some lonely place in the hills behind Rockhampton. *How could I begin to express my joy at seeing in print the language that is my mother, and the sentiments expressed which we have been forced by oppression to embrace.* The *Ekho* was a consolation to the most far-flung of the Russians.

11

I was working at the Stefanovs' one evening under a bare bulb but in the joy of seeing the press stamp the made-up frames and slide forth the wonder of printed paper when there was a curt knocking on the door of my room. Thin Mrs Stefanov was there, frowning and quite handsome. I had a woman visitor, she said tightly. I followed her towards the front door, but as she reached the parlour she stepped into it, leaving me to confront the visitor alone. The energy with which Mrs Stefanov turned away added up to a command that nothing indecent would happen in her house in Merrivale Street. Hence I knew before I saw her it was Hope Mockridge.

So it was – Hope in a dress the colour of duck eggs, her white-gloved hands modestly hidden by a reticule.

I thought I would visit your press, said Hope.

Yes, I said. Ah . . . there is no one there but me just now. Suvarov will be along . . .

So, may I see your printery?

I could not deny her that. On the way along the hall I enquired loudly about her husband's injuries.

Well, she said, smiling, I now see that despite the magazine story about the Russian girl anarchist, there's no glory in dynamite.

We got to the back room and sniffed the air saturated with black ink.

So this is the way newspapers are produced in Russia?

And in Australia. The lies are printed in far grander premises across the river, and on far vaster machines.

I am here to work, she told me, taking off her jacket. Then she walked across to the table in the corner, which held a model of a monorail. Rybukov, my asthmatic friend who had been dismissed as a project engineer by Brisbane Tramways, had brought his model and plans for a special tram/train to be stored with me. It made sense – his own room at Adler's was small. The model was of two white carriages on a small circle of line, but the line was single – a monorail, as Rybukov called it; the People's Train, the future means of moving people in cities. Having been sacked by Bender, he had to await another chance, and hope for possible public interest in an article about his monorail and its unique gyroscopes he was writing for a magazine called *World Engineering*.

It's got only one line.

Yes. That's the trick of it. It could change the world.

Wouldn't it come off the line going round corners?

Not according to Rybukov, I assured her. He's studied the physics and made gyroscope models.

This . . . this is what Bender was raving to us about that afternoon in his office.

Yes. Rybukov calls it the People's Train.

What a name! she said, and moved away towards our self-inking lever press. On a tray by the wall, I had my Cyrillic script arrayed – a pleasant font, *Berezniki*, familiar to all Russian newspaper readers.

I explained that the work ahead of her was tedious – the task of stacking on a bench the six hundred copies of pages printed on both side, pages one, two, eleven and twelve in one pile, three, four, nine and ten in another, and so on, as they came off my press. That task alone would perhaps occupy some hours.

I have a great deal of time, she said.

She set to, and our conversation became basic, like most cottage-industry conversations. After a time Suvarov arrived to stand at an upright desk and subedit some of the articles we had received so that they were ready when our compositor came.

The next time Hope turned up to my supposedly secret printing press she wore a black hat and a dress of blue and white fabric, and a beautiful opal brooch at her neck. It was a night when the seasons were in transition. The heat was not as torrid as it had been, the nights were balmy but not stifling. The so-called winter, so warm by Russian standards, was nonetheless on its way. Since an orgy had not resulted from Mrs Stefanov's last admission of Hope to my printing room, this time she had been let in with slightly better grace.

It was earlier in the evening than her last visit. My assistants Suvarov and Rybukov were presently at their dinner at Adler's boarding house. I had installed a plain, unadorned samovar in the corner. I made Hope a glass of tea with honey, and we sat down on the chairs by the bench where stacked newsprint lay and inhaled again that intoxicating perfume of oily printing ink and newsprint sheets.

Again I asked about her husband and his injuries. She looked at me as if there were more to all that than my simple question could cover.

He's appearing in court with his arm in a sling, she told me. Very gallant.

And there's no idea at all who threw the dynamite?

No. Everyone knew who took Amelia's file. But the dynamiter is a mystery. It was said briskly, as if she were warning me off the subject. She shook her head. It doesn't interest me. What interested me were your remarks on our hypocrisies. That afternoon at Amelia's. You know – that story of the man who was ordered to marry for the cause.

She looked away. She sounded calm but was not.

I was playing games that afternoon, I hurried to say. I think I exaggerated how close a friend the bridegroom was to me.

I don't want you to misunderstand. I am not a stupid girl but of course it's the sort of discussion that made me even more sharply aware my marriage is a thing of very awkward convenience. I don't hate him, though . . . The truth of marriage is that I *know* him. When his arm was broken, I felt anxiety for him, more than I would for an acquaintance. Does that constitute a kind of love? In any case, if you see me as a hypocrite, being here instead of in his house, then I acknowledge the hypocrisy. I have my excuses. But every hypocrite does.

You take all this too seriously, Hope. As if I were here to judge you.

You may not mean to, but that's your effect.

I've got no power to make you feel uneasy, I said.

Why do you own a printing press, which you operate behind closed curtains, if it's not to weigh up the world and find it lacking?

It's just my passion, I said. I might say I need a rest from ideas. But labour on the wharves isn't enough. I need to talk to others too.

In the condition I was in, every sudden contact was amazing. She reached out and took my hand, stroking the back of it with a thumb. I was won by this touch. She laid her face against my cheek, but when I turned my face to engage her, lip to lip, she averted her head. She said, I am near the end of an illness.

Tuberculosis? I suggested.

But she seemed too healthy for that, and her hair was lustrous. She looked at me directly and I knew at once what she meant. Like so many women, she had been infected by her husband.

Artem . . . Tom. I wish to be in your company, for the moment, as a friend. That's all. There is nothing else.

Her tea was finished, and I thought to get her more.

If you have been ill, I said, and such a woman warrior, then I certainly look forward to meeting you when you are well.

She smiled, moved her head from side to side as if balancing things. It's the tail end of my sickness, she said. Medical improvements are astounding, and they sweep around the globe with the mail. But we shan't talk about it any more. Let me fold the papers.

So it began again. The double-printed pages came from the chute at the front of the machine and she folded and stacked them.

And thus we worked together till half past nine, when – as last time – my friend Suvarov arrived.

Rybukov can't come, Suvarov said. Tonight his asthma is cruel.

As I walked her to the corner of Merrivale Street afterwards, so that she could return north on one of Bender's trams, I felt consoled in a fraudulent way. Beyond any doubt, it was best that nothing sentimental had happened, that we had talked and worked together like two friends. This was, after all, how genuinely revolutionary men and women, undistracted by the simperings of bourgeois love, were meant to work.

Yet I wanted to have pretexts to see her again. I remembered a coming event all at once.

Perhaps you would like to visit Buranda Hall on Friday night?

Then I remembered that the play would be all in Russian.

Of course not, I answered for her. It's Maxim Gorki's *The Lower Depths*. You may not know the play, but Suvarov is playing the part of the actor who hangs himself in despair at the end.

That sounds very entertaining, she said, without a derisive smile.

It's a grim and wonderful play, I said. Very realistic, set in a low boarding house, full of tragic figures. But all in Russian.

I would dearly love to come, Tom.

The shining tram she was to catch, protected from anarchists by a wall of social outrage, drew up clanging beneath thunderclouds. She climbed aboard as if she had never had a quarrel with the system on which it ran.

12

We were drinking tea with Suvarov on the dusty stage of Buranda Hall, just south of South Brisbane, where the rags, uprights and timber bunks remained in place, ready for the following night's performance of *Lower Depths.* It was an excellent production, I thought. Mrs Stefanov had had the surprising courage to play Vaselisa, the greedy and unfaithful dosshouse owner's wife. Nastia the streetwalker had, for the sake of propriety, been played by young Zetkin, son of Zetkin of the Waterside Workers. In the wrong boy's hands, this role could have been played entirely for comedy and could have lowered the whole tenor of the play. Although some of his fellow stevedores, Australians, had come to watch the play and had whistled when he first appeared in a dress, he remained resolutely true to Gorki. The Australians knew nothing about this Russian masterpiece but by reading the faces on stage, they – to their credit and my surprise – kept themselves in reasonable bounds from then on. It was a triumph for Rybukov, who had directed the entire performance.

The reason we were still here was that, though I told him Mrs Mockridge had a cab waiting, Suvarov was in one of his talkative moods. He knew a bottle of vodka awaited him back at Adler's boarding house, where he would be greeted by his fellows as a miraculous and transformed being. Thank you, Mr Gorki! He did not necessarily want to rush the moment, and he was one of those generous men who, though of course enjoying the company of Mrs Mockridge himself, had seen that she was my close friend and so put great effort into enlarging on my reputation and exploits.

Now, said Suvarov, when the old German who is the immigration officer here in Brisbane meets our boat, he stamps whatever papers we have to give him. But one young fellow is in a panic, and Artem says to him, What've you got? The young man had a program in his pocket from a theatre in the French concession in Shanghai. Give him that, Artem told him, and the young bloke does and the German stamped it and said, Welcome.

But then, Suvarov continued, the fight begins. We arrive at the immigration dormitory, which is run by an Englishman. And he says to us all, If you join a trade union in Australia you will be deported by the government. The unions are a source of discontent and disorder and if you join such groups we will send you back to Russia to the tsar's army. And Artem speaks up and says, Sir, Mr Englishman, there is no such deportation law as the one you speak of. You see, the Englishman didn't know the law and neither did Artem. But Artem could sniff out imaginary laws just as fast as the Englishman could make them up.

I intend to join the unions of my fellow Australians, Artem told him, and every Russian immigrant knows that he should do the same.

The Englishman assigned Artem to clean the lavatories, so Artem just said, Thank you, Mr Petty Tyrant. I have lived in lavatories in Shanghai and cleaning them is too good a job for me. You understand, *they* see Artem in one light and he turns the light back on them.

Come on, Suvarov. Why don't we go home?

But Suvarov wouldn't be silenced.

So Artem left and found Rybukov, and stayed with him at Adler's. As for myself, I had no money, and I lacked Artem's courage, so I pretended to be a good tsarist and spent a week free of charge in the dormitory.

And so, I said, we all became happy Queenslanders.

But Suvarov wasn't nearly finished.

And then I was sent out to work on the fettling gang, out in Tallwood, and a week later I hear from a Russian travelling through that he saw Artem at Warwick, working on the new line there. I set out to travel to Warwick, because I knew Artem would talk the man in charge there into giving me a job. I had a good swag and slept in paddocks under the stars. The last bit I travelled with some railway fellows on a small rail machine – you know the sort of thing. And I got to this big construction camp with white tents, and found Artem. He gave me tea and took me to see the boss, who already knew Artem even though he'd been there only a few days. Why? Artem can work like a machine, that's why. So we were building a rail bed and carrying rails, and we shared the same tent.

I did not think that occupying the same tent was an accomplishment that would impress Mrs Mockridge. But he talked on about the hearty fellows, the Irish, Canadians, Scots who were the companions of us Russians in the railway camp in Warwick.

Mrs Mockridge must get home, I told him again.

No, no, no, he said, waving his head, as if forbidding her to rise from her chair. Did you tell her about the shovelling contest?

It was true that one Sunday the boss had pitched a Canadian named Lofty Sam against me to see who could fill a wagon with soil faster. Some people ran gambling on it. The railway workers and their families came and watched it; there wasn't much excitement for them except such a sporting contest. In the end I was fortunate and vain enough to win – and was a mess with sweat afterwards, needing pints of water.

I told the bare outlines, so that Suvarov would be done with it quickly and let Hope go, but he couldn't be stopped.

He went on about our Russian choir – we formed it to sing Russian songs to the Irish on their feast day, St Patrick's. They were good fellows and appreciated it. As Vladimir Ilich told me in the letter in which he sent me to Perm, You cannot help organising things, Artem. He didn't say whether it was a disease or a virtue.

Suvarov said, You know, it's easy to like the Irish because they are rebellious, but they have no class consciousness at all. Their imagination is so blotted out by some dream of independence they don't care what kind of independence it is. But they always won the tug-of-war, so Artem went round to all the Russian camps and found a Russian team, full of huge Jews from Odessa and big Mujiks from the Volga. And we ended up winning the tug-of-war too. Artem looks nice, but he can't stand not winning.

I confessed it might be true. Hope looked at me.

The boss liked him so well, said Suvarov, that he put him on the easy job. Explosives.

Explosives, said Hope with a knowing smile. Did he indeed?

Yes, I admitted. But I did not blow up the tram.

She laughed at the idea.

I too know how to handle explosives, said Hope. My grandfather taught me on our property in the Darling Downs.

That's where we worked, said Suvarov excitedly. So your grandfather is a great landowner?

Yes, said Hope, I suppose you could say that. Sheep and cattle.

Dear God, said Suvarov. We are mixing with a princess, Artem.

Yes, I said. Except she is too honest for those pretensions. Anyhow, that's our life story, and you don't have to listen to it ever again, Mrs Mockridge. May I escort you to your cab?

Hope and I left the theatre. She laughed occasionally at this or that aspect of Suvarov's recital as we descended from the stage and started walking out, but when I looked back, Suvarov was still sitting there on the stage, suddenly looking as dejected as the actor whose part he had played. Sometimes some sorrow from the road he had taken would seize him like this, as if he could not move for its weight.

I'll see you at Adler's, I called.

He looked up, and his good spirits returned and, Yes, he said. *Tovarich*, Artem!

13

Walter O'Sullivan and his wife Olive returned to Melbourne on a steamer. I had told him I would follow his directives for local action – he in the Moscow of Australia where the federal parliament sat, me in Brisbane, the Perm or Novgorod of Australia – as long as they did not clash with the program laid out in *What is to be Done?*, the great tract of my party head, Vladimir Ilich Lenin. Given that Walter had also an enthusiasm for that publication, it was unlikely I would disgree with him. I suggested, however, he write out a document of his own beliefs and send it to an address in Zurich I gave him. It would stand as a wonderful proof that the idea of a revolutionary elite devoted full time to action was believed in and pursued, however modestly, across the globe here, in southernmost places.

After the night of *The Lower Depths* I did not see Mrs Mockridge again until May. The executive of the Russian Emigrants Union went down to the wharf to meet eighteen survivors of the Lena goldmine massacre who were touring the world with their story. That very evening we welcomed them onto the stage at Buranda Hall at South Brisbane, where Suvarov had recently had his triumph as the actor. Amelia and Hope arrived together, but I was too busy to greet them as I was introducing the eighteen survivors to our translator for the evening, Setkin the elder, who had been in Brisbane since 1892 and whose English was more than competent.

One of the chief Lena River strikers, Lebedev, was rather impressed by Brisbane – all the sunshine, and the fact this meeting could be held openly. I have to admit that is the excitement I felt when I first came here. On the platform, Lebedev began by drawing a picture for us of life in dismal Bodaybo, between the mountain ranges on the Vitim River, tributary of the Lena, among mountains and in a valley the sun liked to flee. Here the miners had been working fifteen to sixteen hours each Siberian day without a union to protect them. The number of accidents from broken drills and rashness with explosives and gas explosions meant that from every thousand men who worked digging the gold, seven hundred could expect an injury. Tyrannous foremen had the power to fine workers for failing to meet levels of production, damage to equipment and other technicalities, so a part of the pitiable wages went to pay fines. The rest, said Lebedev, was issued in coupons that could be used only to buy deplorable goods at company stores that charged an excessive price.

When workers at the Dhereyevsky goldfield went on strike, led by Lebedev and others, it was like the *Potemkin* battleship rebellion in 1905, claimed Lebedev. It all started with rotten meat. That was all the store had to sell. If you bought meat from the locals along the foothills of the mountains, you were arrested and beaten. The strikers demanded an eight-hour day, a large pay rise, an end to all fines and an improvement in the supply of food. The Lena goldmining joint stock company ignored the demands. The strike spread to other goldfields along the Lena, and troops in fur hats came riding up from Kerensk. These soldiers arrested Lebedev and other members of the strike committee and put them in prison. The following day, thousands of people marched to visit the state prosecutor on the Nadezhdinsky goldfield, where miners were being held in the lock-up, to protest the arbitrary arrest. But before they could reach the prosecutor's office, they were ambushed from both sides and the front by soldiers, who opened fire, killing hundreds of people and wounding hundreds more.

Though the strike was still in progress, sympathisers had got

Lebedev out of prison and then out of the country by way of the east. As he left, he urged the workers and their families to abandon the goldfields, though many did not want to give up the graves of their dead to Lenzoloto, the company. But if the ten thousand miners of the Lena and all their families abandoned the gold company then its directors would learn the lesson that labour was not powerless, and investors such as Count Sergei Witt, minister of the tsar, and Empress Maria Fyodorovna, birdlike mother of the tsar himself, might be similarly damaged.

When Lebedev finished his story, there was great applause from the floor. Amelia was smiling and Hope, for some reason, was glowing, as if first-class ideas had been rubbed together to make warmth. Questions were now asked from the floor. The anarchists wanted to know why, with their access to dynamite, the miners had not blown up the pit heads and the crushing machinery. Lebedev pointed to the presence of the army and the concern the strikers had for their wives and families. A dynamite attack would be a roar from the people, but the state could roar back louder. It was the withdrawal of labour that was most important.

I was leaving Buranda Hall after locking it when I saw in the gloom, glistening moist with an early winter dew, the massive navy-blue Mockridge vehicle. Hope was not in it but appeared out of the dark blue shadow of the building in a yellow dress and white jacket.

A fascinating evening, Tom, she told me. She handed me an envelope. Could I make a contribution to the upkeep of those men?

You are always generous, I said. I'll send you a receipt.

There's no need, she replied, the last word transforming itself into a laugh.

Where is Amelia?

Amelia has too much socialist pride most of the time to ride in my big machine. She yielded to the tram. Will you crank the engine for me again?

There would have been plenty of departing husky fellows who could have done that but she had waited for me. She sat at the wheel, and I jerked the crank and the machine started raging away.

I stepped back and waved. I'll walk home, I cried out.

She did not seem to hear and descended from the driver's seat to the ground.

I wanted to tell you, she said. I am whole. The doctors have declared me recovered.

Her face looked luminous with a wafer-thin gaiety. There was something in it that I was uncomfortable with.

I'm very pleased, I told her. For your sake.

In her exuberance she pulled me to her and she quickly kissed my cheek and then wiped it with a handkerchief.

I need time, she said, to breathe out the last exhalations. Then I will come and stack newspapers with you. And – to speak frankly, Tom, we will be lovers then. We're equals, so why shouldn't I say it? Why shouldn't I be the seducer?

But I saw signs even then that she was a woman engaged on a project, not on a passion. She was straining too hard to be a free woman. What she said was not in her nature.

She drove off then. In the night light the dust she raised looked a shade of mauve.

G'day, Tom, I heard behind me. It was little Paddy Dykes. I had not seen him in the hall but was pleased he was still in Brisbane.

That was a top-class evening, he remarked. A good idea to have a translator, eh. It helped a lot. By the way, he said, dropping his voice to a level that wasn't *by the way* at all, I've come across some interesting news about the dynamite chucker, and Mr Bender's tram. One of the unionists told me he met a man in a pub in Woolloongabba, and this bloke made a very interesting claim about the tram. Just got to check out a few things yet.

Tell me, was it that idiot Menschkin?

Doesn't seem so, he said. Doesn't seem so at all. But that's another story. For all his good work, or to get rid of him, the police have arranged for him to be given a farm allotment up north. Just a little dairy place near Rockhampton. As for the dynamiter, I'll let you know as soon as I know.

Mr Dykes, you seem to be indeed an inquiring man.

I don't want to go back to the big slag heap in Broken Hill, so I have to come up with the good stuff. Talk to you soon, Tom.

He waved and started to move away, but remembered something. Oh, he told me, that company store thing, selling bad food at any price they like, siphoning the wages back? That happened here too. Bastardry! My granddad was stuck at a station in the Barrier Ranges five years because he couldn't pay off the bill he owed the station owner. It's a good trick to play on a man, isn't it? And the owners in Siberia and the owners in Australia thought it up on their own, without sharing ideas at all. Doesn't that beat everything?

Well, I said, human nature unregulated! It explains all the world's sorrows.

The next morning it was reported that Mrs Hope Mockridge had visited her husband in hospital. That news item cast a strange light on her conversation with me. I would need to get used to Hope's mixed messages.

Even so, I dreamed of heroic service to Hope Mockridge, of ridiculous proofs of love, even unto death, and so forth. These dreamings were certainly more excessive than anything I had allowed myself before. The question that arose was: were these fantasies really as pathetic as our scholars would have it? They seemed all at once to be so profoundly planted in me that one wondered whether even the greatest revolution in society could quickly uproot them – the male impulse towards idolising and debasing, the woman's impulse to self-immolation, which I had seen even in Krupskaya. Hope Mockridge had put under siege my agnosticism about a connection between man and woman that excluded all others.

As I had in the past, I calmed myself by thinking of my grandfather. He would reach out and cuff my grandmother without warning and she, wonderful woman though she was, would just shake her head and get on with everything useful to do with livestock and the house – the things he was too lazy or embittered to attend to. My grandfather had a sour heart he never passed on to my father, I am happy to say. But in this situation I imagined my grandfather, so savage later in his disappointment at things, being subject at the start to the same luscious impulses as me, an intoxicating and exclusive devotion to my grandmother's face and body and noble heart, to the extent he could not imagine ever sending blows and curses in her direction.

There was a time when men, including the greatest revolutionaries and writers, played love songs on banjos, simply 'followed their hearts'. Like the young homeward-bound Russian in Turgenev's *The Torrents of Spring* who falls in love with the daughter of the owner of a chocolate shop in Frankfurt, and is compelled to remain in the city, obliged by his infatuation and his outside chance of winning the girl. Why did I love that novel when I was sixteen? Was it for the twists of plot and the barriers and trials of blood put in the way of poor Sanin's love for Gemma Roselli?

On a crasser level, did he carry a packet of condoms in his pocket, just in case?

I could not imagine my friend and mentor Vladimir Ilich strumming too many banjos or fighting too many duels for his wife, Krupskaya, nor her wanting him to. In his youth the Okhrana would have shot him for free, without his needing to invite another jealous male to do it.

Suvarov, who was bolder and more experienced than me in these matters, thought it a great joke to buy some condoms at the Polish chemist's shop in Turbot Street one day. He joked that he virtually needed to tell the chemist he was a syphilitic before the man would sell them. I didn't tell him how this banter irked me. But even my anger was suspect. Why shouldn't love be practical? Particularly if it were not love but a sickness.

Yet, meeting by arrangement in the Stefanovs' curtained room, in the shadow of the modest printing press standing like the patron saint of our adventure, Hope Mockridge and I took to the single bed the place offered and partly sated and partly enlarged our hunger for each other. The bed was enlarged too, so that it seemed a valid arena for us. She proved all that could be imagined: a superb, white, richly curved creation, generous enough to let me see that much. Still, there was a discretion and modesty in the way she went about it – is it crass to say that in large part her outer garments remained undisturbed?

I was amazed with the height and scale of our appetite, and it mattered not at all that Mrs Stefanov might come to her own conclusions, for I had that demented feeling that the world must surely be a co-conspirator in our delight. In any case, judgement had been sent flying. Between our raging bouts, we edited the paper together. She suggested metaphors and emphatic phrases for a letter I sent throughout Queensland, asking the Russians to contribute their florins to a permanent Russian address in Brisbane, where men could stay when they came south from the cane fields, and where newcomers like the Lena survivors could be welcomed after their few irksome days at Immigration House.

Subarov and Rybukov must have both known, and chosen not to know, what was happening. They would time their visits to the room when Hope Mockridge was not there. I don't know how they managed that, and I have to confess that for the first week or two of my frenzy, I took it as part of the way the cosmos – yes, the cosmos! – was applauding and accommodating what I thought of as love.

And in those weeks, rising in my throat like a bubble, was an intention to show her Russia. But what Russia? The Russia of miserable Glebovo? The rail yards at barren Perm? The Russia I felt such a boyish urge to show her was not there to visit. It was mapped along my veins and the veins of many like me. Its future architecture was laid out deep in our brains. It was a Russia as yet unbuilt. It could not yet be revealed to anyone.

One evening Hope and I sat over tea, her hair loose, honey swirling in our cups as it dissolved. She leaned a head on her hand, lost in thought, then said, You are different from Englishmen, Tom.

For some reason I could smell peril and suddenly wanted to stop her. I would be very embarrassed if she began comparisons with her husband. Surely she wouldn't. And despite everything, I found that I did not want her to talk of us now as destined lovers, sentenced to each other's embrace. I wanted that idea to remain in my brain.

Am I also different from Celts? I asked her.

Oh God, yes. She shook her head, and then said deliberately, Your consideration, for example.

I had an urge to bury my head but I said, Of course I should be considerate. We are collaborators in pleasure. Of course I should be!

Not all men think women are meant to have pleasure.

Well, love is democratic. Otherwise it's just a monster and his bait. A violation. A landlord raping a peasant.

I had never had a conversation like this before.

She was smiling broadly at my solemnity. She said, I have done my best to be forward like a modern woman. But it's difficult . . .

I rubbed her arm with the back of my hand. She said, One young man I knew kissed me as if I might break in his hands. I intended to marry him for a time, but I knew his carefulness would drive me mad.

That's why boys like that go to prostitutes, I said. They pay, and in return they are allowed to maul.

As for the landlord and the peasant, I wouldn't say that about my husband. I'd say he was more like a gentleman out riding who accidentally tramples someone's field.

We would never be far from talking about her husband. But, our bodies having moved like delirious machines, I did not yet notice it.

14

The leader in Brisbane of O'Sullivan's Australian Socialist Party was a waterside worker named Thompson, who notified the attorney-general that our first large meeting was planned to take place on a Sunday afternoon at the end of winter in Albert Square.

He received a reply in these terms: Queensland is a Christian state, and the Christians, who are in the overwhelming majority, must be safeguarded on the Sabbath from the ungodly utterances of a few atheists.

Surely enough, we members felt bound to make our point – a freedom of speech campaign. Walter O'Sullivan sent a telegram from Melbourne backing our resolution and wishing he could join us. But despite his mistrust of parliaments, he was attempting to get a resolution concerning Home Rule in Ireland taken up by the elected socialists in the Victorian legislative assembly.

Hope Mockridge and Amelia Pethick also expressed themselves ready to raise their voices in Albert Square in defiance of Hope's former employer, the attorney-general. I urged Hope not to attend the gathering or test the issue. She could then be counsel to those who were arrested, if there were arrests. Giving up the chance to assemble could be her self-sacrifice. As for Amelia, she should stay away on the grounds that the Queensland police had no affection for her after the hatpin affair. I'd had a hard time dissuading Rybukov from turning up – I feared a damp cell might be bad for his lungs.

That Sunday, a drizzly winter's day, I got to Albert Square early. I moved uncertainly around the city council's lawns and flowerbeds as the sun came out and young couples anxious to escape their parents' eyes began to turn up with blankets to settle themselves on the drying lawns.

Paddy Dykes was another early arrival for the rally, to be in one corner of the square. He turned up in the suit he always wore, a ginger-checked affair that would suit most men for a picnic. Because he was negligent about his clothing, this suit had become his uniform.

Expecting the cops, Tom? he asked me.

Not yet. We are an assembly of two.

Isn't that enough to be a crime in this bushwhacker state? He smiled then and leaned towards me. Remember I told you about the fellow in the pub at Woolloongabba? The fellow who made certain claims about Bender's tram? Well I've met up with him. I went to the pub with my unionist friend and here's this big solid fellow, all the charm of a trapdoor spider on a shithouse step. Well, he used to put dynamite in drill holes for the railway. And he claims to have thrown the Palace bomb.

Is it a reliable claim?

He said that for his services he's been given a house in Toowong. He named the street. It turns out to be the case all right. I went to the registrar-general's and filled out a form to see the title to the house. I found it was bought for him by the Queensland Securities Company. So then I enquired into that company.

You're a genuine ferret, Paddy, I told him.

He grinned crookedly. Yeah, but I'm not the one who's hiding up a hole. Anyhow, one of the principal men of this Queensland Securities is Freeman Bender of Brisbane Tramways. There are two other directors of Brisbane Tramways who share that honour with him. I also sighted the stamp-duty cheque signed by Bender himself. Howzat! Clean bloody bowled!

I was genuinely interested now. That means Bender employed the man?

Yes, said Paddy Dykes. Quid pro bloody quo!

Are you going to tell this story in the *Worker*?

Yes, Tom. But the authorities here don't listen to the *Worker*. I've also passed the details on to a scribe of my acquaintance at the *Brisbane Telegraph*, as fine a crusty old rag as you could get. It'll be harder to shut him up. Set deep in his wrinkled face, his eyes blazed. When it becomes known, said Paddy, Bender's credit will be blown in Brisbane. The man in the pub told me Bender's angry because too much mercury was used in the bomb. If it got out he was involved, his toff mates who were injured wouldn't forgive him. Talk about a pork chop at a synagogue! They're the ones who'll drive him out of town. He'll have to go home and pick on coalminers in Pittsburgh.

This exciting conversation was interrupted by the arrival of Thompson with a banner we helped him unfurl. *Australian Socialist Party.* There were quite a few men from the unions, Australians and Britons and others, perhaps two dozen. Since the Salvation Army was allowed to campaign and play band music and march on the Sabbath, Suvarov, with his theatrical tastes, turned up in a Salvation Army uniform with a donation box in his hands. The little crowd was swelled further by a young Lena striker who had decided to stay here in Brisbane after the others left, a hulking young man named Podnaksikov. Freckles on his face, which mining in Siberia had subdued, had come blazing out in Brisbane.

As we stood around the little rostrum, Thompson, a thin fellow whose face looked prematurely seamed, advanced to a low sandstone wall, climbed onto it, and began to speak earnestly about the right of assembly. The ban was not for our sake, and not for the sake of respectable householders whose Sunday rest was in any case disturbed by the sound of massed religious brass bands, but for the sake of capital and its underpinnings.

It was not the best of speeches. I looked around. Families with children were turning up for picnics on the broad lawns behind us. I had a feeling that we were so small in number, and Thompson so little a threat to good order, that we would not be noticed. Ten minutes in, however, I saw the navy blue of police converging from the streets on either side of the square. We were about equal in number and they moved among us, arresting us one by one, taking us to enclosed horse-drawn wagons parked in Ann Street.

Two constables descended on me. The horrors of the old feeling of being constrained, something I thought I'd got over long ago, returned to me as they pushed me along.

Thompson called, No resistance, please, comrades. Show them who we are!

The police had the batons, after all, and were the same big muscular yokels one generation removed from Scotland and Ireland who had broken up the strike march.

Hope, whom I hadn't noticed until then, rushed forward to the senior policeman at the corner of Ann Street.

Inspector, she said, I am counsel representing these men.

All right, miss, said the older policeman with distaste, as if she were declaring her flesh for sale.

You are a base man, I called to him, and he came over to me, raised his elbow (being shorter than me), and dug it into my skull behind my ear. Through my pain I heard Hope cry, Say nothing, Tom, it just gives them further cause.

As I was hustled a few steps, I had the depressing sight of two policemen wrestling with young Podnaksikov. Please, I said, Inspector, please let him go. He was just wandering past.

The inspector spat at my feet and walked away.

Paddy Dykes was at first arrested but soon let go, since a policeman remembered him as mixing with reporters from the better Brisbane papers.

I'll stick with these blokes, he told a police sergeant.

You'll push off when you're told, you bastard.

I don't bloody want to push off and I don't have to.

The sergeant belted Paddy's ear sideways with the stub end of his baton. Here was a gendarme, Queensland-style, beating up a man even because he insisted – unsuccessfully – on being arrested.

In Suvarov's case – though he claimed to be a Salvation Army man who had been looking for donations among the ungodly – they believed not his uniform but his glottal Russian accent, and he shared a wagon with myself and two other men on the way to being charged for violation of the Assembly and Affray Act.

Even then, as we jolted companionably in the back of the wagons off to police headquarters, I thought, they surely cannot punish two dozen men listening to a boring speech on a Sunday morning.

We were taken down to the police cells we had occupied once before. Some men were bored. Not Podnaksikov though, who sat trembling and inspecting his own hands for what palmists pretended to see there: a lifeline.

15

They had taken Suvarov's Salvation Army jacket and cap away and left him shivering overnight. Not a large thing in the history of his sufferings, but in the morning I could see that he was feverish and more hollow-eyed than would have been normal in the circumstances. He had made his assessment more finely and accurately than me, and presumed we would be attacked. The survivor of the Lena massacre, Podnaksikov, looked like a large child who had wandered into a kingdom whose rules he did not understand. The question that occupied us now, as it hadn't that morning, was: could we be truly imprisoned, and in that case how much did the Boggo Road prison of Queensland resemble the prisons of the tsar?

The next morning the public prosecutor let go a few of the men arrested the day before, but no one of Russian background, so poor Podnaksikov was among the twelve of us brought up to the court above to be charged with violating the Act. Bail was refused for such desperate criminals as had dared come together for a dull speech in Albert Square, a frightful assault on society. After we came down, Hope was permitted three minutes to talk to us through the bars. To me it was like a conversation across a river.

If you plead guilty, you'll get lesser prison time or perhaps a fine, she said.

Do you have a defence ready for a not-guilty plea? Thompson asked her, as I held her eye through the bars.

Yes. There is a good argument for not guilty. But this judge has a closed mind.

What do you think we'll get for pleading not guilty?

She put her long-fingered gloved hand to her brow for a second and shook her head. Then she looked up. Surely not more than two months.

I thought, I can manage that. I've managed years!

Obviously Suvarov consoled himself with the same thought. His revolutionary daring came surging back.

Then are we solid? asked Thompson. Are we solid, comrades, all together? Not guilty?

Most growled yes.

Very well, gentlemen, said Hope with great dignity. I shall argue to the limit for you all. But you must help me, Thompson. No inflammatory remarks. You understand?

How I adored her then, but perhaps differently, like a child in a storm finding a kindly aunt.

Cuffed by the wrists and ankles – always a strange unutterable experience and of course reminiscent of our pasts – we were not brought up to magistrates, the lowest order of the judicial system, but taken by cart to the district court, and when our black carriage entered its yard and we hobbled out, the number of police in the yard proved to us that we were in more trouble than we should reasonably have been. Our anklets were removed. Stumbling up the stairs to the court, I noticed that the jury box was empty. The Act, it turned out, did not allow for a jury for our offences – a sign that the authorities desired a certain result. We now stood up on orders from a court clerk. From the dock I saw a black-robed judge enter and sit on the bench. At the prosecutions table, three wigged men represented the state. Below me at her table, Hope turned, looking strange since she too wore her legal wig and gown, a nun of the law, lovely and humane, the gloss of sweat on her upper lip, which madly I took as a message to reassure me that under all the pomp of the court lay the accustomed veins and glands of life and passion.

Suvarov claimed the right to the use of an interpreter, just to hold the court up. He was full of tricks like that, little time-consuming ploys. Annoyed, the judge ordered Suvarov's trial delayed a day, which was probably more of a result than Suvarov wanted.

The state's prosecutor now put his case against us. We had known we could not assemble without the police commissioner's consent, and we knew we would have been very properly refused it, since a British and Christian society wisely did not let those who intended to destroy it discuss their plans in the open air in the hearts of capital cities on Sundays. And unless possessed by a malign spirit of disruption, we certainly should not do so at a time when a recent strike had shown how disaffected many were with society, and when men like these men, Your Honour, men who were anarchists or the friends of anarchists, had thrown an assassin's bomb into the midst of leading citizens!

When Hope rose it was to the evident disgust of the judge.

Yes, Mrs Mockridge? said the judge. I hope your esteemed husband is well.

Thank you, Your Honour, he is improving. And, despite the wild rhetoric of the prosecution, I would not defend the men who had in any way harmed him. There is no evidence these men threw any bomb and it's improper to drag that in.

I see your argument, said the judge, with obvious contempt.

This appearance might be doing neither Hope nor us much good. I began to feel that nausea which the idea of blank walls and foreshortened space brought up in me. The fear of the eye in the peephole in the doorway which, once glimpsed, vanished – or, more horribly, didn't vanish and didn't seem to blink.

Having enough strength nonetheless to endure, I conveyed none of this to my counsel as she bravely argued the common law on assembly. The individual was possessed of a sovereignty that gave free persons the right to associate with each other in exchanging ideas, just as obviously as they could do so to make a commercial contract. Free sovereign citizens considered a crime had been committed only when there was damage to persons or property. The prosecution knew this, and that was why they had raised the matter of the attack on Mr Bender's special tram in court. These men abominate that attack! None of them approved of it.

The prosecution called the inspector who had spat at my feet. He told the judge that some of the accused were lucky they had not been arrested for assaulting police.

I heard a fluting woman's voice from the public gallery. It was Amelia Pethick, holding an umbrella. Shame! Lies! And under oath, Your Honour!

The judge told the usher in the public gallery to remove that woman. Before the usher reached her, Amelia rose. She said, I shall move at my own pace and willingly. I've always despised perjurors.

In his one wise act of the day, the judge let her contempt slide by, and she departed.

Hope called Thompson to the stand. She asked him was he the Queensland president of the Australian Socialist Party?

He said he was.

How many members do you have on your books?

Across Queensland?

Yes.

In the whole state, twenty-seven.

This number amused the prosecution side and the judge.

So when you called a meeting on Sunday did you expect a crowd?

I didn't expect a great crowd, but . . .

He was going to say he had hoped for it, but Hope cut him off and thanked him.

But then the prosecution got to him. If he didn't expect a crowd, why did he go to the biggest meeting place in Brisbane?

In its summing up the prosecution asked for a prison term and a fine for each of us. We will see how deep are the pockets, said the prosecutor, of the Australian Socialist Party and its anarchist friends.

Hope asked the judge to respect the spirit and not the letter of the Assembly and Affray Act.

The judge chastised her in his summing-up for not knowing that statute law overrode common law, a very basic principle. Then he sentenced each of us to two months' imprisonment and a fine of ten pounds. He warned us that he would make it more severe if there was a repeat of our offence, but he had taken some account of the fact that we were working men and our wages were limited. (The next day he took seven hours before giving Suvarov two months but a fine of twenty pounds.)

I looked towards my cherished barrister in her ridiculous legal wig. She was the living water, and I would lose her in my isolation.

16

When a man is imprisoned he goes into a different state. The man walking the shore cannot imagine himself underwater because when he is underwater he is a different being. Prison is like being underwater yet being able to breathe in some diminished way.

Another danger is that though you know the judge said *two months*, something in you, the trapped beast, suspects *forever.*

I had remembered none of this when I had assembled that Sunday at Albert Square. But when I came down from the dock with the others, I needed to battle a new sickness, or a revival of an old one – that sense of my own nullity, such as I had not felt since the days in the Alexandrovski, the Nikolayevski camp, or the miserable cold camp in the trapped valley of Varobyeva.

I had often seen and occasionally passed Boggo Road jail. It was a high-walled square fortress with a gate set well back from the street. Arriving there shackled we were told by the warden we would not be put with murderers, so we had no excuse not to reform our behaviour. We would be allowed to keep our street clothes unless they proved verminous. The section into which we were then marched, each of us with his blanket, his dixie can, tin mug and bar of coarse soap, was three layers of cells high. We were put one by one in cells barely seven feet long and five wide. There was a bed, a chair, a slops bucket in each.

The guards were Britons or else the children of Britons, together with some South Africans from a prison that had closed down at the Cape. They were thus in most cases men who had a strong reverence for the Majesty we had offended. As they moved in and out of our cells, depositing us each in our own suite, they joked along in harsh accents that fell off the prison ceiling like bricks of sound. You could have sworn the fall of these sharp-edged sonic clumps could wound a man.

Once I was locked in I was suddenly utterly well in soul and body again. There, as if delivered by God – the God of equity, not the God of the churches which, as Gorki says, are God's tombs – I saw the trace of stencilling around the walls, as if this tiny dog box had once housed a long-serving prisoner who relieved the vacancy of the walls with little blue fleurs-de-lis. They could still be dimly made out running around the cell at about shoulder height. The little symbols told me that at some time in the past, a man without the writings of Martov or Plekhanov or Gorki to sustain him had breathed here at length and in a sort of resigned version of himself. The immediate comfort drawn from these little blue markings was that I was able to assure myself, You too can certainly remain Artem in this space. The lack of air and the cancellation of dignity need not take you away from what is written at the centre of your flesh and blood.

I sat on the cot and wondered where I could get books to read in the afternoon and evening silence.

In the exercise yard, on some days the guards would let us talk to each other, on others we were required to observe official silence but could murmur, and on others still were commanded at the cost of a beating to remain mute. There was always a knot of Australian Aborigines who stood together smoking thin cigarettes they had made themselves and carried in a little tin. One morning early in our stay, Suvarov lit a self-made cigarette with a match. A furrow-faced prisoner who looked eternally old but probably wasn't more than forty years of age said to him, Mate, never do that, it's a waste. I can show you how to split a match down so you get four lights.

This was a trick Suvarov had not learned even in Siberia.

When it was possible at Boggo Road, we Australian socialists would sit in one of the corners of the yard, and each of us would give in turn a ten-minute speech on theory. Many of them turned out to be anecdotal accounts of the experiences that had made us so-called radicals – we became like Christians recounting the second of their conversion. In the meantime, some warders were kind enough to pass messages and reading matter from one of us to another. A man might end up with a newspaper to read, another with a penny dreadful story about the American west. I must make sure I get some paper from someone, I told myself. I had been thinking of writing an article for a socialist paper, *Proletary*, whose address in St Petersburg I had. Here there was plenty of time, but no paper, ink or pencils.

When locked up we were sometimes able to call to one another until the warders told us to cut out that bloody racket. Boggo Road was just like Perm in that way – the regime varied. One month in Perm we were able to meet in a large room decorated with political posters. Physically we went unmolested. Then a more severe warden would be appointed and the banners were ripped down, we were each consigned to our cells indefinitely, and warders we thought we had tamed were in many cases now willing to beat us with batons and threaten us with pistols. At one period of severity there was a warder who would order this or that prisoner into an empty cell, make him stand spread-eagled against the wall with his pants down, and excruciatingly push the barrel of a pistol into his anus. As the prisoner gasped, the warder asked, What if I fire this now? This obscene liturgy had taught me there was one way of dying in particular I was terrified of – to the point of spending the night hours sitting up.

The routine of Boggo Road began early in the morning when a bell was rung and we rose and dressed. We shivered in the frosty air which came needling in the unglazed rectangle of our cell window. At half past six an enormous voice called, Tubs up and to doors! I lifted my waste tub while carrying my soap and little towel in a pocket of my pants. When our doors were unlocked, we were supposed to advance onto the gallery floor in silence, and since it was a time of day when many warders were on duty, we obeyed.

One of the guards possessed the same dangerous weariness I had seen in prison warders in Russia – the weariness of men disappointed with their choice of profession and waiting for something to enliven their day. He saw me watching and asked if I was fucking staring at him. Who said you could come from some godforsaken shitheap and look at *me*? Who told you you could say any fucking thing you wanted to on our bloody streets? Answer that, you Red bastard!

As a reply I lowered my head. But there was a sense in which I was begging a beating. I could not now remember being as melancholy in Perm as I was then about my little contretemps with the Queensland police. There my imprisonment had been earned or at least expected. But I had come to Australia with other expectations.

As for the warder who asked me if I was staring at him, it reminded me of my visit to the Russian School in Paris – it was just after my first arrest – when we went to a café with an old Parisian from the days of the Paris Commune who had survived the massacre of the Communards at the cemetery of Père Lachaise. In a bar where the glasses were dulled with grease, he told us young Russians, who were of an age where we'd listen to any advice, that there was a trick to imprisonment. It consisted of this, he said: to concentrate one's defiance against one warder, not the whole complement of them but one you chose as soon as you got to prison – the sort of man whom the system worried but who might cover that up easily by losing his temper and being brutal. Concentrate all your prison defiance on that guard, said the old man, who may have been for all we knew utterly mad, though we did not suspect him of that. Concentrate all your defiance to the point of inviting a beating. Getting the beating was important. As you lay on all fours spitting blood, you were to make a harmless joke – for example, to ask him, When did you say the dentist was coming?

From that day, said the old Communard, if you had chosen the right man, you would begin to receive small favours – a gesture, a scrap of food, a book, some paper. Before long, you would be taken aside for conversations. Why? Because the warders are the prisoners as well! You would begin with light discussion, then you would progress to socialist theory. The process – the prison waltz – would enliven you, consume the time, keep the mind sharp.

I had earlier used the old man's trick in the Alexandrovski in Perm. What could I lose? I began to exchange direct looks with a guard named Budeskin, a man with an appropriate temperamental streak, a fellow capable of sentimental kindness and outrageous savagery.

It was this method I tried to use in Boggo Road, making friends with the Irishman. One day, after I smiled broadly at him with a mixture of contempt and oafishness, he led me to an empty cell and beat me severely with a baton and with his left fist, which was his better hand, and then kicked me as I lay on the stone.

They're big boots, I complimented him through bloody lips. I wonder if we have the same shoemaker.

I don't pretend for a second I said it flamboyantly, but with the fragment of composure I had left.

As the old Communard had predicted, here too in Queensland the fellow became a friend, warning me about raids on the communal cell where we were allowed to meet and which was sometimes hung with slogans the warder would have considered blasphemous.

In silence we would march to the sanitary yard, a cold place smelling of human degradation where we emptied our cans and washed ourselves, and then we marched into one of the exercise yards and – on the right days – conversation would burst out. In the exercise yard, old lags taught boys card-sharping and pickpocketing skills quite openly, and frequently the guards did not seem to mind.

Young Podnaksikov, the Lena massacre survivor, was in love with an Italian woman in New Farm and very depressed at having been separated from her. He told Suvarov, There is no place for me in Russia and no place for me here.

Sometimes I was on work details with him and we could converse a little. We would generally be scrubbing floors or tables, or the stones of the sanitary yard if we were unlucky. He had never spent time in prison, and I told him that in the first month everything is strange since there was a build-up of horrifying or absurd things the prisoner had to catch up on. But once you started to do everything by rote, well . . . time evaporated.

To cheer him up, I told him I had been in prison in Perm the better part of two years, then in a labour squad nearby, then marched off as part of the labour battalions to Siberia. Like Hope and Amelia before him, he took an interest in my prison stories. Did I think prison was worse here than in Russia? he asked.

In some ways better, I told him. There are warders who hate you – I was nearly beaten the other morning, I think, when I dared lay eyes on a warder. And then I managed to get some blows out of the Irishman. In Australia, the attitude of the warders is, You've broken our laws, you are guilty according to the court, and we will punish you. In Russia, you'd get beaten up a lot more even while the warders said to you, You know, you are on the side of right, even we can see that, but nevertheless we'll haul into you and smash your pretty looks just because we hate the tsar too. So, my dear Podnaksikov, choose between those two options if you want to!

One thing, I then continued: most of these Boggo Road warders are like mere functionaries – so far they've stuck to the letter of the law. They don't randomly flog a man – they wait for a signal of permission from more senior men. And this place is cleaner. That's because we scrub it every day.

I am very hungry, Podnaksikov admitted. Even after such a little time, I'm hungry.

Oh yes, I said. The meat . . . it's not like the meat I lug for a living. It's the sort of thing they sell from the back door. Knock the maggots off it and wipe it down with salt – that was the process.

I had indeed noticed that there were few fat prisoners in Boggo Road.

One day Podnaksikov and I were led into the long stone shed beneath the prison's back walls where executions took place. I don't like these places – they have a dismal air nothing can disperse, a sort of spiritual stench. In this execution shed, the scaffold had a sort of gantry on which the condemned could be swung out from the platform and over space. Only two months before a child-killer named

Swanston had been hanged here, and the squalor and sourness of his crime and punishment still hung in the air.

While we scrubbed, for my own sake as well as his I started asking about Podnaksikov's childhood. For though the prison was in theory run on the silent system, if you were working in small parties most guards didn't mind if you talked or not.

In answer to my question, Podnaksikov told me his grandfather had been exiled to Siberia in the 1880s and had married an Eastern Khanty woman, a native of Siberia, as had his own father in turn. Yet despite being five-eighths indigenous by descent himself, he looked very Russian, barely a trace of Asia in his eyes. His father had been a miner and was a member of the Socialist Revolutionaries and then ran a small store in one of the towns on the upper Lena, where there was a lot of passing boat traffic.

He was very popular, said Podnaksikov. I assure you, not price-gouging like most shopkeepers. He said publicly he didn't lend money like other shopkeepers because he knew it was the way men were turned into devourers of their own kind. Privately he might make a loan, but not at outrageous interest.

The man was thus a saint, according to Podnaksikov.

After the great Lena massacre of which Podnaksikov was a survivor, certain rich progressives had brought a group of the survivors to Moscow to speak to others of their persuasion. Then he and other survivors were sent to Germany, France, England, the United States – an education in itself. Australia was the last stop and was considered a benign one. Now his friends from the Lena River massacre had departed, and here he was with me, scrubbing the Boggo Road execution chamber and yearning for a girl from New Farm.

But your childhood? he asked me in return.

I laughed. Everyone is like Maxim Gorki these days, talking about childhood, I told him. My Australian friends can't help asking that question and I've given them a detail here and there.

He ground his brush into the evil floor.

Even so, he said. Let's have the lot.

17

Whenever anyone asked about my boyhood my imagination was captured by the patches of colour everyone noticed in villages, the little window boxes of geraniums or pink fuchsias in the midst of dismal timbers. These tiny gestures of brio, of defiance against drabness, were the work of brave women, trying to give a little prettiness to aged structures and hard lives. They were the brightness in the dust. Many women put into them the love they could no longer spare for brutish husbands. They stood for the affection and anxiety of grandmothers and mothers and aunts.

And the other thing – mud. Around Glebovo it had a metal smell as if it was left over from mining, but also an aroma like raw red wine. Chemistry certainly went on in it, and it was the home of the dead as it squeaked and sucked beneath my feet.

As I told Amelia and Hope, when the breeze blew from the south we were near blinded by the emanations of tanneries. We boys swam all the time during the summer in a little stream that ran into the Vorskla River, far enough above the regional mines and tanneries to be safe for children to cavort in. We would sit down as naked as Adam on the mudflats cooking fish we caught, living like little savages in our pre-political, pre-economic existence.

My father was an excellent performer of dramatic parts he had learned by heart. The house was full of his rehearsings. Bits of the heroic saga about the mythic *bogatyri* heroes. Verses about country people, and a finish consisting either of Pushkin or Shakespeare. The orchestras in the province sometimes asked him to do recitations between their musical items. He would perform even for the dinners of the Landlords' Association, and our own landlord, old Scriabin, summoned him up to the big house to enliven his parties. He should have been a full-time actor, but his world did not permit that.

During winter, from the time I was about seven, he would go off on tour for a month or two with a travelling theatre group. My mother, with her handsome open face, forerunner of the face she would bequeath to my sister Trofimova, minded the farm and the accounts and did a better job than my father ever did. She never complained to me about his absence. She thought him a good man and a suppressed artist. Sometimes she would travel to theatres where he was performing and come back reciting snatches from plays. She showed us how Lady Macbeth was haunted by her own bloody hand.

Mother told me about Scriabin's house where she had been a servant. Mrs Scriabin would see a maid yawn after twenty or more hours without sleep and beat the girl savagely, in an absolute frenzy of rage. When my father and mother were young, one of the Scriabins' tenants stood up to them on the rent. Scriabin's sister, worse than her brother, demanded the man be beaten. He died at the hands of the agent and the overseer had him buried in the garden in front of his own farm. Then the sister Miss Scriabin's power over the region was so absolute that she simply let the farm again, and invited a new, submissive tenant family in to live with the murdered man's ghost.

I started school at seven, facing a ferocious but gifted young teacher – a lost soul as I see him now, too brilliant for us and for our poor village of Glebovo, and ready to punish us for it. He told us about his journeys to Kiev and Kharkov and Moscow, the very journeys that had left him discontented with his lot. I think he would have liked to have thrown bombs into palaces, but for lack of the opportunity to do so, he persecuted us. Our rural faces and our coarse smocks showed him every morning the limits set to all his ambition.

My memories of the 1900 strike had to do in part with my mother's brother, Uncle Efim, who worked as a carpenter in the railway sheds in Kharkov, our nearest big city over the border of the Ukraine. To that city, our Russian and Ukrainian forebears had frequently travelled looking for succour or work or to sell a saddle or a pot they had made. I overheard my mother telling my father that Aunt Marta was not happy about Uncle Efim's distant work and addiction to strike meetings. In the towns there were a number of pretty young bourgeois women, operatives of the party, involved in organising meetings, printing leaflets and helping the works committees. These were dangerously alluring young women, who starved themselves to save money for the movement and thus looked angelic with their almost transparent complexions. Uncle Efim, said my mother, wasn't immune to a pretty face, or a bit of starved ankle.

My uncle would visit us with various socialist friends from Kharkov for a Sunday in the country. I loved those days. Uncle Efim was a big fellow, in the image of my mother. He was proud of having escaped the village and of having a job in the city, chiefly because being a worker had given him a new view of the world, a view not passed down by warty old elders and village priests. He belonged to the Union of Railway Employees and Workers, and was a member of the Social Democratic Party. He had ambitions to close down one day the entire railway system in the name of workers' justice. And he sang industrial and political ballads to my father's fiddle.

A black tree grows on our farm.
It sucks all the good from the soil.
It withers every seed, it wipes every smile away.
Whose is this tree?
Nikolka's tree.

The tree, that is, of the tsar.

My uncle and the other men from Kharkov seemed so glamorous to us because they had city things – one of them wore a boater! No one bossed them around at the railway works, or so they said. They told contemptuous stories of workers at the Concordia engineering plant being flogged beside their lathes. They'd like to meet the boss that would flog them! They listened to my father recite, and pleaded with my mother to perform things she had seen in the theatre.

My grandmother sat by the tiled stove, smiling on all now that her brutal husband was bedridden.

In the meantime, my aunt grew suspicious of a particular pretty Jewish university student and party organiser who had moved down to Kharkov from Moscow, but who had been in distant places like Warsaw and Vienna. She was the liaison between the workers and those middle-class doctors, lawyers and engineers who were willing to provide either strike funds or apartments for a secret meeting or for storing printing presses and literature. The young Jewish university student who starved herself for the revolution had complained to the membership that the Kharkov strike committee contained too few workers and too many doctors, lawyers, engineers. This *burzhooi* girl told the largely *burzhooi* committee that they were effete and amateurish. (My aunt feared she might find Uncle Efim too authentic and too passionate.) The girl complained that the committee lacked all the normal subcommittees for organisation, propaganda and agitation. Nobody was even appointed to look after the literary functions any strike committee should hold to raise money.

When my uncle's workers' circle met two evenings a week to read and discuss works of literature and philosophy, the thin young woman from Moscow would attend to urge them to seek election against the mere intellectuals on the committee. She was confident she could get a number of the intelligentsia to resign. Efim stood and was elected. He was also appointed chairman of the propaganda subcommittee, but the committee and subcommittee meetings, and even those of workers' circles, grew argumentative over time. They reflected the old clash in the party between what Vladimir Ilich called the Economists, and the revolutionary Marxists. Economists, my uncle explained to me, applied themselves to a day-to-day battle against employers for better wages and conditions, and often dreamed of having their members elected to imaginary parliaments, ones the tsar had not yet authorised.

My uncle believed instead in the overthrow of any parliament (if ever one existed), and of church and state. Uncle Efim's position became and remained mine, not from imitation – at least I would like to think not – but because of its inherent sense.

Not all socialists thought kindly of Efim's Kharkov committee and so it worked in considerable secrecy, he told us. Yet they were the instigators of the 1900 May Day strike in the city. They had printed and distributed the May Day leaflets that called for a general strike. Stirred by the posters, the men at the locomotive works marched towards the rail yards at the centre of Kharkov and then intended to meet up with other railway workers at Juzny station. But on the way they were ambushed by the Cossacks from among the tall blocks of French-style apartments. A Cossack ran down Uncle Efim and he was arrested and sent to prison in Cheboksary, in Chuvash province, far to the east of Moscow, on the charge of instigating the demonstrations. The thin Jewish girl was sent into exile in Chuvash, a softer fate: she was required to live in the town and report to the gendarmes, but did not go to prison and had the fortunate buffer of family wealth, much of which she spent on food and bribes for the benefit of prisoners.

Weeping and screaming, my aunt turned up at our house in Glebovo, cursing Uncle Efim's radical opinions. I was still at a technical high school, but I had already by then read a great deal in newspapers about the rail workers and carriage workers marching towards each other to link up on May Day in Kharkov. They were blocked by a strong force of Cossacks who obeyed their officers and brutally laid about them with sabres.

My uncle was in the end let go on remand from prison and, thinner but unbroken, told us stories of the sinisterly silent jail corridor in which he had heard no words but only sobbing. He was changed, subdued, watchful. Even I could look at him and gauge that opposing the tyrant was no light thing. But one saw, too, that it had to be done. It was the Russian task. Uncle Efim feared being sent back after his trial, but fortunately – to his own enormous relief – the prosecution was dropped in his case. We found out for the first time that the Jewish girl had been his lover. She had also, in the end, bravely hammered on a judge's door and insisted on imprisonment instead of availing herself of all her family could do. In prison she went on a hunger strike, telling the jail's governor that she had done it to become a skeleton and thus avoid being raped. In the end, she consented to being taken to Vitebsk for medical treatment by her parents.

Uncle Efim spoke of this woman in front of his wife with an admiration that obviously rose above desire. My uncle intended to write to the exile Pavel Axelrod, a friend of Plekhanov's, in Zurich, to get her pulled out of Russia when her prison term was up.

After Uncle Efim's return from exile in Chuvash, I became an attendee at meetings that went on secretly in the countryside among miners. Sometimes I would travel an hour or two by train to meet with others in someone's apartment or squalid rooms in Kharkov. We pretended we knew what we thought, and we did have some concepts via men like Uncle Efim, but really our ideas were circling like birds, waiting for somewhere to land. For example, we all went crazy about a novel called *The Gadfly* by Ethel Voynich. It stressed the revolutionary nature of Christianity, and made us dream we could have our icons and our Marx at the same time. To keep up our Marx, we read editions of *The Southern Worker.* My own imagination was consumed by romantic dreams of Uncle Efim's thin, unquenchable flame of a girl. Sometimes her articles in *Iskra,* the esteemed Vladimir Ilich Lenin's newspaper, would reach my uncle through underground networks. Articles by the aged Plekhanov, by Martov and Vladimir Ilich, turned them into my heroes, the equivalent of Leo Tolstoy or Maxim Gorki. When the Russian Social Democratic Labour Party, meeting in London and Brussels, split in two, I was – like Uncle Efim – with Vladimir Ilich's Bolinstvo, the Bolsheviki. Like him I chose to believe, at that stage almost romantically, that the party should admit as members only those devoted body and soul to the revolution. As a sixteen-year-old I was willing to be one of those. What the powers of the earth will never understand is that in the arrest of an uncle, even for a few months, might lie the making of another revolutionary. There was no doubt that I was attracted, too, by the idea of meeting pale, ruthless bourgeois girls in dim but opulent apartments to plan the end of the tsar and of capital. I also innocently believed that I could handle possible imprisonment and brutality with great composure.

Some of our group, though I confess not I – I was probably protected because of my age – were involved in the rescue of a number of people from the prison in Kiev, when a handmade ladder of sheeting, fortified by wooden rods, was thrown over the wall and an astonishing twelve men escaped. Arrived safely in Zurich, these Kievite escapees were, according to *Iskra,* greeted as men returned from a tomb. The Kievites were shocked to see there were quarrels among the leadership about future directions. Old Georgi Plekhanov, said one of the escapees who went to Switzerland and wrote from there to our group, was grumpy and volatile and in bad health. Vladimir Ilich Lenin was a difficult man to get on with, he said. But then another of the Kiev escapees wrote that Vladimir Ilich lived like a monk and was everyone's beloved uncle and sage, and Krupskaya insisted that everyone was fed properly – the cook in the house was Krupskaya's own mother.

For our meetings in Kharkov and elsewhere, we had developed complicated passwords to ensure that outsiders did not get into our sessions. There was perhaps a little romance to this as well, but I took it all seriously. I remember a challenge, which I uttered myself one day at the top of the stairs to a young man climbing up. *Kostroma, nizhanaya Debrya . . .*

Ah, he said, yes, we are the swallows of the coming spring.

Which was the right answer.

One day it was my uncle's bourgeois Jewish hostess, codenamed Pelageya, returned from Zurich, who came up the stairs. I was very impressed that she had come direct from a meeting in Moscow with Maxim Gorki, my favourite author, whose *My Childhood* had recently captivated me in the intense way only the young can be captivated by writing. I had not nearly as hard an upbringing as Gorki, but his book made me remember the airy callousness with which my father imposed extra duty on my mother, and general male injustices of behaviour and demands. In company with Gorki, Pelageya had actually seen a performance of *The Lower Depths*. She remembered that Gorki was so young, was clumsy on stage, and wiped his brow with a handkerchief all the time. His nervousness seemed so endearing to me – my sweating Russian brother, Maxim!

I now took formal membership of the Russian Social Democratic Party – if Pelageya's example was to be followed, it was the equivalent of becoming a nun or monk taking vows. It was not to be a party of dilettantes, of yearning amateurs, Vladimir Ilich announced again and again in articles. I spent a year in meetings and in study. My energy, I remember, was limitless. I turned seventeen, and to my mother's relief found I was to be sent to the Moscow Technical Institute – what had previously been called the Emperor's Vocational School – on a scholarship.

With one side of my soul I could see the attractions of a student life, of concentrating merely on questions of bridges and railway culverts and being a mere dance-hall-and-café revolutionary. I did study my introductory texts very well, but of course joined the institute's social democratic club. As for the ever-present possibility of arrest for anyone involved in political action, I denied it could happen to someone as young and unexposed to civil censure as I was. After all, many of my fellows were of far more elevated background than myself and had hosted or visited many workers' circles. I went to meetings in factories under the privileged but potentially dangerous description of student leader. The workers I met were likeable and passionate, honest men and women, many of them peasants come up to the city and not much different in background from myself or Uncle Efim.

On a clear winter's day in 1902, the students of the social democratic clubs of the technical institute and the University of Moscow itself proceeded up Volhkonka Street. We were protesting the fact that the education minister had suddenly shipped two hundred teachers to Siberia, and also that the St Petersburg protest march, led by Gorki, had been ambushed by Cossacks.

At the marshalling area at the head of the boulevard, we were joined by workers from the Prokhorov cotton mill and the Stürmer furniture factory, whose progressive owners did not dock their workers for participating in the march. There were railway workers as well, and printers who wanted to be paid for the multiple apostrophes they were required to print but were not rewarded for. As always, the future we marched for meant different things to all the people there. For some – Mensheviks, weak social democrats – a British-style liberal democracy would have done; for many of the compositors a kopek per apostrophe; for others of us only a socialist revolution would serve. And we marched with each other in fraternity since we needed each other's cooperation.

To make us less scared of arrest, one of the leaders of a contingent from the University of Moscow, an impressive-looking young man in a handmade suit and overcoat and a rich-textured homburg, told us that the fifteen hundred arrested in St Petersburg and sent to the Peter and Paul Fortress in the Neva were being supplied with free cigarettes by the manufacturer father of one of the prisoners. Since I had never seen the inside of a prison, all this sounded very jaunty to me, a little picnic of detention. So I marched lightly out under our red banner towards the Pushkin Memorial, and felt armoured in layers of fraternity.

All this I told Podnaksikov as we scrubbed the gallows floor in Boggo Road, with the ghosts of those who had died in that shed hanging about our shoulders like cobwebs.

Well, I told Podnaksikov, that was my first experience of being rushed by Cossacks. It's an alarming thing. The trampling horses seemed to pass on to the marchers their own fright and panic. And then five hundred of us were arrested and sent to Poltava.

And how was Poltava? asked Podnaksikov, interested for once.

It was very . . . brutal. They sent all the troublemakers from the south there. But, I have to admit, it was part of my education.

He could see, though, that I had tired, something like exhaustion setting in for now.

A beanpole of a guard was at the door. He said, I suppose you bastards consider this clean?

Well, I knew from Poltava and elsewhere that it was suicidal to answer a rhetorical question.

18

It was after about a fortnight of our detention that I was called to the visitor's hall and saw sitting there beyond a grille of thick wire Hope Mockridge in an unpretentious tan dress. I was exhilarated but also resented the intervening grille. As I sat down myself, she said, Forgive me, Artem. They did not let me come earlier.

Then she choked on tears for a while. Diffused though she was by wire mesh, I got a sense from her look of health and her outright beauty, that if I concentrated on her I could become part of her and in a way escape with her.

Please, I told her. Don't be distressed, Hope. We're not in here forever.

You should not be in here at all, she whispered. Besides, I miss your company.

And I bitterly miss yours.

She sucked in a lower lip as she wiped her eyes with a handkerchief. She told me then she had heard that Thompson had begun a hunger strike. Was it true? she asked me.

I hadn't heard that, I told her.

If you hear he has, tell him Walter O'Sullivan wants him to stop.

She assured me we had not been at all forgotten. Donations to make up for our lost wages and to buy us comforts were coming in.

But the chief warden had not let any visitors or money reach us yet. Money had been used to buy us food hampers and it should not be too many more days before we received them. The idea cheered Hope as much as it cheered me.

Walter O'Sullivan has not abandoned you either, she told me, beginning to look brighter through the remains of tears. He has sent one of his lieutenants up from Melbourne. A Scotsman named Buchan. His job is to organise the effort on your behalf.

When she laughed, part of the laughter was for scenes from which I was excluded.

This Buchan dresses a little strangely for a socialist, she said, but he's been very helpful. She laughed again. He does a very funny imitation of Olive O'Sullivan.

In a sudden fit of jealousy I thought that shouldn't take too much effort, given Olive's eccentricities.

Does he? I asked stiffly.

My God! Is that bourgeois jealousy I hear in your voice, Tom? Fear not, he's returning to Melbourne next week. By the way, Paddy Dykes – you know, the Broken Hill man – wants to see me. There are all sorts of rumours around about Freeman Bender.

Then a warder moved in. Her visit was curtailed before I could properly thank her for it.

For a time, all exercise was cancelled. I thought that – according to the strange irrationality of jails – it was because of demonstrations outside the prison. Suvarov and I were, however, taken from our cells each afternoon and required to sweep the main floor of our wing. One of the older warders who supervised us was in a rosy mood – he was about to get his pension, and he let us talk.

Has Thompson gone on hunger strike? I asked Suvarov, since Thompson's cell was close to his.

Suvarov told me it was true – that was the real reason exercise had been cancelled for us. I thought at once, A hunger strike is too much. With a hunger strike, one should at least undermine a tsar. But to go on a hunger strike against the Queensland attorney-general seemed a waste of grand intent.

And so does he expect us to join him? I asked Suvarov.

Not yet, said Suvarov. One is enough for the moment.

I agree. I received a message from Walter O'Sullivan via Hope. O'Sullivan wants Thompson to stop. Tell him that!

The food Thompson was renouncing was not so sumptuous anyhow. In the morning we were given a sort of gruel with very little salt and no sugar, and black tea. At lunch it was bread and hard cheese, and in the evening the thinnest stew in the Southern Hemisphere. The Irish guard who had beaten me would, as the old Communard of Paris predicted such men would do, occasionally bring Suvarov and me a chop each, wrapped in cheesecloth, from his own table, and would stay in my cell a little while chatting about the situation of Ireland, for whose cause he was a powerless advocate, and comparing it with that of Russia under the tsars. Whether Russia or Ireland, he said, it's all a matter of land and who owns it! He was right on that.

I told him it was a matter of capital also, and of who owns the means of production and exchange.

Jesus, he told me, just give me two hundred acres up the coast a bit, on one of them lush rivers, and that'll be enough production and exchange for me. But the day is coming, and the question is, who'll rise first, Russia or Ireland? You could put a good bet on it one way or another.

Yet this same man, of kindly tendencies and flaws of brutality, was very contemptuous of Hope Mockridge. Perhaps it was because she came from a pastoral family. And she was a woman, and didn't know a woman's place.

19

The promised food hampers arrived with a note in each. *From your friends Hope Mockridge, Paddy Dykes and Walter O'Sullivan.* A committee of salvation! The hampers restored everyone. Thompson had come off his hunger strike at Walter O'Sullivan's insistence, and Suvarov was permitted into his cell to feed him Scottish broth. And in my hamper came a notepad and a set of pencils. If I handed them through the window to the Irish guard, he would get them sharpened. Don't go bloody cutting your throat with them, Ivan, he warned me, or my job's fucked and I'll have to beat the squealing tripes out of you.

Dear Mr Previn, I then wrote in my cell to the editor of the St Petersburg *Proletary*,

I hope you will find my attached article on the Working Man's Paradise of Australia of interest for your magazine's enlightenment. I have to say that I write it with your eminent Petersburg journal in mind. So we begin:

I write to you from a country which, due to a strange set of circumstances, bears the title 'Australia, the Lucky Country'. We are told by some of the intelligentsia of Russia that Australia is populated by people who have found a solution to all the problems of Europe, that democracy

owns the day in Australia to an extent that cancels the need for a social revolution. Learned men will tell you in drawing rooms of Russian cities that in Australia, they have heard, the class struggle has vanished, classes are reconciled to each other in fraternity, and there exists no wage slavery or industrial servitude. Here – according to the familiar line – there are no strikes, women are equal, landowners and labourers have come to reconciliation, and so no agrarian struggle exists. Here as well is the phenomenon of a national army and not an army of conscripts or mercenaries. And here a party named Labor exercises power, or if not, is capable of doing so.

This is a touching picture of class cooperation, uttered by those who have never gone to the trouble of travelling this far, even though one would think the paradise of it all, the ease of life reported to exist here, would have attracted them to do so. These gentlemen who vapour on about the remote Australian paradise remind me of the Australian advertisements one sees in the offices of shipping agencies and immigration societies in British ports, designed to attract the dregs of British towns to this fortunate country . . .

I write this with emphasis. In the working man's paradise of Australia, I am serving a two-month jail sentence for daring to attend an outdoor meeting of the Australian Socialist Party . . .

For ordinary people, litigation in federal and state courts is a near impossibility, since it takes tens of thousands of roubles to bring the simplest test case. The rights of the citizen, unless he is a millionaire, are less than notable. We are fortunate to have been represented free of charge by a lawyer whose views are similar to those we harbour.

We had served a month and now could have more visitors. Podnaksikov had a visit from the Italian girl, Lucia, and seemed to shed his depression. I was honoured by a visit from Paddy Dykes, who had the look of a man who found it hard to sit still, though he managed it. His brown eyes glowed with excitement.

You might be heartened, he said, to know our mate Bender is in deep shit with his toffy friends – those who got wounded aboard the Palace. I've slipped it all to the *Telegraph* but they dare not publish it. The word and the proof are getting around town though. I reckon Bender's social credit will run out in no time.

The idea of Bender's shame was very pleasing and, as Paddy said, something to warm a cell with in the short term.

I said, You're like a mongoose, Paddy. You have gone down a hole and come back with the cobra in your teeth.

Yeah, but it's more the Queensland taipan, the most poisonous one. And if I wasn't a – what was it? – a mongoose, if I wasn't that, I might as well go back to mining bloody ore.

To continue, Mr Previn:

As for the freedom of people to stand for election, each candidate is required to make a 250-rouble deposit which is forfeited if he polls less than 20 per cent of the votes of the winning candidate. Those who have access to cars and newspapers only need to hire premises for meetings and pay for handbills, but the poor candidates are forbidden by the police from holding assemblies and election meetings in the street. This is the pinch of the law on democracy . . .

The Australian Labor Party has two main objectives – first, the cultivation of an Australian sentiment, based on the maintenance of racial purity, and the development in Australia of an educated and self-reliant community; second, the securing of the full results of their industry to all producers but not to all workers. Society is not to be transformed. It is to be mended in one corner of the cloth and tattered in another.

The only difference between Labor and the conservatives here is that to the conservatives, their nation is the British Empire and not the mere scrap, Australia. The difference between Australia and Russia is that the words 'truly Russian' and other nationalistic terms are replaced here by 'White Race', which means above all British-born, while the 'yid' of Australia is the coloured man, the Aboriginal . . .

But Labor's nationalism makes it willing to send fifteen-year-old youths to military and civilian prisons for failing to turn up at militia training. The great god General Kitchener visited Australia and declared that because of its vastness, all its citizenry must be willing to train to protect it – there must be a working class drilled by Kitchener and Company's batons.

In any case, the country has not yet recovered from its past as Britain's

Siberia. A young man was caned by an officer at a parade. The officer was reprimanded but not cashiered – a Labor minister for defence, George Pearce, former socialist, protected the officer. Such is the Lucky Country.

The article finished, I passed it to Hope one visiting day for posting to the editor Previn in Piter, St Petersburg. She told me in return that word of Bender's involvement in the bombing of the Palace was known throughout the whole of society. What a triumph for Paddy! On the next visit she told me that Bender had resigned his headship of Brisbane Tramways, shut up his great house and put it up for sale, and left on the first steamer for the United States.

20

On the day that we left prison, the pavement across from the gate was thronged with Australian workers holding banners about freedom of speech and assembly. We went out the gate unmolested by police. I saw Paddy Dykes waiting among the crowd, in his old checked suit and a sweat-stained hat. He nodded knowingly and doffed the hat, but as one who had done very little for us, whereas I knew he had done much. More obviously and more regally, Hope Mockridge had her car there and, within its ample seats and on her sideboards, gave us a ride back to Mrs Adler's boarding house along avenues of cheering workers.

Of course I hungered to see Hope in a more private manner, but it would be hard to arrange anything that day.

Rybukov greeted me at Adler's. The Russia House project seemed to be at the forefront of his mind. There were a number of donations, he told me, but this scheme I had felt so keenly about seemed very remote and bloodless today. Finding a house for our people, said Rybukov, was all the more urgent because now the immigration officials gave Russian arrivals only two days at the migrant dosshouse. The People's Train had vanished from his imagination for a time.

I was more interested in my precious printing press, which had gone unconfiscated and which was now ready to be employed again in making a newspaper with a new title, just to confuse the authorities. *Izvestia Russkikh Emigrantov*, I suggested to Rybukov. I would write an editorial in favour of the new house, I promised him.

And a library, he said. I have already gathered some hundreds of books.

After dinner that night he took me to see a two-storey stone house in Stanley Street opposite Delaney's Hotel and suddenly I was back to my former self. The property had stables converted into servants' rooms out the back. It was going for three hundred and ten pounds. The front building, which Rybukov now inspected by twilight, was a sound structure, and the upper front rooms, including a former billiard room, eminently suitable for a library. Downstairs varnished doors could be opened between parlour and sitting room to create a space that nearly encompassed the whole lower floor and provided a suitable meeting room.

In the first edition of my *Izvestia*, for copies of which existing subscriptions to the *Ekho* were valid, I reminded our readers of the late *Ekho* that it had long been inevitable that we must have our own home in Brisbane. Why throw away disgraceful amounts of money in rent if the same amount could cover our own home? Above all, it was important to have a place where we could feel at home and be at home. Which we could treat however we chose, and from which we could not be evicted. The manager of the immigration dormitory had shown a hostility towards Russian immigrants based on the blood relationships between the British monarchy and that of Russia, and upon our obvious ingratitude to our kindly tsar. Our own house would override his prejudices.

Donations to be sent to members of the federation: Artem Samsurov, V. I. Rybukov, A. F. Suvarov.

Then I added the address of Adler's boarding house, our humble but comfortable habitation in South Brisbane – an address that demonstrated that we were not ourselves living like *barins*, noblemen, in the city.

★

After our first needy reunion at the Stefanovs', Hope and I somehow became lovers accustomed to each other's company. Over months, when she came to help me with the subscription records for *Izvestia,* we would choose by subtle mutual signals, not always lacking in affection, as couples do when they have become sure of each other, not to do anything at all except work.

Had imprisonment for two months changed everything? I can't say it had. I began to quibble inwardly about minor traits of her character that didn't matter at all. I began to fret about one stupid thing: she utterly lacked the artful sideways glances, the sway of the hip, what people called coquetry – a welcoming lasciviousness other women were said to have. Though lovely beyond description, she did not have lightness. Though so abundantly beautiful, she was no seductress.

What sort of self-respecting man would bemoan such a fatuous lack in a woman? I am sad to confess I did. A man thinks he can hide such lesser disappointments from a woman. The taking of pleasure is to an extent a shared, animal act. But it is a total confession, too. All is communicated on either side – a slight reluctance in the slope of a woman's shoulder, a slight begrudgery in the man's plenteous seed.

So I did not deserve Hope Mockridge. But after Podnaksikov had loosened my tongue in prison, I saw her chiefly as my confessor. Where I'd been sparing with details of my past, now I could not stop talking about it. It was as if I were trying despite myself to prove to her how alien I was. And I feared, too, that if I did not continue to distract her with tales some inevitable quarrel which was already in the air would be triggered.

I started at the beginning and told her everything I had already told Podnaksikov, then more.

After my first six-month detention in Poltava, I told her, I was not permitted to return to the technical university in Moscow but went back to my Kharkov circle with the reputation of having at least tasted prison. The gendarmes and Okhrana watched me for a while though. Did they want to make me their agent? They never approached me. I liked to think they could sense I could not be turned. But they might have already recruited enough of our people anyhow.

Prison had made me more pragmatic and less deluded as I joined the strike committee of the organisation in Kharkov. There was a strong sense that a general strike was imminent. I and others argued that we needed to involve the troops. In a bar, I had got talking with a soldier of the Starobelsk regiment who turned out to be a well-read young fellow. He gave me the impression of a regiment disgruntled with its colonel and its officers over everything from their hauteur to the issue of rations and the concern that they'd be butchered under such incompetents if they were sent to fight the Japanese. He confided in me a little too easily that there was a secret revolutionary committee within the regiment and I told him I would dearly like to meet the members. A sergeant arrived to meet me one night, a handsome man with a big moustache who looked like a true soldier of the tsar, but once he had assured himself that I had not been got to by the secret police in prison, he proved a very bitter man. When he was a peasant conscript, he had believed all they told him, and when the priest blessed the soldiers he had felt fortified against the bullets of the Asiatic barbarians. Now he believed his officers to be liars and buffoons.

Through carefully extending my contacts, I found the soldiers' committee proved to be broader than I had thought – it included all four regiments of the garrison brigade of Kharkov. I worked hard, meeting my fellows every day and every night, introducing factory workers and our bourgeois backers and new comrades from the army to each other. There arose that undeniable giddiness, warmth and brotherhood of conspiracy. Those who sought that and only that became easy targets for police. They became, in fact, so infatuated by the beauty of a plan they felt they possessed a talisman that made them immune to chance and risk. In the end they sought compliments from the greater world for being part of such an enterprise. They might tell brothers, sisters, parents who – in their concern – went and negotiated on their son's or brother's behalf with the Okhrana.

The events in Moscow in 1905 and Piter were well known to Hope. Our Kharkov strike committee, of which I was elected chairman in October, waited and planned. By November 1905, the waiters and printers, railway and engineering workers, and soldiers of the Starobelsk regiment and the Gabrielov machine-gun battalion joined in a great strike procession – the soldiers marching without their weapons. We addressed the masses of our fellow strikers at the marshalling point. It was a day when, after the strikes and civil war of Moscow, while working-class suburbs were being shelled by the tsar's artillery, no careful words would do. I declared that all over Russia, in every city, this struggle was occurring, and the workers and peasants in the army were involved with their civil brothers and sisters in overturning the tyrant. Later, I would be accused of having said, Long live the armed uprising! Down with the autocracy! Down with the murdering cavalry and artillery! Down with the hangman!

Perhaps I did.

On the eve of the march, one General Nechayev arrived in the city with a regiment from Siberia, made up in considerable part by Siberian natives like the Yakutsk – unlikely, so it was thought, to have sympathy with people so far from their home. The tsarist generals always had a preference for using the bulk of cathedrals or vast public buildings to deploy their cavalry behind. As our procession rallied, General Nechayev set up his Russian machine-gunners of the Okhotsky regiment at the head of the city square, one of the biggest in Europe, the town's pride. The Siberians were obviously detailed to attack us from the flanks. As our march entered the square, I called through a megaphone to the men of the machine-gun regiment, and we had the pleasure of seeing them haul the machine-guns away as their officers – running about with revolvers – raged at them and screamed threats at their troops, who ignored them or, in some cases, yelled threats back. Similarly, some dragoons and the Cossacks waiting behind the machine-gunners were ordered to retreat because their officers could no longer be sure their orders would be followed and so did not give them.

This was a startling, heady moment. The workers and soldiers in our procession marched on carrying red flags and singing:

Comrades, the bugles are blowing,
Shoulder your arms for the struggle.
From our limbs the fetters are falling,
Freedom will triumph this day!

At the heart of the city, the overthrow of tsarism was proclaimed by a number of speakers. The marchers resolved on a strike, including the railway men of the great junction of Kharkov. After the meeting, we members of the strike committee were immediately hurried away with other committee members and hidden in a series of apartments, very opulent ones in many cases, in the city. We changed our addresses every twenty-four hours, sometimes – despite curfews – at night, and with the help of a sympathetic policeman.

At a secret meeting of our committee we set 12 December as a date for a further march, to which my brave sergeant from the Starobelsk regiment committed his soldiers again. The final committee meeting was to occur in the foreman's office at the Poliakov railway ironworks the night before the march. Snow fell steadily on the city – it was an excellent night for the police to stay in barracks. But we became alarmed when no one arrived from the garrison committee even though we were expecting them. News arrived by a fourteen-year-old runner. The barracks had been surrounded by Cossacks, and the Starobelsk and Okhotsky machine-gun regiments had been disarmed and locked up within them.

Before we could break up and leave, we heard trucks and wagons in the street. An officer announced through a megaphone that the works were surrounded by Cossacks and artillery, and that we had a quarter of an hour to surrender before the factory would be shelled. Behind heavy equipment, we took up positions with our rifles, and at the close of fifteen minutes saw from snow-blurred factory windows the artillerymen load and pull the lanyards of their howitzers in the square.

It was my first experience of such bewildering noise, and the roof of the raw-materials shed came in on us, killing many union representatives. I found myself deafened and dazed on the floor with a bent and disembodied leg next to me. The Cossacks were storming the factory and found and arrested one hundred and forty of us from various unions and organisations. As the leg was swept away by the hands of Cossacks, I was roughly picked up, knocked down again, picked up and tethered, and felt I had become a tiny echo lost in a huge cave of skull.

I was taken to a police station. Even there the walls were lined by Cossacks, advising and yelling such things as, Teach the bastards a lesson or we will. I was tripped and kicked but otherwise got to my cell unharmed.

When I appeared before a judge, my sentence was five years' imprisonment. With others of the strike committee, I was moved eastwards towards Kazan in a prison train with whitewashed windows. The Kazan prison had the reputation of being one of the most severe in the empire, supervised by a very ambitious and severe governor. He ordered us to be locked up in the same wing as the death cells. We could hear and see men and women led out late at night to be shot. From glimpses through the eyehole in my cell, I remember how they went, these people, many of them anarchists, some of them political assassins. Most were much older than me – late thirties to fifty years of age – and I saw one woman of about forty, square-faced, well-dressed, holding her glasses in her hand. What had they done that I had not? First, they all looked like people of incontrovertible intellect. I did not want to be shot, but at the same time it was as if the Okhrana refused to consider me serious enough to be executed. Second, they were old enough to have repented of their revolutionary fervour but had not. And third, they had done something enduringly dangerous to the tyrant, an objective in which I had so far failed. As these sacred souls, each of the faces a scar on the memory, marched out, the rest of us hammered on the walls, the plank beds and the bars. The guards in the yard were authorised to shoot at the windows and for ten seconds bullets would go zipping around the walls. Then those in the corridors broke into the cells, beat us with rifle butts, and dragged some of us away to black-walled punishment cells.

One young man, a member of the strike committee, Petya, was

lining up in front of me one day as – chained – we were being readied for the austere exercise yard. For some reason, a hung-over guard hit him across the face with a bundle of keys. The young man stood still, his lips and nostrils bleeding.

Move, said the warder.

My friend would not move.

Are you coming or not? asked the warder.

To hell with you! said Petya.

Since he was already wearing his chains, he would have had to go wherever pushed anyway, but the warder considered that he had committed a small revolution against the tsar's holy dignity, took out his pistol and shot him in the neck in front of me. The blood sprayed the shoulder of my prison overalls. I heard Petya open his mouth to take a huge breath, then his head went forward and he fell back on me. I held him by the shoulders.

Let him drop, said the warder.

We heard later by the prison rumour system that the warder received a reward of five roubles from the prison governor for repressing Petya's rebellion. I am sure it was the truth.

I had nearly two years there. But the person who endured all that is not really known to me and seems an utter stranger. I remember it, of course, the secret selfish bonanza of finding shreddy meat in the soup you happened to get, but then the essential brotherly tap-tap-tapping of one's comrades on the piping – a semaphore you quickly learned. After two months of a purely fluid diet of thin soup imposed by the governor, I began to eat cockroaches, as I would discover others did as well. We tried to convince ourselves this was revolutionary ruggedness rather than degradation. But it was both.

In the late March of 1907 we members of the Kharkov strike committee were amnestied – all because of the birth of a royal child. I was taken out of the Kazan prison gate to be met by my forgiving mother and my sister Trofimova, herself a good radical. My father was off acting in some play, and Uncle Efim was dead.

After a small time resting in Glebovo, I travelled by rail across the Ukraine and Poland and by steamer to Calais, where I attended a meeting at the Russian School and first met Vladimir Ilich. After the conference, I travelled by train to Zurich, and met him again. He had a place for everyone, and my place, he told me, was to organise the party base in the great railway centre of Perm. I returned home via Germany, but what I did there I kept secret from Hope for the time being.

Hope arrived one night at the Stefanovs' door – in what the Brisbaners called winter – to visit the printing room. She received the usual churlish welcome from Mrs Stefanov – quite unlike the hearty welcome in broken English she got from Mr Stefanov, who was what the Australians called 'a sport', if he happened to answer her knocking.

She's a Cadet, I consoled Hope. The only socialist she has liked is Stefanov himself.

Hope said, You have all these bizarre names for parties. Remind me, what in God's name is a Cadet?

The Cadets are innocents, I told her, so-called liberals. They think they will get a government out of the tsar that is like the government of Great Britain, with which they would be very happy. That is all they dream of. As if the British lived in some Utopia.

She shook her head and an annoyed, sucking sound came from her lips. She seemed to have some pain, bordering on sourness, in her throat. Something had happened during my imprisonment, I thought suddenly. That was the change in her, and explained tonight's peevishness

This Russian house? she said.

She squeezed her eyes shut and reached for the big purse she carried, which had carpet patterns on it. She was reaching for her chequebook, I knew.

I put my arm around her shoulders and said, Dear, dear Hope. I think the Russians should do this for themselves. In this case, salvation lies within.

She looked up. There was a weariness in her eyes I wanted to kiss away, but there was also some determination not to be consoled.

Do you want a donation or not, Tom?

Maybe if there's a shortfall after everyone's done their bit.

Is my money somehow unworthy of the Russian cause?

No, no, I insisted. It's just that if the Russian community here in Queensland can't contribute enough for its own home, what are we worth?

I'll put the chequebook away in that case.

Please, do not be offended.

You and your Russians are a closed shop, aren't you? she remarked.

I denied it, of course.

We don't choose the circumstances of our birth, she said. You shouldn't make me culpable for them.

Again I denied I was doing that, but she seemed determined to be disgruntled.

I don't see how I can expiate. Except perhaps with the chequebook. Mrs Stefanov despises me, the men at the Samarkand laugh at me, while to polite society, as it's called . . . well, the less said the better. The whole of Brisbane laughs about my infatuation for you, Tom. It is a small-minded town. They treat my husband with sympathy and contempt. So he pretends, poor fellow, that there is nothing happening.

Please, you're getting carried away. You are a noble soul, Hope, and your generosity has always been welcomed. It's just –

What is it just?

Well, it's not my place to split hairs. But the question that always arises is this: is it *your* money, which is willing and generous money, or is it . . . well, your husband's?

She stared at me hard. She was not normally a woman who took offence easily, although perhaps I had said enough to cause it. Now, though, her offence seemed profound. Flouncing could be survived, but she was no flouncer. She quietly picked up her bag with the offered cheque unwritten inside it.

I think I must go, she said. She looked over at Rybukov's model of the People's Train. Here's us, Artem! Running on the one rail and likely to fall off it. Why does your friend call it the People's Train anyhow? What makes it more of a People's Train than one that runs on two rails?

She was in a mood when any attempt at an answer might annoy her. Nevertheless, I tried to explain.

It's like this. When Bender sacked Rybukov, Rybukov said, this is not a train for capital. This is a train for a revolution. A People's Train.

He might need to wait a good long time for that, she said.

What has happened, to make you like this?

I'm not going to explain, she said. Because I can't. It's indefinable.

She walked out.

In my male stupidity I thought, Something has definitely happened to make her like this. But sometimes male stupidity is right, which might be the reason it runs on such regular rails.

21

A Russian who had done well in the sapphire grounds of Queensland sent us a princely one hundred pounds for the house. I sought a donation from the Trades and Labour Council as well, and Kelly took me for a beer in the hotel in which he was king to discuss the idea. We were drinking, Kelly a beer, me a ginger ale, when three other men entered, one of them my old friend the open-collared, shabby silver miner Paddy Dykes, destroyer of Mr Bender. The second man was one of Kelly's aides, but the third was something to behold. This, said Kelly, is Harry Buchan.

Buchan was tall and looked like the sort of fellow who would always be well fed – women would see to it. His moustaches had been trimmed by a barber, and he wore a cravat hemmed in by grey lapels and a blue and white striped collar. His shoes were two-toned and well polished, and he wore spats over them. He had amused green eyes, and his hat, which hung from a polished hand, was of the kind the British wore in South Africa and which were called Baden-Powells.

He hasn't read your man Marx at all, said Kelly of Buchan. But he works for O'Sullivan. I should tell you, Buchan, Artem Samsurov doesn't like syndicalist bastards like the Wobblies you used to hang round with.

Buchan shook his head. I have Wobbly friends in Melbourne, all right, but that doesn't make me one. His accent was Scottish and charming. None of your libels there, Kelly, if you don't mind.

If you lie down with dogs, you get up with fleas, say I! So, Scottie . . .

Please don't call me Scottie, proud as I am of my Scottish background. I could equally call you Paddy, but I have better manners.

Point taken, said Kelly. But tell me then, surely Buchan you had recourse in your earlier life to the 'black cat' and the 'wooden shoe'?

'Wooden shoe' was the Wobbly term for sabotage. 'Black cat' also implied dynamite and incendiaries.

You know I never went for the black cat, Buchan asserted. I didn't see the sense of sitting around at palaver meetings of prodigious length talking of matters industrial and all the time there was someone with mad wee eyes begging us to use the fire-dope stored in the cellar to burn down Melbourne. We'd be more likely to burn ourselves down if someone dropped a cigarette.

Indeed, instead of lard and mercury, the Wobblies sometimes used something named fire-dope, a mixture of phosphorus and calcium bisulphide. Certain, Buchan admitted, I haven't read the texts. Plekhanov, Marx. But you don't have to study books to find out what ordinary men and women want. Speaking of women, what do you think of Mrs Mockridge, that splendid woman who drives her automobile around the town and does kind works for the oppressed?

There was a second's discomfort, probably more intense than it needed to be. Then Kelly's offsider asked unnecessarily, You mean the poor girl whose mongrel of a husband gave her the clap he caught when prosecuting a case in Townsville?

I was shocked at this, that despite all Hope's work for the trade unions, a union aide would mention so openly and lightly what must only have been to him a rumour. Paddy Dykes looked away, affronted for my sake and Hope's.

My face colouring, I said for the instruction of Buchan and Kelly's aide, Mrs Mockridge has done a great deal for us. She represented the members of your party, Mr Buchan, in court and is very generous to the Russians in town here, too. No one here should slight her.

Dear brother, Kelly's offsider told me, I spoke that way to condemn her husband. Not the lady herself.

Buchan struck a slightly poetic pose. She is a wonderful combination of pulchritude and right-mindedness, he declared.

Kelly groaned. You'll be reciting Robert Burns next.

Oh, said Buchan, there was a man who could praise the lassies. And he intoned:

Of a' the airs the wind can blaw
I dearly like the west,
For there the bonny lassie lives,
The lassie I lo'e best.
There wild woods grow,
And rivers flow,
And mony a hill between,
But day and night my fancy's flight
Is ever wi' my Jean.

Kelly said, I'll have Samsurov lash you with Russian if you don't shut up.

Buchan turned to me. I was up here during your wee imprisonment. Walter O'Sullivan sent me to address the question of your welfare and I hope I achieved something worthwhile in that.

I could tell from his air of self-possession that he was sure he had vastly lightened our pain.

I conferred with Mrs Mockridge, he went on, and she emphatically praised your intellect, Mr Samsurov. Now we in Melbourne have plans for a labour college, in which of course we would lecture on your brave efforts up here. Should you ever be in Melbourne, we would love to hear a lecture from you on the Russian Marxists.

I said that I would be happy to oblige. If ever I was in his city.

Perhaps it'll give Mr Buchan some understanding, said Kelly, winking.

Indeed, said Buchan, I'm no way averse to a little enlightenment. At the least, I have thought up a way to hold a rally without being arrested for it.

We were, of course, all interested to hear.

Well, he said, you could stage a Family Picnic for Peace. They can't stop a picnic. We could hold it at that Roma Street Park. It'll hold hundreds.

Your idea or O'Sullivan's? asked Kelly.

I have in truth to admit it's entirely my own, said Buchan.

Kelly raised his amber glass. Let's drink to Mr Buchan then, because he has something there! And while we're at it, let's drink to this wonderful little bastard from Broken Hill, who ran the mongrel Bender out of town.

So we drank to the ambiguous Scot and to Paddy Dykes. All my mental best wishes as I swallowed my ginger ale were devoted to Paddy.

22

I was often very tired these days, though more fruitfully and pleasantly so than when I first arrived. My compositor had given up on the paper, and on Monday nights I had to do the job myself, which could take me to three in the morning. On Tuesdays there was the meeting of the Russian *souz*, which was followed then by my sitting on a stool for three hours among a circle of men translating the *Telegraph* into Russian for the benefit of those with poor English. I was often booed for what I read, and treated as if I were responsible for the crazy editorials of that rag and others. On Wednesday, there was the affiliated unions meeting at Trades Hall, after which I ran the press and perhaps saw Hope for a few hours, and on Thursday night the Australian Socialist Party met in a parlour at Delaney's Hotel, across from the Russia House for which the *souz* had now made an offer. On Fridays I did the night shift at the meatworks.

On the weekends I worked on assembling the library. I had organised young Stefanov and my jail friend Podnaksikov around town collecting Russian, Ukrainian, German, Estonian and English books for our library. Once we acquired the house we were able to put the books on shelves and send off a list of titles to Russian workers in Townsville, Cairns, Ipswich and elsewhere, and post books to them. Among our newspapers were the German- and Russian-language editions of *Sotsial-Democrat*, the organ of the Bolshevik party, and of *Prosveschenie* and *Novy Mir* from the United States.

I recite my weekly schedule not to arouse pity – I had chosen that timetable – but to indicate that I did not see as much of Hope as I might have wished. She had forgiven me for our earlier scene. I did not then face the reality that, though she and I could make the feast of a day or a year, it would not be nutriment for a lifetime. On the other hand, why should she devote a span of years to a peasant? I was fortunate to have a day, or the remains of a busy evening. With part of my soul, that's all I desired.

Buchan the Melbourne prophet held his peace picnic, with a Russians versus the Rest tug-of-war, but not all union families came. There was a working-class fear that to speak of peace at a time when a great contest seemed to be brewing in Europe could be seen as unpatriotic.

By 1 August, Queenslanders read that Austria-Hungary had declared war on Russia, but that on the grounds of monarchical solidarity Kaiser Wilhelm had appealed to our friend the tsar not to think ill of the German empire. But Russia had already ordered its first mobilisation of its western army.

Despite the calamitous and stupid war against Japan nearly ten years past, I well knew the attractions of soldiering to Russian peasant boys. Some felt duties to ageing parents and were reluctant, but others saw any horizon beyond that which encircled their village to be welcome. When Britain declared war – involving, of course, Australia – all at once the public grounds of Brisbane were full of barking sergeant-majors ordering around the lean volunteers in their mixture of suits and wide-awake hats, button-up jackets and slouch hats. Both Digby Denham the premier and that man of Labor, Thomas Joseph Ryan, who wanted Denham's place, announced that if the empire were attacked, Queensland would be there, and pointed towards the kaiser's men who controlled German New Guinea and must be evicted. The enemy is not as far from us as the people of Queensland might think, intoned Digby, as if Queensland had something to fear from the small launches of the German administration in New Guinea. The great

Queenslander Andrew Fisher, who led the Labor Party in the parliament in Melbourne, desiring to be prime minister yet again, wanted to assure everyone that he was ready to fight too – 'to the last man and the last shilling'. I wondered how many other supposed social democrats throughout the world would make similar statements on behalf of this or that warlord.

But I get ahead of events. On 2 August, the evening of the war, Hope – wearing an elegant green dress suggestive of peace – had come to visit me in the printing room at the Stefanovs'. We drank tea and she told me she was there with an invitation. She and Amelia were organising a picnic for the next day in the hills south of the city – a social event to honour Mr Buchan – and she wondered if Suvarov and Podnaksikov and all the others would come and tell him about our stint in Boggo Road. It would be a good way of pooling ideas on what action to take in the event of a war, she said. I confessed I had already met Buchan. I kept secret my own feeling that Mr Buchan barely deserved being *honoured*.

She smiled. He doesn't pretend to be an intellectual, does he? He is a man of action. Whereas you, Tom, you are both a mental *and* physical giant.

I still felt the tinge of bourgeois jealousy. How would we all fit in her automobile? I asked.

Those who couldn't fit inside, she said, would fit on the broad running boards.

Paddy Dykes? I suggested.

I've already asked. He says he has to work. But I think that for some reason he doesn't like Mr Buchan.

I did not look forward to this event.

The next morning she drew up in what I now thought of satirically as her ocean liner of a car to collect us from Adler's. Podnaksikov had earlier gone to fetch his shy Italian girlfriend, Lucia Mangraviti, who in her blue dress and a straw hat possessed a raw, unconscious peasant beauty. Lucia was admitted to the interior of the car to occupy the back seat with Suvarov. Podnaksikov stood on the running board beside her, as if to protect her from wayside assassins. For the moment I sat in the front with Hope.

While the others conversed, she told me, My husband is very excited at the idea of war. Did you know he's a major of militia? Legal officer to the Brisbane regiment. He spots a chance to redeem himself in battle.

Then, I said, I would pity his soldiers.

He will never go into battle, she said. But I can see the dream in his eye. He sent his old uniform out for cleaning, and he's been to the tailor's to order a new one.

She gave this news about the uniforms with a restrained but total contempt that made me uneasy.

Oh, Hope, I said, you must leave him now if you despise him like that.

She shook her head and laughed. Perhaps I think he hasn't suffered enough yet, she told me.

We crossed the river, blue and spacious on this late winter morning, and as we drew up outside the Trade Union Hotel we saw Buchan sitting calmly and reading at a table under the upper verandah. He did not fold the paper up before I spotted it was a copy of *Direct Action*, the journal of the International Workers of the World – the Wobblies, with whom Kelly had earlier accused him of having sympathy.

When we pulled up and Hope called to him, he began lugging to the car a picnic hamper in which one could hear the cold clink of beer bottles. In his checked suit and his spats and the same veldt-trekker hat he looked to me a walking affectation.

Mr Samsurov, he called. *And* Mrs Mockridge. You have saved me from a terrible fit of the glooms.

He put the hamper down to extract his newspaper from a pocket.

Plekhanov, he declared, my favourite socialist – one of the few a normal man can read – he's come out in favour of supporting the war! Can you believe it? Maybe you can explain this to me, Tom?

He did not wait for an explanation but took up his hamper again and lugged it to the back of the car.

Accept this contribution to our expedition! he announced like a priest, opening the luggage area and dropping the hamper in. Again, that icy clink. Returning, he stepped theatrically into the palatial Mockridge vehicle whose door I had swung open, and settled himself beside me on the leather. All his gestures were nearly forgivable, I decided, a mixture of frankness, apparent boyish passion and exhibitionism.

I had not heard this bad news about Plekhanov. If it were true, then rumours of war sent the best men crazy.

So do you know the man, Tom? he asked as we drove off. Hope says you know everyone.

I met him once in Paris, I said. He is getting old. Then I would have met him again at Stockholm in 1909, except the tsar had other ideas.

By which you mean he arrested you?

Yes. And not solely myself. My friend Suvarov was arrested at that time too, though I did not know him then. I had many to share the misery with.

Oh dearie, dearie me, he said. He shook his head furiously.

He then turned to squint at the people in the two rear seats and on the running boards. And these wee bairns here? he asked.

I introduced him to Suvarov, Podnaksikov, who was still on the running board, and Podnaksikov's beloved Lucia.

Well, he said, indeed we are of many nations, combined together in the brotherhood of Mrs Mockridge's fine auto!

Looking around myself, I saw Suvarov shake his head. God knew Russians could be overly poetic, but Buchan was trying too hard, perhaps fancying himself a prose version of Robbie Burns.

My dear Hope, Buchan continued, I noticed when I put my humble offering in the boot that there is indeed a generous picnic already placed there. Sufficient for a regiment on manoeuvres. Appropriate to the time, eh? But Plekhanov? Ah, Plekhanov!

I remembered Plekhanov's face, its honesty, its no-nonsense moustache. He was drinking tea with Vladimir Ilich and Axelrod in the Russian School. I was sure that either the newspaper or Buchan himself were not accurate in the idea that Plekhanov had come out for the tsar. But I had also read that many Irish and Indians were taking enlistment in the event of war in the belief that they would get greater political rights afterwards for faithful service. Surely Plekhanov did not believe that any such implied promise existed in the tsar's head!

He may have been misquoted mischievously, I told Buchan. Maybe your paper picked it up from the capitalist press. There will be much misinformation in coming days.

But you were to meet Plekhanov, you said.

I was a delegate to the Second International.

You were elected? A delegate?

Yes, I was.

You are a man to be reckoned with, said Buchan, and he whistled.

But I was arrested before . . .

He whistled again, like a man applauding.

A consultative delegate, I told him.

Even so, said Buchan. A delegate just the same.

We rode westwards across the town which, despite the drama of the moment in Europe, was sunk in an Australian Sabbath torpor. Not even the Salvation Army seemed to be out, let alone the colonial armies of King George.

I descended from the car, struggling past Buchan, as Hope drew up in front of Amelia's splendid broad-verandahed place.

We are picking up my friend Amelia Pethick, Hope told him. She was a suffragette and a true fighter.

Until then, I had not known this about Amelia – the suffragette side. But it did not surprise me.

Amelia appeared at the head of her stairs, all sheathed in white, belted at the waist, and looking almost lost beneath her huge sun hat. She had lost weight since I last saw her and had become more twig-like.

I handed her into the car past Buchan, who had the grace to sit sideways.

Amelia protested. Mr Samsurov, there is no need to give up your seat to me.

My dear Amelia, I said, I have just heard of your pedigree from Mrs Mockridge. It is my honour to have you take my seat.

She laughed, the laugh of an ancient, robust, admirable bird.

Though there might have been room enough for me in the back, I swapped places on the running board with Podnaksikov to give him and Lucia room. Then we were on our way again.

23

We rolled south-west through the city's last suburbs on roads that were not topped by tar. Buchan continued a conversation above the noise of the engine, the road and the wind.

You know this syndicalism thing that Kelly accuses me of? I can't ask a fellow like Kelly. He has enough against me already.

I laughed, however begrudgingly, and heard Hope laughing too.

It was a French word at the start, Hope told him. It's the belief in one big union and the use of sabotage to achieve it. Like all big words it's not as complicated as it sounds.

Well, shouted Buchan, I have to say you have brought me enlightenment, Mrs Mockridge. Now I too shall be able to use the elegant sentence, *You, my son, are just a foul syndicalist.*

We had now reached a badly graded and repaired road on the very edge of the country. The last weatherboard houses were left behind.

But how does our consciousness of brotherhood then relate, Mr Samsurov, he asked me, to our unfortunate misuse of the natives of this continent?

The question may have been provoked by a native shanty town we could now see off to the right of the road, below a hill planted with bananas. It couldn't be denied they lived wretchedly, these people, these former wanderers of the Australian earth. In fragments of European clothing they occupied habitations of bark and cardboard and corrugated iron in so-called 'missions' like this one. From the steeple of the mission church the cross rose above them and cast its shadow like a knife – or so it was easy to surmise.

Their camp is named after a J. C. Slaughter, said Hope. A man who did his best.

His best wasn't of the highest order, Buchan shouted.

In fact we were now travelling at perhaps no more than five miles an hour on the bad road and could barely speak to each other without shouting.

So, Mrs Mockridge, yelled the unstoppably conversational Buchan, again I must ask you, as a native of this colony, how do you feel about these Slaughter people and their piccaninnies?

She drove on for at least ten seconds before answering at high pitch. They confuse me. My grandfather had them work for him and they lived in the black stockmen's camp and were wonderful horsemen. And yet there's something in them that has nothing to do with the world of capital and labour. They come from before the world we know and are too hard to think about. It's *much* easier to think about capital and labour.

We entered on a smooth patch.

Sadly, said Amelia now, they *will* die out. It is our duty to smooth the dying pillow. They are not made for our world.

Buchan looked across at the shanty encampment again.

He had the wit to say, I don't think it looks like a very smooth dying pillow, Mrs Pethick.

You are no doubt right, Mr Buchan, said Amelia.

Now we were among dairy farms and herds of cattle, and then we entered the hills with their tall shafts of eucalyptus trees. Hope parked her great vehicle in a clearing, pointed up the hill and said that we must walk on a track from there.

When we had all got out of the car and Buchan had shouldered his hamper and I Hope's, we began our little climb. I heard Amelia cry, Everyone go ahead. I shall be slowest.

It was not arduous hiking and Buchan stopped and pointed out the occasional clan of kangaroos or wallabies – advancing and retreating with that easy unfrightened lope – ahead of us or to our flanks. I was always excited to see them, bounding like this, fluid among the verticals of trees. We climbed steps of sandstone and natural shale, but then we began to descend again a little to a clear space and a big sunny rock platform. A creek came down from the further heights and made a small cascade where it went over the lip of the rock. Putting down the hamper, I walked to the edge of the falls and saw the impressive drop, the grey and gold of wet sandstone, and the silver thread of descending water. When I returned, Buchan declared, I don't dare do what you have just tried, Tom. Hikes and cliffs are my terror.

It was hard to dislike a man who could be so frank about his fears. From the basket I had been carrying, Hope took and spread a blanket and then, hard by it, a tablecloth onto which she and Buchan and I unloaded food. Hope had brought sliced beef and delicious chicken legs and a bowl of lettuce, huge bananas and mangoes and a rich fruitcake. It was wonderfully warm there, that August, on the rock platform. We were all exhilarated, and I was close to forgiving Buchan for being Buchan. We seemed to be out of the world there – it might have been another planet, and the trees rose behind us with an upright indifference to the designs of humankind, tsars and kaisers though they might be.

We started a fire, an easy business in Australia where the eucalypts shed their bark and branches all the time, and whose wood burned with a very powerful fragrance that was said to flavour the tea in the billycan. When Hope had distributed plates, we ate our meal, the chicken, beef and ham garnished with mustard and chutney. Suvarov had been quiet today, intent upon the superior food, something for which I could not blame him. Podnaksikov and his Lucia sat to one side and occasionally he would whisper reassurances towards her along the lines of: My friends are not all as strange as they seem. Mrs Mockridge and Mrs Pethick are women like you and they wish you well.

In the meantime, Buchan described for Amelia his dream of a labour college in Melbourne.

Amelia nodded, cocked her head with a certain scepticism, and then asked politely how he liked Melbourne.

Oh, he said, I'm a true Melbourne patriot – it is a grander city than either Edinburgh or Glasgow, and as for Aberdeen . . . In my book, the Botanic Gardens of Melbourne are a wonder of the world. The Exhibition buildings are splendid. I would say it was one of the greatest cities of the empire.

Of the empire? I wondered.

On the other hand, Buchan went on, given your general strike and the mass arrests over the right of assembly, it's amazing how Brisbane attracts attention for its size. It is a cockpit. I wanted to come up here and look around and meet you all. And to hold the peace picnic.

As for the labour college, he told us, returning to his theme, the Victorian Railways Union was ready to support him in arranging classes in economics, philosophy and industrial strategy. It might take a year or two to set up, but it was bound to happen. From there, the college could spread to Sydney where the Labour Council had been similarly interested.

The question was, if he pretended to be so unread in the major socialist texts, why did he dream of a college? I was surprised to see that Hope listened to his vapouring as a provincial lawyer in Russia might hear the doings of Moscow or St Petersburg. I thought, I stand the risk of losing her to that southern city. I had to admit, though, she could be freed of her Brisbane history in a place like Melbourne.

And how much longer are you here for this time, Mr Buchan? asked Hope.

Another two weeks, I'd say. O'Sullivan wants me back to report.

You must let me take you down the coast next week, said Hope. And to Mount Coot-tha.

A stupid jealousy seethed away in me then. For I had never been taken to Mount Coot-tha in Hope's automobile.

Here, said Hope, sighing, a forkful of beef in her hands, the world of drums and rifles seems a long way off, doesn't it?

Thank God it does, sighed Amelia, for a second over-burdened by all the posturings of Europe.

We all drank big mugs of raw black tea, in which the taste of eucalypt and fire remained. It was not like Russian tea. Laced with white sugar, it was a taste I had had to get used to and was so hot it absorbed a taste of the metal of the billy and pannikin. I found it very agreeable. When we had finished drinking tea and eating fruitcake, Hope, Amelia and the nearly silent Lucia suggested they retreat over the hill carrying their parasols and leave the men to talk – an old-fashioned proposition if calls of nature weren't taken into account. I could see, as they went, Amelia talking to Lucia very kindly and without condescension, including her, trying to overcome her natural reticence.

Buchan put on his adventurer's hat and stood like an African explorer, before going a little way uphill himself and urinating behind a fern. Coming back he suggested that we gentlemen go beating along the brush-lined creek that came down the hill to feed the waterfall.

God knows we might start some animals, he said. Out of pure passivity, Podnaksikov, Suvarov and I groaned but agreed, and packed up the hampers and set off, walking beside bracken and ferns, climbing the occasional boulder, parting the fronds of fern trees to see the deep plum-coloured pure water of the stream running below.

What are the chances, said Buchan, that a Scotsman and three Russians go beating about the bush like this? In Queensland, I mean. Who would have laid the odds to that?

Suvarov wore no hat and his reddish hair blazed beneath the sun. He said, But we are not ashamed to let a Scotsman into our Russian Queensland.

Podnaksikov and I exchanged amused glances. Suvarov hooted.

Through bracken and ferns we came to a further platform of sandstone from which the city could be seen. Above us, in the fork of a eucalypt, was a ball of dreaming fur, a koala, which Buchan at first pointed out to us as a wasp's nest until he excitedly revised his opinion. After we passed on, Buchan turned to examine the small so-called bear again and then pointed up the hill and said, Look up there!

What is that person doing? he asked. He kept his own eyes on the scrub around the creek, like someone pretending not to have spotted anything. But the rest of us stole a look up the hill.

My God, it's the lunatic, I said.

My God, it is, Suvarov agreed.

It was Menschkin.

Suvarov shook his head and laughed. I heard that the Russians in Rockhampton had run him off his land, he said. And here is the bastard back again!

We looked at the figure, darkly suited, up the hill, and knew that he was about to run.

He's a lunatic, I explained to Buchan and Podnaksikov. A Russian agent of the police here. But surely the police haven't dispatched him to watch a picnic in the bush!

Menschkin now vanished behind a tall tree on the ridge and stayed there.

I'm going to catch him, said Podnaksikov suddenly.

Yes, said Suvarov, and the big youth from the Lena and Suvarov both set off at a jog, Buchan trailing in his less pliable spats.

No, I called. Let's see if we can attract him closer.

They stopped in mid-stride.

I argued that if we pretended we had somehow lost sight of him and simply sat on the rock platform, he would creep closer and then perhaps could be caught.

So we all sat on our haunches and even got chatting about Boggo Road. I noticed how sunburned Podnaksikov's Siberian complexion was. It was not one designed for this place.

Buchan took a chance to move closer to me and began murmuring. I must take this moment to say to you two things, Mr Samsurov. One is that I apologise, for I was not aware that you had a close . . . a close friendship with Mrs Mockridge.

I was confused by this. A close friendship, I agreed.

I will not be such a hypocrite, he then said, as not to desire your friend. Could you tolerate that much, Mr Samsurov?

That is a matter for you, I said, my skin prickling with a new rage.

We could see Menschkin moving downhill among the ferns now. The man who wished to sell details of our conversation to the police or else to the consul-general, McDonald, an Englishman who had lived in Russia for a time.

Tell me when we go after him, muttered Suvarov, pretending not to see Menschkin.

Yes, tell us when to fly, murmured Podnaksikov.

We could clearly hear Menschkin wading waist-deep in the creek-side ferns.

Go! I yelled, and we were all up and after Menschkin.

What? yelled Menschkin when he saw us coming. Comrade Samsurov!

And he pulled from his coat pocket a revolver, which gave us immediate pause. We slowed down twenty yards from him.

You would hunt your fellow countryman like a fox? asked Menschkin.

It was you stalking us, I told him.

I am sorry I was ever born of the race among which my mother dropped me, said Menschkin.

Too late to amend that, I said. I felt no fear of the gun in his hands, though in any other hands it would have been different.

My fellow countrymen in Rockhampton terrorised me, cried Menschkin, burned my cowshed, threw huge rocks on my roof, broke my windows. What am I to do? Didn't I suffer with them? Am I not their comrade?

No, I told him, not while the police pay you. Not while you report to McDonald.

If you had not chased me, I would have simply stood here, looking at your innocence, enjoying it. I would have gone downhill, walked all that way, and somehow got to town and said, *Today, some of the socialists had a picnic.* Is that a harmful thing? And yet you hunt me.

Suvarov went to move in on his flank. Menschkin turned the gun and fired it in Suvarov's direction. The birds, the very air, seemed shocked at the noise. My friend Suvarov put his hand to his upper arm, which was gushing blood.

You have wounded me, you son of a harlot, said Suvarov in his native tongue.

I wanted to kill Menschkin but first moved to Suvarov. By some happy chance the bullet had scored the flesh of his bicep and, though the blood fell copiously, it did not appear that any extreme damage had been done.

It seemed enough blood to shock Menschkin too.

God's curse be on you all, he cried and raised the pistol, so that we shied away. But then he fired the revolver at his own head, creating another terrific detonation and felling himself backwards.

The women were coming back from their walk, summoned by the two shots and hurrying bravely towards us.

Menschkin lay crookedly among the ferns, and I felt a fraternal pity for him. Perhaps the fellow *had* been hounded to death. Less than satisfactory to the police and despised by every Russian in Queensland. For a man who could be comical, this shot to his own head was far too large and tragic a gesture, and I could sense that as well as giving himself peace, he had at last created a great threat to us.

Podnaksikov went forward to Lucia and stopped her from coming closer. At his example, Buchan and I moved up to reassure Amelia and Hope.

It's Menschkin, I told them. He was spying on us. When he saw us coming, he shot himself.

Oh God, said Hope. Genuinely? Shot himself?

Amelia, who had the air of someone who had seen everything, moved in with me and looked down on Menschkin. I had of course hoped he had done neat damage to himself. But I saw the bloodied top of his head whose skull was partly lifted away from the rest and he was shocking to look at. Just the same Amelia, beside me, was unflinching above the corpse and the drain of blood and grey matter.

Does he have a heartbeat?

I kneeled outside the circle of the mess he'd made of his head and felt for that and a pulse, but there was nothing. How could there be any throb of life left?

Meanwhile, Suvarov produced from his pocket a little flask of raw liquor and poured it on his wound. His paleness increased. He staggered and raised his eyes to heaven. I reached out and grabbed him to prevent his fainting away.

Hope moved in to look down on the dropped revolver.

I asked her, What should we do about the police?

Tom, of course we must let them know what happened.

And they won't believe us.

Even so, Tom. Think clearly. It is so obvious that the man did himself the harm that there is no chance any of us will be arrested. Or if we are, we won't be held for long.

It was decided as a fair thing that Amelia should be taken home, and that, after we took Suvarov to hospital, Lucia should be dropped off too, and only myself, Buchan, Podnaksikov and Hope should face the police.

Buchan bent over to pick up Menschkin's revolver, as if to study it.

No, leave it there, Mr Buchan, Hope called urgently. They can tell if anyone else but Menschkin has handled it.

This chastisement made Buchan feel as if he had lost face.

How would they do that? he asked.

Fingerprinting, Hope said brusquely. Even backward police services have had it for years.

The corpse was covered, at Hope's insistence, with the picnic rug. Amelia herself bound up Suvarov's wound with a tea towel and, with nothing further to do other than look at Menschkin, at length we left him lying there on the edge of the ferns.

24

Suvarov seemed clear-headed but silent during our return to the city. Indeed I would have called his demeanour brooding, not at all like the old Suvarov. Even so, his wound was staunched and he bore it without complaint.

Now they will try all their nonsense on us again, he murmured to me.

At Suvarov's insistence we dropped a distressed Lucia off in South Brisbane, then Amelia at her house on stilts, before driving across the river and coming at last in the dark to a private hospital named Greenslopes. Hope, Buchan, big Podnaksikov and I helped Suvarov in from the car, and up the garden stairs to the hospital door. A stocky matron answered the bell.

Heavens, what is that? she asked. Did you cut yourself, my dear?

Hope said, It's a gunshot wound.

The matron blinked. But she had seen most of what could be presented for mending and dressing, and she said, Yes, come in to our outpatients room and we'll sort out that mess.

In the sharper light of the clinic, where she sat Suvarov down beside a steel table, she could see better. Off-handedly she said, Mrs Mockridge, how are you?

Hope said she was well and introduced us. Tom Samsurov, Mr

Buchan, and the victim here is Mr Suvarov.

My God, said the matron, what a crowd! Do you all need to be here?

Hope pretended not to hear. This happened at a picnic we were enjoying, she explained. We were intruded upon by a man armed with a revolver. After wounding Mr Suvarov, the assailant shot himself.

You know, said the nurse, looking up, this will need to be reported to the police.

We are about to do so, said Hope. Can we leave you here, Mr Suvarov? We'll be back later to collect you.

Yes, go, he said, but uncharacteristically began to weep.

It's the shock, opined the matron.

Hope said, Don't fear, Mr Suvarov. No one can blame you for this, I promise you.

Don't leave me alone, said the nurse. In case he becomes . . .

I'll stay here, said Podnaksikov, looking pale. He didn't want to present himself to the police yet.

His offer didn't seem to cheer the nurse. She warned Podnaksikov, You behave yourself while you're here, young man.

Hope, Buchan and I went out to the car and drove off to tell the police that up on the mountainside south of the city lay a corpse and a revolver.

Arriving within a few minutes at the Roma Street police office, we left the car and entered the lobby. There was a sergeant standing behind a desk who looked like a monument to boredom.

Hope Mockridge took a card from her purse and gave it to the sergeant. I would like to see the duty inspector, please. Who is it tonight?

The man said it was Chief Inspector Kirkwood. He looked at us, Hope in her elegance, me in my bad suit, Buchan in his two-tone shoes. We were a strange trinity, I suppose. We would have made, in our contrasts, a good travelling theatrical group.

A constable arrived to take us upstairs. We mounted a broad staircase past photographs of stern attorney-generals and police commissioners who all seemed to me to be sure of the guilt of anyone who ascended. At the head of the stairs was a portrait of Geoffrey Cahill, into whose leg Amelia had once dug a hatpin. Inspector Kirkwood waited outside his office door to greet Hope, but it was written on his face that he did not like her, though he was clearly determined to treat her with courtesy.

Can I be of service? he asked her in a dubious growl. He looked Buchan and me over with an acid amusement he didn't try to hide. He said we had better come inside. On the wall of his office sat a picture of the commissioner and of the King of England, who was about to call his brave boys forward for the fight. Hope introduced us to Kirkwood as if we were fellow lawyers, explained to him we had been at a picnic, and what we had seen, and the extraordinary thing Menschkin had done when surrounded.

She told him where the body could be found, at Slaughter Falls, some hundred yards up from the rock platform. She told him that we had paused on our way to report this tragic event only to drop off Mr Suvarov at Greenslopes private hospital.

I believe the matron has or will be reporting the wound, Hope told him solemnly.

Just to humiliate her and us, he made a meal of spelling my name. I always have trouble with these Irish names, he told me, and winked at Buchan malignly.

I wonder if you would be so kind as to call my husband and inform him of what I've just told you. It seemed important that I come here before consulting him.

But you did not bring this corpse, suspected to be that of Menschkin, back with you?

The top of his head was blown off. I thought it important, too, that you see him as he lay, in the suicide posture.

Life was extinct when you left him? asked Kirkwood.

Life was obviously extinct, Mr Kirkwood, Hope told him. As the saying goes, he had virtually blown his head off. Had there been the slightest sign of life, he would have been brought back with us.

Intending to be helpful, Buchan said, That wee troublemaker couldn't have been deader, Mr Kirkwood.

Kirkwood ignored him.

And where is the spot you abandoned him?

Hope didn't like that word, *abandoned.*

We left him where he fell. None of us touched him or the revolver, though we closely inspected him. Could you telephone my husband, please? Or send a messenger?

You realise you must stay here until the body is retrieved? Kirkwood asked with savage joy.

Inspector Kirkwood, said Hope, we certainly expected to be held and questioned.

Kirkwood asked who the other members of the picnic were, and since Podnaksikov had been so prominently standing on the running board on the way out of town, it was better for him to be named than not, though it seemed strange to do it with him still waiting at the hospital with Suvarov and still, in theory, a free man. Hope also named Amelia, who was not within four hundred yards of Menschkin when it happened, and whose age and frailty seemed to warrant dropping her at her house. And then, of course, the wounded Suvarov. She didn't mention Lucia, however. If challenged on that she could put her omission down to the shock of events.

Now Hope was permitted to occupy a primitive waiting room where she sat at a table with a police matron who had been summoned from home on this Sunday evening and did not seem happy about it.

Buchan and I were taken down to a communal cell. After an hour there we were quite genially served some stew, but, pensively spooning it, Buchan told me, They will put this drear death on us if they can. This stew is just the prelude. This will make us a stew in another sense before the night's out.

It's impossible that they can do that, I said. Not even to Suvarov and me.

They would love to put the blame on you Russians, he said. They would love it better than a night with a harlot.

25

Two hours later an agitated Podnaksikov was brought in to join us in the cell. He told us that Suvarov had been allotted a bed and was told by a doctor that he was well but to pray against septicaemia. Podnaksikov himself was worried that Lucia's honest Italian parents would think him even more of a criminal than when he was sent to Boggo Road.

So we're off to prison again? he asked us, wide-eyed. I'd rather die. I wish the Cossacks had drowned me in the Lena.

I had spent the intervening time chatting with Buchan about Vladimir Ilich's *What is to be Done*?

So we have a long wait, according to you, Artem?

I don't think so, I told him. Capitalism is thundering towards the extreme. This war may very well be the extreme we look for. It may in the end turn men against their officers.

Not in the British army, he said. Not in those fancy-dressed Scottish regiments or the Irish Guards or any of that crowd.

But now, in the immediacy of Podnaksikov's panic and genuine anguish, we moved away from theory altogether.

Mrs Mockridge, Buchan comforted the young man, says we'll be questioned and let go. You too.

I took Podnaksikov by the shoulders. When you are questioned, you would not let them put words in your mouth, would you?

How do I know I wouldn't? he asked me.

Because we are innocent, I told him.

Buchan entered the discussion. They will tell you they'll let you go if you say we killed Menschkin. But they'll let you go anyhow. Mrs Mockridge's husband has been called, and he's a powerful man.

I said, He's not a shadow of Hope but no judge will treat him the way judges have treated her, because he's one of them. So please have courage, Podnaksikov. Remember your brothers and sisters who died in the massacre. If you go along with what these police say, these Australian gendarmes, you disgrace them. Remember that.

Indeed, as soon as enough detectives could be summoned to undertake the job on the Sabbath, we were taken away and questioned. Kirkwood himself questioned me with a half-smile that implied he had new information of my guilt.

You hated Menschkin, didn't you? he asked me in a room painted to match the colour of a migraine. He told us about your sly grog. He told us you had a supply of fire junk. He told us about your printing press. He told us about you and Mrs Mockridge playing jig-a-jig. And now you produce a weapon and shoot him, and plant it by his hand.

I resisted the temptation to be angry and denied it all, of course, but with a weary sense that the night had merely begun.

He came within fifty yards of you, you say? If he was spying on you, why would he come so close?

I had to confess I did not know. It was part of his mental disorder, I told Kirkwood. He has always been mentally unsteady.

You're his doctor, are you? Well, you doctored him this afternoon. You killed him with a dosage of lead.

Somewhere, in parallel rooms, Buchan and Podnaksikov were being questioned. And somewhere, condescendingly, Hope Mockridge.

Listen, you Red bastard, said Kirkwood, gathering himself. There will be no rest for you tonight, nor tomorrow night, until you tell us what really happened. I know what you socialist pricks are like. You fuck Mrs Mockridge and you think you own the world.

You think you can aim a gun at a fellow like Menschkin, poor hapless bastard that he is. But you will be found out. You will be tried. And you will be hanged.

Everything about my resentment of Menschkin was again listed by Kirkwood. I hated him for causing the *souz* trouble, didn't I? I'd incited the Russians of Rockhampton to drive him out of his home. Now the poor fellow had been following me around in the hope of finding something that might restore his credit with the authorities. He might indeed have seen something happen at the picnic that would very much interest the authorities. And as a result, I had shot him.

I have never owned a gun, I told him, not on this side of the ocean.

As I went on denying everything, he repeated his questions again and again. I was anxious about how Podnaksikov would stand up to similar treatment. For some reason I trusted that Buchan would. There was a lot of instinctive determination in him.

I wondered had the police been out onto that dark hillside where Menschkin's berserk blood dampened the ferns, and collected him and brought him back to town.

You forget he wounded Suvarov, I reminded Kirkwood frequently, but he was not influenced by that.

Well, what *if* the gun was Menschkin's? We have yet to test it. So he wounds your friend Suvarov and, enraged, you take the gun from him and blow his skull off.

I could see the many ways that they could depict Menschkin's death, and I was suddenly not so sure that I'd avoid treading the boards of that long, evil-spirited hall whose tainted floor Podnaksikov and I had scrubbed.

Kirkwood left at last and was replaced by a detective sergeant, who pursued exactly the same line. I dealt with it in the same way, even though I knew that in the end they would make me plead for sleep.

I had learned as a prisoner and an escapee that it was possible to endure in the second, to enter the instant and say I am safe here in this little nut of time. And all the more so if they were not beating me.

They thought they could get me – or one of the others – without a beating. It was a belief convenient to me, but perhaps more terrifying. They knew how wonderful it would be for them to prove a Russian murder in the first days of the war craze. You go, my sons, they could say, to fight alien things – while we fight society's good fight here.

I think I might have been questioned for five or six hours before a man in a military uniform, holding what the British called a swagger stick, opened the door and sat by the wall, crossing his long legs. I saw a crown on his shoulder. His cavalry boots squeaked. His features were lean, he had a delicate mouth, a waxed moustache and worried eyes.

At the first chance the police sergeant greeted him as if he was a man of great significance, and then walked out and closed the door, leaving me with him. He rose and came to the interrogation table but did not sit.

Mr Samsurov, I am Warwick Mockridge, said the officer, without extending a hand. I know of Hope's enthusiasm for strange causes, and I have already spoken to her. She's made a statement. But at the moment she's not being questioned in the way you chaps are. It's essential, whatever they do, that you refuse to touch that firearm, the one the Russian ended his life with. I have told the police not to try it on, and I think I've dissuaded them from it – I know them well. I don't mind them verballing and arranging things for people I know are guilty. But I am sure, Mr Samsurov, that you and that strange Scotsman and your friends are not guilty. I know because Hope told me.

I was more confused than was usual. I had never been in this situation before, where I was being favoured with the advice of a man for whose wife I had some definite feeling – a passion or infatuation or need or love?

Have they tried it already, by any chance? he asked. The gun?

No.

Good. Now we may be a remote part of the Empire. But the police have been using fingerprints for nearly ten years now. You don't seem to have been beaten?

No.

He frowned and then said what I had already surmised. Well, in that case they must be confident they've got you.

You are very kind to advise me, I managed to say at last. But have you warned my friends yet?

No. I intend to, however. Because if they fix you to a supposed murder, they'll directly or indirectly fix my wife with it too. I have no interest in wandering Russians, Mr Samsurov. My aim is to help my wife, who for all her faults of enthusiasm makes a very unlikely accessory to murder.

I understand, I assured him. But I am worried about one of my comrades: Podnaksikov.

No, if I were them I would try it with your wounded friend, Surov.

Suvarov, I corrected him.

Yes. He has a powerless hand. I would press his hand around the butt, if I were them.

I had noticed that he had no drink at all on his breath, that he was as sober as I was. Had Hope exaggerated his drunkenness to save her – and me – from conscience?

I have seen this war coming, he told me suddenly, as if it were part of our legal situation. Ever since Japan fought and beat the tsar, the kaiser and the Austrian emperor have been yearning to take on the Russians themselves. His eyes actually twinkled at the idea. Yesterday I was a mere mess dinner-jacket soldier. Now I find myself the adjutant of a battalion.

I hope you are well used by your generals, I told him.

Unlikely, he said. I think that, for the beginning, my generals will be as confused as me. In any case I intend to use *them* well. I should warn you now that, being a certified patriot, I will have the chance to sue my beautiful but silly wife for a divorce. She is a wonderful woman, and she has her reasons to embarrass and exploit me. Just the same, I have employed a private investigator – they are all semi-criminal former constables, but they are skilled at observing adultery. So I am saving you from the courts now so that I can bring you to court later. I also wanted to tell you that though you cuckolded me, Mr Red, you in turn have probably been cuckolded, and so it will go on with our dear Hope.

Amid my embarrassment I noticed how his conversation darted around erratically. His explicit opinion that I might be replaced by someone else in Hope's mind made me squirm. Particularly if it were someone like Buchan.

He held up his hand then, to end that stanza of the conversation.

Oh, I've asked my old friend Fuller KC to keep an eye on you all vis-a-vis what happened with Menschkin. You must prepare to be charged with homicide even pending the coroner's report. But remain cool. Beware. And keep watchful. That's all I can tell you. By the way, if you survive this, you might redeem yourself by joining our expeditionary force.

If I'm innocent I don't need to redeem myself.That's what I should have said, but it would have been discourteous. Again I was aware of how irrational his whole argument had been. Maybe he was embarrassed too. He suggested I become a private soldier and then, as far as I could work him out, wanted to name me as the culprit when he sued Hope for divorce! The whole thing was crazy.Yet he was a lawyer and a commander of men.Then I wondered if it was pure uneasiness that made his mind jerk around the map of the world, from wise to savage to philosophic to melancholy.

Well, as they say at the bookmakers, he continued strangely, all bets are off from here on in.

I nodded.

Goodbye, he said, looking downwards and full at me. I hope you don't end up in that shed at Boggo Road.You know, at the end of a rope.

He flourished his swagger stick, and his boots creaked in a way they would not after he had been on some front line for a time. At the moment, though, the gallantry of leather, of his belt and diagonal leather strap, could be smelled.

I wish you much safety, Mr Mockridge, I called as he went.

Major Mockridge, he said over his shoulder.

So, later in the night, when they presented me with the revolver to inspect, I was pre-warned against the trick. All due to the mercy of that strange but canny officer, Major Mockridge.

26

Back in our communal cell at dawn, Podnaksikov had his face in his hands and I did not know what it meant. It turned out that he had behaved sturdily, but he was a man in fear for his life and might have lost Lucia. That was his grief. The survivor of the Lena massacre was no revolutionary but a man who wanted domestic felicity above all, who wanted his Lucia and a little house in South Brisbane, and some freckled Australian brats, Russian-Italian as they were, running to greet him with voices like crows in the humid afternoons of long summers.

Morning broke beyond the high-up slit window of the holding cell. By now Menschkin's body must lie in the police morgue, and soon doctors would come in and look at it and weigh up its fatal wound.

Mr Fuller KC, a jovial older man with a meaty face, came to visit us in our cell after we'd enjoyed a breakfast of stale bread.

Your comrade Suvarov, he told us, I'm afraid they *did* manage to get his prints on the gun. Mockridge thought the blighters would. And sure enough, they seem to have taken the chance to force it into the hand of his maimed wing. Not that I was there. Would I were! That at least saved you from a beating, or as they say, *a fall downstairs*. Just the same, it's bad, it's extremely bad for you.

He seemed entertained by the idea and combed a splendid mane of silver hair with his fingers.

You will all be charged with being accessories to murder, he said. And first we need to face the coroner's court.

Later in the day he spoke to us individually in a dismal interview room. I did feel as cool-headed as Major Mockridge had urged me to be. I knew Fuller was exactly the sort of man to whom other lawyers and judges nodded with respect at Doomben and Eagle Farm racecourses, or at civic balls. As he sat across the table from me, his eyes were nearly closed in a look of Asian amusement. The layers of his big face were brick red either from the climate or from liquor or both.

Hope Mockridge sends you all her regards, he told each of us. It's understandable why – for your own good – she can't visit and why she's lying low and leaving the business to me.

Is she paying for your services? I asked him.

Ah, what a question. Yes. But trade rates. I'm a friend of Major Mockridge. He's a very complicated fellow, our Mockridge. Now, as we speak, the police are targeting your hides very zealously. Have they had you in that common cell all this time?

Apart from questioning, yes.

Oh dear. They don't mind if you confer. Mockridge did tell me they're supremely confident. They begin with the proposition that all Reds are liars and degenerates and they go from there. I would like to ask you once more about the events of that day.

It was a joy in fact to tell him, without dissimulation. Menschkin had drawn near us and we'd caught him at it. Menschkin had said that he'd been driven off his farm and that Russians were an accursed group, and then Menschkin had wounded Suvarov with a wide shot and shot himself all too accurately.

How long have you known Mr Suvarov? Fuller asked me.

We travelled in Siberia and then Japan together, and worked in Shanghai.

It was such a brief statement of our adventures – if you'd call them that – that it sounded untrue to me.

He is an honest fellow, I assured him.

Nonetheless, said Fuller, they got his fingerprints on the gun.

I told him about Suvarov and the tea towel that had been used to staunch the flow, and the tourniquet of similar origin that Amelia tied around his upper arm.

He bled a great deal, in other words?

I told him the severe bleeding had stopped before we were back to town.

But, asked Fuller, he was dazed by blood loss? Not himself? Please say yes.

Yes, I said.

He asked me what hospital we brought Suvarov to. I tried to remember. I said, It had something about green in its name.

Greenslopes, he asserted. Very well. Now, be of good heart. There's a chance you might get off.

Only a chance? I wanted to ask him. His bare, unqualified idea of a chance suddenly pitched me back yet again into that evil long shed at Boggo Road.

Later that day we were separated into individual cells. We were exhausted by then and to an extent Podnaksikov had infected me with his depression. I had not thought imprisonment and execution would be part of my contract when I chose Australia, but as I had said in my article to Previn, it was I who had misread the deed of sale.

Caveat emptor.

27

Now, held at His Majesty's pleasure (or, more realistically, that of the Queensland police) on suspicion of murder but not actually charged – a special arrangement of the Queensland judicial system – we were taken to the remand section at Boggo Road. We were to be questioned in the coroner's court and that was what would lead, if the prosecutor there succeeded, to charges and a murder trial. Our solitary consolation was that the women, Hope and Amelia, were not charged. It had been accepted that they were absent from the events that followed the sighting of Menschkin.

The warders did not let us exercise together, in case we conspired at our story. Again I feared that if the police now asked Podnaksikov to alter his testimony in exchange for freedom, he might give it.

Somehow the other prisoners in the remand cells knew we were there and called out, They're going to hang you fucking Reds! As always, there was something about prisoners that made them even more feverish to see others punished than the authorities themselves.

After a few days, Suvarov was brought into the section, his wound dressed and closed up. Though we could barely talk as he passed down the corridor, he turned his tormented face to me. I am such a fool, Suvarov called out suddenly in Russian. They put the revolver in my hand while I was still dosed with laudanum. They say they have my fingerprints!

Occasionally he would break out in talk addressed to no one, to the ether, and his voice from the cell was quavery and depressed. I had never heard him like this, not even the time when a ship's captain locked us up in a latrine for days under threat of return to the tsar's justice.

At a morning parade I was able to slip a note into Podnaksikov's hand. It said, *If you give way to them you will be their creature for life like Menschkin*. I was consoled to see that in the best tradition of prisoners he read it and swallowed it, with quite an easy jerk of his prominent Adam's apple. But then he stared at me so bleakly.

I became stupidly anguished about whether Hope had been to visit Buchan, or whether she had written to him and not me. Buchan looked steadfast and ruddy-faced when he was escorted past my cell for exercise.

At last a guard, possibly sweetened by our friends, brought me a letter that came from Hope.

Dear Tom,

I wish to tell you that our committee – yes, we have formed a committee on your behalf – is working very actively for your case, and our friend Paddy Dykes has written much and spoken to other journalists about it as an example of police malice. We held a public meeting at the Buranda Hall. The hat was passed round and people gave very generously to your defence and your comfort.

I wanted to give you the sad news though that Amelia, who has been working very hard as the secretary of the fund, has suffered a stroke. One side of her face is paralysed, and one can imagine her as a genuine old lady for the first time. It's very sad. But be assured, I am spending a great deal of time on her care.

Yours with affection,
Hope Mockridge.

I was disturbed by the chasteness of that *Yours with affection*, even though I knew she did not say anything more than that for fear the letter might be intercepted. But as I had begun to suspect in my last stay in Boggo Road, I did not feel as sturdy as I did in my earlier detentions.

Old Fuller visited us once more before the coroner's court was due to sit on the death of Menschkin, and I asked him for an opinion on how the other prisoners were holding up, chiefly because I felt my own isolation from them hard.

He said he thought they were very well.

They haven't become like that police creature Menschkin, if that's what you mean.

The Brisbane Coroner's Court on the corner of George and Turbot streets was a fine, yellow-stoned, only slightly sooty building in the British style, with the symbol VR on its cornice. I had passed it often enough in my journeys around the city. We did not enter beneath the cornice, however. We were taken there in handcuffs by enclosed black wagon, each this time accompanied by a constable who had instructions not to permit us to talk. On our arrival in the small courtyard we were taken down to a communal cell where a sergeant of police and two constables continued custody of us in relays. Suvarov began suddenly to speak and was told to Shut up, you murdering Red bastard!

Our eyes were eloquent though.

They took Podnaksikov up first. Since we were a mongrel mixture of accused and witnesses, we were not to be in court for the duration of the trial but only for the period of our testimony. Yet testimony was long. Podnaksikov was gone nearly two hours and waiting for him was hard. Buchan seemed particularly good at it, leaning his head back and dozing. He still wore, scuffed, the two-tone shoes, but he'd given up his spats. Above all he did not share the pallor of Suvarov or Podnaksikov.

At last Podnaksikov came back, wan, but able to look us in the eye and put his head on the side and perform a shrug in a way that seemed to promise us he had made no foolish concessions, or at least thought he hadn't.

While the court was in recess they brought us some stale bread and a thin soup and the cell was full of the clatter of our spoons like the clatter of shuttles in a factory.

Buchan was then taken up and his interrogation took up the entire and endless afternoon. Across the room Suvarov shook his head at me as if he might rather be beaten than wait this long. Like me, he might not have been the prisoner he once was. Our separate escapes from our exile to the Pacific coast of Siberia had left us unsuited for jail life and I could see that if he were sentenced to a long term, he would not live, and that strangling for a finite period at a rope's end might be easier.

Down again, Buchan smiled and said aloud, with that prison pallor we'd seen on Podnaksikov, They're not getting it all their own way. That wee Fuller is giving them gypsum!

He too was shouted at to be silent by the policemen watching us from a nearby room.

We'll come in and beat the suffering fucking liver out of you bastards! one of them roared.

We had been permitted to urinate in a waste bucket in the corner. Buchan, for having spoken, was given the job of emptying it in the sewer down the corridor, and then we were cuffed again to be returned to Boggo Road. As we made our way to the back of the prison truck Buchan whispered, Hope was in the court! Beautiful!

This sparked in me enough asinine speculation to keep me awake in the dark, until I fell into an hour of nightmares deep in the vacancy of the prison night. The fact that I knew where he was – in a cell down the corridor – and that no jealous lover was ever as certain about his rival's movements as I was, did not help at all.

28

The next morning it was only Suvarov and myself who were taken out and handcuffed to make the journey in the big black wagon. I was still irrationally angry at what Buchan had said and in a petulant lather about Hope being in court when I appeared. First up the stairs to the court that day, as I rose up to the dock I scanned the public gallery and could not see her. Paddy Dykes was obvious in the press box with his withered, sad-eyed face. But then I spotted her in the far corner of the court, sitting by a sadly shrunken Amelia, half-reclined in a wicker wheelchair. At once I thought, The death of Menschkin did this to Amelia, tilted some delicate balance. Reconciled and chastened, I gave a nod in the women's direction, though not with enough emphasis to cause them trouble.

On the bench, the coroner was quite aged and white-haired, wearing not a black gown but a brown suit. It was not his age that worried me as much as that dangerous look some old men have that something essential in their lives vanished at some point, and they intend to exact punishment for its absence. He was as stern a presence as any judge.

The clean-shaven crown prosecutor, robed and wigged, questioned me at great length. The travel to the picnic, Mrs Mockridge driving – a fact that he managed to convey did not impress him at all – the exact route to the picnic place, who sat where?

Oh, said the prosecutor, the witness Podnaksikov told us that Mrs Pethick occupied the front seat of the vehicle.

I explained that she did for a time, and that all of us men took turns riding on the running boards.

All of us? asked the prosecutor like a hawk, and had me argue that useless point to the extent that even I thought my own account became blurred and uncertain. From a supposed small lie about who sat where, he intended to build a vaster picture of our guilt.

Fuller, rising, appealed to the coroner that all this had been covered already and was not germane to the case. The coroner disagreed, but with some sign of respect for Fuller, whom he called *the esteemed* Mr Fuller. Then the prosecutor continued, probing for all lapses of memory, dressing them up as malice and lies, interrogating me on our progress up the hill, among the trees, asking where we sat at the picnic, when the women went away, where they were when Menschkin was sighted.

Let us go into the many quarrels you had had with Mr Menschkin, the prosecutor said. You quarrelled with him when he found what is called sly grog at a meeting of the Russian Emigrants Union, commonly known as the *souz* or *soyuz*?

I told him Menschkin had not found anything there – he had put it there himself.

The prosecutor behaved as if he hadn't heard this version of the sly-grog fiasco and shook his head.

Then there were some reports of fire junk and incendiaries being kept in that same building, Buranda Hall.

No, it was not kept there, I said.

I suppose Menschkin brought that too?

Yes.

Ah, said the prosecutor. If he was guilty of so many insults to the majesty of your union, you must have found him even more acutely annoying? And therefore, I suppose, you would all the more have dearly liked to see him dead?

I informed the coroner, Sir, I did not touch him.

But the coroner groaned, Your fellow Red Russians drove him off his farm in Rockhampton. Was that authorised by you?

No sir.

The coroner growled, *No sir.* Like a school teacher assuring a child that he was not believed and that punishment was waiting.

The prosecutor asked next if I knew where Major Mockridge was at the time his wife was cavorting about the bush with us Reds?

I was angry that Hope was being drawn in by this awful fellow, who would try to flay her even though no charge had been laid against her.

I do not know where the major was, I said. I know only that Mrs Mockridge does not *cavort* but has been very kind to us immigrants.

There was a giggle among the spectators, as if Hope Mockridge and I were a melodrama they were all familiar with, and had seen Act One of, and were now back for the laughter and shock of Act Two.

I do not know where Major Mockridge was, I managed to tell him. I am sure he was engaged on work he considered worthy of his time.

Fuller had already objected to the coroner – what could it matter what Major Mockridge was doing at the time?

I can tell you where he was, said the prosecutor, overriding him. While Reds disported themselves with his wife, he happened to be working with my brother at the headquarters of the Ninth Battalion, organising billets and transport.

Fuller said, Very worthy, very worthy, and I applaud those patriotic endeavours. But what's it all meant to signify, Your Worship?

The prosecutor shouted, It means that given Mrs Mockridge's choice of company she is not a woman to be necessarily trusted, any more than your clients are to be believed. In other words, there was no *reliable* or *independent* British citizen there to verify what befell the deceased, as there would have been had Major Mockridge been there!

People laughed again, at the idea of Major Mockridge KC picnicking with Buchan and me. It was an argument far away from the issue of supposed murder, but it was somehow powerful and the coroner let it all go on and seemed pleased with it.

So when did Mr Suvarov wrestle Menschkin's gun from him? Before or after Suvarov had been shot?

I said that at no time had Suvarov seized Menschkin's gun.

Perhaps you're right, said the prosecutor. Was the gun even Menschkin's in the first place? How can we know it wasn't Suvarov's gun that he had taken to the picnic? Or, for that matter, yours?

I had a sense of the solid ground threatening to move out from beneath my feet. I struggled with panic and urged myself not to sound desperate – such was the political prisoners' code in Russia, but it seemed to have become blurred in Brisbane.

No, I told the man slowly and with emphasis, none of us travelled with weapons. We had none to travel with.

The prosecutor said in a dubious voice that my guarantee on that point was very welcome. But he suggested we surmise the gun was ours, the picnickers' gun, and not Menschkin's. Suvarov shoots Menschkin, argued the prosecutor, since his fingerprints are on the gun. Then another of you, with a pistol you had many chances to be rid of, bravely agreed to give Suvarov a flesh wound in support of the story.

I was aware that the idea made perfect sense to many in the courtroom. I stole a look into the corner where Hope and Amelia sat. They were gone.

29

I was not at the time aware of all that was happening in the trial – we did not have the benefit of daily papers. To be one of a number of accused is to see simply one grim corner of the event. The truth was, despite the snide laughter that had attended the mention of Hope Mockridge, beyond my gaze and that of my friends, the Queensland bar and the Queensland judiciary were uneasy about the process to which we were being subjected. I saw the coroner as an individual of great and unquestioned power, sufficient unto himself, a god who could release thunderbolts without creating comment. In reality he was just another old man among other men, and the other men, even as their minds were seized by the international crisis, were also seized by the unsoundness of the procedure we were suffering under.

This did not mean that they wished us well, but that they harboured certain principles they believed the police had violated. On top of that, it appeared that in every liberal newspaper in the country, in the newspapers of little towns along the rivers of New South Wales, and those south and north of Brisbane, the nature of the prosecution had raised doubts. Though we knew nothing of it, there were editorials that said that on the one hand we were an unsatisfactory element in the society of Australia, but that on the other it did not mean that we had committed a murder.

On top of that, every day the court was surrounded by Kelly's clamorous trade unionists carrying banners, asking that we not be sacrificed to the fervour of the moment. Neither Buchan nor Suvarov nor Podnaksikov nor I knew about any of it. Though we sighted him in court, we knew little of Paddy Dykes's part in it all – the writing, the discussions with like-minded journalists from the respectable papers.

Nor did we know that Mr Fuller had subpoenaed the matron from Greenslopes Hospital or that she was a woman of independent soul. Since she was the gatekeeper to an important source of Brisbane's medical care, she seemed to have no fear of anyone, and she was a woman accustomed to authority over nurses, doctors, patients. We were not in court to see and hear her testimony and so had to rely on reports. She entered the court like a secular nun, a great symmetrically draped and starched veil hanging from her head, an unarguable red cross at the white centre of her breast. When asked questions by Fuller she answered with the innocence of a woman who had no reason to fear anyone. She claimed that the police had visited Suvarov with the gun late in the night of our first questioning. She had led them to him at their insistence, and against her advice, and she had seen them press it into the slack fingers of his right, his good hand, while he was still full of laudanum, faint from blood loss, and had no strength. The matron made it clear how uneasy she had been about it all, and had remained so for some time until at last contacted by Fuller KC.

What did one make of such perfected ruggedness of the kind the nurse possessed? It was an honesty that evaded the net of politics and theory. It was what it was, like a glory of nature. There is no ideology for sunrises.

On the street, though we did not know it, people were already accusing the police of making their own evidence – the Queensland police having a reputation for being a blunt instrument.

But the coroner's hearing continued and, without books or writing paper, we dwelled interminably in our cells. I wonder how the others endured when my own endurance was so fragile. Then one morning I heard cell doors crash open like thunder, like a biblical tomb door split by lightning. I heard warders shouting. My door opened with sudden fury, and a warder stood there. He said, All right, you Red bastard, you got away with it this time. The coroner caved in. Piss off out of here!

His presumption was that we had been loitering here of our free will. Soon we were all walking out of Boggo Road's big gate to be greeted by a cheering crowd. We shook hands with our supporters and smiled and pretended we had not been touched by what had happened. What was remarkable was that, although we emerged into a mass of men and women who considered our fraternity noble and unbroken, each of us went his own way that night. Even Suvarov and I had been separated in the crush of well-wishers outside the prison and may have been glad to be. I'm sure that fact mystified even us. But with people cheering us we felt bound to pretend to them we would lead our lives as before – then secretly didn't. Though I could see Hope's big automobile on the edge of the crowd, for reasons I could not understand I returned home to Adler's in a unionist's dray. Did we think of each other as bad luck?

While we were in prison declarations of war had exploded across the globe, involving country after country in subtle alliance and confusing the world's socialists. I gave myself a few days' rest and, as I waited to start my job again, I saw a crowd of men outside the town hall, anxious for the coming slaughter. I looked at their long, straight bodies, tufts of hair beneath straw hats and well-blocked felt, all of them wearing suits as if presenting themselves to a bride. It was said in the papers that only the finest, the antipodean Adonises, should be taken. Men unworthy of the national template need not apply. They joked with each other on the town hall steps and believed that somebody loved them, girls or governments, mothers or monarchs, and the God of the Highest and Most Blessed Things.

I met by accident that day my former prison warder, the Irishman who gave us chops in Boggo Road, our imprisonment before last. I had not seen him during my recent imprisonment, since he had left the prison service to start his own small dairy along the coast. He saw the war as a mechanism to drive up the price of setting up a homestead, the last vengeance of the British against him and his people. They won't get me in uniform, he assured me. They can fight their own fucking war.

All along I thought that there must be at least in St Petersburg and Moscow some sceptical ageing officers and NCOs who remembered the Japanese and sought to dampen the fever of the young. Whereas the British Empire by its very existence exercised a pull on the young. The history they'd learned in steamy classrooms assured the young Queenslanders that they were on the winning team.

Suddenly sturdy, tall boys, in new baggy army uniforms instead of suits, leaned from the trams in Roma Street, calling to girls. The impact of all this jollity was that the price of bread and tea and sugar and beef, all Australian staples, had – as my former warder had told me – suddenly leapt. Workers were laid off by manufacturers. People with German names had their windows broken. All the usual silliness, the human race returning to its vomit as predictably in Brisbane as ever in the cities of Russia.

Over the next two months nearly sixty thousand men, or so I would read, joined the ranks, although the Australians needed only twenty thousand of them for now. Surely the Russians these days, conscious of the Japanese victories of 1905, weren't clamouring like the innocent Australian boys to get into the battle?

But there was a sense in which I understood the Australian enthusiasm. The blank eye of the Australian sky seemed oblivious to many Australian masculine virtues. Considerable virtues indeed I had found them to be in the railway camps. A straight sort of people! Now history was reaching towards them, including them, inviting them – to use the words of the newspaper editorials – to the great global corroboree, the dance of gallantry. The *Telegraph* attributed it all to love of empire, and I had seen the same complicated if jovial earnestness in the young men who would be slaughtered by the Japanese at Port Arthur in Korea.

30

I was by the first evening after my release back in the print room at the Stefanovs', admitted by Mr Stefanov who pumped my hand up and down in congratulation. I was delighted to be re-acquainted with my printing frames and machines, and amazed at their loyalty in waiting there faithfully for me – though dear old Rybukov, through frequent visits, had been able to issue an *Izvestia* news-sheet now and then, a one-page bulletin telling the Russians of Queensland that I had been wrongfully placed in prison and informing them of the progress of our ordeal. Soon I would move all the newsprint and apparatus to Russia House but I did not want the trouble of that yet.

I wondered now how our conversation would get started if Hope arrived. The strange interview I'd had with Major Mockridge made me more than uncertain. But sure enough, she came that same night, knocking on the Stefanovs' door after looking for me at Adler's. I was putting into type an article warning Russian workers against being swept up in the war hysteria, or getting the idea that it was a way to prove they had a right to be in Queensland. The earth was theirs. They had a right to be where they were without having to put on a uniform or take up arms.

As she came in, we kissed like brother and sister, she as uncertain of me as I was of her.

As a safe move, I asked first about Amelia.

Isn't she a sad sight now? Hope replied.

I told her how I'd glimpsed them from the dock.

She raised her head and shook it for a second. That's why I may not be along for a week or two. I'm busy with helping Amelia out. And with a committee of wives.

A committee of wives? I asked. It sounded crazy.

I'm raising money for soldiers' comforts. On behalf of my husband. I know you won't approve, Tom.

All infatuation had been burned out of me by the Menschkin affair. I knew that I owed her and her husband my freedom. But even that seemed part of the disorder of their minds and their marriage. You are both mad, I thought but did not say. You have caught madness from each other. Why play at being dutiful to each other when the world knows that you aren't? I wondered how the other wives treated her – but, I began to suspect, she was not oblivious to all contempt. She actually liked it, playing the game that way!

I know there's folly on both our parts, she said. But he thinks all this will make up for some of the errors of his life.

Such as giving you syphilis? I asked in a murmur.

She wasn't appalled by my bluntness. Yes, she said. That too. I hate the war, as you know. But in this I must be loyal to him.

But you haven't been loyal.

I know. But I must be now. I don't know if I can help with *Izvestia* much longer.

I felt relief to be escaping what I now saw as the whole Mockridge mess. I stared at this beautiful, demented woman.

We kissed then. Despite everything some animal feelings were raised, but she excused herself and left. Just as well. It had all become impossible. If Buchan wanted her, well . . . She could brew up a further madness with him.

Yet now she was going, it came to me that all her generosity could not be explained by madness, by a manoeuvre within her marriage. I was overcome by sorrow that I'd been curt to her.

It doesn't mean, I said as she paused by the door, we don't all owe you so much.

She nodded and went through.

I would see less of her now than at any time since we had first met – including the prison periods. Before Christmas, Major Mockridge was one of the officers who led the Ninth Battalion of Queenslanders through the streets, behind a brass band, to notable enthusiasm from families on the pavement. Their exhilaration seemed to rise and add lustre to the sun. As the major and Hope had both implied, battle could obliterate the memory of what could barely be spoken of. At the level of such parades as this, military fervour could approach a religious ecstasy.

The grinning martial ardour of the younger men was heartbreaking to behold. They thought a brisk dash against the enemy would settle things. The glad unknowingness of their womenfolk could sting tears from the eye.

Russians were fighting the Germans in the forests of Tannenberg, and, lured forward by success, were surrounded. The cables printed in the *Courier Mail* indicated that the Russians were in a triumphantly encircled condition. I suspected that they were the victims of a slaughter. It seemed no time afterwards that the French and English were fighting in front of Paris to save it from the Germans. But even before that, I was horrified to see two young Russian waterside workers turn up to a meeting at our *souz* house wearing the Australian uniform. One seemed slightly embarrassed, as if he did not quite know why he had volunteered – indeed, he said he'd done it while drunk. The other was unapologetic and said, tsar or not, Russia is in danger. I feel I must help. And heaven knows, he said, the tsar might become kinder after this war.

Then, at the Russia House we had by now acquired, Podnaksikov presented himself without apology in the cap, tunic and leggings of an Australian soldier. The war changed everything, he said.

Like the boy earlier, he used the argument that Russia must be helped, and that the tsar would become more democratically minded through the process of the war and his alliance with the British and French. In the light of his height and broad shoulders, and despite the dismissed charges against him, the recruiters had taken him and he was grateful. Lucia still saw him, he told me, and the parents were almost reconciled to him. He said, My future is an Australian one. And I can't tell them that better than by putting on the uniform of the Australian Imperial Force.

We shook hands. As if I were his uncle, I asked him to be cautious.

Despite all you say, he told me with a smile, this isn't as bad as Russia.

The Australian unionists who now came to Trades Hall wearing uniforms had similar arguments. If the workers stood by the empire now, said Billy Foster of the Tramways Union at one meeting, there'd be no denying their claims afterwards. I read in the *Telegraph* that various Irish national leaders had made the same statement. Stick by the old empire, and it will behave well to its subjects after it has been saved! As if empires had been built without savagery and with every promise honoured! The idea seemed as stupid to me as the belief that the taipan snakes who slithered before the Russian cane-cutters would, if sung to correctly, decide to be non-venomous.

The next week there were two more Russian youths in uniform.

I had a visit from an officer, one of them told me. He was accompanied by a fellow in a starched tie. They told me all Russians who did not join the Australian army were being deported.

I was seized by familiar outrage. They told you that? They can't do it. That's ridiculous. Why didn't you check with me?

But they didn't seem too upset by the idea of the horror awaiting them. If the Russian–Japanese war had been so deadly, why did they think this war would be easy on flesh, bone and spirit? And in all wars the early recruits are fed into the mincer first.

I was getting sick of Queensland anyhow, one of them whispered to me, as if he'd chosen a sea cruise.

31

In those first weeks of the war, Rybukov had suddenly been recruited as an engineer by Queensland Government Railways and – being a man who liked his own place – moved out of Adler's once more to occupy a nice little house in Merrivale Street. In its front garden was the plant they called the jacaranda, blooming deep-blue in the front and strewing the ground – as summer came on – with a fall of vivid petals.

He invited me to tea, and we sat in his living room. He had fruit-cake a fellow worker's wife had made for him, and he brought in the tea like an Englishman, in a teapot. My Australian friends aren't keen on samovar tea, he explained. In some ways, this is all less fussy.

He asked me did I want to rent a room from him at very lenient rates. I told him that I thought I might accept his kind offer. Then he poured his cup and mine and sat back and lit one of those cigarettes designed for asthmatics.

Are they any good for you? I asked. They smelled like bitter menthol.

They do me no harm, he said, and began at once to cough.

And the People's Train? I asked him.

I've built a new model in the Railways office.

I can keep the other one?

Yes. We're running this one as hard as we can, adjusting the miniature gyros with tiny screwdrivers. But now everything is war, war, war. We might have to wait.

He coughed some more. Then he said, I wanted to let you know – and you won't like it. Just as I've settled in here with my new job . . . Well, I'm being sent to Britain.

Being sent?

Pretty much. From an article I published a little time back, the British War Office knows about my work. They want me to work on similar schemes.

Everyone's being called to the colours, I complained. Everyone!

They said as a British resident and a loyal subject of the tsar, I would help them. They also implied they'd deport me if I didn't.

Do you think they were bluffing? I asked.

I'm no longer a fire-eater like you. I cannot survive a detention camp here. And of course I don't want to go back to Russia under guard in the bowels of some steamer. Artem, I won't fool you . . . I don't push things like you do. I can't, if I want to live to see the day. And don't forget, if this war is as bad as 1905, it will bring the fall of our little friend Nikolka. That's what I want to live to see!

He studied me for any sign of accusation, and my silence was complicated. I was aware of his earlier sufferings. He'd been imprisoned first when less than twenty, had spent five years in Siberia and then two consumptive years on the run before he got to Harbin in Manchuria. And hadn't he given up a solid job with Bender to take a low-paid, draughty one out of solidarity with us? And wasn't I, by loading beef carcases, helping the military too, fuelling the empire and its capitalists?

I said, So, lucky old Rybukov! You'll be close to home now.

He smiled, grateful to me.

I am sick of Queensland, he said – like the young Russian volunteer earlier. I am literally sick. These seasons here are killing me. It's all too tropical. You see that beautiful tree outside? For a quarter-hour after I pass it I can't breathe. But I can't cut it down because it's the most beautiful tree in the world. A peculiar thing – my lungs were always much clearer in Harbin.

On a sunny afternoon in January he departed, first class, on a steamer named *Carlisle Castle*, whose lower decks were crowded with troops bound, according to rumour, for Egypt.

Then – of all people – Suvarov. Late that night, when I was drinking tea at Adler's, Suvarov, stooped and holding a full glass of vodka, approached me. He still had not found his old spark, the whimsy that had once caused him to dress as a Salvation Army officer for that Sunday meeting in town that led to our first arrest.

I'm sorry, Artem, he told me. I'm away from here! I have not had any rest in Brisbane. I've been to jail twice, and the tropical weather doesn't make up for that. I'm going south to Hobart.

I urged him to stand his ground. Tasmania might be better but would be close enough in character to Queensland, since the two of them were bound in a federation. But this argument did not sway him.

He told me that he hated to leave me – we had been together so long that it was like a divorce. But he had to find a place, he said, where he was not blamed for every disturbance on the civic landscape.

Sadly, I tracked his departure. He spoke to shipping agents. There were always ships that wanted men for the voyage to Hobart – it was the way of things. He vanished one day while I was at work. He left a note saying simply, *Goodbye, my old comrade*. It was signed *S*.

32

Suvarov and I had become brothers on the difficult road out of far eastern Siberia. But before meeting him I had to go through an initial, time-consuming flight, and though it would have engrossed Hope and Amelia, it was no different in essential detail from that of many others.

I mentioned earlier a guard in the Alexandrovski prison in Perm and then in the Nikolayevski work camp nearby. His name was Budeskin and he became my personal governor, confidant and disciple. He told me sad stories about his wife's family, about his sister-in-law who was the bastard child of the landlord. His daughter had gained a scholarship to the regional polytechnic and was the family's hope. As well as telling me such intimate things he began to bring me books, and food from his own kitchen. And just as I thought I had found a friend for the duration of my sentence, I was deprived of his company.

One early evening in the spring of 1909 we were ordered from our cells and told to bring our caps and blankets with us. We were lined up in the prison forecourt where armed guards – whose faces were unknown to us – were drawn up with carbines. Budeskin had not warned me of this movement and it might have been a surprise to him as well. But it was always on the cards that we would be marched out to Siberia, and the marches were never measured in mere hundreds of miles – the tsar always rewarded his prisoners with marches of three to four thousand or so *versts*, two and a half thousand miles, to work camps or to exile in small towns.

Now, wrapped in our blankets, we started out through inner and outer gates, waiting while one was closed and the next opened, until we emerged into the streets of the town. Perm is not a pretty town but it looked delightful by the light of the torches the guards carried. When we entered the zone of streetlights and evening street hawkers, we could smell the day's bread from bakeries – at that time of day about to close. Smoke fumed from the chimneys of the armaments factory where the night shift was at work. On my right I saw the ornate windows and turrets of the railway administration building and then the Magdalen Church that, except for its dome, looked more like a bank.

Only the better roads had escaped the thaw, and long before we got to the double-eagle columns that marked the city's outer gate, our boots were not only sinking into the mud of the season but filling with it as well.

Outside the city we were rested for a few hours in a tobacco warehouse, then marched off in the mild day. That night, wrapped in our thin blankets, it was an old schoolhouse we sheltered in. At unexpected moments on the march they would tell us to stop and strip off our clothes so that they could see whether we had somehow stolen anything on our passage through the villages, but all we'd stolen were the shit-stains and vermin we'd picked up in prison.

Now my memory of the journey blurs a little. We were walked for weeks or then months on end, sleeping in fields as the nighttimes became warmer. Those who grew ill were towed along in farm wagons commandeered by the guards, or travelled along rivers in barges while the rest of us trudged along the tow path. It was endless. We forgot Perm, we barely believed in a destination, and the road became our home.

When in the first few weeks the awesome peaks of the Urals presented themselves like God's wrath, they put us on a train with barred windows for the journey through the mountain passes. So we crept up the great gorges and then came down in switchback turns to the fields and, ultimately, to the swamps and forests of Siberia, where again we sometimes had the luxury of travel by farm cart or by barge. We reached a transit prison surrounded by birch forests, and were left there for some weeks in barracks. Here random beatings were routine, and though I avoided them, I was not there long enough to benefit from the sort of relationship I had built with Budeskin. The meat the local traders sold the camp governor was already putrefying, but succulent smells came from the officers' cookhouse.

On calm nights in camp on some tributary of the Lena, I could almost believe that I was on an excursion with friends. We sang choruses of folk songs and music hall favourites – 'Juniper, Juniper'; 'Moscow Nights'; and 'Steppe All Around'. 'Steppe All Around' is like an Australian song I have heard – the one about the drover who asks to be buried under a coolibah tree.

Steppe, endless steppe,
The way lies far before us,
And in that endless steppe,
A coachman lay dying . . .

A barge took us to a village named Zhigalovo, and our officer, a decent fellow, let us meet some of the citizens of the town in the communal hall. These men were Russian exiles, men permitted to live in Siberian towns who had married Siberian women and had stayed on in the region of their punishment. A small number of those we met in the hall had served time in prison camps, not merely in the torpor and misery of Siberian villages. They seemed not quite as prosperous as the exiles, and quite possibly worked for them as clerks and shop assistants. But the kind officer wanted us to meet them so that we could see a future for ourselves if we behaved well and – knowing what camp life was like – so that exiles of Zhigalovo might send us food packages and write reassuring letters to our families.

So the exiles took down our names and promised to write to our relatives and tell them we were well when last seen. But one of them, a gruff man with a huge black beard, passed me a paper. Learn it, he muttered. It consisted of the names of three river towns. The names of three men. Later in the night, I learned these items off by heart, knowing I'd been given an escape route. I remember still the first name – Zerbikov, K. F., of a little town named Martynovka which served a number of work camps. The mystery of why the man had chosen me remained unexplained. Had others been similarly helped?

As they dropped prisoners from our column off at this and that timber camp, we were left with a party of sixteen and were taken by our remaining guards up the Aldan River in boats made of canvas, and afterwards were issued horses and rode without saddles across the taiga to the village of Martynovka, where Zerbikov, K. F., lived. Beyond that lay mountains snow-capped even in summer.

That's where we ended, ten miles from the village in a camp on the edge of a dreary swamp. Our generous officer was gone – he had reported to a larger camp some miles west. Midges and mosquitoes infested our new camp, but in the hut in which I was placed the veteran prisoners took a strange joy in telling us that when winter came we would yearn for the warm mosquito days.

I was warned by several men that there were informers in every hut, but what surprised me was the decent, noble sturdiness of purpose of some, those who had come to terms with their situation, even if those terms were death by attrition. Or else by accident.

We went out cutting trees each day and manhandling them to a mill. The easier milling jobs were allotted to trusties who got extra food. An occasional timber-gang prisoner was known at an opportune moment to put his neck in the path of the steam-driven buzz saw. Men called it the Siberian guillotine.

As the short autumn came, morning parades continued despite rain or sleet, wind or mud or snow. I stood numbly at attention with the others to watch men flogged for trying to steal off-cuts of timber from the mill to fuel the tepid hut fires. I was hungry all the time, but without a mirror could not see what that was doing to my appearance. We talked a lot about the unknown merchant in Martynovka who was doing well supplying meat so far along the stages of rottenness that it was not fit for sale in the towns and villages. Only the niggardly amount we were fed saved us from food poisoning and dysentery. Just the same, a young man died of the meat and we carried him to the camp cemetery, a swamp two miles along a track leading from the camp town. Into the bog the young intellectual was thrown – with all his ideas locked up forever in his dead brain – without a word of ceremony.

I decided I must try to visit Zerbikov, K. F., of Martynovka, even if the attempt killed me. There was just enough of autumn left to try it in.

The day I edged away from a timber gang, everyone was distracted by a young man who'd been injured. A larger fir tree, in falling, had snapped off a sapling which – as it flew whirring among us – flattened one of the prisoners. Guards came striding up to inspect the bloody injuries. And I sidled out of the clearing. I left without any ambition and doubted I would get ten miles, and I had two thousand or so to cover as the bird flies to reach the Pacific coast, but was no bird and must deal with north-flowing rivers and ferries and railway lines that sometimes moved south and only sometimes honestly and accommodatingly east. To tell the truth, I don't think I was quite sane at the time. As I rushed away through the shafts of trees I had what a religious person would call an angelic visitation. A golden conviction of being in the hands of some providence filled me – a crazed idea that the whole thing was designed to turn out happily. First, however, I had somehow to cross the Aldan River. I did not know how. I more or less expected to be translocated by magic.

And, according to my delusions, I *was* sent a messenger. As I came down to a ferry landing through a fringe of trees, I saw a young Yakut, a Siberian native, who was caulking the seams of his beached skin-covered boat with thick clay dug out of the riverbank. His weathered face was like an assertion of hope. I was meant, according to the lunacy I was afflicted with at that moment, to take the chance of speaking to him. I offered him my prison jacket in return for passage in his boat to Martynovka. He took it but told me, Not Martynovka, too full of gendarmes. Kerensk, though.

Kerensk seemed so far south and thus upriver as to be beyond my present imaginings. But I went along with him. His suggestions seemed statements of infallibility. When he was finished caulking, he lifted the boat and set it in the river, took me on board and began rowing. The river was not so strong and he was able to skim past the grey houses of Martynovka and my unwitting comrade K. F. Zerbikov. It turned dark. As I slept in the bottom of the hide boat, we entered the great Lena and edged towards Kerensk. In Kerensk my contact was to be one Deshin, F. V.

When we arrived within sight of the town and saw its golden cupola, my wise Yakut put ashore, hid the boat among the branches, then suggested I should skirt around the town, go to the first teahouse at the southern edge of the town – it belonged to a former prisoner – and ask after my contact, Deshin. But I knew I had to be careful. I was dressed in a ragged jacket and pants, and if it hadn't been for the discolouration of dirt and mud and sap I would have been an advertisement for the work camp. But given their condition I might just about pass as a pauper.

The last I saw of the Yakut, forever *my Yakut*, he was darting across the river on the slight, contrary current. I didn't even know where he was headed.

I did as he suggested, finding the south-east road into the town and walking into the teahouse. Fortunately the only two customers were engaged in playing *durak*, as engrossing a card game as you could hope for. Reckless with need, I asked the owner straight out for Deshin. I felt I had a right to aid but later, when less demented, I was awed by the man's open-handedness. He took me out to his residence, gave me tea and cake and fitted me out with a smock, trousers and boots that had belonged to his dead son. And then I went, in his child's clothes, and never saw him again.

Armed with an address, I approached Deshin's house, a big place of logs with a broad wooden balcony. Deshin was my second angel – for once I didn't hesitate to use the word in my head. He came to the door – a small but vigorous man who had made his fortune as a timber merchant – and rescued me from a suspicious servant. He seemed amused, and his eyes twinkled; when he took me down to his cellar, he introduced me to two other escaped felons there, one from a camp to the south, the other an exile who couldn't stand his village any more. We three rested and ate single-mindedly. Fresh bread, butter, meat. I was sometimes shamefully sick afterwards.

Deshin would come and chat with us in the evenings. He was a Siberian patriot. If a man wanted to live freely and occasionally express his opinions, this was the place! You could almost forget the tsar here. Deshin praised the taiga and its mysteries, and the swift-flowing rivers that were fed by its mountains and drained into the faraway Arctic seas. He had made himself happy with a Siberian wife who had since died, and with his business and his imaginings of rivers flowing to unimaginable estuaries beyond the Arctic Circle. His life seemed enviable to us escapees. But it wasn't available to us.

Deshin's group of former exiles had gathered passports from men who had died, and they knew how to remove the original details with acid and then insert other details. They did this for the three of us escapees, and my passport made me Konstantin Fomin. These documents we escapees called 'boots', because they let us take to the road with a sense of security, even though we still had to be careful. At four o'clock one morning we were taken down to the Lena banks and boarded a large wooden lighter with a boat-steerer standing in the stern. It had been recommended we should go north again, with the current, to reach this or that river village from which we could more easily embark on escape than we could through the open country around Kerensk. We floated off, each with our own plans. The other two intended to land at a ferry stage downriver where a steamboat would take them up a tributary running east. But I chose to get off earlier at a landing south of that, at a village – so the boat-steerer said – big enough for a fellow to lose himself in if he needed to. From there I could walk three hundred kilometres to the railway that I could then follow all the way into Vladivostok.

On arrival, for fear of being spotted or reported despite my new identity as Konstantin Fomin, I did not enter the village and instead found a south-east, hard-baked road. The first slurry of winter mud had earlier formed on it and then been rendered solid by a few unseasonably warm days. I was hurrying on this surface to get to the rail before the snow started. I avoided towns and – by choice – traversed forests and slept in barns in clearings or abandoned woodmen's huts, and despite some stinging rains made the distance to a ferry on the Angara River in sixteen days. I offered a hair comb I had been given the day I had met the exiles and former prisoners as a fare to the hairy ferryman so that he'd take me across. Then, two days later, emerging from a birch forest, I saw the rails glinting away to a west I had been denied, and an east where I was a stranger. No traffic seemed to run here. I walked past many noxious-looking swamps for two days on the hard rail bed, my feet suffering as they had not in all their previous abuse.

I began to wonder had the world ended, and if so was I in Christian hell with the two parallels stretching away to meaningless eternity. But on the third morning I heard a train whistle. I hid in grass and saw the locomotive go by, then emerged to tumble into an empty truck that smelled of livestock, and pulled the door shut. It was the best berth I'd had since leaving Kerensk, and when I woke up I opened the door and saw the domes of something akin to a full-blown city coming up on my right. I jumped out and walked down a road, through columns patriotically adorned, leading to the wooden houses on the outer edge. I stopped a Russian-featured schoolboy. A silly question, I said, winking, but what town is this? This is Irkutsk, he told me with civic pride.

33

Mr Deshin had given me an Irkutsk address, which I had memorised. I went there and found a good, substantial timber house like Deshin's, and was able to rest there with a Russian-Siberian family for a week. Here the first snows began. I did not just then possess a warm enough coat or heavy boots. Yet even if I could have stayed I did not want to. Fitted out by the family, I set off again. My journey was a long, long way from finished – had I known how long my escape would still take I might even have reconsidered.

I went down to the river and took a job as a stoker on a steamboat bound for a town on the Chinese border. Jumping ship immediately I landed, not waiting till evening when the gendarmes would come through the town looking for missing sailors. I travelled by foot, sometimes by third-class railway, sometimes in kindly farmers' wagons, into Khabarovsk, where the border turned a corner and ran south towards Vladivostok. Here was the biggest and liveliest town I had been in since Perm. As well as Russians and native peoples, the streets were full of Chinese, Japanese and Koreans labouring on buildings or sitting in teahouses. I felt very safe there, lost among the port's population of labourers. But ships were carefully watched and searched, so I was nervous about attempting the final leg of my escape. I got talking to a clerk at a timber yard and he let me shelter in the shed at night. Then, in the mornings, I lined up with Koreans and Japanese on the docks of Golden Horn Bay to get jobs loading lumber into scows.

It was here, while we waited, that I got talking to the tall, ruddy-complexioned Grisha Suvarov. Though his passport name was Fyodor Bannikov, Fedya for short, he would soon tell me his name was Grigorii, and from the beginning he asked me to call him Grisha. I can't remember what we talked about at first, but I remember it was at once amusing and companionable. The false name confirmed my instinct that he was an escaped political as well. We discussed how to get out of Siberia and catch a ship to Japan.

I think it's going to be easier further north, said Grisha. But I can't travel yet. I need money.

I too was in that position. I was living off a small daily bowl of fish and rice here. I did not know any former exile to appeal to for help.

One morning at the wharves, Grisha Suvarov turned up and told me he had got a job with a Russian manufacturer of marble washbasins as a polisher. I could do the job too, he said. When I applied, I was allowed to live with the genial Suvarov in a workshop. Winter came on but I, Konstantin Fomin, could now afford a coat and fur-lined boots. We worked in a long shed with an iron stove in the middle, and the boss fed us. The main food at that season was salted fish.

There I let him have my real name. If caught by the gendarmes we could use our false ones quickly enough, and I could swear he was Fedya Bannikov as readily as he could swear I was Kostya Fomin. One morning, in fact, police came to the marble works and looked at all our papers. We presented our false passports. We were in the habit of using our false first names in public – Suvarov calling me Kostya, me calling him Fedya. After so long working under the name of K. Fomin, it came naturally to me. The police took our details and departed, but I had a feeling they would be back.

About midday a moustachioed man in a good suit arrived at the works. Smoking a cigarette in a holder, he began to look over the polished basins. He was building a large house, he said, and would need perhaps a dozen, for one wants one's servants to be clean too. As he passed Suvarov and me, he growled, Central Library five o'clock. Because of the suit, which was not the kind a police agent would wear, we decided to risk that he was one of our people. We worked the rest of the day then went to the splendid neo-classical library to meet him, finding him at a long desk in the reading room devouring a history of Japan.

Get yourselves a book each, he told us, and we did so, reference books; *The Almanac of the Siberian Provinces* – that sort of thing.

I know who you are. You have to leave the marble works. The police will come back. Find your way up to Nikolayevsk, where the ferries leave for Japan. Go straight to the public library there – someone will have new passports for you.

He went on reading again as if we were not there.

What's delaying you? he asked after a time.

Suvarov said, Between here and Nikolayevsk?

Stay hidden. If you have to use the old passports, so be it. Get off any train you're on as you get near and just walk into town. With any luck you won't be challenged.

And so we set off on the fringe of the railway, occasionally catching a freight train for a small distance but avoiding the stations. The spring had arrived again now. There were cherry trees here and they came into bloom, a sense of resurrection filled the huge sky. And the ironic, teasing Suvarov and I were good company for each other. He too liked Maxim Gorki and Gogol as well.

We walked around intervening towns, at least one of them quite substantial. Trekking through forests into the pleasant Pacific port of Nikolayevsk, we walked down the town's hills to the public library, sat at a table as the gentleman in Vladivostok had told us to, took from the shelf two copies of *The Report on the Resources of Siberia (1898)*, and waited. A gentleman walked in wearing an overcoat, which he draped across the desk. All the former exiles here in the east seemed affluent. He took new passports from one of his pockets and passed them to us. We had new names.

Memorise those, he said.

And he went. As we left the library, we saw a line of police. The long flight has finished, I thought with surprising acceptance. One of them looked at my papers and asked me, What is your name?

I very nearly said Fomin, whereas my new papers said Bulatov.

So I told him Bulatov.

And what are you doing in Nikolayevsk?

Having a holiday, I told him. I'm a sailor and I think I might get a job on the ferries to Japan. I've never seen Japan.

It was in fact exactly what we intended to do. Like a nihilist I was defying peril, inviting calamity in. There was something inside me that quavered like a sapling in the storm, but also something carelessly confident in my behaviour. I didn't give a damn. If this was to be death, virtually at Russia's eastern limit, then let it be.

They patted us down and we left. The man with the overcoat had given us a little money for a reasonable dosshouse that night, whose owner told us that the police were looking for a jewel thief who had plundered the biggest jewellery shop in the town. At the dosshouse, money had been handed in at the front desk for us by some unknown and blessed person. A message was delivered that we were to meet a nurse at the botanical park and we went there, into gardens where all was blooming, Japanese and Chinese vegetation, and even that of North America, far away to the east. Wearing her cap and cape, a nurse arrived at the park and without a word – she might have been leading us to the gendarmes for all we knew – escorted us to the home of some friends of hers. Again the capacious wooden house of a former exile. In this case of a former convict too, for the father of the family had been a political convict on Sakhalin Island before the war with the Japanese. He had seen the tsarist guards bayonet and shoot many prisoners there, and feigned death to escape the massacre. Our host told us he had passed on to his large family a hatred of the autocracy, and now lived as far from its reach as he could.

Now he was a prosperous dealer in Siberian and humpback salmon, since the Amur River estuary was rich in these fish that crowded from the ocean into the fresh waters to spawn. Japanese and Russians were paid to catch the salmon with nets and even by hand. Ashore, they gutted them and dried them in the sun on bast matting, then coated them in salt and laid them out in the form of a pyramid. There they awaited sale to the grocers and fish merchants of the city.

After a pleasant week there, being spoiled with fruit and chocolate by the old prisoner's children, he offered us work vending fish to stores in the area. Suvarov and I built up our stocks of money from wages and occasional bonuses for signing up orders for salmon. The ports were still closely watched, we were told, and we felt safe with our salmon merchant. But salmon was, above all, a summer business, and in the autumn, with our summer money in our pockets, we wrung the hand of the salmon merchant. We knew we were now in reach of Japan. The idea that in a few hours we might have got to the end of our escape made us both delirious and fretful.

But the high walls of the fort ramparts, built by an earlier tsar, hung above us – a promise that Russia didn't let go of her delinquent children too easily. Suvarov alerted me to the fact that, at the wharf gate, some of Russia's easternmost gendarmes were checking documents and detaining a number of men who looked more or less like us, in serge pants and boots and greasy, creased jackets and caps, in a line of the damned and rejected. The men being pulled out of the line were being taken by guards to line up under the ramparts, as if for a firing squad.

They're escaped prisoners or army deserters, an old man told us cheerily.

We could not risk having that happen to us.

You slip out first, I told Suvarov, and he did, like a man who'd been farewelling a relative. I kissed a surprised elderly woman and left in my turn. We were not stopped.

34

Presenting ourselves at the home of the good salmon merchant again, he advised us to lie low until the new spring. Our patron arranged a safe job for us, felling trees with Koreans in the nearby forests, sharing the Koreans' huts for accommodation.

It was a harsh winter toppling trees with crosscut saws held in mittened but chilblained hands, rushing them back into gloves every few minutes to prevent the horrors of frostbite. But the Koreans treated us as their pet Russians and Suvarov entertained them with a sequence of risqué Russian musical numbers, which they loved, being a very earthy bunch.

When we came back to town in the spring, I had been in the process of escaping for nearly two years. It was still snowing in Nikolayevsk, and the streets were full of troikas. According to what we heard, the gendarmes checked the guests of dosshouses closer to the harbour. We avoided the docks where the trouble had happened late the previous summer, and instead went to one of the harbour inlets used only by small fishing boats, and hired a Gilyak native with creased Asiatic skin and an unceasing smile, in his uniform of velvet trousers and a heavy coat, to row Suvarov and me out to a ship named the *Kiyefu Maru*.

We chatted to the man as he pulled hard. A good coat, remarked Suvarov. What animal?

Dog fur, said the man. It's the best one. It lasts.

It was pronouncements like this that made it easy for Russians to sneer at the Gilyaks. Venerable European Russia devoured men and gorged, virtually, on the skins of the miserable, but chose to be fussy when it came to the skinning of a dog.

Suvarov and I came up the steps of the ship onto the deck, showed our papers, and spent our winter money on a cabin. As the ship pulled away through the broad calm estuary of the Amur, we went walking forward.

On the foredeck, in very thin clothing, sat a number of Chinese and Japanese coolies, travelling as deck cargo and returning to their families. A Japanese officer stood in front of two of them, beating them with an iron marlin spike. Hey, we called in Russian. Stop that!

Fortunately the officer ceased. He told us in a rage that these deck passengers always crept aboard without paying their two and a half roubles. Suvarov clattered down the companionway, faced the officer, counted from his pocket five roubles that I was sure we would ultimately need, and gave them to the man.

But for Christ's sake, he said, stop beating them!

The two Japanese coolies, their faces distorted by the spike, tried to kowtow to Suvarov but he told them, whether they understood or not, that they were men of equal value as the fellow who had beaten them.

We had enjoyed such patronage from the Russian exiles of Siberia that we came to expect the Russian émigré community in Japan would do us the same favours. I think it is fair to say that even my good friend Suvarov had become accustomed to this help, though not to an extent that it disabled his native wit. Yet how else to explain that we lashed out to buy cabin tickets, all to share a main cabin in which Japanese fish and timber merchants strutted. When we saw these merchant princes of Japan smoking and talking emphatically, we began to wonder why we had not saved our money and travelled with the Chinese and Japanese on the foredeck.

*

We landed one misty morning four days later in Niigata, and travelled southwards on the railway, trying to talk to the Japanese families on board the train. We did not tell them that three of their countrymen had expired for the sanctity of class on the foredeck of the *Kiyefu Maru*.

We changed trains in Kyoto, and galloped up a hill to look at a temple, where we met a Russian who told us there were exiles living in Nagasaki over the straits in Kyushu. Then we rushed back to the train. In Nagasaki we wandered the streets looking for a Russian face but spotting none. We entered the premises of a few Russian merchants who made it clear they didn't particularly want to know us.

In Nagasaki Suvarov and I sank so low that we bought a net and caught shrimps, and picked up sea cabbage and shellfish. One day, while I was studying a Japanese grammar in our dosshouse, Suvarov came home to announce that he had met a wealthy merchant who wanted to learn Russian from him. We were both invited to join him as his guests at the *kabuki* opera. We all sat there in the semi-darkness, watching a tragic play in which the main character performs ritual suicide. Before that a comical character appeared, who was either American or European, and this was signalled by the fact that he was dressed in a checked suit, rather fresher than the one I'd later see on Paddy Dykes. The Japanese laughed heartily at him, which showed that they welcomed making Europeans a target of scorn, and explained why we were sometimes treated with hostility on the streets.

As we sat listening to music to which we lacked the key, I began to suspect by the man's gestures and eye movements that he wanted Suvarov for a lover. Suvarov had already visited some teahouses in Nagasaki where one could find the company of women, and I did not want him to sell himself to the merchant out of pure financial need.

In fact, Suvarov rebuffed the merchant and we were forced to leave our accommodation, and slept in a cave in the side of one of Nagasaki's coastal hills. We shared it with Koreans, who were also waiting for a change of fortune. We visited the docks every day to see if Russian ships had put in and to try to start a conversation with the sailors. It was hard without our being able to afford to buy them rice wine.

Two sympathetic sailors we met in the street and visited a teahouse with became friendly with us. This time Suvarov was not scrupulous. He and one of the sailors disappeared for a time. After they returned, the sailors agreed to sneak us onto their ship, the *Khabarov,* which was leaving for Shanghai – where there were, they said, hordes of Russians. Knowing we might starve if we did not take this chance, we got a boatman to row us to the ship by dark and climbed a ladder to its deck, where the sailors met us and hid us in lifeboats. We lay there all through the night and until dusk the following day. But on the verge of sailing the captain and his officers, making a final inspection before leaving, found us. There is nothing more ridiculous and few things less dignified than emerging from a lifeboat, stumbling upright, and being asked by an officer whether we had shitted in there.

He had us rowed ashore again, yelling after us, It's a good thing you're Russians.

We were back in our smoky cave, with Koreans who somehow knew about our adventures and found them hilarious. These Koreans knew how to cook good rice with a mere smattering of sardine, and they gave us some in repayment for the pure comedy of our situation.

The next ship in, also bound for Shanghai, was the *Primorsk*, and Suvarov and I expended our last coins on taking a *Primorsk* sailor, Sanya, to a waterside teahouse. This time Suvarov did not have to pay any price of the flesh to get aboard. Sanya took us down to the wharf and showed us where the shore-leave boat picked up men every hour after dark. If we got into the boat muffled up and appeared a little drunk, we could get away with boarding the *Primorsk* because the coxswain wouldn't count us. To prepare for the journey we filled our pockets with bread and Korean dumplings, farewelled our fellow cave-dwellers, and went and met the shore-leave cutter. Then we motored out to the *Primorsk* and clattered aboard with the others. There had been no officer at the gangway and Sanya had assured us that even if we were caught the captain was liberal-minded. Just don't mention *me*, said Sanya. That was all.

We hid in an equipment locker on the main deck. The next dawn an officer discovered Suvarov urinating through the taffrail, and I heard him taken past the locker where I still hid. Obviously there would now be a search, so when it began I threw open the locker door and gave myself up.

The bearded captain to whom we were taken on the bridge did not seem the creature of generous socialist impulse that Sanya had described to us.

You scum! he roared. You turds floated across from Siberia. Don't think I don't know who you are! Criminals! Disturbers of order! Bloody anarchists! I'm going to hand you to the Russian consul in Shanghai. Until then, you'll be locked up and starved.

We were pushed into a latrine and the door was locked behind us. The water closet was there so that we could be left indefinitely without fouling the ship. The hopeful sign was that they brought us the same food as the crew ate – rice and steamed fish – and jars of water.

But since the captain had said he'd starve us, an old prison instinct made us refuse the food. We kept it up for a day and a half. Then the captain appeared, his fury evaporated.

You are a pain in my arse and I hate having you aboard. But don't worry – if you don't put on airs like refusing to eat, you'll get on all right. Eat up now. You can bunk with the crew.

He considered us a while, tugging on his moustache.

No wonder the tsar had trouble with you two.

We were put to work scraping and painting, and then one dawn the colour of pearl, we entered the port of Shanghai. The density of the traffic in the mouth of the Huang Po, the scows and barges drifting past anchored European warships and freighters, by its nature made one feel hopeful. My two-year escape had brought me to this fascinating place. But the prospect of being returned soured the day.

The agent of the shipping company came aboard, interviewed the captain, inspected the ship's log, let stevedores aboard to unload a cargo of Japanese lacquered furniture, and then told us to accompany him to the Russian consulate. At the bottom of the gangway he had posted a tall Indian armed with a rifle, and the guard and agent now escorted us to the Russian legation located in a European-style building on the road called the Bund. We were already depressed, but the tsar's picture, which looked down on us with a kindly severity in the outer office, left us dismal. At last the door to the consul-general's inner office opened and there stood a young man with a beard trimmed like Nikolka's. This young man thanked the guard and the shipping agent, permitted them to leave, and then called us into his office. On his wall was a very handy map of the region, the sort of gift of information I felt bound to devour.

What can I do with you? the young consul-general asked us. Had the shipping agent, with so much on his mind, left without telling him we were stowaways?

We thought it best not to show the consul our false passports. We told him instead we were sailors but we'd missed our ship in Nagasaki and our papers and belongings were on that ship. The consul told us he was swamped by stranded Russian sailors. He gave us a few dollars of local money – he did so for every stranded sailor. He would send us back to Vladivostok on the very first Russian ship available, but in the meantime we should live in the Russian Sailors' Home in Fuchau Road.

We were sent off without any guard or any orders about our behaviour. Standing in the densely peopled street among rickshaw men and coolies and Europeans in the most elegant suits to be seen in the world, we had trouble believing what had just happened.

He doesn't want to see us again, said Suvarov in wonder, and it seemed that that was so, that the harried young man would be pleased for us to disappear into the streets that had all the liveliness of the harbour. Huge banners advertising pawn shops were everywhere. Chinese pharmacies stood in every block with their unguessable rows of drawers and big urns full of cures. Men carrying live crabs on a string walked from food shop to food shop, and from the top balcony of a furniture store a Chinese band played. Every three or four doors was a coolie restaurant selling food very cheaply. Men who pulled rickshaws would eat here, replenishing their strength for hauling further humans.

Lost amid such traffic, we felt our freedom had been achieved at last.

35

Suvarov and I would become familiar with the coolie restaurants where the steamed buns or crab tofu was made in a great earthenware stove in the middle of the room.

With the freedom permitted Europeans here, we wandered in the International Settlement, where we would regularly see teams of coolies, twenty at a time and four abreast, hauling wagons loaded with timber or cobblestones by means of ropes over the shoulder or straps across the breast. They were all thin men, their faces like parchment. They were successors to those slaves who built the pyramids. The rickshaw drivers carried foreigners to the doors of their banks, their concession offices and trading firms, then back to their villas. We learned by observation that the white Shanghai European princelings, once arrived at their broad house-gate, would get down without a word and toss a coin on the pavement for the Chinese driver to pick up.

In French Town, where beautiful European-style villas could be found in the quieter streets, there was also an area of bars, cheap restaurants and dosshouses frequented by French seamen. For leisure these men reeled around in rickshaws using the rickshaw puller's braided queue as a rein and whipping him on with a cane. In this area we rented a whole room to ourselves in a cheap hotel owned by an Armenian. It was always sepulchral, even in the day, and had little room for anything but one large bed for us to share. In a nearby street, though, we came across a Russian bakery. Paying rent a month ahead, we had only a few dollars left, and so went looking for work at the bakery.

It was a cold season. Fog haunted the streets. We wore grey caps, our Russian belted shirts and thin black overcoats. Suvarov had in his hand a pocket dictionary of Russian and phonetic Mandarin.

When we arrived at the counter of the place, and stood before the display of bread and delicacies on glass shelves, a Russian cashier and the baker who cooked the bread in the oven at the rear of the shop came forward, each with a grin on his face. Brothers, one of them said. They looked at our clothes and our thin faces, and they knew the story behind them since they had maybe made a journey like ours themselves. The cashier shook our hands, the plump baker wiped flour off his palms with his apron and offered his hand too. They introduced themselves as Radich and Yevgeny. We presented ourselves in turn by our real first names. It felt safe enough to do that. Radich the manager was rueful when we mentioned jobs. He told us the bakery was in fact owned by a Chinese merchant from beyond the margin of the International Settlement, and doubted he himself had the power to employ anyone. But, he said, they'd been authorised to employ Chinese to work on a new bread run in French Town – it was taken for granted that it was always Chinese who delivered bread. Can't you use us instead? Suvarov pleaded. Russians are half Asiatic.

Yevgeny wondered about that. White men have never been used for deliveries here. The English were fussy about that, and the French were nearly as bad.

But we can't afford to be fussy ourselves, argued Suvarov.

The two bread men looked at each other. No money at all? asked Yevgeny the baker.

We have two settlement dollars.

Holy Mother! said Radich. But now, let's be clear. You'd have to be here at four o'clock in the morning. You'd *have* to be here. *At four.* And never let me down. Even if you're ill.

We swore. From then we paid the Armenian's Chinese servant a few pence to wake us at three each morning, and by four we were at the bakery door and Yevgeny let us in. We counted the loaves for delivery against the French numbers and names and set off hauling the cart by its shafts southwards into an elegant region of French Town. White mansions rose in misty gardens, and a Chinese servant was always waiting at the high gate to accept the European family's bread.

Suvarov and I developed a system for the bread delivery. Since I was a broader-shouldered man, I took to harnessing myself to the cart while Suvarov pushed from behind. Suvarov, with his good humour, quickly charmed all the Chinese women servants to whom he handed the loaves. By eleven o'clock we were back at the bakery with an empty cart, and we'd drink tea and discuss socialist theory. I told them stories about Russian immigrants in Paris from when I had been there ten years before, and about Plekhanov, Martov and Vladimir Ilich Lenin. It turned out that neither of our employers was very political. Radich had escaped the police on Sakhalin Island, while Yevgeny had fled an enforced marriage in Khabarovsk.

I grew a little entrepreneurial. We took some bread down to the harbour, and started to sell it to various Russian freighters. The SS *Poltava* was a regular visitor to Shanghai and we would always have lunch with the stokers in their mess. The stokers harboured secret feelings of rebellion but had a low quotient of class-consciousness. Women and liquor seemed to be at the forefront of their minds.

In the end we moved out of our sepulchral dosshouse and into one of the small rooms behind the bakery. From our deliveries of bread to various ships, we got to know deserting sailors and absconded convicts and paid their dosshouse rent. In a small way, Suvarov and I repaid the kindnesses of Siberia.

One day the British paper in the International Settlement – the *Courier* – carried an editorial item condemning certain Russians in the French quarter who had undermined European prestige and violated the concept of face by taking the work that properly belonged to Chinese coolies. I had not had the mental room nor the ease in which to write a letter reporting my movements to the leader, Vladimir Ilich.

Now – spurred by the grand imperial attitude of the *Courier* – I did so, reporting on all I had seen in Eastern Siberia and beyond. I raised with Vladimir Ilich the question of moving, a matter that occupied a great deal of Suvarov's and my time. America was the obvious place. We also had a number of ships from the Australia run come in to the port of Shanghai and that seemed a possibility. The attraction of Australia as a supposed working man's paradise where labour representatives were elected to parliament was powerful. In the end, I was drawn by that idea and so was Suvarov.

More than two years had now passed since my first escape, and Suvarov and I had built up our accounts to the point where we could afford a steerage passage to Australia. Radich and Yevgeny decided to come with us, as did a Russian deserter, but they intended to leave the ship in Melbourne whereas Suvarov and I had read plenty about the warm weather of Queensland. We travelled for three weeks in a cabin for eight people. Some nights we simply had to sleep on deck, since the air below was barely breathable.

South of Borneo the captain kindly filled a large tarpaulin frame with water to make a swimming pool for us and we would strip to undervests and sit in it by the hour.

And that was how, as brothers, Suvarov and I reached the great southern continent and lived and worked together until the Menschkin case drove him away to Tasmania.

36

It was in the early southern summer that we came into Moreton Bay. From the deck of our ship, we could see the Brisbane wharves and sun-leathered waterside workers pushing hand carts loaded with bales of wool and other goods. If one were to believe the British paper in Shanghai, they were letting down the prestige of Europeans as well. The streets seemed more full of lorries and cars seemed more numerous in the streets beyond the wharves than they were in Russian cities, and it was then I noticed the tram cars, their cleanliness, their good order and – as I would find out – their put-upon drivers and conductors. The working men of Brisbane wore singlets, which was the Australian equivalent of the Russian smock, and overalls and sturdy boots and broad-brimmed hats. I would find that this – perhaps with a woollen jumper in the winter – was the standard uniform.

It had been interesting that before leaving Shanghai we had acquired false passports but in our real names! This, despite the remote risk that people in Australia might have a list of escaped tsarist prisoners. It was a liberation to travel under one's genuine name and to present oneself on those terms. Landed from our ship by launch we were processed for entry into Queensland in a little portable tent set up by a German-born official, and it was obvious he was very sympathetic to our situation. In a season when labour was needed in Queensland, the German-Australian official and his two auxiliaries placed very little obstacle to our landing.

This generous attitude was not reflected when we went walking in the city, however. We sat on a bench in the botanic gardens and were moved on by a policeman for fear that we were vagrants. Strolling in the streets of the city, we decided to buy something to wear less disconcerting to passers-by than Russian smocks. We went into a store like the one I worked at in French Town and a curt male shop assistant sold us shirts and singlets and pants. Before we could return to the immigrant dormitory, where we were allowed to sleep for seven days, we met a friend of Suvarov on the street. Even I thought it was a strange sight, two Russians embracing each other on a street corner in Brisbane.

The man's name was Cherlin. He took Grisha by the shoulders. Do you know those bastard gendarmes hanged Kolya?

I did not know Kolya, but suddenly Russia seemed closer and I knew that complete escape could never be achieved.

The dormitory supervisor tried to recruit us as scab labour to go to a place named Bundaberg where members of the Australian Workers Union were on strike. He said that we would be sent back to Russia if we did not and that there was a law to that effect. Many of the Russian new arrivals joined in a walkout, including Suvarov.

But now, Suvarov was reduced to nervousness and was on his way to Tasmania or there already, and it would not surprise me if by his own efforts he became an itinerant again, a negligible figure to the authorities.

Out of the blue, there was sudden, graphic news. The Queenslanders, the Australians, the New Zealanders had been used in the Hellespont – on the peninsula named Gallipoli – to make a landing and try to capture Istanbul, and so give the tsar at last his warm water port by which his armies could be supplied. It was as if the land I'd fled to had been drawn into some great plot to pursue the benefit of the tsar. The Queensland newspapers claimed that the Queensland battalion, the Ninth of the Third Brigade of the First Australian Division, had been first ashore. I wondered what Major Mockridge made of that fierce landing under fire.

Two weeks later, battalion adjutant Major Mockridge was killed at the head of some dusty and meaningless ravine while leading a party of Australians in a probe. He fell at the head of his men in an assault on the upper escarpment on top of which the Turks were well dug in. I don't know why I felt such grief for the man and the boys he had led into the ambush. In the eyes of the *Telegraph*, this former militia officer had *laid his body upon the high altar of the Empire*, and the ravine was thereafter christened in his honour – Mockridge Gully.

Russia was never mentioned as the mainspring of this operation, though all of us in our boarding houses discussed it endlessly. In Gallipoli, slaughter outran the capacity of newspapers to record. For a country of small population, Australia was indeed laying many on its empire's altar. There were mothers' sons in Mockridge's probe whose future had been dependent on the judgement of a flawed officer whose wife had rebuffed him, with whom he shared a shameful disease, and who thus had a taste for immolation.

I wrote to Hope. I remembered, I said, that Hope and he worked together to save our very necks. *I feel that if things had been only a little different he would have been more closely your ally.*

I met Paddy Dykes sitting on a bench at Trades Hall drinking tea. He looked up at me from a newspaper, then he stood.

You heard about Major Mockridge? he asked me.

I told him I had.

Shouldn't have been there in the first place. The blind leading the blind.

Something similar to that, I agreed.

He held up his newspaper. I'm reading about these bloody ministers of religion. Coming home from leave in England. And all of them say the English have cleaned themselves up for the war effort, reformed themselves completely. Living angelic bloody lives it seems. Hardly a pub open and as for prostitution . . . But the Australians are still too interested in cricket and football, and the races at Eagle Farm and Doomben. And beer, of course. What total balls!

And he sat down to write something in his notebook. I was sure he was writing along the lines of, If labour gives up cricket, what will capital give up?

After the landings in the Dardanelles, parsons and priests became busy in another sense. I saw them on the streets of South Brisbane walking the pavements, telegrams in hand, on their way to deliver them and to comfort newly desolated women.

At Trades Hall Kelly was angry. Capital will drive the essentials of life upwards! This idea captured him and made him a radical; the Labor government he so fervently believed in, despite all, wanted a wage freeze! Workers could tighten their belts while capital got rich on selling them the food for their tables. We also became aware of our people losing their jobs. They came into Russia House from the metal factories and joinery works, where machinery was being packed up to send to Britain. Men were also sacked from the coalmines, since governments were wary of the dangers of exporting Australian coal all the way to England, across oceans filled with raiders and U-boats. At Russia House we looked after our own as we had promised to. In saying 'our own' I display the ethnic bias that has been the bane of socialism. But that had been the promise of my earlier appeals for funds.

I was suddenly living on my savings too. The owners of the meat-works had closed them down in the face of Premier Ryan's newly opened state butchers' shops and from the unfounded fear that their meat could not safely be shipped to hungry Britain. It would be a fear they would get over quickly.

I'll tell you a strange story, Paddy said to me at Trades Hall one evening. The miners at Broken Hill know Germany bought most of Broken Hill's ore before the war started, and now it's being aimed back at Australians in the trenches.

In the absence of Suvarov and Rybukov, and in the remoteness of Hope's behaviour (and mine, to be fair) I felt bereft of my normal sounding boards, and Paddy Dykes fulfilled the role. We worked on an account of the Menschkin case so that the *Australian Worker* could publish it in a small pamphlet ultimately named *The Persecution of Workers and Their Friends: The Story of the So-Called Queensland Murder Case.*

I enjoyed Paddy's company and the way he released news to his friends in energetic murmurs. Like me he was not much of a drinker; his father had been too much of one, with the outcome unhappy for Paddy Dykes and his frazzled mother. So we drank tea a lot, sometimes at Adler's, sometimes at the printing press of *Izvestia* in the Stefanovs' spare room in which the model of the People's Train remained like a whisper of Rybukov's imagination.

That Scotsman, Fisher! Paddy would complain of the prime minister. The Gympie miner! he sniffed. For him the war is everything.

Yet, with the great mincing apparatus of Gallipoli still operating, Fisher gave up his prime ministerial position and took a grand job as agent-general of the Australian states in London. He left a little Welsh chap named Hughes, whom Amelia had met frequently in her younger years, to lead the government of the Commonwealth of Australia. Hughes was also in a sense a Queenslander. He had come into the small but intense political cauldron of Brisbane, having arrived here as an assisted migrant. Everyone seemed to come through Queensland, and then leave it without regrets. A working man, Hughes had trained as a lawyer and became an organiser of unions. The little Welshman had campaigned for a prices referendum to take place – an aim in which he failed. But the longer the war went on, the more he was determined to go on feeding young blood into that furnace.

In the period when the Gallipoli campaign had become a deadly and predictable stalemate, so that the news each day was as identically woeful as that of the day before, Dykes and I spent a lot of time in the room at the Stefanovs', talking about articles in *Izvestia* and working together to translate some of them into English. He was a very fast learner, this withered little man in an old checked suit probably tailored in the 1890s and who had enjoyed only four years of school. He took an interest in Cyrillic type, too, picking up this or that leaden letter and asking, What sound does this one make? As far as I knew he had no domestic arrangements of his own. It struck me that when it came to women and working-class marriage he had something of the same reticence as he had about drinking.

Sometimes he and I would catch the tram over to see Amelia, who seemed to be sadly wasting, as if she had decided that her lack of capacity to be heard as an opponent of war was the end of her usefulness.

Did you read in the papers? she would ask me, short of breath. Like many older people whose movements were curtailed, she read them down to the most insignificant column-inch. That Billy Hughes! Always talked like a peacemaker. Knew what travesties wars are. Now he's in love with this one. Oh, what a fall is there!

Amelia for now avoided the question of the widowed Hope and Buchan and myself and concentrated on broader politics than that.

Have you heard of Emmeline Pankhurst? she asked me one day.

I said that of course I had – she was the famous English suffragette.

She is the most beautiful of women, Amelia told me. Old now, of course. But when she was in full cry . . . well . . . Her hair is in absolute clusters. Her bones . . . Her long neck. She was almost painfully beautiful when she was young in Manchester, where I knew her. And her marriage – she married a lawyer who believed in her work. I joined her organisation a quarter of a century ago. Yet Englishwomen *still* don't have the franchise. But what I was talking about . . . ? Folly. Yes, folly as grand as Billy Hughes' – if not more so. I would sit here in Brisbane in previous times and read of the exploits of Mrs Pankhurst and her daughters with awe. Their endurance! Their hunger strikes!

She is like the Wobblies a little, I said, your old friend Emmeline Pankhurst?

Indeed. She's blown up churches in her day! But the suffragettes were not frightened of turning violence on themselves. Remember that racing incident? That pleasant and pretty girl Emily Davison, who threw herself under the king's horse at the Epsom Derby and was trampled to death? I believe the king's horse was called Anham. They say she suffered terrible injuries from it. No, that's not right. Anmer's the name. Anmer who trampled Emily to death. And Pankhurst herself and her daughters, off on hunger strikes in prison. Not playing at it – really starving themselves. The warders feeding them by tubes down their throats. Emily Davison, too, before her accident. She'd barricaded herself in her prison cell, and the authorities flooded her cell with iced water. Makes me furious, Tom, even now!

She would always grow quiet at the end of such a stanza of outrage so that she could recruit her breath to go on.

The Cat and Mouse Act, she murmured.

Cat and Mouse?

Yes, said Amelia. It allowed the authorities to release the hunger-striking followers of Emmeline once they had become dangerously weak, and then to rearrest them when they had become healthy again. But still women went on hunger strikes in prison. Emmeline Pankhurst's daughter . . . Sylvia. She went on silent hunger strike, and you can imagine the damage to her health. Yet what did Emmeline Pankhurst do as soon as the war started? The same as Fisher, the same as my friend Billy! She blasphemed against all the suffering they'd been through. She devoted herself and her women to the war effort in the hope of getting the vote afterwards. She told them to turn the same fervour they'd taken to jail and into bombing churches to pursuing the Hun, or persuading young fellows to do so. Beside such rank foolishness, our friend Hope is a modest sinner. And whether a sinner at all, she is one beloved of me.

The lesson ended there for the moment. I didn't know if its point had been Emmeline Pankhurst or Hope.

My father was a lawyer, she told me one evening when I walked her along the riverbank. And a member of the House of Lords. He was progressive too. But he was absolutely appalled when I sought to marry a stevedore. He would do anything for the working class, my dear old papa, except give one of them his daughter.

She laughed. And I was determined to do it, just to shock him . . . or punish him. What for? All children punish their parents, though – perhaps for having begotten them. Anyhow, at the stage I was courting my husband I was a very prim and argumentative little creature indeed. Thus, I used my fiancé, later my husband, as a stick to beat my parents with. This was unjust to all parties. Except for myself. I was having a very good time.

She had a coughing fit, and her crooked mouth was cruelly twisted by it. Afterwards she leaned on her stick, panting.

You see. I have committed my own crimes. It is not surprising at all that a woman should behave like Hope, given the provocation offered by her late husband.

Then why hadn't she abandoned him long ago? I asked. Nowadays it astonished me more and more that she hadn't.

I don't presume to know, said Amelia. He's abandoned *her* now, in any case. But whatever Hope's small sins, they don't come close to matching Emmeline's grossness. She let those young women dynamite, she let them starve themselves, she let them throw themselves under the king's horse, and yet, as soon as the war begins, she becomes a conventional rallyer of the troops. At least Hope restricted herself to membership of a benevolent society for the troops – the young men are going to need it when they come back maimed.

37

Sometimes, in the early evenings, I went round to the fruit shop owned by Lucia's parents and would be brought into the parlour at the back of the shop. The Mangravitis were wary of me but pointed me to a settee above which hung a black, blue and gold tapestry of Naples and Vesuvius. It was not their home – they came from a small volcanic island in the Tyrrhenian Sea.

I began to wonder if Lucia was as shy as she appeared. She was, for example, powerful enough to persuade her parents to have me as a guest. On the other hand, she was dutiful. Her life was spent in mutely serving out the fruit and vegetables her father bought every pre-dawn at the Brisbane markets. She was brave enough to give me one of the letters Podnaksikov had sent her. Another had obviously been too private, but she said that he had been impressed by the journey to Egypt, the blueness of the Red Sea, and then riding a donkey around the pyramids. He had made many Australian friends, he'd said, and they'd nicknamed him Igor. That was obviously the sort of cachet he wanted to achieve. That and survival.

The letter she gave me, despite a gesticulating quarrel with her mother and father, was a very primitive card, on which was printed:

☐ *I have been wounded*

☐ *I have been sent back to base*

☐ *I am well*

☐ *I am convalescing*

Podnaksikov had ticked *I am well*, and that was all there was. It was hard to tell where he was now, still in Egypt or working with the wounded in Lemnos or toiling at the cliffs of Gallipoli.

I heard news second-hand from Kelly, who was discreet for once and did not blurt it out all over the Trades Hall Hotel: Hope had left her widowed home now and gone to live with Amelia. And apparently Buchan came courting there.

One day – telling myself I was going for Amelia's sake – I caught the tram to Amelia's house and climbed the stairs. Knocking on the screen door, I was answered by Hope, her hair a little astray.

Artem, please come in. Would you like to see Amelia?

I wanted to see you too. Your husband, Hope . . . It was a tragedy.

She bowed her head.

Such a waste it all is, she said. He should have married someone else. So should I. I am both bereaved and liberated, Artem. But marriage has a power beyond the sum of its two members and it holds people in place even when they dream of being free. I have to tell you, I wept for him. As for Mr Buchan, I suppose you think I am an abandoned woman.

In my world, there is no such creature, I said.

I will marry Buchan, she said. Although you are an excellent man . . .

This statement would have been a matter of serious grief for me only a few months before. Now, I barely needed to hide my true feelings.

Well, I said, I don't know that he's any more suitable than me. Do you know who you should marry? Paddy Dykes.

She made a face and laughed. She was relieved by my attitude and thought it was a joke.

It's the truth, I insisted. He's the most honest man in Brisbane.

Do you know what my husband wrote to me? she asked. Well,

you wouldn't. He wrote, *Here in the Gallipoli peninsula, I am making an argument no one can rebut.* And we can't rebut it. So I am attending his public memorial service, and the hypocrites can say what they want!

I had time to notice that she made the most exquisite widow on earth. Before I really knew it myself I'd tried to kiss her – in part as a goodbye. She turned her face away.

No, Tom.

Justly feeling a fool, I went in to see Amelia. Her mouth was even more cruelly twisted. I wanted to take it and mould the muscles back into shape.

Hello, dear Artem, Amelia told me. I am on the way down into the shades.

Not yet, Amelia, I said. You can't orphan me so easily.

Don't patronise me, Tom. Once the brain and its veins turn on one, it does not stop, it's all set on betrayal.

She dropped her voice and grabbed me with her thin parchment hand.

I'm not taking sides, Tom, and it is not my duty to work everything out. But I allow nothing improper to occur on my premises.

If Amelia was right, when Buchan called at Amelia's place he called not as a lover, but as a suitor.

Then she sat up and resumed full volume.

Look, I want to ask you, would you ever desire to return to Russia? After all the acrimony poured on you here? I have an estate. I can finance you. You are a remarkable man and I would like to see you restored to your true scene of activities – if it were not too dangerous.

This offer stunned me. I covered my eyes. It was so tempting, now with Suvarov and Rybukov gone, and the wearing thin of the connection between Hope and myself. But it was not the time yet. I was as active here as I could be in Swiss or French exile, and if I returned to Russia I would probably become a conscript.

There will be a time, she said with certainty, when it's appropriate for you. I see you as a returning Russian, not as a Queenslander. I am not even sure I have become a Queenslander myself!

I uttered my thanks and took her hand.

I would certainly like to go when I am no longer a subject of the tsar – though that's hard to imagine, even with every Russian front line in crisis.

We said goodbye. I kissed her hand, which was half blue for want of oxygen. When I came out to the verandah, Hope was not there.

The next Sunday the odious *Truth* called her Red Hope and expressed the wish that now she had taken part as an unworthy mourner in her husband's memorial service, she might mend some of her radical socialist ways.

Accompanied by Paddy Dykes, I went down to the offices of the *Telegraph,* where a map of the Hellespont had been placed by the doors to educate Australians on where their sons were being killed. There behind Anzac Cove lay the ravine out of which Mockridge had tried to lead his men to the heights above. A pasted marker pointed to the place and declared: MAJOR MOCKRIDGE FATALLY WOUNDED HERE. A brave few had captured the top of the escarpment, but then had been ejected by fierce artillery and machine-gun fire.

Jesus Almighty, said Paddy, you've got to give it to him, getting all the way up there!

Kelly grew wistful for the faces of many of the men who had enlisted for whatever reason – a renewed sense of nation, a spiritual intensity or a desire to leave their squalid working day behind. He was supporting the widows and children, even though the government had made noises that they would do this. But they were still buying the desks and pens for the public servants who would give out the government's mite to the families. The war had changed Kelly, who had begun by supporting it as a means by which labouring men would earn the gratitude of the government. Now he refused to consider the deaths a holy immolation.

38

A week or so after I visited Hope and Amelia, a note came to Adler's in which Hope asked me to meet her and Buchan at the Samarkand. I thought she could have chosen a better place, a more anonymous or neutral one, to reveal whatever joint decision she and Buchan had reached. The steaming samovars of the place, the little cakes, the atmosphere were all reminiscent of the times we had sat there trying to charm each other. But they reminded me too that I had soon enough grown into the habits of a bad husband, and had loved her negligently. And now – like all the people I felt affection for – she was going to go away, I suspected, to Buchan's city, Melbourne.

How soured love debases us! I noticed with a grim satisfaction that afternoon that she wore a black dress as if she were entitled to both mourning and Buchan. Buchan was beside her, wearing a restrained suit but the spats still. His clothes attracted the covert glances of the Russian working men and humble clerks who frequented the Samarkand.

He nodded. Tom, he said. The way he said it was eloquent: We can both be men about this, but if you take offence and throw a punch, I believe I can beat you that way too.

When we were all seated, and before the daughter of the shop came to serve us, Hope told me, frowning and with careful phrasing, Amelia is somewhat improved. She's a determined woman and is telling me to go. She knows there's some urgency for us to go to Melbourne.

I looked at Buchan and felt a sudden, if perhaps brief, relief that her history with all its contradictions and (quoting Amelia) *follies* would be his business to attend to now.

Buchan enlarged on the Melbourne idea.

From this distance Walter O'Sullivan seems to be doing the right thing. But he dominates a weak committee down there, and he's got the unions so offside they won't attend the peace rallies he puts on. So he sits there like Buddha, above the vulgar crowd. He sees the party as consisting of him, the supreme Number One. If he ever doubts that, his wife is there to believe in it harder than ever. I know him though. I reckon I can get him back on a more effective path.

I said nothing. I could imagine ordinary union members having a choice between Walter and Buchan.

It's a wonder you didn't go earlier then, I said to Buchan. Given that you see such an appalling crisis down there.

Only Hope looked away, embarrassed for the moment. I thought of how often she had saved me, and I felt ashamed.

If you're telling me I'm a procrastinator, he answered, then I agree with you. I don't mind telling you I didn't want to leave Hope, but I am a friend of Amelia also, and Amelia had something to do with it. So be it.

Hope reached for my hand. Tom, aren't we all in the same fight?

Even Walter O'Sullivan and Olive? I asked.

Buchan told me, There is right thinking and then there's total delusion.

I shook my head. I didn't say aloud that he was not exactly Vladimir Ilich when it came to right thinking.

Hope said, the labour college needs looking after too. It's defunct. Walter doesn't approve of it, because he didn't think of it. With the war . . .

Buchan finished the sentence for her: . . . O'Sullivan has let it all slide. As if educating people doesn't matter any more, or is an idea you can dispense with.

You finish each other's sentences, I observed, like married people.

Buchan said, Indeed. We hope to be married by a free commitment innocent of any minister of religion.

I'm sure Hope's inherited wealth will help the college greatly, I remarked.

Hope was angry and no doubt entitled to be. In that light her cheeks genuinely looked like alabaster, even to a jaded lover, and now they took on a rose colouring. But she swallowed and refused to be baited by my backsliding rancour. They both watched me and I thought, How stupid of me, how gross, how bourgeois to play the aggrieved lover. Just like some fool in a drama not written by a first-class talent.

As soon as I get to Melbourne, Hope told me, I will send you our address. If Amelia has another stroke, send me a telegram immediately. Can I rely on you to do that, Tom?

Of course I will, I mumbled. As if a man wouldn't do that much . . .

I'm not saying you wouldn't do it. Please don't be offended. This is very awkward.

I suppose so, I said.

You will send me a telegram, Artem? Amelia is very precious to all of us.

You realise, I said. You realise . . .

I had been going to remind them that even if she received a telegram one day, it would be at least three days by steamer or a combination of rail and steamer before she was in Brisbane to see Amelia. I had been going to say that I had enough charges in my life without being burdened with the sole care of Amelia. Again, I had become a miserable, whining soul under the weight of their decision to go to Melbourne. Now I repented, and not before time.

I want you to know, I wish you well. But Buchan, I believe you should read more if you want to be a leader. Despite Plekhanov's betrayal, you should read *The Role of the Individual in History*. You should also read Vladimir Ilich's 'Our Programme' and *What is to be Done*? It's not as if they're as long as *Kapital*. You should also read Martov, even though he's a Menshevik. As you know, men don't always follow the wisdom of their original words, but that doesn't cancel the words. You have to understand what we stand for by understanding exactly what they – the people we disagree with – stand for.

Sure, Buchan told me equably. Of course. Mind you, I have my own encyclopaedia.

He put his hand on Hope's shoulder, and that nearly started the whole madness in me again. But I steered away from it. This crazy fellow who, totally unread, wanted to have people give a series of night lectures he dared to call a labour college. This woman who, while insisting on wearing black, wanted to decamp to Melbourne with a Scot in spats.

Yes, I said, you are a fortunate man. But all the leaders are thinkers too, and Walter is at least a thinker.

He took this with good grace.

Perhaps if we could combine Walter's intellect and my capacity for action, we'd have a complete being.

Good luck, I said when I realised there was no profit in talking further. I wanted to ask her, more from curiosity than anything, Do you really love this joke of a Caledonian? But I rose and at last behaved properly, kissed Hope's scented hand, shook hands with Buchan, and went to the counter to pay for the whole farce.

T. J. Ryan now sat over Queensland as its chief minister. With his round, fashionably bearded Irish face, he sang his siren song to the people of the state – the control of prices and new laws to improve the lot of labour. There were many who expected the moon, said Ryan, but he declared the best that could be delivered was a few moonbeams. Ah, the old cant, I thought, dressed up in Celtic-style imagery, in Celtic-style palaver.

He did begin state enterprises in milling and producing food. The growers of sugar cane were promised a fixed price for their product, and so the cane-cutting brethren who had come down, disconsolate, to Russia House in Brisbane were now able to return to their fields and take up their machetes again. State insurance and a state bank were set up. But the old venal banks were not obliterated. An arbitration system for labour was put in place. While not perfect, Ryan's was indeed the best government I knew of in the world until that stage of history, yet his curtsies towards capital and the war continued and meant that he could not utterly win over a true socialist such as Walter O'Sullivan or make a restless Russian like myself a happy and grateful unthinking citizen of an antipodean Utopia.

39

On my visits to Amelia, she would now always ask me, How are you, poor old Tom?

I had become poor old Tom. I hankered for vanished faces. Her maternal feelings for me were now an enduring and nourishing aspect of my uncertain life. I called on her at least once every two days, since I needed her as much as she needed me. These days she had the company of a nurse – I suspected Hope had installed the woman.

I'm very well, I always told her. At least I'm not serving on the Galician front. Or any other futile front for that matter.

Podnaksikov was on some futile front. As I came into Adler's boarding house one evening from the room at the Stefanovs', I found Mr Mangraviti waiting in the front room. He rose to greet me. His demeanour was much friendlier than the last time I had seen him.

Did I speak Italian?

I told him, *Poco*.

Podnaksikov e morte. Nella Hellesponte.

Podnaksikov? I asked stupidly.

E morte. He imitated a machine-gun. Ratatatatat. *Lucia a riceverato una telegramma e una lettera assicurata. Lucia . . . Eristissima.*

He wanted me, as Podnaksikov's friend, to visit his daughter and assuage her grief.

Mr Mangraviti led me two streets around to the shop and into a stuffy back parlour that seemed to be humid with Lucia's tears. Lucia's big-bosomed mother surrounded her with her arms and soothed her. To my shame, and for the first time, I noticed how remarkable the tear-blurred, dark-headed Lucia looked. Her father pointed out my presence, and she smiled through her grief.

We all sat at the Mangravitis' parlour table and, with her parents' approval, I held her hand in mine and spoke to her in English, in which she had more skill than her parents. I am sure you were his last thought, I assured her, only afterwards understanding what a double-edged comfort that might be.

Later I asked her to go for walks with me in the evenings. If she were as shy as she looked, of course, if she did not secretly exercise some authority over her parents, they would have stopped her coming out with me. I began to see in her the will, the capacity, to command. I would fetch her from the fruit shop and her parents would turn their eyes to heaven, her mother touching a small picture of the Virgin, which hung over the cash register. Russians must indeed have seemed like a mixed blessing to them.

She remembered the island she had lived on as a child, remembered her village, her parents arguing about the lack of food. She remembered, too, how common idiocy and rickets were in that place – children gaping without understanding of the world, or creeping around on legs bent by hunger. The longer I sat with her by the river, the more confidently she began to rail against landowners and money-lenders. Brisbane was better, she said. Her parents stood in their shop among oranges, pineapples, cabbages and melons in astounding bounty.

As I sat beside her on a bench, smelling the plain, unscented soap of the Mangraviti household – her chief perfume – I could feel her thigh against mine and was aroused in obvious ways, but in other ways as well: a wish to find a home in her. I wanted to caress her but I was cautious. If there were a pregnancy, marriage would be necessary. Otherwise she would be sent to one of those convent institutions for fallen girls. I was aware that her remaining affection for Podnaksikov might nonetheless give me an easy run into the enjoyment of such kindnesses as she had extended to him, but though I felt driven to meet and walk with her, I tried to resist her honest scent and the feel of her flesh through fabric. I did not want to end up living in a stilt house – even with as surprisingly robust a girl as Lucia – and raising an indefinite number of Australian children. Many sane men would have thought it my tragedy that I did not want to end up tending a vegetable garden in some lush Queensland valley, standing in my own thicket of pawpaw trees.

In the spring of that year, the troops abandoned Gallipoli and the graves of Mockridge and Podnaksikov. Never mind, said the jingos, they'll be fighting in France soon.

Increasingly, in those later months of 1915, Paddy spent his evenings with me – sometimes helping me, sometimes writing in the printing room at the Stefanovs', trading concepts and figures of speech, asking me about Russian factions. His presence created no scandal with Mrs Stefanov, who, now that I wasn't undermining her husband's moral fibre any more and had been taught a lesson, was much kinder to me.

I was aware of a changed atmosphere in other quarters though. By this stage so many had died, people seemed to think more must risk death! People became furious at the idea of anyone calling a pause. I would find that demonstrated to me vividly, bruisingly. I had met Dykes after work one afternoon as summer was coming on, and we caught a tram across to South Brisbane.

As we neared Adler's boarding house, a large group of men in suits and Australian army uniforms rounded a corner ahead of us. They were talking among themselves – like an oblivious group of youths returning from a cricket match, say. I saw that some had axe handles and – appropriately – metal-tipped cricket stumps in their hands.

When Paddy Dykes and I instinctively looked behind us, we saw another similar crowd of soldiers and civilians, blocking any chance of escape. They knew we had seen them and they approached faster, especially the soldiers, the men in suits waving them on with their hats in a parody of older men waving the young into battle.

You Red bastards! one of the civilians called to us, and a few others cheered and the young soldiers began to sprint, waving their clubs and cricket stumps. A man in an open-collared shirt and suit approached from the front, a wooden club in his hands.

Holy hell, I heard Paddy Dykes say, but with a strange tone that betrayed curiosity about the outcome. Dykes went into a crouch. You wanted to declare me on, you bastard? he roared, I'll declare *you* on. And he put the fellow on his back before I could appreciate what had happened.

Why now? I wondered as the man with the open collar started in on my shoulders with his club. I had not written or published anything different from that I had written or published at the outbreak of war. Had one of these older men been suddenly alerted to my existence? Had they taken umbrage at Paddy's writing? Someone got a good blow in against my ribs. I felt an excruciating expulsion of breath and the faint but sharp vibrations of a *crack* too muted to be heard by the yelling men who surrounded Paddy and me. I was aware that Paddy Dykes was fighting much better than I could, more ruthlessly, with greater cunning. Even as I felt a terrifying whack on my ear, I was aware that Paddy was still causing men to hang back and stamping the ribs, heads and genitals of those who didn't. The one chief cry penetrated the tolling of my head. *Red bastards*, with an occasional chorus of *Kaiser's poofters*.

I was on the ground now, receiving more blows, and then one that made everything distant and still for a second. Then Paddy Dykes was still speaking, defying them, telling them that if they were so keen on fighting, France was only a boat trip away. I thought, What a man – to be able to fight and orate at the same time. I have a dim remembrance of police turning up and counselling all the young men to go home, and leaning over us and saying we shouldn't have started a fight and we deserved to be charged. My head still rang, my vision was jaundiced.

Constable, said Paddy Dykes, are you seriously telling me that two blokes walking home from the tram took on twenty lunatics? Are you telling me that?

One of the policeman sighed. He had beery breath and an Irish accent. Now look, son, he told the mad-eyed Dykes, who was standing while I was sitting, being unfit for any vertical position. I don't like that little fucker Hughes either, but we're not going to have street brawls in South Brisbane. Do you understand? What would your mother think?

My mother died of tuberculosis when I was five, said Paddy, and I could now see his eyes gleaming by the streetlamps.

God rest her, said the Irishman. Now you two go home and no more trouble tonight.

Aren't you going to arrest those men?

They'll soon be suffering bad enough to satisfy you, said the policeman.

The other of the two coppers pulled me upright. Can you stand, you Russian bastard? he asked fraternally.

40

For the next two weeks I stumbled my way to the *Izvestia* printery. Mrs Stefanov had heard that I had been involved in a street riot and been seen yet again in the presence of police. She was cool to me once more in case I brought suspicion down on her house. There had been a time after our supposed trial when she called me by my formal, baptismal names, Fyodor Andreivich, but now she would call down the hall to her husband, Samsurov is here. Just to rile her, honest Stefanov would cry, Need a cup of tea, Artem?

I would have been off work except the superintendent was a native-born Australian resister of the war. He kept me on the wage books. After three days' rest I was back on hauling. The healing was thus slowed – indeed, I could never recover from a stab of pain every time I lifted my right arm from that day on. Yet whenever I remembered that street attack, my chief impression was of the ferocious warriorhood of Paddy Dykes.

As I approached Adler's boarding house one evening, I was delighted to see Suvarov leaning like a bent scarecrow on the front fence as if he had never gone away. He looked thinner but sun-bronzed, and wore a seaman's leather cap.

Grisha, I called out. Tell me it's you!

Smiling, he straightened up, came to the gate and embraced me.

Where have you been? I asked. Tasmania? Or even further afield?

All the cities, he said, in this part of the world. To Hobart as a stoker, then Melbourne. Then, I regret to say, Sydney.

You *regret*?

He shook his head. I got to know a girl there, he explained. I think I'm being chased by a private detective. So I'm afraid I'm just here for a moment, Artem, I'm signed on a Chilean ship bound for Valparaiso – a sailing ship, so it's just as well I've got experience with sails from working on the schooners on Lake Baikal.

He had done that long before I met him.

But you can't be serious, I told him. I can't afford to lose you again. And Valparaiso's no closer to home than Brisbane.

I took him at once to the Samarkand. Of course I wanted to know all that had happened to him down south. Under the Samarkand's dim electric lighting, he began to speak about his experiences in Hobart, and I saw that his Australian travels had been as complicated as his Siberian escape. Are we designed, Suvarov and me, for complications and only for complications? I wondered.

In Hobart, he told me, he lived for a while in a Greek boarding house that catered to fishermen. But, out of cash, he had taken his tent to a beach on the west bank of the Derwent, and camped and fished for whiting. It was all so much a repetition of our existence in Nagasaki. He took a job on a schooner making for Melbourne and, on landing there, rented a room in Port Melbourne from a widow who lived in a ramshackle house along the bay. Then, in between working on Greek fishing vessels, he went for a tour aboard a visiting Japanese warship and found that the guns were marked with the name of the Putilov works in St Petersburg, where he himself had once been a metal turner. This ship had been captured from the Russians in the Battle of Tsushima ten years before.

He survived on heaped plates of shark meat discarded as useless by the Greeks and cooked by his landlady. She could tell Suvarov was on the move and, being lonely and maternal, she begged him not to leave. But he knew he would go on to Sydney, as if to find or even to flee the Russian echoes he had discovered in Melbourne.

One day he left a letter for the old lady and took the train that carried him to the north-east limits of the city. He had kept his tent and now lugged it with him on the road to Sydney. At night he shared the ground at the edge of pastures with ox-cart drivers, gold prospectors and sheep shearers, to whom he was generous with his limited tent space. Arrived in Sydney at last, he worked with poor fishermen at Watsons Bay, sharing their wooden shacks. The Pacific Ocean came booming in the Sydney Heads, the same ocean in which the Russian fleet, venturing beyond its proper place, had been defeated. He admired the sandstone of the great heads and cliffs of Sydney.

Now he fell back on one of the skills he'd learned on Russia's Pacific coast – he got a job at a marble basin factory as a polisher. The factory was in the beach suburbs of Sydney, reached by tram from the city. In a house at Bronte Beach lived an old widow who had made her fortune selling soft drinks and lollies to summer bathers at the string of beaches around there. Suvarov could afford to take one of her rooms up at the top of the house, where the chief sound came from waves bullying the sandstone headlands, and from seabirds. The widow, Mrs Clancy, held parties to which she invited her own friends and her children's, and it became apparent to Suvarov that these parties were designed to suck in young men who might marry Denise, her pretty, pleasant but not overly clever eighteen-year-old daughter. Suvarov saw that the widow dominated her daughter to the extent that Denise would obediently marry any man Mama nominated. Suvarov did not consider himself a potential suitor, but one young man in particular, a clerk, a very well-brushed but innocent young fellow named Michael, seemed to be the frontrunner for the hand of the daughter. Because he was a lively conversationalist, which the older woman liked, Suvarov was invited to take his meals at the main table downstairs whenever the other young man was present.

On the cliffs, watching the strong Pacific currents and the occasional sounding whale bound for northern breeding grounds, Suvarov realised again that he was fatally homesick for Russia. On the nights Mrs Clancy held her parties, his chief relief from the suffocation of the house was to sit on the headland in the teeth of prevailing southerlies, buffeted by winds and yearning for the unpretty northern suburbs of the Vyborg district in Piter. There – in his entire lifetime – he had been happiest. One evening, as he sat there on the cliff, he saw the daughter climbing towards him in her long green skirt. The last light was bouncing off clouds and favouring her with its glow. He stood for her. Of course he could not avoid asking her to share the seat with him.

She suggested teasingly that he had been avoiding her. He denied it. All at once she had her arms around him, and her shyness turned to tears.

My dear Russian, she said, you are the only one who can make me happy. Mother steers me towards Michael, because he makes lots of money, but you're the only one I can love. You with your jokes and your sadness . . .

Suvarov was carried away by this. He noticed all at once that she possessed sad green eyes, and decided she had undiscovered maturity. Staring into her eyes he promised not to avoid her any more. At the next party Michael the clerk could tell from the glances Suvarov and Denise exchanged that he himself no longer had the chief claim. Michael started to come to the house less. Suvarov and Denise would wash up after dinner and he caught the widow and her brothers and sisters, Denise's aunts and uncles, exchanging winks. He came to the conclusion that he had passed some test, that doing the washing-up with a girl in Australia meant an intention to marry.

Then, with the same suddenness as its onset, at the sink with her one evening, he awoke from his infatuation. A lifetime of accepting the wet dishes from this woman? He couldn't believe he had ever wanted it.

Off the beach below was a rock platform, a shoal on which the sea pounded. On a grim winter's Saturday, beset by his melancholy, Suvarov took to the waves and made for the reef, half hoping he would be pounded to death against it. He would find an end in this same ocean that had ended the tsar's navy. On the promenade above the beach, a small crowd gathered beneath umbrellas and exclaimed and pointed. He saw them when he turned to look back without regret at the shore that harboured monsters like Mrs Clancy and her daughter. Ahead, the rock platform was bludgeoned by surf and it, too, like the spectators ashore, kept disappearing beneath the swell and revealing itself again. Portuguese men-of-war wrapped purple tentacles around him, and their long strands stung him, but that merely added to his perverse glee. Off the rock platform he chose to tread water for a while, tired now and ready to consider whether he should let himself sink or return to land. He turned in the water. When the swell revealed the beach to him, he could see even more people there, intruding on him with their concern. He was sure he could see a frantic Denise in a navy-blue coat. That was a good reason to drown. But a simple desire for breath made him drag himself towards shore in the end, a failed suicide in his own mind. When he reached the sand, his body was marked with purple strands of stinger. Denise rushed to him and he tried to hobble from her rather than collapse in her arms. But he did not manage to avoid it, and the crowd rushed up to them as to a pair of lovers saved from tragedy, and she towelled him and gave him water and then was gratified to lead him home. The Sydney papers said that during the southerly gale a Russian had swum out to sea to the reef and back with a knife in his teeth, apparently to catch shellfish. In the meantime, against his best instincts and purely from pain and tiredness and despair, he said affectionate things to Denise and suddenly the widow was calling a party.

She did not ask Suvarov before doing so, and it was not till the event had started and the first drinks were poured, with everyone being very jovial towards him, that she announced that Denise and Suvarov were engaged. The widow's older brother made a speech in which he applauded Suvarov's good fortune, and his pluck worthy of a Briton. A man who can escape a barbarous country like Russia and set himself to a trade in a civilised place like Sydney must feel very blessed indeed, the uncle said. He invited the guests to look at the spacious spread the widow had provided – a long chalk, he said, from the sauerkraut, offal and sawdust bread we read about Russians eating. Now perhaps with Denise you can get over your horrid past, he suggested. Directly you are married, we will help you become a proud Australian subject.

Subject? asked Suvarov mentally. If a subject, then he chose the tsar and all his crimes over the British monarch.

The end of the would-be engagement party in Sydney found Suvarov dazed. He doesn't know what to say, said the speechifying uncle, laughing. And indeed Suvarov didn't.

A few days later, Suvarov's misery reached its deepest point. Chinese gardeners delivered some vegetables to the house, and while separating out a hand of bananas, Denise said how much she hated the Chinese as lecherous, diseased, opium-smoking fiends. Perhaps I should be pleased you don't hate Russians, said Suvarov. But suddenly the last atom of infatuation was gone, and for good. It was a worse destiny than accepting doused plates from her! Suvarov could foresee a lifetime of listening to narrow, uninformed complaints from this complacent woman.

He did not sleep that night. He left the house early, as if for work. The tsarist prisons were calling to him, he thought. They seemed so much sweeter than the prison of Denise's arms and the grasp of her unthinking mind.

He went straight to the city on a tram. A week's wages waited for him at the marble polishing works, but he knew that the premises would soon enough be watched by the relentless widow. Walking northwards in the city, he saw an unbelievable sight – a young man with a Russian peasant cap carrying a balalaika under his arm. Suvarov immediately began talking to him in Russian. His name was Bondar, he too possessed only small change, and he too was a homesick Russian.

This Bondar had worked in Newcastle in the coalmines. Before that he had worked in mines around Vladivostok. He had come to Sydney looking for work, had found none, and now was returning with another purpose – to sign on a ship in Newcastle that would get him at least part of the way home.

The two Russians camped in a clearing by a creek on their first night out of Sydney, and after a smoke Bondar reached for his balalaika and played 'In the Mountains of Manchuria'. Then he began to sing songs he'd picked up in the mining towns of Siberia. 'The tsar does not know how I slave and ache here in the hungry dark.' He'd also acquired some Australian, British and American songs, and had a wonderful voice.

Within a few days on the road, their food was gone, and Suvarov suggested Bondar might earn a bit of money playing to farmers. Bondar wandered up to a dairy farmhouse on a hill, presented himself to the farmer and sang on the verandah – 'You Can't Keep a Good Man Down'. But the farmer's muscular wife emerged onto the verandah and shouted, Get out of here with your bloody music, you bloody foreigner. You're waking the kids.

That night they crawled into some wagons at a railway siding – bags of cement were covered with a tarpaulin. Between the cold sky and the cold cement they had no hope of sleeping. They could hear people laughing from a hotel that stood on the dirt road by the railway track. Bondar grabbed his balalaika at once, said he was going to try it again. In his absence, Suvarov heard the noise from the pub grow louder. An hour later Bondar was back, telling Suvarov to rouse himself. He had enough money to buy them a night's stay at the hotel and to buy railway tickets to Newcastle.

In the beautiful harbour at Newcastle there were Danish, Italian, English, Peruvian, Norwegian and other ships. As Suvarov surveyed them with his new friend, he saw the harbour police launch returning to vessels with sailors who had deserted. The deserters had chains on their wrists. On the docks stood a shipping agent watching with satisfaction as the men were taken by force back to their ships.

Bondar and Suvarov made their approach to the agent and were taken aboard a Chilean sailing ship. By the time they paid for their uniform and blanket, and the captain had given a quarter of their advance pay to the shipping agent, they had little left. But at least they felt they were on their way. Then a collision with a whale left them with some damage to their bows and so they had put into Brisbane. If not for that whale I would not have seen Suvarov before he went. He would be going as soon as the ship was repaired.

He could not be dissuaded, and the next morning, while loading the refrigerated sides of beef on the north side of the river, I saw an elegant sailing ship, gleaming white and black-trimmed, under way down the mangrove reaches of Moreton Bay. I decided, If he's going to Russia, I must go soon as well. I felt the strangeness in what had become familiar. Brisbane. I suddenly realised that Brisbane was a ridiculous choice of exile for me. The aspects of it I had liked were now repugnant, and as vacant as the sky-splitting raven-like cries of my fellow workers.

As I fought the temptation offered by Lucia Mangraviti, I had a letter from Walter O'Sullivan, telling me that Buchan and Hope were settled in the suburb of St Kilda. He also told me that the war census bill and its gauging of all Australian human resources was the first step in a plan to begin conscripting Australians into an army that until now had been made up purely of yearning volunteers like Podnaksikov.

O'Sullivan urged me, along with Thompson, our leader in Queensland, to write and argue about the iniquity of such a war and of forcing men to fight it.

I would discuss all these issues with Amelia when I went to check on her and see that she was well. On a stick, looking as if she might be toppled by a mere breeze, Amelia still tried to fuss around me with tea and cake – she saw it as her duty. When we discussed the times, the perfidy of the little Welsh prime minister of Australia, Billy Hughes, she would always tell me, I've had a letter from Hope.

She must write to you every day.

Every second day or better, replied Amelia. About eight letters a fortnight. I always believed her a wonderful girl, Mockridge and Buchan aside.

In the balmier evenings, we would walk along Roma Street with her nurse, a very glum Englishwoman, and the trams that had brought Amelia and me together as friends went clanging past.

I told her that in Russia, where it was the start of summer, the tsar's soldiers held their line from the Caucasus to west of St Petersburg. But the scenes of my childhood had been overrun by the kaiser's men. My brave sister, whom I'd adored in childhood, and her husband Trofimov, who suffered from a black lung, moved for a time to Moscow. I tried to imagine their lives in that hungry city but found I had lost the gift.

41

The attack on myself and Paddy Dykes was a harbinger of more numerous attacks by soldiers and thick-browed citizens on anyone who doubted the war's wisdom. The long argument remained the same, whether in France, the Middle East or Mesopotamia. In that time there was no woman in my life except Amelia. I did not often ask her for news of Hope and my sensitivity about it all might have prevented her from telling me too much. In the meantime, Amelia survived through her gentle outrage at the politics of the time. She was appalled and invigorated when Billy Hughes left Australia to visit the Western Front and the Australian troops newly arrived in England and France. He will come back, she predicted, roaring for the conscription of every son of woman.

Sure enough, when the renegade returned from his visit to the Western Front at the end of that failure named the Battle of the Somme, he wanted more lambs to the sacrifice. The physical standards required for the great abattoirs of the Western Front had been reduced now. Anyone would do. But on top of that, Billy Hughes wished to introduce, by referendum, conscription of any and all.

You might ask who opposed all this – apart from Amelia and myself. An extraordinary alliance of people came into being to oppose the conscription vote. Kelly and Trades Hall, of course, and we denizens of the Russian shadows of Brisbane. But also the Catholic Archbishop of Melbourne, an Irishman who perhaps remembered that earlier in the year – when the Irish Nationalists rose and seized the Dublin Post Office – little mercy had been shown. Australian farmers, too, would prove to be against it. Having already given one son to the furnace they were unwilling to give a second or third who were needed for farm labour and as cherished remnants.

So we all appeared on the town hall steps: Kelly, Amelia on a stick with the nurse holding the wheelchair handy in case, even the premier, Ryan – thanks to political pressure. My normal speech centred on a description of the regime – the regime of the tsar – for which the young Australians had been sacrificed in the Dardanelles. One could feel the air crackling about one's ears with danger. Young men who had just joined the army stood on the edges of the crowd and hooted at my accented English. But the police – many of them Irish – were themselves not keen on conscription. Some offered tacit protection to meetings that were in theory illegal, though not so in practice now Ryan had been elected to leadership of the state. The worst that happened to me in those days was that I was jostled – a very minor price to pay for a bad accent and a fundamentally revolutionary intent.

I followed avidly what was happening in Russia and discussed it all with Paddy Dykes in our little printery at the Stefanovs' and with Amelia. The major campaigning season had ended in the Northern Hemisphere. Mr Hughes still despaired that not enough Australians were coming forward to immolate themselves – he said he needed sixteen and a half thousand a month for the mangle.

As for Russia, a general named Brusilov had done good work for the tsar against the Austrians, but incompetence reigned on all other fronts. Even in the Brisbane papers there were imputations that the empress was under the evil influence of the mad monk Rasputin and that the tsar – bravely taking over command of the front – was not up to the job.

I was reporting these matters in *Izvestia* when two black marias pulled up outside the Stefanov house. An army intelligence officer and senior police hammered on the door and demanded to know if there was a printing press on the premises. Mrs Stefanov began to harangue Mr Stefanov. The sky had fallen in exactly as she'd predicted. Stefanov himself called me out from the spare room and the officer presented me with a warrant empowering him to seize all printing equipment on the premises. *Izvestia*, he said, was closed down by order of the War Precautions Act and section 49 of the Defence Act.

Sir, I told the army officer, this press does not belong to me – it belongs to the Russian Emigrants Union.

Then you can tell them to forward all enquiries to the Commissioner of Police, he told me. This is an authorised seizure and there will be no compensation to anyone.

He pointed the way to the police and the hallway filled up with them. Mrs Stefanov jabbed her hand towards the room in question, saying in a piteous voice, I know nothing. I tell my husband don't.

Thus, while I watched, the cellar was emptied out – newsprint, printing frames, print. Disassembled, the printing press itself was carried out of the house while I stood passive, not knowing quite what to do, feeling dismally that the past year had unmanned me.

Best to take it calmly, Artem, Stefanov said in Russian at my elbow.

At least I did not seem to be under arrest.

It was a letter from Grisha Suvarov that gave me comfort. He was back in Piter after only three months' wandering and was right into the melee. He had got a job as a metal worker in the new Lessner factory in Vyborg. It was a matter of a mere few days before he was attending a party cell. He said he was working with a handsome young man named Shliapnikov who was said to have been the lover of the beautiful but much older grand dame of Russian socialism, Alexandra Kollontai, herself in exile for the moment in the United States.

Almost whimsically he broke into party code we had used when we were young. He and Shliapnikov were seeking active Bolsheviks (*plenty of metal frames*) for the party (*the floor of the factory*). Shliapnikov and he had visited – this created a pang of literary envy in me – the apartment of the great Maxim Gorki himself, supreme Russian writer and generous soul, who lived in Kronversky Prospekt across from the

Neva in the fashionable Petrograd district. Gorki let the party use his apartment – for contacts, exchange of information, meetings. It was a wonderful act of open-handedness and foresight by a genius. The great writer, said Suvarov, feared what was happening to his country, both the country of the trenches, where human flesh and blood had become the one amalgam with snow and mud, and in the cities. That winter (sweltering summer in Brisbane), Gorki bemoaned the savage cold, the worst of the war so far, the respectable women begging or acting as prostitutes on the street, the tearing down of fences and even of houses for firewood, the shuffling armies of jaundiced child prostitutes. He told Suvarov about going to one of the little girls and giving her a bundle of money to enable her to escape, but a grubby man came up to him and said, Do you want to get her killed? The others will kill her for that! So gestures of generosity were no good any more.

What was obvious from the letter was that despite all the misery and challenge of the times, Suvarov was happy.

Paddy and I translated this letter, I putting it into immigrant English, he rewriting it in the English of the *Australian Worker*, where it was published.

Paddy Dykes had gone away for a time to write about a failed strike in Broken Hill, but now returned to Brisbane as fast as he could, as if it were the Paris of 1789. It's like you told me, Tom, he said once, and I did not remember having told him this at all before. It's the railways that're the key. Silver's silver, and wheat's wheat and beef's beef, but they only stay put if the railways go out on strike. For a national all-out blue, to put a government in its place, it's the railways.

Without a newspaper to edit and print I spent more time still at Amelia's as the summer passed. She was too ill to be out on the winter's night in 1916 when the referendum result was announced outside the offices of the *Telegraph* and the movement to bring in conscription was defeated. There was a great meeting at the town hall where girls from the unions handed out red feathers, to counter the white ones that women gave out to men who weren't in uniform.

Only Paddy Dykes, taking notes, looked melancholy. Do they

think the bastard won't try again? he asked. Australia's stuffed, rooted, done for.

I had to tell Amelia all about the joyful aspects of this scene as she sat so shrunken in a chair that it seemed the thing was devouring her. As the winter passed, she was still fighting. In the torrid summer days, when Hughes had announced a second conscription vote, a waxy gloss of sweat would appear on her face as she sat on her verandah, yet she survived to be invigorated by the events of late summer, and news from Russia.

42

Though I had never been to Piter I could see these things as if on a film in the flickering pictures. Workers walking from Vyborg – stark figures, angry and black against the frozen river, nearing the centre of St Petersburg, shouting, Bread! and Down with the tsar! It was 1905 again. Cossacks not wanting in their hearts to attack them, riding up to them as if to terrify them, then backing away. On the famous Nevsky Prospekt, a young girl with apple cheeks approaching the Cossacks with a bouquet of red roses. The Cossack officer taking them, and peace being thus established. Soldiers leaving their lines to join the people, and when the crowd was fired on, falling to bleed in the snow. Veterans marching in the streets, roaring, They are shooting our mothers and fathers! NCOs of the Preobrazhensky Regiment, the Lithuanian Regiment, the Finland Regiment all joining in the uprising and shooting officers who tried to stop them. Workers and soldiers capturing the arsenal, fitting themselves out with rifles and pistols, taking over the ordnance depot where the cannons were, as well as occupying the St Petersburg railway stations.

And more graphic detail still. My hero and Suvarov's acquaintance Gorki was charged with taking over police headquarters, but when he got there found that the crowd had already arrived and set fire to the place.

The Queensland papers published a report from *The Times* that spoke of the good order and good nature of the crowds. The people wore red armbands or red buttonholes as they marched together on the Tauride Palace, where the tsar's retrograde Duma met. There they cleared some bureaucrats out of their offices and occupied them with a committee (a soviet, that is) of the Councils of Workers' Deputies – to act as a parallel government.

They attacked the Peter and Paul Fortress in the middle of the river and let imprisoned soldiers go. They seized the less bizarre jails of the suburbs and – as at the Bastille – let the prisoners go free. The naval cadets at Kronstadt began to shoot their officers. Indeed, it sounded like the day might have arrived.

Members of my party, the Bolsheviks, were among those elected to the first sitting of the Soviet. In the Soviet, though, there were all sorts of other men and women and opinions – Mensheviks, Trudoviks, the quasi-liberal Cadets. Nonetheless, this Supreme Council of Soviets, of all the workers' and soldiers' own works and regimental soviets, put a point on the great javelin of Russian discontent.

The news is a tonic, Amelia told me from the depths of her chair.

But waiting on letters from Suvarov and others, we heard conflicting bulletins. There were announcements of the end of rebellion. The forces still loyal to the tsar were marching on St Petersburg. A gentleman named Kerensky tried to bridge the Duma and the Soviet with a further temporary committee aimed at restoring order.

What was undeniable was that a red flag now flew from the Tauride Palace. That was what excited Amelia and teased my stagnant soul. Then, through clenched teeth, the respectable papers printed the astonishing news – the tsar had abdicated! I found this harder to believe than any mystery of religion. Countless Russians had put all their lives and energies into opposing this man, and he had fallen in the end while caught between the outraged soldiers of the front and the workers of St Petersburg – or, as they were calling it now, Petrograd. The now eternal and glorious Piter! The press was free, the prison doors open, and I was no longer under sentence. So suddenly had this come that I would forget it, waking in my exiled state in the small hours and then the reality rousing in me: No more a prisoner, Artem. No more!

Even from the distance at which we sat, we could sense the chaos of Russia like the chaos of a Creation. The bulletins reprinted in the Brisbane papers from *The Times* and other sources depicted soldiers making rough camps in the corridors of the Tauride, attacking the Astoria Hotel and bayoneting so many officers that the revolving doors could not turn for blood. When Sukhonlinov, a former minister of war, appeared, the crowd outside had to be dissuaded from shooting him, but they tore his epaulettes off instead. Most astoundingly of all, the Soviet in the Tauride Palace voted that from now on the military should take its orders not from the government but from the Supreme Council of Soviets itself. The cry was born: All power to the soviets!

It used to be said that a backward country like Russia could not achieve a revolution until it went thoroughly through the industrial stage like Germany or England or America. But despite all the mutual bloodshed, Germany and England remained loyal monarchies. The revolution was with *us*. And so suddenly.

Everyone was congratulating me. Kelly was wringing my hand.

Marvellous, marvellous, he said. The best news since the war started.

Russia's the only country going ahead, said Paddy Dykes. The rest of us are all piss and vinegar. I just can't believe that bastard Hughes. It's hard for a man to live with. But it's all rosy with Russia.

It was hard to deal with the tumult of what I felt. Since Kerensky and his comrades promised to fight on against the Germans, it became apparent even on the streets of Brisbane that the majority of locals thought it a good thing, an end to backwardness. Meanwhile, in France, their children were hurled against the wire to enfilading fire.

A telegram came from Hope and Buchan. DELIGHTED PLEASED FOR YOU AT RUSSIAN EVENTS. ARE YOU GOING? H & B.

I could have sent a bitter telegram back: CANNOT GO IN VIEW AMELIA HEALTH.

Of course I was pleased I talked myself out of that meanness.

Yet everyone was asking, When are you going back?

One night, Paddy Dykes asked me, If you go back, would I be able to come too?

The idea astonished me.

I've got funds, he argued, and it's the only place on the move. I could write about events and send back reports. Admittedly, I don't know the language yet. Would I be in the way?

I assured him he wouldn't. The question of how I would raise the necessary funds myself remained open.

If you went back, Tom, he asked after reflection, what would be the best way?

Least expensive? I'd take work on a steamer to Japan, and then across to Vladivostok. It'll be cheaper to travel from there by train to Ukraine and then take another one to Piter.

Within a few seconds our discussions had become very concrete. I still had my duty to Amelia – to abandon her in her growing weakness seemed unthinkable. But what was thinkable was the matter of how deep and serious a revolution it was after all. After the early turbulence, peace was said to have been made between the Soviet and the Duma, and Prince Lvov – an old liberal with backsliding mystical ideas – had been appointed chief minister. And when many wanted the return of Nikolka, our tsar, would revolution stick?

It's not worth going yet, I told Amelia when she raised the question. She lowered her head and looked up at me in doubt. No, I assured her, I could get there if I took a job as a stoker. But then it would take months for me to work my way home. Anything might have happened by then.

But you mustn't think of staying for me, said the Amelia no one but a callous man could leave. I have my nurse, and my letters from Hope and visits from all the girls in the secretarial union.

No. I should wait and see if the tsar comes back. If he does, he'll return like thunder.

Yet I was getting tired of Australian battles, which suddenly seemed minor by comparison with every bulletin from Piter.

⋆

At the end of the Australian summer there are contrasting days. It might be over one hundred degrees Fahrenheit one morning and blowing a brisk gale from the sea the next, enough to make the stevedores don their tattered jumpers. It used to be the time of year that most afflicted Rybukov. Now, in that uneven weather, Amelia suffered a chill. Within a day or so of renewed heat, the chill had turned to pneumonia. I went to visit her and found her unaware of the world, lying in a bed veiled with mosquito netting. The rasping of her breath was cruel to hear. The nurse, who sat by reading, looked up and said, She feels very little. The doctor has her on laudanum. To make her comfortable, you know.

I did not like the sound of that.

But she will get over it, I asserted.

Perhaps, said the nurse lightly and got up, lifted the netting and, looking at a watch attached to her tunic, took Amelia's pulse. Then she said, I think you should prepare all Amelia's friends for the worst.

I left and sent a telegram to Hope. She arrived three days later by steamer and by that time Amelia was even more profoundly in a coma and even more pitiably searching for breath.

Sometimes Hope and I drank tea in Amelia's kitchen. I could look at Hope now without resentment or any mixed feelings. There was a shadow of age over her as she bent her lips to her tea. It made her more lovely but less of the woman I had adored. Passion had, at least, with a sane heart, given way to affection and even – since she lived with Buchan – pity.

And I had my own distraction – a rueful suspicion.

I keep thinking, I told Hope, that she's doing this for me. To free me, so I can go to Russia. I wish I could call her back and have a conversation. I wish I could say, You don't need to sink down into the shadows.

No, said Hope. Don't fret yourself. Even when she's unconscious she's still captain of her own ship. It's ridiculous to think she'd die for your convenience, Artem. You could have gone anyhow. It's not as if she's your mother.

No. But she is one of my dearest friends.

I went home after midnight – Hope remained to sit out the vigil. At dawn there was a hammering on the door of Adler's which, emerging from my room on the ground floor, I answered. A tear-streaked Hope was there.

Four o'clock this morning, Hope told me. It was sudden, otherwise I'd have come for you.

We fell into each other's arms, I felt a click of grief in my throat, and we shuddered with mutual tears.

The funeral was on a bright, temperate day, the golden mean of the Queensland seasons. The coffin was carried by Kelly and me and two unionists who had known Amelia, and it was accompanied, four each side, by eight of Amelia's young typists dressed in white and wearing sashes. After the interment there was a wake at the Trades Hall Hotel where toasts were made to her, one of them being a half-tipsy, half-weeping tribute from Hope. Those women you saw, Hope told us, the women either side of the coffin – they were there out of gratitude. She had given them dignity and better wages – sixty per cent over the past five years.

The statistics ran a little strangely in the saloon bar near the close of a hymn of praise for Amelia. But they arose honestly from Hope's lips; they were the statistics of her loss.

When it was time for me to leave, Hope rushed after me.

Artem, stop, please. Don't go yet.

She stood in front of me and fished from her reticule an envelope.

This was in Amelia's 'death file', as she called it – a list of the things she wanted done after she died. Her nurse pointed it out to me. Inside, there was money for her funeral, of course. So upright to the end! And this one is for you.

Dubiously I took it. A letter of farewell and encouragement, I thought. But it was thickly padded.

It's none of my business, said Hope. But aren't you going to open it?

I know she would never have asked this normally but she had drunk too much gin.

Very well, I told her.

Inside were fifty-pound notes amounting – I would discover – to three hundred pounds. A fortune.

And a note.

Artem, this is for Russia!

She means that you ought to go direct, Artem. You needn't work your passage.

My lids slammed shut with the sadness of that skeletal creature going to this trouble. I thought better of the nurse, who knew all that money was there and had left it untouched.

The next day I took an early shift and after that Paddy met me and we walked together to the shipping offices of the NYK line. The *Yawata Maru* was due to sail from Brisbane to Yokohama and Nagasaki in two weeks' time. We paid our deposit as steerage passengers. We left the office with the sense of having accomplished great things, and walked into the sunshine of the early Queensland winter.

Russian winters aren't like this, I told Paddy, but he shrugged.

There was time to talk to the committee of the *souz*, to leave some cash for the purchase or hire of a new printing press and the upkeep of Russia House – Amelia would have approved of such expenditure. I said goodbye to Lucia, to the Stefanovs, who had found an enduring home in Queensland, and to Kelly. But the palms on the streets, and the shuttling trams over which we had fought our first battle, seemed visible only through a remote lens now, through the wrong end of binoculars. Australia, the passions I had deployed there, the fights fought, the adventures endured, the bright air, seemed precious but all the more so since, even before the *Yawata Maru* sailed, and under the weight of Russian events, it was sinking beneath the horizon of my concerns.

And there I stood with Paddy Dykes, the most unexpected companion of all – a substitute, perhaps, for Amelia's immortal spirit.

Part Two

Paddy Dykes' Russian Journal

1

I'm an accidental Russian, led here from a far-off place and by a famous man. This is the tale of my travels with Artem Samsurov, well known enough to have a stamp dedicated to him in the 1930s when others were being shot and removed from the record. This is also the story of myself – in the year 1917. Many still think of it as the year of years! Many write about it. Here I'm adding my voice to the *many*. Anyone who was there in the summer and autumn of 1917 and could read and write but still doesn't take up his pen and put something to paper about those times – he'd be rightly judged a failure.

On the ship I spent every morning studying Russian grammar with Artem. I think by the time the first part of the journey ended in Japan I could speak the language like an eighteen-month-old and read it like a three-year-old. I'll give little time to Japan. For a little while, though, Artem and I found ourselves among these lovely fish- and rice-eating people who had thrashed the Russians in 1905. The skin of Japanese women, I saw, was silken after all. Artem thought me a dry old fish myself – good only for stoushes and reporting. Indeed I'm a desert man, coming from Broken Hill. Hunger and the sun hollowed me out. But if I'd been on my own instead of with Artem, I might have been delayed a bit longer among those people in Japan, and grabbed any job, as an inland sea fisherman, say, or even mining.

Enough of that. I've got my path in life, and I'm writing about my Russian education, which began, as I say, when I was still a child even though I was thirty-five years old. Innocent as one of those kids presented in a long embroidered gown at the baptismal font. Like most children, I was a witness instead of an actor on life's stage. But others were active, and when it came to activity, you couldn't beat Artem Samsurov.

To get to Siberia we caught the ferry across from Fukura on Honshu, and we watched the great mountains disappear behind us. I loved the look of snow as a novelty. But Artem told me I'd get enough of it next winter and come to curse it.

We came up Golden Horn Bay towards the great terraced streets of Vladivostok. They shone in a bright mid-summer sun that would stay up for most of the day. The ferry landing was right next door to the big white palace of a railway station, and I'd find as I travelled that the Russians put a lot of work into their railway stations. Standing in front of that one, I thought I'd finally arrived in Russia. The fact is I've been arriving every day since.

The last time I was here, Tom told me, we were running away up the coast to Nikolayevsk. Suvarov and me.

There were soldiers in their grey uniforms everywhere in the streets and around the railway. Many of them had Asian faces from the tribes of Siberia. They'd been stationed here, Artem told me, because the tsar had feared the Japanese might attack Russia while its main army was in the west. A lot of the soldiers I saw had tuberculosis and stopped in the street to spit into bloody rags. They looked ragged, restless and dangerous – men who were fed up and might have shot their officers. At intersections we also saw the rifle-bearing civilians, factory workers in bits of uniform but mainly their poor old clothes – their red armbands were what really identified them. These were a new militia and called themselves Red Guards. They took themselves more seriously than the soldiers, and didn't look any more war-weary than me.

I'd got a geography lesson from Artem – along the lines that to get to Petrograd from Vladivostok is three times Sydney to Perth. I'd always thought there was nothing bigger than Australia. But there in Vladivostok we were facing three Australias. I thought Europe was all small, I told him. It was what Australians consoled themselves with. Europe is small and every ten miles there is someone that hates someone else, and Australia is large and we love each other – or so the story goes.

At the railway station, Artem didn't go anywhere near the ticket counter. It was as if he knew the geography of the place. We went down some steps, crossed some rails and Artem knocked on the door of the railway workers' barracks. A young man with grease-stained overalls opened the door and listened to Artem. Then he opened the door further and we went into the dimness of a sort of laundry room. On this clear humid day the smell of wet Russian socks from the barracks was just like the smell of wet miners' socks at Broken Hill. Beyond was a common room and the young railway man pointed us towards it. There was a crowd of drivers, firemen, guards and fettlers sitting and talking and smoking rough tobacco in pipes. A cheap samovar of tea steamed away. Almost straight off Artem was recognised by an engine driver.

Now a lot of what was said to us in Russia early on I didn't understand. At first I asked Artem to explain and later – after maybe three months – began to understand it a bit. So I'll do my best to say – or sometimes take a stab at – what talk took place. This engine driver said something like, Comrade Samsurov, I was with you in the Perm railway yards. Have you been all this time in prison?

Artem was straight away treated with respect. I don't pretend they all knew him, but a number had heard enough about him, his arrest, work in Perm, his escape, to want to wring his hand. They invited us to sit. Artem sat down and began to talk with them, now and then turning to tell me what they were saying to him, and what he was saying to them. I'm letting them know Australia is a wonderful place, he informed me as if he'd become a Brisbane patriot. But the workers have no proper class consciousness – except for you.

Indeed all eyes were on me as if I was a strange and special creature. I would get used to this.

From the railway barracks – where we were fed soup and rye bread – we were taken that evening out into the streets past grand stone buildings and decrepit wooden houses to the municipal offices, a building like so many Russian buildings that tried to look French. Here the Vladivostok Soviet of Workers and Soldiers met. There was a stove giving off heat in the middle of the hall – even in June – and I was too close to it not to sweat buckets. Some hundreds of people gradually gathered. But with the warmth I drowsed off among the speechifying of the Russian workers, and I missed half of Artem's speech, in which I believe he said that the thousands of people the tsar had driven out were returning from over the seas to work in the new republic.

At the end of Artem's speech, an executive member of the soviet presented Artem with a signed pass that would allow us to travel on the Eastern Railway free of charge. So the next day we got on a real bone-rattler train and travelled in fair comfort on black padded seats. At every railway works and junction they had got word Artem was coming and we were treated to the hospitality of the rail crews. We got to the big town of Khabarovsk, and the same happened there. Artem told me we were only a walk away from the Manchurian border. But why would a person go there now? A lot had though, in the tsar's day.

When I see these towns again, Artem told me, I get the idea I'm still on the run.

Even in Khabarovsk our journey was just starting. I began to get depressed, thinking we'd be on trains or waiting for them for a year, but I didn't say anything to put a dent in Artem's spirits. Our next train was ready to steam due west at last and this time we were put in a red velvet first-class compartment – welcome because we could sleep. The one businessman who also sat in the compartment read his newspaper and tried to ignore us. And so we went on via fir forests and the frozen swamps they call the taiga and across great open plains and with a view of mountains streaked with snow. We stopped at a medium-sized town, and a peasant even more husky than Artem entered the compartment. He was large and strong but greeted us in a quiet voice. The Russian good morning, or whatever he said, sounded endless to me – lots of vowels in there. He smelled of sweat and though he had a good smock, his shoes were made of bast fibre, a sort of straw stuck together with pressure. He quickly latched on to the *burzhooi* – the middle-class man – hiding behind his paper and deliberately walked across to him, hauled the paper down, and said in a basso voice what was probably, Good morning, comrade. Then he sat down. As the train left he pulled out a knife and began to cut the velvet backing out of a vacant seat. He called something friendly to Artem as he did it. Artem began to laugh.

He wants it to make shoes, Artem told me. He says red velvet'll look good in the mud.

Artem thought a while, with the smile dying on his lips. Then he said, There's a time for ripping out velvet and a time to stop. This is a time to rip.

The peasant nodded to us as if he understood Artem, folded the velvet on his lap and began to sleep noisily. The gentleman traveller sighed to whatever gods were still on his side.

We'd see a lot of scenes like that as we crossed Siberia and southern Russia on our journey to Chelyabinsk. Locomotives were changed over but we stayed with our plush compartment because, said Artem, we were going further than anyone and would need the rest it provided.

Sometimes soldiers with a bugger-you attitude came into our compartment and sat down and frequently Artem got into conversation with them and they rumbled away about hopeless campaigns and idiot generals and how in the end they had walked home to see to the family farm or visit girlfriends or both. Why they were travelling west again now I didn't quite understand. Maybe they were going to make trouble in Moscow or Petrograd. As in Vladivostok, some of these men were stocky members of the Asiatic tribes – the children of Kublai Khan, said Artem.

We made occasional excursions to the harsh wooden third-class carriages where men in caps and smocks and women in shawls were jolted around by every fault of the track. Grain was scarce, they told him. Requisitioners from the army and the government came round to grab the harvest. The cities must be very hungry, one woman said. Some told us how the landlords' barns had been burned – with the horses blindfolded and led out by young men and returned peasant soldiers. All the women we met in these carriages were like those we passed in towns along the way – those who stopped in their tracks, looking up and frowning at the passing trains from under the shadow of their shawls. And the men in the streets too in their black or red or grey smocks and hats and shoes made out of straw.

We would get out at watering places to wash ourselves at the pump. Bare-chested men crowded around, waiting to throw water over their stale bodies.

It took only twelve days even with some waiting in sidings to get to Chelyabinsk, two-thirds of the way, where our train with the velvet seats terminated. Now everyone Artem met told him what a quick trip we'd had. They said sometimes soldiers formed gangs, lived in camps in the forests and raided and delayed trains. But it hadn't happened to us.

Like Omsk – a town we'd already been through – Chelyabinsk was a real city. Rolling in towards the main station I could see great homes of white and reddish stone and then at the station itself soldiers begging, a lot of them on crutches or missing a limb. The Red Guards paraded around in their bits of uniform, and as we left the train I saw men who looked like bandits, in round hats and tight-waisted coats decorated with storage holes for bullets and a dagger at the waist. These coats were called *chokhas*, and were favoured by men from Georgia. In the station lobby you could buy postcards of Kerensky and other leaders inspecting troops in grand opera uniforms.

Artem reacted to the postcards with rare bile. Look at the pompous bugger, he said. His father was an honest headmaster and taught Vladimir Ilich. Kerensky must get all this rubbish of his – wanting to fight on in the war and so on – from his mother.

There was to be a day's delay before we could catch the train north-west. We went to an unpainted cranky-looking teahouse. As we walked, Artem relished the smell of coal and metal in the air. He was used to this sort of city.

That night we were guests of a Bolshevik journalist and his young wife – their address had been given to us by a Bolshevik engine driver in Omsk. The journalist had been shot through a lung serving under General Brusilov in 1915 and a sort of shade of future widowhood hung over the young wife and gave her face a bruised look.

And again I was like the unwitting child in this group. The couple sat at this dinner table with Artem and me over a plain meal of cabbage soup with a bit of onion and horsemeat and talked by the hour. I had had my first encounter with horsemeat when I ate it one night from a café near a railway station in one of the towns along our way. It tasted strange enough but I was eating it in such good company it didn't matter.

Artem was – as always – a great talker – though he wasn't alone. The whole country seemed to me to be yapping and arguing. And because I didn't really know what they were saying, everything I heard sounded just as important as the last thing.

The journalist with the bad lung made his wife cry by saying he wouldn't end up seeing what became of it all – of this wild and woolly time. But I got a sense that to them everything – absolutely everything – seemed to be just around the corner. These were people with a light inside them.

Before we went to sleep in the room that we shared Artem and I talked. Artem's conversation was all about the mess the railway system was in. He had an old railway man's eye for that sort of thing. Should the trains serve the army? Or should they take food to Petrograd and Moscow? And if they did that, how did you stop speculators getting hold of it?

The next morning the young journalist – with a lot of ceremony – presented a telegram to Artem. Apparently it was from the party leadership. Even though we had been headed for Moscow and Petrograd, this telegram instructed him to go to Kharkov and the coalmines of the Don. That's where he was to get going – in country he knew.

That day I wrote a report of what I'd seen for the *Australian Worker* and left it with the journalist's wife for posting. Soon we were rolling along on wooden seats among a big crowd of peasants and mine workers across the Don basin. There were lots of coal towns and they looked grim. Smoke blocked the sky and the slag heaps were higher than mountains and spread their black grit over everything. But it was possible now to believe that the coal was the people's coal. No one dared to say anything different these days.

Artem assured me we were near the Black Sea and all its beauty spots, but it was hard to believe. The grass was green on the hillsides though. On granite knolls on top of green mountains, you'd see a monastery now and then. When big Artem smiled across at me it was because it was all familiar to him. Even the slag heaps had their poetry to him. He was really coming home – he would even see his sister Trofimova who lived in a town on the railway line to Kharkov.

2

We got off the train at a mining town called Kresnopalovka and climbed down to its flat station. There were flowerbeds some railway guard was tending in spite of the times – when nobody had any time for flowers except peasant wives and a few determined fellows. And a big-boned woman with a pleasant face was waiting there – a telegram from her brother had told her when we were due. What was I to call her? I asked Artem. He told me to call his sister Evgenia Alexandrovna until I got to know her. Then I could call her Zhenya or else Trofimova. There would come some point, he told me, when she would look at me with the light of affectionate friendship in her eye and then it would be time to call her Zhenya, her short name.

Trofimova was a few years older than Artem, but she had the same broad face and strong features. They kissed each other three times. Then I was introduced, and Artem turned to me. When Zhenya first married Trofimov, he said, I missed her so badly I used to catch empty coal trucks all the way down to Kresnopalovka to visit her.

What struck me from the start was her great good humour. She and her brother laughed all the way. And you could see Artem's style of liveliness in her face.

Trofimova had brought a dray – a borrowed one – to the station and we threw our luggage – my kitbag and his suitcase – in the back and she drove us through dreary streets, past tiny little workers' terraces as cramped as the corrugated-iron terraces of Broken Hill but here made of blackened stone and brick. On the edge of town the houses were wooden and had gardens. Artem's sister and her husband lived in one of these.

Artem yelled as we drew up, Are you in there, Trofimov? His sister – with her hands still on the reins – gave him a friendly nudge. She got down, took the horse out of the traces, and with the reins in the grip of her large hands led it to its shed at the back of the house.

Even though it was early summer the night was beginning to get cold. Inside the house there was a smell of linctus and a ceramic stove in the middle of the room was putting out heat. A thin man – barely older than me but hollowed out in the face – struggled up from the stove's surrounding bench and coughed and greeted Artem. They hugged and kissed. I recognised that cough, I'd heard it in other places. Silicosis. Trofimova signalled us all to sit down quickly at the table. The brother and sister talked like mad. Trofimov would prepare his lips as though he were about to say something and they would pause. But he never managed it. There was never any doubt about Artem's sister's power to speak. She talked like the clappers – her eyes and her auburn hair appeared just about ready to burst into flames. I thought, What a family!

Trofimova was telling stories – about her brother, how clever he was. He read genuine books from the time he was eleven; he sang like an angel and he played the clarinet in the institute band.

Suddenly Trofimov got talking. The brother and sister turned to him straight away. All the fun went out of them but not all the interest. I could tell he was talking politics.

He had served for a time in the army in 1915 but had been pulled out of the ranks when his disease became apparent. That he was called up at all showed you how desperate they were, Artem said later. But sleeping in wet or icy bivouacs had hastened his illness along.

As Trofimov spoke he gestured and scowled like an actor. I still find it amazing how much of a person's politics you can pick up when listening to a language you don't understand just by observing gestures and faces. What is emphasised. The sudden anger. It makes me think that behind the different languages ideas hang in the air as a kind of common language without words – and that we all understand it. By the time I left the Trofimovs' I had a pretty good idea of what was going on – Artem had explained the Ukrainian Rada, the parliament in Kiev making a bid for Ukrainian independence from Greater Russia. The Rada was full of soft-headed make-believe socialists, he said. And all this was distressing to Trofimov, who though living in the Ukraine was a Great Russian through and through.

Next morning we were due to catch the train to Kharkov itself, the big smoke. Artem's sister came to the station to wave us off. She showed no embarrassment or regret at all about what had occurred during the night.

She had given Artem his old room and sent me to sleep in a hut in the garden. At three o'clock or so I was awoken by Evgenia Alexandrovna in a big white nightgown levering herself into my bed, uttering a few soft sentences to me as if we'd been married for a long time and she was attending to some needs I didn't even know I had. Then she'd patted my face and was gone. It was a revelation to me but I couldn't help thinking it must have been a dream – though not one I could tell Artem about.

But at the railway station saying goodbye to Trofimova. Her brisk tender way bowled me over – the lack of words let alone of any blame. I wish I could say I felt guilty for Trofimov. But I didn't. I had always avoided the idea of marriage because in my lifetime and experience it always led to the hollowing out and ruin of the girls who went in for it. I had a fear of making a girl old before her time – that's what happened to miners' wives. But I'd never met anyone like Trofimova before – someone who couldn't be undermined or embarrassed by whatever she'd said and done or by whatever I'd done.

I believed then I'd found a woman. Or the other way round.

3

The railway station at Kharkov was another cathedral of steam, slung between two stone towers. We could see it ahead of us as we were coming over the Don railway bridge. When we pulled in we got down with our belongings in a suitcase and an army kitbag and were bowled over – I was anyway – to see the Railway Workers' Union brass band playing in Artem's honour at the ticket gate. Our suits were greasy and we carried our belongings in knocked-about luggage, but we – or at least Artem – were like arriving princes. There were a number of people standing there with the band – members of the town soviet, some of them in the grey uniforms in which they had fought the war, some educated workers, young women of good families in summer dresses and light coats of blue and yellow, and men with trimmed beards, *burzhooi*, men who looked as if they owned an engineering plant or were doctors or lawyers – and they all applauded Artem.

After he'd shaken each of their hands, I was presented to them. They clapped and grinned as if I deserved it for being an Australian – something exotic, a living sample of the working class from the other end of the world! Roll up, roll up and don't trip over the tent peg! In my poor suit I was the proof of international fraternity.

One man in the welcoming party – boasting a tailor-made suit and a pomaded moustache – led us past the band to a large car into which we and a number of the welcoming committee all squeezed, including a grizzled soldier and two of the young women. This impressive-looking man introduced himself as Izaak Abramovich Federev. He was a lawyer, he said. A uniformed chauffeur held the door for us, and a pale, very good-looking blonde girl in a white dress and sky-blue jacket sat on one side of Tom, and the *burzhooi* in his frock coat sat on the other. The handsome girl's sister sat across from them and so did I, on a sort of dickie seat with my back to the driver. We drove through the town, down long avenues of apartment buildings that like the posher buildings in towns further east looked to me exactly like pictures I'd seen of Paris. Occasionally the big sweaty soldier added a few words to the conversation and his voice was as deep as a cave. Yes, there was stale sweat – some of it my own – in that big automobile. But it was like an argument in itself. The well-bred girls did not wrinkle their noses.

In Australia I'd never got anywhere near a car like this one. It was far bigger than Hope Mockridge's. I was excited both by its engineering and by the closeness of us all. All brothers and sisters – everyone from the man who owned the car to the soldier to the two girls with their knees together so as not to take up the room of the arriving heroes. The sun shone on the finest city I had ever seen. But there were also street meetings being held on corners – soldiers and deputies or others standing under red banners and haranguing the crowds. It was a season in which nearly everyone was claiming to be the *true* Reds. And on a closer look some of the buildings were gutted and rags of blackened curtain blew in the warm breeze from the east. Soldiers kept guard outside a handsome villa whose door stood wide open. The furniture inside had probably been taken away by people and the liquor from the cellar gone to satisfy the thirst of soldiers. We rolled past a great green sunny space and the man in the frock coat – Federev – leaned over and said in accented English: The city soviet have named this Zbody Square – Freedom Square. It is the biggest square in Greater Russia. Bigger than the Kremlin itself.

We arrived at a grand building and Federev invited us to his apartment on the fourth floor.

We took a lift to his flat – a glorious place with a main room big as a ballroom. An old woman served tea and small cakes and after that the others left in small groups. When they were all gone, Federev advised us to rest and refresh ourselves in the bedrooms he assigned us and promised to take us for a walk in Zbody Square later in the afternoon. Before going into our separate rooms Artem and I had a little chat in the corridor.

His English is good, I told Artem.

A lot of the *burzhooi* speak English. Most of them speak French too. You see they had tutors when they were kids, and then they travelled a lot when they were young. French is the one they really like but they can take their English for a spin as well.

In my room I lay on my soft bed and felt too lucky to sleep and too tired to write anything for the *Australian Worker*. For the moment I felt I was a breathing part of a great attempt to reach out for the light. Houses might get burned down and velvet ripped. There might be fury. That had to be expected. In the meantime I felt this stretching of the skin.

I was turning into a different human being.

4

That night the apartment was more crowded than it had been earlier in the day. The young women were back, the railway men, workers in suits no better than mine – worse in terms of stitching because in the new republic thread was scarce too. Two well-dressed aesthetes were there as well, their complexions nearly as soft as those of the girls. No passwords seemed to be exchanged but I noticed that a worker had been put on watch by the front door. Federev spoke in Russian then English and introduced Artem as a leading figure of the committee who had organised the strikers in 1905 and who had been punished and driven to the limits of the earth by the tsar's malice. Then the lawyer pointed to me as a brother from the end of the world.

Artem rose. He was very fluent and spoke with a half-smile on his face as the room filled with the smell of the soldiers' cheap tobacco. It stung the eyes but neither Federev nor the two young women we'd travelled with that morning complained about it. I noticed one of the two soldiers in the room had been reduced to using newsprint for cigarette papers.

I heard Artem utter the names Fisher and Cook. Hughes and T. J. Ryan were referred to occasionally, and I could guess what he was saying – that the Labor Party in Australia had failed in its great chance, that it'd been tamed and become party to the war just the way the German social democrats had. Just as surely, the Cadet liberals and Mensheviks in the Russian Duma were insisting on carrying on the war against the Germans and Austrians, even though there was a ceasefire for the moment.

When he had finished speaking he answered questions, and when it was over he came straight to me with his usual half-smile on his broad face and said, Paddy, I have a favour to ask. Will you find out from our host who is the girl in the blue coat?

Then he whispered, How she smouldered, Paddy! She's out for vengeance – Nikolka had better watch out.

People drank tea and shook hands earnestly with Artem and sometimes with me and then left by ones and twos. The two artistic-looking young men shook our hands vigorously before speaking quietly to Federev then departing. The blonde girl in the blue coat smiled and called him Tovarich Artem – a name the Russians pronounced *Artyom*. Artem spoke to her briefly – his eyes were ablaze and his face full of good humour. Then she and her sister were gone too and we sat down in the state room with Federev, who drank some brandy and inspected his moulded ceiling for a bit. After a while he leaned forward to continue discussions. He was proud of his English and determined to speak it.

An excellent group, he said. Stout souls. You noticed the young men? One is a lecturer in philosophy at the university, the other a great connoisseur of the arts, a friend of Stravinsky and Cocteau. And then the men from the Starilov works and the veteran soldiers. Not to forget the women. What an alliance!

Who are the sisters? I asked, remembering Artem's request. The girl in blue? The one in yellow?

The blue coat is Tasha, Federev said. Tasha is her party name. She spent time with Lenin's family in Geneva – this was after she had been in exile in Voronezh. She was in prison too.

Jesus! said Artem. He stroked his brow.

Now their name is Abrasova, said our host. The one you ask about is Orika Varvara Abrasova – Tasha. The sister is Olya. He grinned knowingly at me. Men always ask about Tasha first. Poor Olya is an afterthought yet she is a sturdy little creature. Their father is a surgeon. They're Jewish – as am I.

Jewish? asked Artem. With that hair?

Perhaps some Cossack violated her great-grandmother, our host said matter-of-factly. These things happen. Anyhow, she is not as shy as she looks. You're lucky she did not jump up and take the speaker's rostrum from you, Comrade Artem.

The conversation then drifted away from the good-looking Abrasova sisters. Artem told Federev about the peasant who cut the velvet from the train seats. Federev laughed, shaking his head – as if cutting the velvet was a sign of progress. Which maybe it was.

Everything has to be brought down and rebuilt! he said. I know. I know. Even this apartment. Even if I am given a room and a half to live in, brotherhood is more important than splendid isolation.

You take a very enlightened view, said Artem. My literary idol, Gorki, is more shocked by the mess he sees in Petersburg.

It is peculiar, said our host, that a great writer such as he cannot see that all this is necessary. What did we have before, when the streets were clean enough to satisfy Gorki? We had people crushed under the wheels of authority. My father for one!

He rose and reached for a decanter of French brandy on a sideboard – he offered us some and when we declined asked if we minded him having some. Sitting again, he continued, You see, my father was a captain in the engineers. An educated farmer's son. The cavalry was closed to him on both counts: that he was self-educated and a Jew. But he was appointed to an engineering unit. Twelve years ago there was a great Japanese slaughter of Russians at Mukden in Manchuria. Have you seen that painting of the Russian officer standing among his dead, screaming, with his hair turned white?

We hadn't seen the painting.

Well, there is such a painting. Now my father was a wit and he had a sharp tongue – certainly he did. He was famous for parodies of his colonel. My late mother and I got the bitter details of what happened from a junior officer who survived. Before the battle, the Japanese had advanced as far as a place named Fuhsien when my father and his men were ordered by his colonel to stay by the river, building a pontoon bridge under the barrels of the Japanese artillery. My father made the point that his company of engineers would be overrun – the Japanese would use the pontoon bridge itself to get to them. That shouldn't be a problem, said his colonel. After all, you can make the Japanese fall over laughing. You make the other officers laugh soon enough at me.

Our host shook his head.

My father wrote a letter in the half-hour left before he returned to the site with his sappers. He wrote to my mother, You said, my darling, many times, that you would kill me. Our colonel is saving you the trouble.

Federev let the awful story hang in the air.

You see, according to some it is barbarous to shoot a thief or let the garbage build up in your courtyard. But what about the barbarism that out of pure vanity throws an entire company of engineers away? And for nothing. The colonel himself was killed two days later in the Japanese onslaught. Let us hope there is a hell for his sake!

Our host was trembling and reached for his brandy again.

Anyhow . . . if you keep people in a barbarous condition, he said, you can't expect them not to break a few windows when you let them loose. Their barbarism is not their fault. It's the fault of their former masters. Who would have them back under subjection in a second, given the chance.

Tom murmured, All power to the soviets, would you say?

Precisely, said our host. Not to the Duma, not to the Rada or any other body. But to the soviets. A regimental soviet would not have killed my father.

5

I slept very soundly that night. I was excited by the surroundings and the pulse running under things. And it would continue to do that. I'd been promised by Artem that he would speak at a public meeting at the technical university the next night.

In the meantime our host was off very early the next day and left us to wander about the city. We crossed the avenue and walked maybe three hundred yards and were in the great square. As yesterday every street corner running off it was full of ragged men listening to speakers of all kinds. Between the groups I saw women in what had once been good dresses and with boas around their necks hoping a man would pay them for the obvious. There were a lot of war widows, said Artem, and people who had lost their jobs through factories being burned down.

We pushed on past a scrum of newspaper sellers and maimed soldiers and pencil vendors until we were in the parkland beyond. Here we started down a pathway by a river that was – I think – some tributary of the Don. I remember it was running well – it looked as if the snow of the last winter was still in it. I enjoyed walking in a bright day in a city where no one knew me.

This park though wasn't quite like the Botanic Gardens in Brisbane. I could see among the trees humpies where soldiers lived and

Artem and I could smell the smoke of their cooking fires. These weren't soldiers under command; these were men who were striking out for themselves – refusing to follow the orders of officers unless their regimental soviet voted to do it. Artem told me they were survivors of General Brusilov's Polish offensive that had killed millions. But though they were mutineers, they seemed very well-mannered and unlikely to trouble anyone who passed by.

The conversation between Artem and myself was slow and easy as we strolled. We were discussing our host's claim the night before that he was prepared to lose his apartment – which would mean putting up with garbage in the courtyard and queuing to use his own lavatory. Tom believed Federev was sincere but that he was in for a few shocks.

Because he's our friend, said Artem, we're all very respectful when we go into his apartment. The soldiers are respectful. A respect for property is implanted in us. But he might get a surprise when people really believe that his bedroom is theirs. There's something in Gorki and our lawyer friend and me that we want all peasants to be novelists. But they aren't. Oppression's made them rabid. There aren't so many noble souls. My sister is one.

I didn't know if he knew anything about Trofimova's adventure with me. Something of the leftover Catholic in me wanted to confess to him, but I couldn't imagine the words. I didn't have the gift for describing that sort of thing – or even the other thing: that his big sister came to my mind when I was half asleep. And when I was full awake too.

From among the remnants of park benches that hadn't been totally used up for firewood there appeared a determined bunch of threadbare soldiers. Three of them were pushing along a wiry young man they had hold of and two others behind had their rifles aimed at his back. Their captive was bleeding from his nose and mouth. Tom called something to the soldiers, his whole approach a mixture of humour and authority. What has gone wrong here? he seemed to ask. One of the soldiers explained to Artem that the fellow they held prisoner was a thief.

A debate began between Artem and the others. The soldiers were young and a little edgy at being challenged. They told Artem that bullets had to be kept for the ultimate enemies of the people, not just for common thieves. So they weren't going to waste a bullet on this man – who had stolen one of their coats. They were going to throw him in the river and let it look after him.

Some kids turned up and started dancing and yelling and skipping because it was just a theatre piece to them. But the soldiers weren't acting. One of those with a rifle advanced on Artem and began yelling. Artem got angry and told him to go to hell. Touch me, he told them, and you'll answer to the city soviet. I am Artem Samsurov who led the uprising in Kharkov in 1905, when you were still shitting your baby pants.

It's a study to see how even men with rifles will back away from someone so certain of his authority. Even though these fellows had lost faith in their officers they still seemed to believe Artem. Still, they were determined to have their way, and the man was taken onto a little boat pier and hurled off it. He went under then rose to the surface and thrashed around a bit, clearly a man who couldn't swim a stroke.

As he was swept away the kids went running along the bank, chanting and cat-calling.

Please! he screamed. *Bulbtyo Dobry*! Please. I'd been numb till now but I all at once felt his terror. I couldn't swim, but I had a mad impulse to dive in after him. Mercifully, one of the two soldiers who held a rifle stepped onto the pier and took aim and – regardless of the desire to save bullets – shot him between the shoulder blades. The man in the water gave a shriek and then surrendered to the current and sailed away.

In a daze, we walked back to the square and Tom bought a paper. He stood scanning it while I waited, as if he was looking for something to take the weight of what we'd seen away. He whistled.

It's all happening in Piter, Paddy.

Piter was Petrograd.

The cat's among the pigeons.

He frowned. While we were settling into Kharkov something massive had been happening in the capital. A vast crowd of people – sailors, workers from a huge Vyborg factory (the Putilov works where Suvarov had once been employed) – had marched on the Tauride Palace and begged the Supreme Council of Soviets – who shared the building with the parliament, the Duma – to give them leave to do away with the Duma, the government and the war itself. This was the moment, they cried.

We were attending worthy meetings in Kharkov. But the main action was in Petrograd. Would Artem rather be there? That's what I wondered.

6

If Artem was disappointed not to be part of the events in Piter, he didn't show it. He seemed excited as we travelled with Federev in his large car. This time it was protected by a number of Red Guards either sitting inside with us or riding on the running boards. In a narrow street somewhere between the centre of town and its older wooden outer reaches, we picked up the two sisters from what looked like a half-finished block of flats into which the windows had not been fitted. The sisters lived in the basement.

Artem greeted them with a smile large enough for the two of them to share. They were all obviously rattling on about the events in the capital – what it all meant – and whether this was *it*, the promised day.

Again, said Federev, there's every sort of beast in the menagerie tonight. There are anarchists and Ukrainian Nationalists and Great Ukrainian Nationalist Mensheviks. There are Great Russian Mensheviks. And then us. The absolute lot!

The hall was grander than anything I had ever seen. Big Greek columns and a great arch held up a group of plump angels. This was going to be a bigger version of all the meetings I'd been to and seen on railway stations and in halls while we chugged our way across from Vladivostok. The welter of ideas contained in here seemed to make its own heatwave. But the Abrasova sisters didn't seem timid about it at all as we fought our way in.

Some soldiers had wrestled others off to keep seats for us near the front. I noticed Tasha's eyes as she sat down. She was a creature on a leash, sitting forward with her white fists on the knees of her dress. She was coiled. Her sister Olya meanwhile was looking around as if she were trying to count how many people lay between her and the side doors. Artem in turn sat beside Tasha and made some remarks that caused a laugh to stutter up over her bottom lip. She leaned across Artem and told me in thick English, I speak tonight.

So we're off to the races, Paddy, Artem told me, beaming.

A Ukrainian Menshevik spoke first, a man in dark suit, collar and tie – not the kind that come from the best tailors. Every sentence was yelled out in a lusty way. But he had to roar and rage like that to be heard. The Ukrainians had their own language, as it turned out, but Russians used to say it had come late in history and was based on Russian anyway. It was like the difference between Portuguese and Spanish, Artem would tell me. But I got the idea that anyone who spoke in Russian believed in a great All Russia, and those who spoke in Ukrainian wanted a separate republic of the Ukraine. So this first speaker had started to talk sentimentally about the glories of ancient Kiev, and how they wouldn't come back – that brotherhood of knights and warriors – without Ukraine being separate from Russia.

A fantasist, Artem told me, shaking his head.

Some people in our group – soldiers and factory workers and others – began roaring questions at him, along the lines of who cleaned out the nobles' shit in golden Kiev? His face grew red with the effort of pushing his dream on people and the noise was bigger than a cattle auction.

Next there was a member of the Rada, the Ukrainian parliament, a socialist who was listened to a bit more respectfully even by our crowd.

After that we had a Cadet in a frock coat and collar not much different from Federev's. It turned out he wanted the Ukraine to ally itself with Germany. In some other forum he might have got a better reception – here he got a lot of boos. He kept on asking whether the crowd wanted continuing tyranny from St Petersburg. All our crowd were on their feet asking where the tyranny was.

Suddenly it was Tasha's turn. By now her sister Olya had anxious bulging eyes and her forehead was waxed with sweat. Federev escorted Tasha to the stage and seemed determined to stay to protect her from the insults the other speakers had copped, but she shooed him back to his seat.

When she started speaking she was like a woman transformed. Not that I could understand a single word she said. Well, that's not true – I understood a few. But I could tell that she was a spellbinder and seemed to grow in height and in substance as she spoke. Her voice was contralto but it didn't have an ounce of yield in it. And the audience was stunned for a time by this combination of the angelic and the political.

She's like a muse, Artem whispered to me.

Among other things, she argued that if the Rada continued its plan for an independent republic there would be civil war. Some people yelled out that if Bolsheviks were so brave, why didn't Vladimir Ilich surrender himself to the provisional government who'd now issued a warrant for his arrest?

Mensheviks were holding up newspapers. Reports from Piter said that Kerensky had issued an order for Vladimir Ilich's arrest and that he'd fled the city and was in hiding.

Federev seemed less confused than Artem and was immediately on his feet, raging away. No doubt Kerensky would have Vladimir Ilich killed on the way to prison! So why wouldn't he hide? He knows you fear him enough to kill him!

On the platform Tasha leaned forward from her hips and both her fists were clenched. She sang out her own answer above the racket of the hall. But the debate was going to take a further slide still, because all at once a cry was raised. A man's voice directed at Tasha. It yelled, *Zhidy Bolsheviki!* Bolsheviks in the audience, various soldiers, workers,

Olya and Federev stood up at this and turned around to the crowd behind and screamed at the accuser. The cry *Bolshevik Jew!* was one I'd get used to. The interjector kept on shouting it and others took up the chant.

Total pandemonium!

The offender – who like the first speaker wore a suit halfway between that of a gent and a worker – made a further speech. He asked his fellow citizens of the Ukraine if they wanted to starve the way the Russians were doing in Petrograd. Would they want their children to starve because of Jew speculators and Jew Bolsheviks?

I could tell now Tasha was getting to be less attractive to the crowd. I've never seen people hate a Jew like they did then. The family of Jewish drapers in Broken Hill, the Lendls, had snide things said about them. All the less so because young Lendl was a champion fast bowler – at least by Broken Hill standards. But all this was on a different scale. Tasha didn't take a step back. In fact she took a step forward and in her anger looked more in charge. She moved without any concern from here to there as fists reached up and pounded the floor of the rostrum. It sounded like she might be eaten alive. They'd discovered a spy among them – someone who had deceived them by dressing herself up in a fashionable gown and Ukrainian or Russian hair. To a lot of them, it appeared, she was a witch in disguise and they couldn't wait to have at her.

We'll have to get her out, Artem told me as people rushed into the aisles to charge the stage. There was already a crowd blocking the way to the stairs and we had to fight our way through it. I'm not using that word lightly: it *was* fighting. Artem was willing to push people to the ground – even women – to get onto the stage. Over his shoulder he was yelling, Come on, Paddy! as if he really needed me. I followed, kicking and pushing. The more I was blocked by this mass of human stupidity – who wanted to punish Tasha instead of Kerensky – the more my old state of barbarism started to come over me: I saw everyone in an extra-sharp way. I saw beforehand how I could break their jaws and grind their bones. It was a strange feeling – unfamiliar to me normally. But I more than enjoyed it. I was let loose and everything I did felt as if it was permitted – by who I don't know. A gaping mouth full of hate presented itself and I smashed my forearm into it and wanted to hear the cartilage in the nose snap – though that would have been impossible over the noise of the crowd.

When we made it onto the stage there were maybe thirty others who were already there with unkind intent. I could see our host Federev on the far side of Tasha with a hold on her arm and trying to get her away. Tasha was still yelling some point she wanted to make. I kicked a man who was trying to drag her by her right arm towards the mob who wanted to devour her. I'll beat the bloody lot of you, I was yelling. Bastards! Fuckers! I drove a flank of men and women away from Tasha to the back of the stage. It wasn't one-sided. Someone slammed me in the ribs. But some fierce-looking moustached soldiers and some of Federev's Red Guards – who often stood on the running boards of his car – came up around me and we held one side of the platform while Tasha and Federev and Artem made a retreat towards the wings. With the soldiers to help me I fought a rearguard down the steps leading to a stage door. I saw Tasha's shy sister Olya in front of me. Somehow she'd fought her way out too without anyone caring for her in the same way they looked after her orator of a sister.

Outside we ran for our host's car and the Red Guards standing on the running boards had rifles in their hands. That made the crowd pause and think. We all tumbled in – our host and Tasha, Olya and Artem, his big hand reaching for me.

Make way for the little tiger! Artem cried in English, hauling me aboard.

Inside the car, everyone was laughing, even though people outside were pounding the windows and our host's Ukrainian driver was yelling curses at the hundreds who stood in his way. We were suddenly all laughing like crazy and when some of the mob threw stones and horse manure at the back window of the car it made us laugh even more.

That's nationalism for you! our host told me – shaking his head. That's idiots of all classes going for old nationalist fairy tales about

Kiev the Golden and *The Protocols of the Elders of Zion* – the dreadful Rasputin's favourite book by the way. And the tsar's as well.

But they tried to arrest Vladimir Ilich? asked Artem as all the jollity died down.

I know, said Federev. Don't worry. He'll be hidden. They don't have the whip-handle they did once.

7

I thought that we would now be heading down the long avenues to our lawyer's house but instead we turned off into a side street – Botanical Street – and pulled up outside the shell of the two-storey building where the sisters lived. As we all got out an old lady in a scarf came from a room under the stairs that led up to nowhere as yet and stood scolding the lot of us. Tasha and Olya responded cheerfully and let us into their place. This looked to be pretty pleasant – and expensive even. However there was no electricity and the quieter sister Olya set out to get the place illumined – like some Queensland dairy farm – by a kerosene lamp. Tasha quickly got the samovar working on the tiled stove. But before any tea was served they settled down to hold – yes, a meeting. These were serious people.

The people in the Abrasova sisters' rooms – and me less than most – didn't know anything about the turmoil going on in Vladimir Ilich's closest circle. He had come back to Russia in April and straight away he had old friends from exile, like the intellectual engine-driver's son Lev Kamenev – sniping at him but not wishing to shoot him – as no doubt Kerensky did. And now he was on the run anyhow. The internal arguments were things I and others would find out about from later reading. But here in Kharkov nobody wavered and the circle who sat in the Abrasova girls' flat was a united one. First up of course they wanted to discuss Vladimir Ilich's escape and whether he had managed it and whether it was complete yet. Would he try to get back to Western Europe by way of the Baltic? No, said Federev. He'll never go that far again. He'll hide maybe in Latvia. Or in Sweden or Finland.

In the minds in that little apartment it was not the Jew-haters who believed the words Jew and Bolshevik to be the same thing who were the greater threat. To people like Federev or Tasha the Mensheviks were to be feared more than the Cadets and Golden Kievites. Because Mensheviks actually believed that by taking seats in the Duma – not to overthrow it, but to get on with everyone – they'd be able to talk everyone else round to their view.

Our little meeting lasted three hours all up. Olya talked enough to show she was no cat's paw either. Some time about two o'clock we drank the tea with some sausage and bread. Everyone was talkative still and very jolly about their escape. I found I was too. I had not yawned during their long confabulation. I was entranced. And I was learning – a word at a time.

Over tea, Artem told them further stories about Australia. To them it was like hearing stories about Antarctica. And after that Tasha had her own story to tell – Artem would relate it to me later. It was about how she'd been a regular at Vladimir Ilich's house in Geneva. If Bolsheviks were likely to be boastful about anything it was how close they were to Vladimir Ilich Lenin. It was clear Vladimir Ilich had the power to make them feel they played an essential part and that they were valued for it. Before her sister joined the party, Tasha had been already working as a party agent in a city called Tver on the Volga – a city associated with Pushkin, Dostoevsky and Ostrovsky. She'd already written and dispatched two reports to Piter on the activities of the local cell and was writing another when she heard a knock on the door. It was the gendarmes. She threw her report into the fire, but when she let them in the police could smell the burning paper and from that point on there was a watch on her house.

And so she was spirited away. The party machine had contacts with people smugglers and employed one to take her out of the country in return for ten roubles. Once she was in the tsarist part of Poland she was handed on from smuggler to smuggler so that it cost her a lot more than ten roubles in the end. Finally, dressed in peasant shawl and riding in a farm wagon, she was driven to the German border by a Polish Jew who kept on stopping every time he saw a haystack to steal fodder for his horse. Soon he had a huge load in the wagon, which groaned its way into East Prussia. Tasha found out when they crossed the border that far from being a poor man who needed all the straw he could find to feed his horse – he owned the inn she was to stay at.

According to her new travel documents she was Akilina. As the smuggler and his wife argued about whether she ought to be fed or not, Tasha pretended she couldn't understand Yiddish. And why would a golden-haired Slav such as her have any grasp of the Jewish dialect? In fact the girls' granny had spoken it when they grew up in Kiev – that Jew-baiting city (so I was told) where their father had tried to protect them by giving them full-on Russian names like Natasha and Olya.

Tasha admired Germany. I would find the Great Russians always admired Germany – even in those days when the German army was still inside the Western Ukrainian border. Tasha thought German farm people looked well fed. The theory was that because Germany was more industrial Western Europe would turn to revolution before Russia. But the good houses of the Prussian farmers made Tasha wonder about that. It wasn't until she saw the slums of the cities and spoke with other members of the party there that she saw things were not right. In the meantime they looked after her and advised her how to carry herself when faced with policemen and officials. She got to Berlin – carrying herself as they'd advised her – and caught the train to Zurich.

In that city Tasha stayed in the house of some exiled Russians who kept complaining that Vladimir Ilich was trying to split the party over clause 1 of the membership rules, which determined who was eligible and who wasn't. Lenin didn't want or respect anyone other than active full-time campaigners like Tasha. All the others were just useless tea-drinkers and merchants of palaver, he argued. By contrast the Mensheviks were quite happy to let in anyone who agreed with their program and who did an occasional service – such as giving out handbills or newspapers – when it suited them. Tasha believed with Vladimir Ilich that revolution wasn't work for amateurs.

Olya came to join her in Switzerland and the sisters started to meet up with other political escapees. The legendary old Yuri Martov – now on the Menshevik side – was so kind even though he disagreed with Vladimir Ilich. Tasha and Olya lived in a pension in Zurich and Martov – the veteran their parents had known and respected – would visit her and her sister and offer them help with money and food. But when during one of Martov's visits to the sisters Tasha told the old man what she really thought about the party issue, that she sided with Vladimir Ilich and his all-out revolutionaries known as the Bolsheviks, he became angry and yelled and screamed about fanatics. Afterwards the landlady of the pension called Tasha to the office and told her that if her Russian friends didn't stop coming and creating mayhem she would have to leave.

Tasha and Olya moved to Geneva. Even though Vladimir Ilich lived there she did not want to bother him. But the elder of the Marxists in Switzerland – Georgi Plekhanov – stepped forward and filled the fatherly gap left by Martov. When Tasha caught influenza, she was treated by Plekhanov's wife and Plekhanov himself came round like a grandfather and brought her pastries and told her it would be better for now not to trouble her mind with talk about the party split and the arguments between him and Martov on the one side and Vladimir Ilich on the other. After all, he said, we are all brothers. Just the same, he was sad to hear that she'd lined up with Lenin's battering rams. Some of them were bullies, he said.

Despite his kindness Tasha thought, Yes, you don't want me to discuss it but you'll come around here using terms like *battering rams.*

She first met Vladimir Ilich at a large social democrat meeting where he spoke on what party people called 'the agrarian question'. He always preferred a box or something like that to speak from if he could find one because he wasn't a tall man and the way he spoke would have been a bit flat unless you actually saw him and felt his presence.

Afterwards Tasha and Olya were introduced to him for the first time. He didn't put on airs, said Tasha. In fact he made ordinary people feel at one with him while he spoke and even more once he'd finished talking and came down and became one of the crowd. And though he was hard on such people as the Mensheviks and the Socialist Revolutionaries from the platform, he was very polite to them on the floor. Tasha was surprised that he wanted to talk to her. (Maybe even Vladimir Ilich knew a good-looking woman when he saw one but Tasha seemed unaware of how beautiful she was.) Vladimir Ilich wanted to know all about the local committee of the Bolsheviks in Tver and how much it knew about splits in party theory that were happening in Switzerland. These things might be only a conflict of ideas now, said Vladimir Ilich, but when the revolution comes they could become clashes between armed men.

Tasha told him not everyone understood as clearly as she did now she was in Geneva. They all read *Iskra* of course – but they needed meetings to have things explained.

I have come to enlist with the Leninist Rams, Tasha told him, and Vladimir Ilich laughed a lot at this and called his wife Nadezhda Constantinovna Krupskaya over so the story could be repeated. Krupskaya was known to work long days typing Vladimir Ilich's endless string of speeches and pamphlets. Her face was lined and pinched but she smiled at the mention of Leninist Rams. She invited Tasha and her sister to come and visit them at home.

The sisters caught a tram out to Secheron, the suburb of Geneva where Lenin lived with Krupskaya and Krupskaya's mother Elizaveta Krupskaya in a two-storey rented house. The largest room was the kitchen – where Vladimir Ilich's mother-in-law stood at a large stove. Vladimir's study was up a trembly staircase. There was an iron bed in case he needed a rest and a few chairs and a white table heaped with writing and papers. All his books were packed into rough home-made bookshelves. All very primitive – a poor monk's room as Tasha imagined a monk's room to be. Nadezhda Krupskaya's workroom wasn't any more comfortable. It wasn't unusual for Swiss houses to be as bare as this but Tasha was awed by the bareness.

She found out that the old lady Elizaveta did all the housework because her daughter – apart from the other work – had to translate into code the letters being sent to all the cells inside Russia. It took hours to do that just for one letter.

Tasha wanted to visit this Aladdin's cave for revolutionaries every day – just so that when Vladimir Ilich came down from his office he could educate her ever more. But she and others restricted themselves to Tuesdays and Thursdays, the days set aside by Lenin for visits. Whenever they arrived Krupskaya's old mother would call out, Go on, go upstairs. Drag them out of their caves. Dinner's on. There's enough left over for you.

Sometimes Lenin would have been working in a shabby suit and sometimes in a blue cotton smock just like a Russian farmer. But he always came down laughing his famous laugh – people later would forget that laugh and judge him only by his photographs. Even though he was in a lot of ways ordinary looking – bald, a bit harried – his jocose manner would spread to the young visitors and they'd spend their time making political jokes. They were like the disciples listening to Christ, said Tasha, and they breathed easier with him. One night Tasha and Olya missed the last tram and Vladimir Ilich offered to see them home – he said he needed the fresh air. For Tasha in particular it was a chance to talk to him further. She admitted she was scared – she didn't think she had any of the qualities required to be numbered among the sort of party members Vladimir Ilich was looking for. She didn't have any great skills for persuading others or explaining theory. Sometimes she felt so inadequate that she thought she was close to a nervous breakdown.

He said not to worry. The important thing, he said, was that the revolutionary's personal life and party life had to be one and the same – the way it was with him and Krupskaya. But it needed strong young people who were in touch with the masses. He said that just for now this was where they had to begin – out of these hard little circles – until the time came. As for talking to others in the groups back in Russia, it was only the science of being certain about what you were certain about.

Under Vladimir Ilich's spell, she reached her pension. Lenin twinkled by the light of a lamppost. You have to have more confidence in your abilities, he told Tasha and Olya.

And so with her Bolshevik bishop's blessing she and her sister went inside to bed while Lenin himself walked a long way home clearing his head for new ideas.

Tasha said – that night in her flat in the basement when she was talking to us after barely surviving the Jew-haters – she was guilty about the time she'd taken from Vladimir Ilich. But no one ever *made* him leave his room.

We knew that that night Vladimir Ilich was hiding somewhere. After returning from exile in April he and his Bolsheviks had set up their headquarters in a mansion named after a ballerina – Matilda Kshesinskaya – who had owned it once. It was near the Peter and Paul Fortress, the prison Vladimir Ilich would have landed in if he'd surrendered to Kerensky's warrant and they hadn't killed him in the car on the way there.

Olya said, There's a rumour that a subterranean passage runs from the mansion to the Winter Palace.

Federev laughed. I doubt that's the truth, he said.

But it didn't matter. Now Lenin and some of his Bolsheviks were on the run – blamed for the big march by the soldiers and sailors that July which had wanted the Supreme Council of Workers, Peasants and Soldiers Soviets in Petrograd to do away with the parliament. Or if the master and his disciples weren't in hiding in the city, then they were in more far-off quarters.

8

On the way home that night in Federev's automobile Artem said with a wink, No need to mention my friendship with Hope Mockridge to Tasha. She might be fussy about these things.

With that he started whistling. They were Russian songs I didn't know. They made me homesick – I couldn't work out why. I've got to learn this bloody language, I told myself. Then I'll be at home.

Good night, dear Kangaroo, Tasha had said to me in English when we were leaving. Gradually that became my party name – not that I'd signed up to join anything. Since it came from beautiful Tasha even Federev started calling me that. I didn't like it – Tovarich Kangaroo – but didn't have much say in the matter.

There was a letter waiting for us at Federev's. It was addressed simply to F. S. Samsurov, Kharkov Municipal Soviet, Kharkov. The people at the soviet had obviously forwarded it.

It's my sister's hand, said Artem. He tore the letter open and scanned it.

Ah, he announced, and looked at me as if he was weighing me up. Poor Trofimov is dead. Zhenya says it's a mercy. No more gasping like a landed fish.

I looked away. I had this weird idea that my adventures with

Trofimova might have hastened Trofimov's death.

Well, said Artem. A good man . . . a good man.

I'm very sorry, I told him in confusion.

I'll pass on your condolences, he assured me.

Poor Trofimov – a fellow miner, and I'd betrayed him. Yet I found it hard to think like that – like a man with a conscience. I thought: Here now is Trofimova! And she had already put down a claim on a future with me – or so I hoped.

I thought of how Trofimov's passing would have been treated had he died of black lung in Broken Hill. The other miners would go to the widow's house and parade by their brother's coffin and pat the heads of the dead man's kids – and mutter something to the bowed widow and slip her a few bob . . . That's where the comparison broke down. I couldn't imagine Trofimova as the despairing widow.

Artem yawned now and moved on from the memory of Trofimov. His sister had said that when Artem was young he almost saw Trofimov as a rival for possession of his sister. If it were true then that rivalry was at an end.

He yawned again. If I can jot my speeches down in English, he said, I wouldn't mind if you could edit them and send them back to the *Australian Worker.* Not that I think I'm the last word when it comes to oratory. And why stop at the *Australian Worker*? Let's send the message everywhere – the *Weekly World* in New York, *Daily Worker* in London. Few people are in your position, Paddy. To be able to spread our particular news.

I thought, As long as I can understand it.

In the following days we were often at the basement flat in Botanical Street – or else the girls were often at Federev's apartment. At a meeting in a railway workshop attended by soldiers and workers, Tasha's name and Artem's were voted on to attend a regional conference of the Donbas area. Artem came in first in the vote, a little ahead of Tasha. According to the party there was supposed to be no prejudice against women. But there was. And especially against pretty women and maybe especially against pretty young women who were Jewish.

When delegates were elected, an engine driver who was a Menshevik got up from the floor and moved that no one get a free ride down to the congress. That was his way of trying to stop some of us getting there. He accused Bolshevik guards and drivers of giving everyone free rides here and there. That just helped the railways go to hell, he said. They needed the fares and no one should travel free. If you or your party can't afford the fare, he said (with reasoning that would have gone down well in Queensland), then you can't afford to be a party and you can't afford to send delegates.

There was a lot of clapping from the floor. But Artem said, Are we really going to argue over train fares? Does my comrade believe that my fare will rebuild the whole rail system? Is this what the people's revolution has come to? That it can't afford to carry us?

Then he lifted his voice. As for me, he roared, I will damn well walk there. I have the shoe leather, I have the legs and they are good Bolshevik legs.

Instead of cheers, everyone was falling out of their chairs laughing with him. It seemed to be funnier in Russian than in Federev's whispered English translation.

There was a time I walked from the banks of the Aldan all the way to the suburbs of Irkutsk, he told them. I did not do it legally either. But I'll go to Ekaterinoslav legally. Ekaterinoslav does not scare me as a destination. I have come back from Australia to be with my brothers and sisters. And now my good Menshevik here wants to stop me being among them by waffling about fares. If he decides to put this branch meeting at the South Pole, he will find me there. If he puts it in the Arctic – there I'll be. If he puts it in Rome, he will find me there. If he puts it in London, he will find me there. Voting for my party, for the power of the people.

It was obvious that a lot of the soldiers and workers – if not the railway men – were on our side. Because they could grasp the message. An end to the war, land for the peasants, factories for the workers.

Nevertheless the Mensheviks did win their point and it was our host Federev who paid for our tickets – even mine – and we set off with the girls to Ekaterinoslav in early August. The weather was sweltering in our compartment, but the sisters in their summer dresses looked as if they carried their own shade with them. All Artem's conversations with Tasha and her sister seemed simply political. In argument his eye moved from one to the other. He did not behave as if he were lovesick for either of them.

The outer suburbs of Ekaterinoslav – a city Artem and the girls had praised – was like outer Kharkov at first with coal dust on everything. But it was beautiful at the centre where all the delegates were put up in a hotel called the Europa. The organisers of the congress had arranged a ride down the river. From a pier set on a lake in parkland we boarded a little steam ferry and Artem sat with Tasha and Olya inside by an open window to catch the breeze from the water. I went walking the deck – this was new country to me and I had the bushie's habit of dashing around trying to see new things from every possible angle. A few people stood near the open prow where I thought I recognised from behind a particular sturdy-looking woman in a long dress. She wore a peasant shawl a bit like the way some of the soldiers wore their uniforms – to show where they had been and also to show their hope about where they were going. The woman's dress was white but with a sash over her shoulder that was tied at her hip. She was looking at the shell of a rickety white mansion on top of a cliff on one side of the river. It was Artem's sister. I skirted her to the front as if she were a dangerous creature.

It is Australia, she said when she saw me.

Zhenya, I said, forgetting I was to call her Trofimova. Are you a delegate? I asked in Russian, amazing myself (though *delegate* was easy to say – it was *delegat*). Nevertheless I had to say it twice.

No, she said, shaking her head.

Later I'd find Artem had asked her to come here as an observer and in the belief it would help her with her grief by giving her a sense of a new dawn.

Artem tells me, come! she announced in English.

Trofimov? I said. I'm sorry.

I had to go back to English for this, and I blushed as I said it. I saw the sash she wore over her right shoulder did not carry a political slogan but was pure black – the sign of her widowhood. The rough map of the Ukraine I carried in my head told me she had not had far to come. Europa Hotel? I asked her.

She nodded. Tasha, she said. Olya.

Then she smiled at me – it was an innocent smile but it seemed to know everything about me. She looked away at the shore but then smiled again at me and nodded. She touched her black sash. Trofimov, she told me. And then more softly, Trofimov, and raised both her hands. But it wasn't in prayer and it wasn't asking for any mercy. Once more I was reassured to see a woman no man could make into a victim. This was a full-bodied woman with her brother Artem's lion heart – that's how it seemed to me. We stood on the prow together – silent. We watched the way the ferry broke up the reflection of trees and buildings in the water.

The congress of the various wings of the Social Democratic Party was held in a theatre that still had the scenery of a living room painted on canvas at the back of the stage. There were more peasant delegates than I'd seen at the Kharkov meetings – they wore boots and smocks cinched at the waist with big belts and were probably yelling that the land belonged to them. A chairman was elected – he was a Menshevik. He read out an agenda. He was booed a few times and it was clear that our side – though maybe outnumbered as delegates – had a lot of support. I made notes in a little notebook I'd acquired. *Social Democratic Party very divided*, I wrote. *Mensheviks would fit into Holman's Labor government in New South Wales or Ryan's in Queensland.*

After a while everyone settled down and the speeches seemed fairly polished. It was the fumbling Duma in Petrograd – and Kerensky – who wanted to be another Napoleon and dressed as if he was – who got most of the abuse.

★

At the hotel that evening Trofimova kept very close to the sisters, Tasha and Olya. I passed her once in the corridor on the way to dinner. She smiled and opened up her arms – just as a gesture though. It said no instead of yes. I found myself doing something I'd never done before – I tapped my left chest twice with the first two fingers of my right hand. Where had that come from?

Meanwhile I made myself busy writing about the congress for the *Worker.*

Comrade Artem Samsurov formerly of Brisbane was welcomed on the stage. After a brief charming speech was elected by acclamation a member of the Regional Committee of the Russian Social Democratic Party.

Later in the day there was a side meeting of the Bolshevik delegates in a little concert hall. This was a very ornate room and made a mockery of our ordinary clothing. Here Artem was elected secretary of the Donbas Central Committee of the Bolsheviks – one of the tasks for which he'd been sent to Kharkov by the people in Piter.

Among the others elected was Tasha.

At the railway station that night, Trofimova – who was going east while we were all going north – pecked me first on one cheek then on the other and looked me in the eye with what seemed to an uninformed man like something close to affection. I wanted to say her name, Zhenya, as she left for another platform.

I was what I never expected to be – a disappointed admirer – as I watched her make her way over a connecting bridge.

Our train steamed in and I boarded, then pretended to write in my notebook through all the happy conversation of the others. I fell asleep with the jolting of the train and had some sad dreams about my mother. I woke in the first light of morning and found Artem still flirting with the Abrasova sisters as if he hadn't let up all night. I was pleased when we pulled into the grim vaulted old station in Kharkov. The Abrasova girls looked tired and so we took a hackney coach to their place.

From there Artem and I walked to Federev's – we didn't have unlimited funds for hackneys. I want to dictate something to you right now, he said. For English readers. You're not tired are you, Paddy?

Federev was not at home, so we sat in the living room while Artem gave me his English notes for his Russian lecture of the following evening at the technical university. As well as Australia, the Second International occupied his speech. The Germans and the Belgians had got together in 1889 and started it. Its last meeting had taken place in Brussels just before the war started – around the time Menschkin killed himself during Hope Mockridge's picnic. Then war was declared and Kautsky of the German Social Democratic Party caved in to the hysteria the way T. J. Ryan and Fisher and Hughes had done. Therefore the Second International had failed from pole to pole. What had failed in Sydney and Melbourne and Brisbane had also failed on the shores of the Baltic Sea. Universal brotherhood was killed off in the trenches and the swamps on the Galician border or the forests of the north-east as surely as it was killed off at Gallipoli.

Artem left me to make what I could out of his notes and then we slept a while. Then – writing on my own. Nothing kept me awake better. I finished the piece and posted it to the *Australian Worker* that afternoon at the Central Kharkov post office. It was strange to think the lower end of government still worked – the mail and the lamp lighting and the trams.

9

When Federev saw us at breakfast the next morning he announced that *our* Bolshevik group would take over a fine house that had belonged to the family of the late General Gubin. The family were gone and the house stood unoccupied. Gubin himself – Federev told us – had died a mysterious death. Last spring his corps had got out of control on the Polish front. These probably included the men we'd seen in the park the day the thief had been thrown into the river. Federev said it was not certain how General Gubin had died. He might have killed himself in despair when his soldiers set up bars and theatres and brothels in their dug-outs and invited German scouts across the lines to enjoy themselves there in a brotherly spirit. Or he might have been shot by his own men. In any case, the rest of the Gubin family had fled and were living in Italy.

When we occupied the house, said Federev, we would have a great number of soldiers and Red Guards to call on to protect the place. Because the Bolshevik faction was the only party promising an absolute end to the war.

So the Gubin house was to be our fortress – even Federev would have a bed there in case he was too busy to come home. We packed our kits and were driven the short distance to the Gubin mansion. And there we walked through a double door with columns on either side and from the large entrance hall went up a broad staircase to the upper floor, to the room where it had been decided – I don't know by who – we would be working and living from now on. I could see the places on the walls where the Gubins' paintings had been and wondered where they'd disappeared to.

The day before we moved in there were mainly meetings. Then suddenly there were jobs. All at once Federev and Artem and Tasha had roles they seemed to know how to play. In a big room on the ground floor, Federev was to be the chief of security – he would guard the premises and the party's principles. He was supposed to gather intelligence about our enemies and about the armaments other groups had. Almost straight away his clothing changed. He wore a military cap and a well-tailored military jacket. A number of soldiers put maps up on the wall for him to study. He began his work. Immediately his office was full of housewives and good-looking boys bringing information from the suburbs and the bars and teahouses and Turkish baths of the city.

Tasha and Olya were given an office at the head of the stairs. They headed some sort of secretarial and propaganda departments. They kept in touch with the members of the party. They wrote speeches and articles for our newspaper – it was named *Izvestia* just like Artem's Brisbane newspaper. It was published from a cellar across the city. Olya typed letters for the rest of us. Equality between man and woman hadn't reached the typewriter yet. Anyhow – as dear old Amelia would have said – it doesn't matter as long as the shorthand typist is valued.

Artem was to be military liaison, chief of supplies and propaganda – he shared that task with Tasha – and I was taken on as his informal aide. I felt shy about this. The most I could do was work up a bit of an English-language story out of the English speech notes Artem gave me and to write in longhand and with my direct rough style for the *Australian Worker* and anyone else who'd give me the time of day. But my Russian was still like that of a child. Did I belong? Of course I didn't. But I didn't want to go home either. I couldn't believe everything that had happened. The people who'd met us at Kharkov station a few weeks ago had just moved into a house without taking any lease. They'd said at the little meetings they had the army and the Red Guards on their side and now – going by the numbers of armed men around the house and in the guardroom downstairs – it turned out to be true.

And if you're here in the first place, I told myself, no sense creeping around as if you aren't a welcome guest. Artem must have known I'd go home if he told me to. So until he said it . . . here we were.

In our office across from that of the sisters, army cots were put in place for us to sleep on. Though everyone seemed to be making up their work as they went along, there wasn't a doubt that we were on what the English call a war footing.

The mansion was well guarded, as I said – the guardhouse was in the big reception room across from Federev's office. It seemed the city knew we were here and protected by soldiers. Now and then there'd be catcalls between our guards and the young men and women from the finer academies who marched past in white cadet uniforms or summer skirts shouting insults at Vladimir Ilich and everyone inside the building. Sometimes more mature men and women marched past holding banners that said the soviets should be abandoned and the Rada obeyed in the Ukraine and the Duma in Russia. We'd look up from our work and hear the yelling in the street. We'd hear our sentries calling their own insults back.

One of Artem's first problems was feeding everyone in the Gubin mansion. Our kitchen and communal dining room were downstairs at the back of the house and what the army cooks prepared there came from the municipal warehouses. To reach them Artem and I would travel by truck with the documents he signed as a member of the Donbas Central Committee of the Bolsheviks. Whatever party the men in the warehouse came from, they didn't want to refuse us or our truckload of soldiers and Red Guards. Artem had flour distributed to the barracks around the city where soldiers dossed. Other officials of the city soviet were doing that – some people resented that they were not willing to cooperate in the noble business of being slaughtered by the Germans and Austrians. But if they weren't given bread they would just seize it from civilians. Artem didn't want that. At heart he was a law and order man.

We arrived at some municipal food storeroom one mid-morning in a convoy of trucks. Things were getting serious for people. On streets nearby there were queues of men and women outside the bakeries from midnight waiting to buy a loaf. You could just about imagine the bakers getting to be the kings of life and death.

We passed the bags of flour from the heaps that rose into the lofty interior of the warehouse and then I got rid of my coat – the old checked one – and sweated like a happy labourer ought to. Artem and I then helped the soldiers to load consignments to the bakeries in the outer suburbs. We had no choice but to sell it to them at a fair price and warn them against running up the price and keeping any aside to sell on or give to their girlfriends. It was a less than perfect way to do things but at least the bakers were scared of the soldiers who occasionally turned up at the premises of some baker they suspected and led him onto the footpath outside and shot him. So Artem was the boss, but he hauled sacks beside me and it wasn't a condescension – it wasn't like Tolstoy doing the harvest with the peasants – because Artem was a peasant too.

When it was over we washed our upper bodies in some pump water one of the Red sentries at the warehouse had fetched us in a pail.

Blowing water out of his mouth, Artem told me, We've sent people out to scout places we can put public bakeries. Undercut the damned hoarders.

Like T. J. Ryan's butcheries, I said as a half-tease.

Maybe, he admitted. I'm going to get Trofimova up here. She can find places like that and get army cooks. Pay them with bread. And she's got quite an ear for information too. What do you think, Paddy?

Keeping my head down and splashing water on my own face, I said I thought it was a good idea. Even so it might mean a lot of frustration for me – that's what I thought privately. Trofimova had repented of me by now.

Back in the truck we set off again towards the Gubin mansion. The other trucks of the convoy had peeled off to their various destinations around the city. Artem and I sat in the front of the truck with the driver and we were approaching the National Hotel – one of the best old hotels in Kharkov. It stood above a vast white staircase – maybe designed for an emperor and all his staff to walk up. Standing on it in the sunshine was a family group. They were being photographed by a man placed slightly down the staircase with a camera on a tripod. The family was well dressed – the women in their big hats and spotless dresses and a father and another middle-aged man both wearing morning suits. The young officer at the centre of the group made an amazing picture – the reverse of the bedraggled soldiers we saw around the city in his braided cavalry jacket and white pants and shining boots. On his head was a crimson headpiece the Russians called a *bashlik* – a sort of leather hood cum hat. To go with all that a big Caucasian sword hung at the boy's waist. Was he really a soldier or did he come out of some play? And I wondered whether the women carried bread with them in their handbags when they went out – and little silver boxes full of sugar cubes for their tea and coffee. It was rumoured the best of people did it in these hard-up days.

The family stood proudly around their golden boy who had clearly just graduated from a military academy. It was a strange sight. Who would he command, this young sprat? Where could he fight in such fancy gear? When we were getting close, our driver put on the brakes for three soldiers who were running across the avenue. We saw them kneel on the edge of the pavement beneath the white stairs and raise their rifles. Even over the engine we heard the combined blast. The young military officer fell and his *bashlik* rolled down the stairs. The two older men stooped and tried to lift him upright. A woman with blood and brains on her white dress fell into the arms of two others of the family. The soldiers who'd shot the boy simply turned their backs and crossed the avenue again.

I was shocked and somehow offended that these *burzhooi* had been so badly punished for pretending it was 1914. Artem must have been suffering the same sort of shock and got down from the truck cabin.

The soldiers crossing the avenue turned back and confronted Artem as he bawled at them. I too found myself yelling at them in a language they'd never heard.

Artem pulled me back.

Not worth the effort, Paddy, he told me. He could understand what was in the men's mind. By his uniform, this kid was a future officer, so they had nipped him in the bud. They'd cut him out of the family photograph. And they felt justified and very gamely argued back at Artem – one of them had his fist clenched as if he was going to hit him. Then they turned away. I wondered what Artem had told them. Maybe it was that after the *real* revolution the kind of people who were on the stairs would be dealt with in a more orderly way.

Above us two women were stopping the blood-stained third from hurling herself full-length on the body of the boy. Artem climbed towards the family and I followed him. He offered to take the body of the boy inside. Though the men harangued us as if we'd shot the boy ourselves they let us help. I took the booted ankles and Artem carried him under the armpits. In the lobby we sat him in a chair where he lolled. The lamenting women followed us inside. I'll never forget how delicate this young officer's lips looked, as if he were about to say something as the bullet ripped into his head.

The hotel manager rushed away to ring a doctor. There was nothing more for us to do. We backed towards the door. Suddenly the father of the boy and various of the menfolk blocked our way out and began raining blows on us. I quickly had enough of this and knocked one to the ground and then was drained of all anger and felt sorry for the man. Artem was not at a loss to defend himself but the father and uncle or godfather – blinded by anger and loss – were smashing into him. We forced our way out through the hotel door.

That night I dreamed of a conversation the young officer had with me. In the dream I knew exactly what he was saying but when I woke I remembered it only as stumps of words. The sense was all gouged out of it.

10

It was a day or two later that my education in guns resumed. A man in a bowler hat and frock coat came to the gate and spoke to the Red Guards and was let in. We were upstairs in our office but we heard the fellow enter Federev's office yelling. Artem raised his head and said to me, I know that voice. But surely it can't be . . .

He stood up, his face lively with anticipation. Come on, he said, and we went clattering down the stairs. Through Federev's open door I saw a true gentleman with a fancy walking stick and a crooked grin – for all the world like a hayseed who'd struck it rich. Someone who'd come into money instead of being used to it.

Not *you*! Artem yelled at the man.

It is me, said the man. How is my old Artem?

How is my old Slatkin for that matter? roared Artem, and they walked up to each other and swapped energetic kisses and hugs.

The man was shorter than Artem but he was well fed and had a little pot belly. When I was introduced to him he spoke English to me as well as some of Artem's people in Brisbane. It turned out he'd worked more than two years on the London docks.

Timofei Maximovich Slatkin, said Artem. There he stands in all his bourgeois glory. Wouldn't you just like to shoot him?

I deserve it, said Slatkin. Without a doubt. Do you like my suit,

Artem? I had a little trip to France last year – yes, to France despite the war – and I had it run up there. I wanted to impress you today so I had my servant get it out of the cupboard and send it with me.

You clearly have a hard life, said Artem, beginning to laugh. How is the divine Mrs Slatkin?

Delighted with her husband still, he said. Because – after all – he never complains.

Even Federev – a very serious man – was smiling at all this.

She is also discontented with the so-called revolution, said Slatkin of his wife.

But she'll lose her fortune and her house in the end, said Federev.

She can't wait for that liberation, said Slatkin. She believes in brotherhood, not in Mammon.

That's handy, said Artem.

Artem, I had to see you.

See all you want, Artem invited him.

Is there somewhere we can talk?

Upstairs, said Artem.

Artem and Slatkin said goodbye to Federev and we went up the stairs with Slatkin flourishing his cane like someone in a play. I left them to talk alone in the office and went into the sisters' room where Tasha was dictating an article to Olya. They *were* like Martha and Mary in the gospel. One of them knew what theory was and the other did a lot of the work. I was not really welcome there so in the end I took a chair outside to the head of the stairs and began writing more notes about things I had seen here – half hoping something new would come from them that I could use for one of my articles. Certainly not an article on the killing of the young officer.

The light started to fade. A mixed smell of sulphur and candle grease came from Artem's office where the old friends were advising each other in Russian with slightly raised voices. Then they came out onto the landing. I stood up. Artem told Slatkin in English that I was totally reliable. I felt vainly proud of that.

Slatkin looked at me directly. Did Artem tell you about the banks we used to rob? And he began to laugh.

Artem laughed too. Comrade Slatkin's talking about himself, he told me.

No, said Slatkin. You were our quartermaster, Artem. You were a sneaky little supplier. He put a finger to his nose in a gesture of secrecy. See you tomorrow then, Artem. Good afternoon to you too, Mr Dykes.

As Artem saw Slatkin off the premises I went into the office and began working up the notes of a speech Artem had given me earlier. But I couldn't help sitting back in my chair and wondering, *Robbed a bank?* I understood but did not forgive the fact that he hadn't told me earlier.

Artem returned and got straight back to work. But the question was aching in the air. He looked up.

He exaggerates, Paddy, said Artem. It was on my way back from France all those years ago. I bought pistols in Germany, the ones Slatkin and his crowd needed. I passed them on. Using them they robbed a bullion shipment on its way from the docks to a bank in Kaliningrad. That's all, Paddy. I wasn't there – maybe I wasn't considered tough enough for that. But I've got to be frank: I would have if ordered. The party needed the funds, and Slatkin was a man for funds.

I had read somewhere that the Social Democratic Party had voted to end bank robberies. But after all – even I understood this that afternoon – the revolution was the revolution and had to be paid for. I still stupidly felt offended, and I didn't know why. Why was the idea of bank robbery itself a genuine shock to me when the usury of the banks – their licensed thieving – wasn't? If it was a shock to me, what did it say about me and my timid approach to things?

Artem explained further: Vladimir Ilich didn't ask me to be a bandit but he asked Slatkin – because Slatkin was a true man of action, a bank robber right out of the Wild West. And then Vladimir Ilich asked him to marry the heiress, Miss Stürmer, as I told you in Brisbane.

No, I said. You never told me that.

It must have been Hope Mockridge, he said. Or perhaps I was talking to Amelia.

He explained that Slatkin had been ordered by Lenin to marry the sister of a deceased industrialist who had been a party sympathiser and one of its financiers. And sure enough he'd charmed the girl and done it, just as ordered, and it was the former Miss Stürmer whom Artem had asked after when we were downstairs in Federev's office.

Internally I gave myself a good talking to. How did I think the party had been kept going? Was it by nice sentiments? Was it by timid little prayers? Of course it was by big, tough plans. Yet it was as if Artem himself didn't want me to think too much about that.

Anyhow, he said, changing the subject, Slatkin said they want me to go to Piter. You'll come, of course?

At once I wanted to, but I asked, Why?

Artem shook his head, confused by my resistance.

Because you're my partner, Paddy. Do you think you're ever going home again?

Well I might, I said. But I managed a smile.

He looked down at his desk and grinned almost shyly. No, you won't go back. Trofimova – she has her hooks in you.

What he knew, and what he didn't – that was the question. And how did he know it? I didn't want to ask him.

When are we leaving? I rushed in to ask him.

As soon as we can. But there's something we need to do here first. With Slatkin.

11

Later that evening Artem came into the room and put a black and white bandanna on the desk.

You'll need that, Paddy, he told me.

What for?

Slatkin will be along in a while. You'll see how things work.

He looked at his watch and decided that we should wait downstairs.

We're not robbing a bank, are we? The idea excited me – I was surprised how ready I was to go.

Not a bank, Artem told me.

We didn't disturb the sisters across the hall but went down the stairs and out the front door past columns of Red Guards who – in our new military mode – Artem saluted. Then we waited on the pavement.

He shouldn't be too long, said Artem.

We were there about ten minutes before a large French car pulled up. The auto was driven by a man in a uniform like Federev's chauffeur wore – a better uniform than those of the soldiers or Red Guards. Behind the car a large truck pulled in, its back covered with a canopy. The uniformed driver got out of the car and opened the doors for us to enter. The well-dressed Slatkin was waiting for us inside.

Seat yourselves, gentlemen, he said. The performance is about to begin.

As soon as our backs hit the upholstery and the car took off he did something amazing. He fetched from a deep pocket in the door of the car a pistol and handed it butt-first to Artem. Artem inspected it like an expert. My attention was riveted on the thing too. It had nothing in common with the six-shooters in the books I had read as a child – and it seemed all the more sinister for that. The trigger was placed between the brown handle and a thin rectangular box. That box-like appendage – Artem told me – was the magazine for bullets. Then Slatkin fetched another pistol from the pocket and handed it to me.

Paddy's not trained in firearms, said Artem. Perhaps it would be better –

No, no, no! said Slatkin. As long as he doesn't shoot one of us, he should carry one. The odd accidental shot – what does that matter at this moment of history? Keep the safety catch on and he can wave it about like an actor on stage.

Artem sighed. The hard steel thing in my hand excited me and frightened me at the same time. He took the thing away from me and assured himself the catch was on. Then – with a warning stare – he gave it back to me. He was right – I was not ready yet for such a weapon – but at last I felt like a true actor in the scene. I had the idea that I was being, as people say, initiated or *blooded*. I didn't mind at all that Artem might be adding me into what the old part of me thought of as a crime.

Slatkin himself opened his jacket and fitted a gun into a leather holster he was wearing. Meanwhile I could see through the back window that the truck stuck to us. I wondered how many men were concealed beneath its canopy to help us in whatever adventure we were embarked on.

Is this a bank robbery? I asked again.

Slatkin laughed. Not exactly, Mr Dykes, he said.

Artem told me, We're just going to collect a few items we need. Sorry to be mysterious but . . . you'll see.

We drove north-east, towards the workers' section of the city. It was a dreary place full of hollow-faced men and women, the kids barefoot in the autumn chill. We rolled over cobbles towards what could only be called a fort at the top of a hill. I could see two sentries on its main gate. They had not abandoned the army like others – perhaps they had had an easy time of the war. Even so they looked bored and not very much devoted. Slatkin's auto swung to the right in front of the gate and the truck braked only a few yards from the sentries.

In the car Slatkin said, Bandannas, gentlemen.

And we pulled them on, like children playing cowboys. Slatkin's driver opened the car door and we all bundled out, Slatkin first. The area smelled of busted sewers and cooking in which sour cabbage played a big part. I saw that men wearing caps and bandannas had piled out of the truck and two of them already held pistols to the sentries' throats. The rest of those from the truck broke the lock on the gate and swung it open. In barely more than a second the truck rolled through the gate and disappeared.

The three of us walked in behind it. From a guardroom a number of soldiers carrying rifles appeared but our fellows threatened them with Mausers and rifles – the same Mannlichers with which the tsar had equipped his troops. We three caught up to the raiding party and Slatkin gave the commands.

Two officers appeared from the main stone building ahead – it looked like the sort of place that would have once housed two dozen officers and hundreds of men. But not in these days of chaos. Slatkin and Artem spoke with the two men while I stood by, armed with a pistol if not with the language. The more senior of the officers led us – nearly invited us – inside the barracks. On the walls there were crossed swords and dim paintings of battles that had meant a lot to the tsars but which now meant nothing. The officer opened cabinets full of rifles. We had many hands to carry them down into the courtyard and load them into the truck.

Some of our men – helped by NCOs – fetched machine-guns from a cellar and hoisted boxes of ammunition for them into the truck. I put my pistol in my pocket and helped carry a Maxim gun. The whole thing was done in a quarter of an hour. We were like locusts stripping a field. Our men held the gate open as the truck went through and then they climbed into the back. We slipped out ourselves – Slatkin and Artem and I – and returned to the car we'd left only a few minutes before. Slatkin's uniformed chauffeur even held the car door for us again – as if we were going home after dinner at a hotel. We left by a different road than we had arrived on.

Artem inspected his Mauser in the back seat.

He said, I should get one of these, Timofei Maximovich.

You *should*, said Slatkin. But I can't spare that one, I'm sorry.

Artem gave it back without regret and I pulled mine out of my pocket and handed it over.

Well done, comrade, Slatkin said. You waved it at those officers like a true bandit. I couldn't tell you before, but the hold-up was a bit of a fake. The men on the gate and half the guardroom were our fellows. We had to threaten them to make them seem blameless. You were never in great peril, Paddy.

I don't know why but I felt a little disappointed – I'd wanted the peril to be real.

As far as I know, neither before or after our adventure at the fort did Slatkin tell Artem exactly why he was wanted in Petrograd. But I met Federev in the corridor and his face had a sourness it had never had while we were his guests.

He said, Off to Piter? So soon! While the old campaigners stay here whistling as best they can in Kharkov.

We'll be back, I told him.

Unless Vladimir Ilich considers you too valuable to lose. But better watch out. The gendarmes will be on your trail. He turned and went into his office.

Slatkin had the tickets for us. The next morning Artem took Tasha for a walk in the city gardens – the very ones where we'd seen the thief shot and drowned. When they got back Tasha looked flushed in the face – as if there'd been an intimate conversation and not just an exchange of political ideas.

Finally we said goodbye to Federev. I hadn't told Artem about my earlier exchange with the lawyer and to Artem's face he pretended he was impressed by the summons to Piter. He hadn't known he was harbouring someone so essential to Petrograd, he said. He asked Artem to tell the Central Committee what was happening in Kharkov and how the revolution was on a knife edge – the Germans might renew their offensive or the forces of the Rada might try to take Kharkov. I wondered – was all this talk of knife edges designed to make the people in Petrograd think he was important?

Federev provided his car to take us to the station – a sure sign he wanted Artem's backing and his words to be dropped into the right ears. Then we were off with Red Guards again draped across the fenders and standing on the running boards. Their rifles protruded either side of the car bonnet like a porcupine's spines. So we got to Kharkov's main station – a place I was used to by now. There were people all over the platform. Women sat on bundles of luggage looking weary. Men smoked their pipes and kids made the best of things by chasing each other around the columns. They had borne the summer but wanted to get away to the country for the winter. There were no regular services any more. They waited there on the off-chance that a train would go where they wanted to go – to relatives in the countryside where there were cows and butter and chickens. I knew this would be the scene at any station we visited.

A small delegation of railway workers had met us at the station to lead us to our carriage. Artem – seeing himself as a railway man – was always disappointed that the Mensheviks had now captured the leadership position in the Railway Men's Union.

Artem said to them, I thought you were all Mensheviks.

Too many of us are, said one man.

In the allotted carriage we had our own compartment. People who wanted to travel north climbed aboard our train and men sat on the roof. Railway guards went along the length of the train yelling at them that they'd get their heads knocked off when the train entered tunnels. They yelled back that they'd lie flat for the tunnels. Soon we were off, overcrowded but leaving hordes of people still on the platform. Slatkin slept and Artem read while I looked out the window and continued my education in Russia – the churches and the country streams. The mines. The clumps of birches. Every country village with houses of old grey wood that looked like stacked and weathered timber. You'd expect crows to come flying out of the windows and flit over the fences of plaited black branches. Children ran after the train, holding up their hands and touching their mouths – they were willing to catch money or food. So much for the countryside! Grain dealers had driven the price up so the poorer families couldn't afford wheat or rye and might have already eaten their seed crop.

I saw a bare-footed idiot – poor creature – standing without his pants in the dust and holding his privates. Was he the national symbol? I wondered.

As we travelled I also read an English–Russian phrasebook, a ridiculous little book – like a pop-gun aimed at my gigantic ignorance. I felt I would need it more than ever though. Because Artem was right. I did not believe I would be going back to Australia soon. There's nothing like language lessons to put the teachers – Artem and Slatkin – and student to sleep. I woke as the train was grinding into the Vitebsk station at Petrograd. I saw the platform here was as crowded as the one in Kharkov – maybe more so.

There were sailors, soldiers, families. Pedlars went amongst them selling wizened little apples and oranges and even cups of water from a bucket. Men playing balalaikas and others, strumming a sort of banjo made out of just a few strings stretched across a hollowed-out pumpkin skin, strolled through the crowd hoping to be paid for their music.

When we got down on the platform ourselves a smell of piss and uncollected garbage hit us like a blow. It was the stink of a government falling apart. But strong enough – as Slatkin had told us – to force Vladimir Ilich to flee and to put Trotsky in jail along with the woman hero Kollontai who'd come back from America with him earlier that year. They'd been Mensheviks but they'd since come across to Vladimir Ilich's side. I would notice that up in the capital the divisions weren't as sharp as they were in Kharkov. Men and women who weren't as schooled as Artem or Tasha moved all the time from one group to another.

Outside the station another giant auto pulled up; apparently it was Slatkin's. We got inside and there sat a tall woman – long-faced and pale – in a summer hat and a long white dress: Mrs Slatkin. Slatkin kissed her on both cheeks and she looked delighted. He sat down, holding her left hand, while Artem kissed the gloved right one.

Kiss her hand, Artem advised me softly. I did it. The glove was of a sort of netting or gauze and I could see the bones running underneath it. Then Red Guards with rifles climbed up onto our running boards – to signal to any mob this was not the sort of *burzhooi* car ripe to be seized or attacked or fired upon – and we were off.

12

I felt wide awake as we rolled through the broad streets. There was a peculiar smell to this city – something different and more complicated than at the railway station. Artem told me, You can hear the voice of the earth up here in the north. Yelling for rebirth.

Piter had brought out visions and poetry in him – that seemed to be one of the jobs it always did for Russians.

As the sun rose we crossed a canal the colour of soiled gold. Slatkin swung around in his seat.

Two carloads of gendarmes were behind us. They followed anyone who might lead them to Vladimir Ilich.

We rolled down very wide avenues quiet at that hour and full of apartments grander than the best in Kharkov. We pulled up in front of one that even had its own doorman.

Slatkin's driver left his seat in the front and opened the door on the pavement side. He handed Mrs Slatkin out and she was followed by Slatkin. He watched the police cars roll past as if they weren't interested.

Goodbye boys, called Slatkin.

Since Artem did not move I knew this was not where we were going to stay. I could see Slatkin giving the driver further instructions.

We moved on a little – the Red Guards still on the running

boards – and stopped by double wooden gates further along the street. The driver pipped his horn and the gates opened. We were driven into a cobbled courtyard and through an archway that led into a dim lane. From here we emerged on another street of reasonable size. We did not travel too far from the flasher part of town – the building we eventually pulled up at did not look shabby. We shook hands solemnly with the Red Guards – just boys but determined ones. They came from the factories in the northern suburbs. Slatkin's chauffeur insisted on carrying our stained kits and led us into the lobby and up the stairs and then rang the bell for us. Once it was opened by a young servant woman the chauffeur saluted us and ran back downstairs. The apartment we entered seemed very still. But a good-looking middle-aged woman appeared from somewhere inside and greeted Artem. She seemed to know him and her lively green eyes flashed on seeing him.

Speaking softly to him – it turned out the rest of the family who lived here weren't up yet – she kept her hand on Artem's upper arm while she gave her orders to her maid. Then she exchanged an earnest hug and kiss with Artem and shook my hand before the maid led us into the kitchen and sat us down at a big scoured table. She fetched us bread and broth and made us tea. Then she said something under her breath. Artem laughed and looked at me.

She told me things cost a lot here so we must appreciate what we're given. She thinks we're tramps.

We were still eating when an older man with a shock of grey hair came into the kitchen. He and Artem embraced. This man was a renowned Marxist named Sergei Alliluyev – the owner of this apartment. The woman who'd met us was his wife. Alliluyev grinned at Artem, and Artem grinned back at him – two fellows who'd been through it and were now meeting up again in more promising times.

Artem crinkled his nose. There was a pretty strong smell of tobacco wafting into the kitchen. *Makhorka*, he complained. It was a word I knew. It was the sort of tobacco smoked by peasants and hard-up workers.

Koba, said Alliluyev.

Ah, said Artem.

The reek got closer to us now and a man about Artem's age came into the kitchen. He looked at first to be built for endurance and I suppose you'd call him strong. He had pockmarks on his face but I thought he was good-looking in a dark sort of way. His collarless shirt looked no better than mine. And I noticed one of his arms was shorter than the other. I would find out later that it had been like that since his childhood. He stood in the doorway with his eyes twinkling and sang a few lines of a song. Then puffed away and put on a performance fart that was meant to go with the smoking. But then he put his pipe down as if he'd never take it up again. He'd had enough.

The greeting between Artem and this new man Koba was not as warm as the one I'd witnessed between Artem and Alliluyev. There was a simple explanation – they had never met before. Koba – as all Russia would one day know – had been in prison or at least in exile in Siberia for most of the time Artem had been in Brisbane.

Artem kindly introduced me. Koba shook my hand roughly – grinning at me as if I were a hayseed.

Paddy, I mumbled. Pleased to meet you.

In reply he just opened his mouth and let out sounds that imitated my accent. Wah-wah-wah! he said back to me and looked at Artem and Alliluyev inviting them to laugh with him. Alliluyev laughed but Artem abstained.

Now we all sat down and began to drink tea. The conversation grew serious and I was left with the crumbs of it – a word here and there. I realised again that apart from being his travelling companion and taking down his English notes I was as useless to Artem as a two-year-old.

We were still drinking tea when two young women burst bubbling into the kitchen. They wore house gowns and light slippers and one of them had curl papers in her hair. They were as pretty as their mother, who had followed them in and stood slightly behind her husband with her hand on his shoulder.

The girls seemed flirtatious with Koba who turned in his chair and smiled at them. Their mother smiled too – though a bit sourly. The girls looked across the table questioningly. Artem introduced himself and once more announced where I was from and the girls covered their mouths in amazement. Then they sat down with us.

At the end of the meal their father Alliluyev said goodbye and went off to work. He managed an electricity station somewhere in Petrograd.

Olga Alliluyeva – the handsome wife and mother – showed us around the apartment. She explained that Koba was living and working in the third bedroom. This left only the sewing room for us. We found two truckle beds there by a table with a Singer sewing machine on it. After she had left we lay on our backs and looked at the ceiling and waited for sleep to hit us.

Artem said, Alliluyev is a brave fellow. But he's very stupid with his wife and daughters.

I said nothing and let him talk on.

Olga and his daughters all desire that rogue, Koba, and Alliluyev doesn't seem to notice. Koba's a likeable fellow in his way but I'd say he's unreliable with women. A typical Georgian. What do you say in Brisbane? *A bullshit artist.*

I would find out that Georgians were like the Sicilians of the Russian republic.

Artem told me, If I had two daughters, I wouldn't let a fellow like Koba sleep between them and me. Not for a second.

More silence. But uneasiness about Koba kept him from resting.

I suppose he's been very useful to the party. And he's pretentious – Koba isn't a good enough name any more – it's just the name of some Georgian Robin Hood. He's started to call himself Stalin now. The man of steel. His real Georgian name would be four times as long as that!

By now Artem's voice was drowsy.

I'd watch those girls, he repeated sleepily. All eyes for Koba.

I still had not heard why we were in Petrograd or what job Artem had been given. But Artem was asleep.

*

When Alliluyev came back from his job in the evening there was a merry dinner. (Koba wasn't there because he stayed out late editing *Rabochii Put – Workers' Way* – in the cellar it was produced in.) Wine was passed around and even Artem had a little. The Alliluyevs' eyes were a circle of admirable Russian smiles under the light of the apartment's chief electric globe. They told Artem stories and – without being asked to – left gaps for him to translate for me. The reason Lenin hadn't surrendered to the authorities in July – as Trotsky had – was that he found out from his sources among the gendarmes that there were two officers assigned by the provisional government to shoot him dead on the way to prison. And so he'd left his sister-in-law's flat and come here – into this very apartment.

I looked around, amazed. This man they talked about as if he were the centre of the earth had been here, maybe in the kitchen or resting in the sewing room.

So Vladimir Ilich Lenin had to be got away, the tale continued, but he needed a disguise. Koba turned up and started working with the Alliluyevs to disguise him. Olga swathed his head in bandages but he looked like a mummy. Alliluyev suggested he wear a dress. But everyone laughed that idea off the face of the earth. Koba offered to shave him. He became Lenin's barber, covering Vladimir Ilich's face with soap and wielding the razor in front of a shaving mirror in the anteroom. Soon the job had been done and the moustache and beard were off. Lenin thought it was a pretty good job and was very pleased that he looked like a Finnish peasant now. Then Koba and Alliluyev took him to one of the railway stations – better not to say which one – and off he went and was still out there somewhere.

We went to bed before Koba came home – though the women were determined to wait up for him.

All right, Paddy, Artem told me when we lay flat on our beds, I'll be met by a man tomorrow morning, and he'll take me to a railway station. And from the railway station to a secret place.

There was quite a pause then.

They don't particularly want you to come along. But I do – because of the people you'll meet. You see, I want you at some stage after the danger's over to write a piece for the *Australian Worker* and the others – to show people how autocrats treat men of great talent. Again, mentioning no geographic names. You won't know a thing about where you're going even when you get there. But the thing to bear in mind is this: you could in theory be arrested by the gendarmes or the Okhrana and be grilled by them.

More deep thought.

Anyhow, he went on, I talked to Alliluyev and he said it would be okay on those conditions. So do you want to join me on this mysterious excursion? He laughed as if he did not need an answer.

I told him I'd tag along.

You know what? he asked. They suggested we give you a stick so you can pretend you're a blind man. But that takes some doing.

Yes. I don't like that idea.

He grew quiet and I didn't hear from him again that night.

13

Koba was just stirring himself as we left the apartment the next morning. He appeared from his room in his collarless shirt and pants and embraced Artem and then me. Bon voyage, Comrade Wah-wah! he yelled.

I thought that today there was a bit less malice in it.

We went downstairs and this time there were no Red Guards and no car. Just a wiry little man even shorter than me and with a tugged-down cap. He was smoking and when he saw us he stubbed out the cigarette and put it in his pocket. He said nothing but led us outside to a tram line.

Artem whispered, See the gendarme on the corner.

In case we were followed we kept changing trams, rushing from one to another. Then we'd get off and hurry up a string of laneways until we reached another avenue and a different line. The little man seemed happy with the third tram we caught. We crossed the famous Nevsky Prospekt and I won't bang on about all the great buildings there – just that it was magnificent with the great white buildings stretching away, as well as a string of palaces and church domes with hammered gold all washed with rain and glinting in the dawn.

Lots of people were already on the streets selling things and holding signs. The poorer prostitutes were still working. There were so many of them standing about. It looked like the city couldn't satisfy its hunger any more and turned to this army of street women.

Artem pointed out a four-domed church, and then a fortress on an island. That's where Trotsky is. The Peter and Paul Fortress.

A few minutes later we pulled into the forecourt of a railway station – smaller than the one we'd arrived at the day before. I didn't ask its name of course. Much later I would find out it was the Sestroretsk Station and its line ran along the coast of the Gulf of Finland.

Our little ferret of an escort hopped off the tram outside the station and told us to hurry after him. He rushed us through the grimy columns and raced along a platform and onto a train. The three of us settled ourselves down on the ancient tattered upholstery of a carriage just as the doors were closed.

Not too comfortable, Paddy, Artem told me with a wink.

We rolled out past factories and factory barracks where the workers slept on the premises. Suddenly we were on the shore of the Baltic – though in what direction we were headed I took a lot of trouble not to calculate. Factories gave way to villages and dairy farms.

I saw off the coast what I suspected was the naval island of Kronstadt – where the sailors were in control and had their own soviet that Kerensky's government and the Duma hadn't been able to get under control. It was its own republic. But I turned my head away from the view and didn't ask Artem about it.

We journeyed for two hours among low-set forests and villages that looked less dismal than the ones further south, then we got off the train at a country station. Children in dresses and sailor suits looked down at us with real pity while we stood looking lost at our little siding. Why would we be getting off at a dump like this? they were asking themselves. We turned and began to trudge through the village attached to the siding. The sun was very high. The clouds were milky and the air hazy. Just like in an Australian town, dogs curled up in the dust of the main road. But everything else was different. There was a stone police barracks like a fortress near some local bigwig's two-storey stone house. Everything else was the usual weathered black timber. At the other end of the street we could see and hear a timber mill buzzing away. When we strolled along the road no one took much notice except a sleepy copper on a chair in the gateway of the barracks. He was in his summer uniform – a white soldier's shirt with a wide belt and black pants and boots. He looked at us but didn't think we were any threat to good order. Our escort said he probably thought we were farmers going to the mill to buy timber.

Our guide led us now down a side street to a path that ran around a shallow lake with reeds. The humidity was worse than in Brisbane and the whole area seemed to be alive – sizzling and frying with insects and frogs. The sun bit into our backs but then we came to the shade of birches and the strong-smelling kind of tree they called Russian olive.

Our escort now took us off the track onto a narrow pathway. Ahead of us – set above a field of hay – was a tiny wooded hill and on its slope a little hut with a thatched roof. As we approached we could see the door of the place lay open. Our escort knocked and then took a nervous look into the deep shadow inside.

An older man in shirtsleeves and trousers came to us out of the dimness. He was holding a copy of a Petrograd newspaper and his blue-grey hair was dishevelled. He shook hands with our escort. Then he pumped the hand of Artem and smiled. After a while Artem turned to me and said, Let me introduce Mr Yemelyanov. We're on his property.

Another man in shirtsleeves appeared. He was somewhat younger but he was totally bald and looked a bit Asian. This fellow was a little too thin to be called stocky. He wasn't a peasant and he didn't look like an athlete. But he was an impressive-looking man with the air of someone used to being in control of the room.

Yemelyanov stood back and let Artem say hello to this new man. As he did that our escort took a fresh Petrograd newspaper from his breast pocket and handed it to Yemelyanov. The bald fellow embraced Artem and shook his hand warmly and kissed him on both cheeks. They spoke to each other and then Artem told the other man who I was but did not give me the fellow's name. The man frowned a little and looked at Artem. It was clear I was unwelcome.

Artem spoke up as if explaining me. He didn't seem embarrassed at all and in the end the man extended his hand a bit crookedly and shook mine. His eyes looked Asiatic – Tartar maybe – and though they were half-closed they were beaming. Slowly – from memories of photographs – I realised who it was. This was Vladimir Ilich. He was here – in a humpy that would have been considered rough quarters even in the Barrier Range. I felt the amazement Tasha had felt in Geneva about the ordinariness of Vladimir Ilich's household. This was a very plain old hutch in which to find the leader of the party, the man most feared by Kerensky.

My shock at that was nothing compared to the fact that my first moments with the famous man were marked by his disapproval.

Vladimir Ilich gestured that Artem should join him in the room beyond. I could see a bit of it through the doorway: a desk and heaps of papers and books. Did he bring them with him into exile or had they been supplied by Yemelyanov?

He led Artem through into his little room and shut the door.

In the outer room, Yemelyanov fetched the escort and me some tea in glasses. Then our escort went to sleep as Yemelyanov was more and more absorbed in the newspapers on the table and I just waited – not even taking notes in case they were later found on me by gendarmes – while the day got hotter. It was about noon that the door to the inner room opened again. Vladimir Ilich came out leading Artem.

Vata, Vladimir Ilich said to me – a word I understood. Water. He looked me in the face and said slowly, *Zharaa*. Swimming. Two words in a row I understood!

We followed him out the door and down behind the hut to a little gravelly beach by a pond. There we took our shoes and socks off and then our clothes and we all went running into the water. I was expecting it to be cold since it must have been frozen solid all winter. But in fact it was really pleasant. I saw Vladimir Ilich's bald head as he leaned back in the water and closed his eyes and sort of smirked at the sun.

I went out along the silky bottom till the water was up to my armpits. I couldn't swim – I'd grown up too far from the coast for that, seven hundred miles from Sydney and nearly three hundred from Adelaide. In a desert where there were no pools like this one. Yet I felt comfortable here. I watched Artem swimming – where had he learned? – and Vladimir Ilich's skull breaking the surface and coming up shining with water.

After the swim we tried to get the mud off our feet – a job that didn't seem to worry Vladimir Ilich as much as it worried me – and then sloped back up that ordinary hill to the shanty. Artem asked Vladimir Ilich if I could see his room. The great man agreed and I was taken into it. It astounded me how many books he'd managed to get in there. He was still working flat out on a book or article. He had a number of French-language books on the Paris Commune. I would read in time that what Vladimir Ilich learned from the Commune was that the doomed workers of Paris – the Communards – tried to take hold of the state machinery. But taking hold hadn't been enough. One way or another they should have smashed it – that was the concept Vladimir Ilich was busy with.

Vladimir Ilich and Artem went back to work. The escort had vanished. Yemelyanov lay down on a low cot against one of the walls. I sat at the table framing in my mind the further details of the ultimate piece I would write on this extraordinary visit.

A mop-haired man in a good suit without a collar arrived late in the afternoon of that first day. He carried a small-bore rifle in one hand and two hares in the other. Hearing his voice Vladimir Ilich and Artem came out to greet him. He told them he'd wandered off Yemelyanov's land and onto a neighbouring estate where the gamekeeper had caught him and wanted to have him arrested. But he pretended to be a visiting Swede unable to understand the gamekeeper.

Now the man handed the two hares to Yemelyanov and sat down very happy with his day's work. But he didn't look like a hunter at all – probably one of the reasons the gamekeeper let him go.

I found out later this man was one Grigorii Zinoviev – fellow exile of Vladimir Ilich and a man who sometimes irked him. This supposed hunter still had traces of rabbit blood on his fingers as he began a lively conversation with Artem about things going on in the capital and then about moving pictures. Vladimir Ilich laughed when the matter of the flickers came up and went back into his office but this time left the door open. Zinoviev asked Artem had we been to see Vera Kholodnaya in *The Song of Triumphant Love*, based on a book of Turgenev's I eventually read and found overblown. The picture was just out and apparently packing them in in Piter. But Artem explained to the hunter that though the cinemas were still crowded in Petrograd we hadn't had a chance to go yet. The hunter said he believed Kholodnaya would be a great actress of the revolution and that Sarah Bernhardt was drab beside her. It would be essential – come the day – that we would make lots of big films to get the message out to people. It would be the best way.

At the end – exhausted by his adventures – the hunter lay down on his cot in the hut's third room separated by a curtain. The rest of us went out with Yemelyanov in the long twilight to help him cut his hay. I took up a sickle instead of a scythe – since it looked easier for a beginner. Artem – who'd done this sort of thing when he was young – cut like a machine, in big semicircular swathes. Vladimir Ilich was a better reaper than you would have guessed too – as if he'd once taken a few lessons from peasants.

We went back to the hut where an outdoor kitchen had been set up – probably by some unseen servants of Yemelyanov's. There was a samovar sitting on a steel plate to one side. On a spit above a fire the pink bodies of the skinned rabbits were being roasted. Yemelyanov turned the spit now and then. I watched him and wondered how he had become a Bolshevik. He didn't seem like a city bourgeois or the owner of an estate.

The rabbits were served up in bowls once they'd been cooked through and were so succulent I forgot all about politics. The fire kept the insects away from us and our repast.

When it was time to sleep Zinoviev and I chose to bed down outside. I went to the privy down the hill a little and – as I later comically boasted – sat on the same seat as Vladimir Ilich had. Once I settled on a blanket in the twilight I found that the air was thick with mosquitoes again. But I slept.

The dawn came up very early and rain began to fall. Zinoviev and I went inside.

Vladimir Ilich had already begun talking to Artem again in the office. Later, Artem told me what he and Vladimir Ilich had talked about on the first morning and the second of our visit. On the first morning he told Artem he wanted him on the Central Committee of the Bolsheviks and that voting him in could be managed. (What would Federev think of Artem's promotion if that happened?) He could then go back to Kharkov and begin to ready the party for an armed uprising against the provisional government and the Ukrainian Rada and all the rest. We must act soon, Vladimir Ilich told him, or the autocrats will use the All-Russia Congress – due to meet in October – to wipe us out. The slogan *All Power to the Soviets* was all very well, but Kerensky's provisional government wasn't going to allow all power to go to any Council of Soviets. The council was full of temporising Mensheviks anyhow – they'd never rebel! Kerensky – flitting between the old tsarist parliament the Duma on one side of the Tauride Palace and the Council of Soviets in the other wing of the palace – wanted to put the two together like a donkey and a horse to make an impotent creature. It was a useless mule of a thing.

This is at least the way I put down Artem's version of the whole interesting conversation.

The rain went on. In the outer room the rest of us moved around to escape the leaks that were even more plentiful than in your average bark-covered hut in Australia. When Artem emerged from Vladimir Ilich's office it was well towards noon.

Artem told me he had asked Vladimir Ilich whether he knew Suvarov – our old friend from Brisbane. Vladimir Ilich said Suvarov was active in Vyborg at the crucial Putilov works – important since its workers numbered in the tens of thousands.

That afternoon – a miserable, humid, drizzling affair – Vladimir

Ilich started packing his books into suitcases. It was normal for him to move around to avoid arrest and it would turn out that he intended to go north into Finland. For that he and Zinoviev needed passport pictures taken. A photographer they called Dimitri turned up with a bag full of wigs and moustaches and a camera. Vladimir Ilich and Zinoviev tried the wigs on and then the photographer told them to lie on the ground and he took passport pictures of them from above. He printed them – using emulsions and chemicals and whatever photographers use – in the curtained section of the hut. It took a while. But he came out smiling.

Lenin and Zinoviev then clasped Artem to their chests and shook hands heartily with me. Yemelyanov arrived with a farm wagon and into it Vladimir Ilich and Zinoviev piled with their suitcases. In the twilight – with a blue-coloured sun falling downwards very slowly in the sky and making the Russian olives shine – Artem and I started back along the road to the station to catch the train to Piter.

Artem's insistence that I come with him would eventually pay dividends. In time – when Vladimir Ilich was safe again – my narrative was published in all the socialist papers from Australia to London to New York to Chicago. The world could see what a tyrant Kerensky was to chase good men into the wilds of Russia and Finland.

14

We had to stay at the Alliluyevs' for two days waiting for the Sixth Congress of the Party where Artem was meant to be elected to the Central Committee. I was – to my shame – ignorant of when the other five were held. The first day at the apartment I spent finishing my article and translating an article Artem was writing for *Proletary* into English. The next day we went with Alliluyev and caught a tram across town to the gate of the Smolny Institute. This building – very beautiful on the outside with high windows and decorated cornices and archways at ground level – was where all the radical groups had their offices now.

We stepped off the trolley car and walked across to the heavily guarded gate. In the grounds, machine-guns were dug in – some of them manned by sailors from Kronstadt. The soldiers were from the machine-gun regiment and the Red Guards were from Vyborg. Some of the Red Guards wore bowler hats and others caps to top off their mix-and-match uniforms. There were also girls in factory pinafores and jackets – armed with rifles and looking martial. The idea was that Kerensky was going to think twice about sending troops to rout our people out of this building.

Alliluyev got us past the guards at the gate. We walked up an ornate staircase and along a corridor. The room the Bolshevik Party – now given a capital P – were to meet in was a big old classroom. For the institute had till recently been a school for the daughters of the nobility. As I would find out there were much flasher rooms in the Smolny Institute, but they were for general meetings between the factions. In any case we didn't quite have the authority yet to take one of them over for our meetings.

Classroom No. 18 was full of soldiers and workers communing in the usual fug of raw tobacco smoke. I didn't mind mixing with the unwashed for the good reason I was one of them and added to the overall aroma, which after time a person got used to. But that tobacco smoke! Artem went up to a table that a number of men sat around sweating over lists of names. When Artem came back to me he had a piece of paper in his hand.

This says you're an observer, Paddy.

Artem had also shown the men at the table a note from Vladimir Ilich that made him a full voting member. I could see the good-looking Alexandra Kollontai up there at the front table – the finest figure in the room and looking fresh after her exile in New York. America didn't seem to age people like Zurich and Geneva did. A bespectacled man named Lev Kamenev coughed harshly to bring the room to order and everyone sat down on chairs or leftover desks or leaned against the walls. There was an agenda before the election – there always was. People spoke at great length and without notes. The big debate was – and I would read this in history books that would elevate classroom No. 18 to a position you wouldn't have guessed possible if you'd seen it – the very same question of that day.

I know from transcripts published later what was said there but I could have guessed it anyway. A young factory worker started out. If all the organs of government were seized here in the capital of Russia – well then – with the help of our brothers and sisters in Moscow and elsewhere all else would have to follow. An old Bolshevik named Yvgeny – whom Artem had known when he was organising the railway workers in Perm – shook his head. He'd read his Plekhanov and even his Vladimir Ilich of the past. It was a given fact that there had to be a proletarian revolution in the West before backward Russia could stage one. In fact Vladimir Ilich himself had once said that. Another man yelled from the floor that that was all very well. But Russia was the only place where the iron was hot.

Just the same, delegates – the civilians and the soldiers and the young women wearing ammunition belts over their summer dresses – were surpisingly polite to Yvgeny. His motions against the revolution were put on the agenda paper and they were read out and soundly defeated.

Then an amusing fellow, Nikolai Bukharin, came to the rostrum. He was treated with respect – he had been with the Bolsheviks a long time and suffered exile. He had written a great book on imperialism which at a later date I would read in Russian. He was a good speaker, smiled a lot, and occasionally people in the hall laughed. But he also had a motion on the agenda – he too argued a revolution wasn't possible at the moment.

You could tell most of the men and women in the room didn't want to hear any of this. They knew the Mensheviks were along the hall devising means to continue the war 'defensively'.

Alliluyev was now recognised by the chair. The soldiers in the garrison towns in the rear would follow us to a man, he argued – the Bolsheviks were the only ones who wouldn't send them to the trenches to fight for something that didn't interest them at all. Especially when they know that they wouldn't get proper food or proper clothes when winter struck.

When Bukharin's motion was put to the vote, it was voted down too. Across the room I suddenly saw Slatkin's sharp face. He hadn't dressed down to suit the proletarian company. He was keenly watching everything.

Koba was up by now and could have been entertaining the crowd as a comedian if I hadn't known he was talking politics. He'd helped Vladimir Ilich escape and declared himself now in favour of his leader coming back to Petrograd and appearing in court – but only if his safety could be guaranteed. No one should surrender without guarantees. But if he came back the trial itself might bring on the revolution.

The congress ran till close to midnight and after the last round-up conversations ended we caught a tram back to the Alliluyevs'. And next morning it all started again. No one could say that Russians were shy with their oratory or their contrariness. Koba's motion from the day before – that Vladimir Ilich should turn himself in – was voted down. He took the loss without emotion – I'm tempted to say with good grace except there was something about him that made such polite terms irrelevant. The tiger doesn't take the loss of the gazelle with good grace!

So at last they got around to electing a Central Committee of the Bolshevik Party. Vladimir Ilich got the most votes, of course, but among the others was a thin Pole named Dzerzhinsky and Alexandra Kollontai. Artem was elected eighth and got more votes than Koba. He now had the full authority of the Central Committee with him.

We caught the train to Kharkov that night. The list of the Central Committee was already published in the papers – in which I searched out Artem's name and pointed it out to him. It was mid-morning the next day before we were back in Kharkov and took a tram to the Gubin mansion. Here we went past the guards and up the steps into Federev's study. When he saw Artem, Federev's eyes glittered too fiercely – like those of a man trying his level best to celebrate in a way he didn't feel inside himself. But he had a letter from Australia for Artem. He'd collected it from his postbox at the apartment and now handed it over.

Artem held the letter in his hand as he and Federev inspected a map of the city mounted on the wall. Then they moved on to a further map of the outskirts. I went out and waited in the hall and when he emerged Artem held up the letter as if it were a treasure to share and led me to a parlour behind the guardroom. He sat at a remaining occasional table and read it carefully. When he was finished, he passed it to me.

It's from Hope Mockridge, he said.

At the top of the page was her address in St Kilda in Melbourne and a date from three months earlier.

Dear Artem,

I hope things go well in your native country. The newspapers here say that the provisional government is falling apart, and that must be good news for you. I know you must be very busy now, but I needed to report to you on what is going on in Australia.

Walter O'Sullivan and his demented wife are still running their party as their own small cell. They make no effort to go into the factories and talk to the real workers in hope of raising their perception of the world. I think that at heart they have contempt for working people and soldiers. In regard to soldiers, let me say incidentally that the casualties from France have multiplied horribly.

When Buchan and I undertake the tasks the O'Sullivans neglect, and go to speak to the waterside workers and the men in the heavy engineering section of the railways, O'Sullivan attacks us in his newspaper using words such as 'syndicalists' the way other people might say 'scoundrels'.

We have got our labour college up and running, and all manner of men and women attend – the range of our lecturers is much praised by the people who attend. Of course, nothing like it has been done by O'Sullivan's branch. In the meantime I trust that you and Paddy, and Grisha Suvarov if you have met him, are all in the pink. Every news report from Russia tells us that food is scarce. And the accompaniment of hunger is, of course, disease. So please take care of yourselves.

Could you please write us a letter supporting Buchan's and my labour schools, which are open to anyone who wants to attend – except, naturally, agents of the police. If you could express in your letter the opinion that Walter O'Sullivan is mistaken in his attitudes, it would be a great service to the movement and to socialism generally in Australia. For O'Sullivan does nothing but meet with his small band of supposed conspirators – in reality sycophants – who have done nothing, absolutely nothing, but talk among themselves. Do you have similar men in Russia? Men who think that the revolution will be achieved by angels, not by men and women who sweat at their work? I suppose you do, since human nature is the same everywhere on the globe.

In the hope that you are free of all threats, I remain,

Your sincere friend,

Hope Mockridge.

I finished reading the letter and Artem looked at me in the way Dickens used to call 'quizzical'.

Too early, wouldn't you say, Paddy, to ordain a socialist pope in Melbourne?

Especially Buchan, I agreed.

Yes indeed. On the other hand, speaking of Kharkov, my sister Trofimova is too good and competent a woman to be left in her little miner's cottage wearing her black sash. At the end of the month we have a meeting in Ekaterinoslav again, and I've asked her to turn up at that. We'll bring her to Kharkov with us.

I felt anticipation and nervousness. It seemed he had his womenfolk well organised – Tasha and her sister in the office opposite ours and Trofimova on her way. That sort of skill was beyond me.

15

So there we were at the end of the month standing under the great murky rafters of the Briantsk factory in Ekaterinoslav. The uplifted faces Tom spoke to seemed pale and anxious, but expectant as well. Federev and his aides were also in Ekaterinoslav and Trofimova was due at some stage, but – for whatever reason of organisation – Tasha and Olya had stayed in Kharkov.

I had noticed that Artem and Tasha had recently gone for many secretive walks together and shared long conversations in the basement dining room at the Gubin mansion. Other people – even the guards – were sensitive enough not to sit down with them. Olya seemed a bit awed and bemused by what was happening and looked lost as she dined among young women from the Red Guards.

It had been a hectic month since we'd seen Vladimir Ilich in his cabin. My main memory is of great factory ceilings and dimness. And of oratorical heat and fire. Businessmen in Kharkov were frankly telling the press they'd like Germany to advance – in spite of the ceasefire – and take the Ukraine and Russia over and subject them to their gift for administering foreign nations. That's the size of what we were up against. Yet when I think of that month of crisis and arguments and meetings I remember above all Artem's good humour in debate – in a month when other people's faces and delivery were getting grimmer and more sour. Up in the north-east the great General Kornilov decided he was going to capture Piter and save the provisional government from the soviets. Artem would ask audiences, Do you agree that we need to be saved from ourselves? Do we agree with Kornilov? Are you a man, are you a woman, who needs to be saved from yourself?

One night Artem and Tasha and a host of newly elected officers and NCOs from the barracks around town hurried into Federev's office. For a telegram had arrived at the Gubin mansion announcing that Kornilov's Third Cossack army were on their way to Piter under his command. Even in Kharkov everyone other than those who would benefit from Kornilov's success was thrown together by fear. Kornilov intended to put an end not only to Bolsheviks and the Council of Soviets but even to Kerensky and his Duma. There was an emergency meeting of the Kharkov soviets at the town hall. The soviets comprised all sorts of people, even some of the Cadets who didn't want Kornilov to win, who didn't want to do away with what had happened the February before and didn't want the tsar back. Even the Rada delegates, from the Ukrainian parliament, were as scared as anyone in Petrograd by Kornilov's advance. Because – under Kornilov – the tsarist oppression would be back.

Artem moved a resolution at the municipal soviet – attended by soldiers from the regimental soviets – about placing troops on the main roads leading to Kharkov. It was passed not only by our people but by the Mensheviks and socialist revolutionaries as well – the threat of Kornilov made us all brothers. Dear Olya herself rose and moved that a military council should now be created to handle the defence of Kharkov and all the hands went up again. Artem – with the great authority of being a member of the Central Committee – was elected. So was Federev and a sergeant-major named Brevda – a veteran of the Galician front – and a strong-minded factory foreman by the name of Ismaylov.

I was up early at the Gubin house when Federev's young men started to arrive by car and come into his office. They seemed to like wearing leather jackets and army pants with glistening boots. This morning as they brushed past without looking at me I smelled cologne on them and something else – something peppery and clinging. I'd smelled it infrequently before: it was cordite. I knew at once what had happened. Federev had sent them around the city to shoot the men who would have welcomed Kornilov and his tsar. He had built up his list with the help of these clever young aides and now he had cleared it.

I chose to tell myself we were at war. The idea of revolution would not protect itself by its own force. It had to have its acolytes. Federev's boys? I pushed aside the question of whether Artem knew. I also pushed aside the question of whether it mattered to me whether he did or not. Soon I was busy enough myself. I found myself travelling out of town with Brevda the sergeant-major and Tasha and Olya – who wore army coats themselves – in trucks laden with boilers and mobile ovens and army cooks we'd gathered up from army barracks. We'd done it all without having to ask anyone's permission. Tasha and Olya sat forward on their seats. They were defiant and tense. Brevda was a man with such a huge grey moustache that you had to look at him closely to see how young he was – maybe twenty-five or so. A person could only imagine what had turned his moustache grey.

We laboured together with other men and women to set up a field kitchen and bakery in a meadow of rank grass on the side of the Sumi road. The sisters worked cheerily and seemed to enjoy the country air that might soon be full of the Cossacks' shells. I reflected while we worked that the matters in which I had been educated by now ran from stealing firearms to putting together makeshift field bakeries to rudimentary Russian. And I was as good as anyone else as a packhorse and a collector of timber and water for the boilers.

Some of the NCOs my sergeant-major knew came across the field from the woods or camps on low hills to chat with him. Many of them were commanding regiments and they were too serious to tease or flirt with the women working on the bakery as soldiers usually might. They were the first fair-dinkum field commanders I would meet and most of them were much younger than the colonels or majors who had once commanded their battalions. These men out here – wearing red armbands over their sleeves – were willing to fight under their own authority to beat back Kornilov and his Cossacks. One of them told Brevda that Kornilov couldn't beat the Germans so God would make sure he didn't have a chance with us. God was still powerful in the minds of some of our soldiers even though the tsar no longer was.

That night the sisters and I took a truck back to Kharkov. I crept into our office and found Artem still turning in his bed obviously awake.

What is it like out there? he asked.

I told him how hard the sisters had worked and about the impressive regimental elected leaders I'd met. I heard him sigh.

After a while he said, It's a wonderful thing that they've all been elected. But when they give orders, will the men obey them or take a vote?

I remembered the smell of cordite on the leather jackets of Federev's men. Artem must know about it – that's what I decided. He was a member of the military council of Kharkov. Surely Federev just didn't do it off his own bat without saying anything.

So I thought – in a way I hadn't thought about it that morning, in a way that seeped through me like a dye – it *is* war!

I fell asleep but seemed to be instantly awoken by Artem. He roused me with the idea that like Olive O'Sullivan I could and should write about absolutely everything. A person should be awake to see all there was to see. In any case I woke up quickly at that stage of history. We drove around at the head of a convoy of trucks all the rest of the night and collected rifles and machine-guns from warehouses – accumulating as many as we could fit at the mansion. We packed out the main building and the stables and even the garage and a garden hut. From an early hour we handed them out to new Red Guards who came tramping through the Gubin mansion saying they were ready to go to battle for the city. I saw young factory girls in army caps and wearing red armbands taking rifles as if glad to get hold of them. Some of the slighter girls would slump a little under the unexpected weight of their firearms. Over the next day or two, Artem and the war committee would start arming the rest of us.

One morning I woke from a two-hour sleep on my cot upstairs and found the room empty. I dressed and then ran downstairs. Artem was in the entrance hall, fresh-faced though not shaven and wearing his soldier's jacket. (I still wore the old checked suit I'd bought in Broken Hill but it was getting worn and might not last the coming winter.)

In the avenue beyond the gate I saw a crowd of soldiers and Red Guards. The street was choked with them and though they weren't in strict columns they seemed ready to move on orders. I had never seen so many armed men and women in the one place and it was intoxicating in its way but also took your breath with a kind of dread. The sentry on the gate knew me and nodded his head. He too was in good humour. He called me Tovarich Dikesh. I noticed men in football uniforms – blue and white – from one of the Kharkov teams. They looked strange with their rifles slung on the shoulders of their jerseys.

Back inside the building I saw Federev and Sergeant-Major Brevda cross the lobby with three aides and signal to Artem; Ismaylov the factory worker must have been attending to business elsewhere. Federev was dressed up for the excitement of the day in a snug leather jacket and military pants and boots. He smoked Turkish cigarettes non-stop – many more than he had in previous days in his flat. He had taken to barking at his young men in their trim uniforms in a voice full of nervousness and urgency. I took the time to look at the closed and neutral faces of the three young assassins. I decided I'd think about what they had done after the coming battle.

Artem called to me once the conference ended.

A big military procession today – right through the square. Just so Kornilov's spies know we're not under strength.

Then he beckoned me and I followed him across the hall into the guardroom that had been a small ballroom or a large parlour. I had not actually been in there before. I found it messy – a dosshouse for soldiers and Red Guards. But the open spaces on the floor among the blankets were crowded with stands of Mannlicher rifles and the empty racks from which rifles had been taken and put into the hands of the citizens outside.

Isn't this a sight? You should get yourself one while there are still some left.

I don't think I'm a military man yet, I told him.

You looked military enough with that Mauser.

Artem took one of the rifles and forced it into my hands.

Best to take it now, he repeated. He picked up four clips of bullets. Put the clips in your pocket. We'll get you some rifle training when we can.

Did he foresee some final stand against the Cossacks in the Gubin house? I leaned the heavy rifle against the wall. It would never feel like an extra limb to me the way it seemed to be to the soldiers. When I walked I was half embarrassed at the unfamiliar weight and clink of the ammunition clips in my coat pocket.

As Artem had described there was a great fraternal march of soldiers and Red Guards through the middle of the city at noon that day. He and I watched with Tasha and Olya from the running board of a truck in the square near the Russian Cathedral of the Epiphany. It was led by two members of the military council – Federev and Sergeant-Major Brevda. Artem did not want – or else need – to be seen as a general.

At the end of the march, Federev – standing on the tray of a truck – gave the final exhortation to the troops. The parade broke up into detachments and marched out on various roads to the outskirts to join troops already in place. It bowled me over that all this show of force had been put together inside the walls of the Gubin mansion.

Back at the Gubin house I wrote my article on the events of the day while Artem and the other members of the council met in Federev's office. Red Guard dispatch riders constantly came in on motorbikes with their reports for Artem and he was woken many times in the night so that he could read messages from the defence line. He'd wander out of our room and once came back in to say, They wake me up to tell me nothing's happening. Hooray!

It was about three o'clock in the morning when someone woke me again. The moonlight from the uncurtained windows was so bright at that moment that it looked a solid mat of white-blue thrown across the floor. It was Olya who had shaken me. Her eyes looked panic-stricken. She whispered to me in simple Russian, *Kyda Tasha*? Where is Tasha?

I noticed Artem's cot wasn't occupied. Fortunately I was wearing my old suit pants and shirtsleeves, so I stood up crookedly and shook myself out of a messed-up dream of Trofimova.

We went out onto the landing where some Red Guards had chosen to sleep. Some stirred, and one of them laughed and growled in an encouraging way – as if Olya and I were ourselves setting off on some sort of tryst. It was a fair assumption. I knew the day that had passed was exactly the sort of day on which a girl might give herself to a man. Such an exciting day in which Artem and Tasha had their important roles! By the bright moonlight through a glass dome above the stairwell and the hallway I could see the dark distress in Olya's eyes as we went down to the lobby. She knew and I knew what was happening somewhere not far away.

Artem tramped in the front door while we were still on the stairs. As he came towards us he stopped. He had a new presence to him – the idea that he'd crept out to the lavatory to answer a call of nature was out of the question. Olya rushed down the stairs, hoping to see her sister. Artem called after her to reassure her.

I saw Tasha come in from the night with her sister. She looked radiant and flustered but her sister was lecturing her.

The hell with it, Paddy, Artem told me softly. I was with Tasha but nothing happened. The girl needs such a lot of tender reassurance. It's not Olya's business to lecture us. Does she think I'm some animal? Worse still, does she think her sister is?

Artem – who had probably entered first out of gallantry and to save Tasha's blushes – turned down the stairs again and when he reached the bottom linked his arm defiantly with that of Tasha. Olya glared. But it took stronger people than Olya to put Artem in his place.

We separated from the sisters at the top of the stairs. Artem chastely kissed Tasha on the cheek and then her sister took her back to their room where we could hear them arguing. The Red Guards on the landing stirred. Artem stood a second at their door and hissed an angry command at Olya. Olya immediately began to weep and sought out her bed. Then Artem and I went back in to our cots.

Artem began speaking like a conspirator. There are in fact three Cossack armies over in Novocherkassk. Someone woke me up earlier to tell me. What their intentions are I have no idea. But they could swallow us whole if they tried.

It was a good distraction from the question of Tasha and him.

I asked, Is Trofimova in a safe area?

I had heard all sorts of things about Don Cossacks being terrible raiders.

I told her to wait for us in Ekaterinoslav. But you can't depend on her to be obedient. Or on the Cossacks to stay where they are.

The thought of Cossacks and Trofimova kept me awake two hours. Surely Artem wouldn't have been so calm if he thought his sister in danger. I looked over at the corner where I could see clearly the rifle I'd been issued. It was impossible to imagine using it in anger. But to save Artem? To save the sisters? And Trofimova!

Federev might be a different matter . . .

16

After a week, the Cossacks had not moved. The brave railway men over in the east at Novocherkassk – Mensheviks though many of them might have been – had made things difficult for them by holding up the arrival of fodder and grain in that town. It was decided to be safe for us to attend a coming congress in Ekaterinoslav. When we arrived there by train we went by truck straight to the technical university where I searched the crowd for Trofimova's face. Artem's speech had been so well advertised that if she was in the city she could not *not* have heard about it.

It was when Artem came down from the platform to almost universal applause that Trofimova presented herself, smiling and wearing a green autumn-weight dress with an embroidered neck and not a shawl or a sash but a citified felt hat. I felt a stab of warmth for her. She kissed her brother on both cheeks and then me – smiling but giving no signals. Maybe she wanted me then or later to make some new gesture towards her, but I didn't have enough experience to know what I was meant to do.

She kept her mysteries to herself as she travelled a few days by train around the Donbas with us – to Krivoi Rog and Zaporozhye, where she stayed overnight in the women workers' room in any hotel or party headquarters available to her. We stayed in the men's barracks.

She was a very jolly travelling companion and would wink at me at times. But they were not amorous winks. I'd seen other men in the state of confusion I was in and had always thought what idiots they were. Now I was the idiot.

In Krivoi Rog they put us in a mansion. Artem started work with the local military committee to put outposts on their approach roads. Would that hold the Cossacks? I was wondering as I waited in the lobby. I saw Trofimova appear from the back of the house. She said in Russian and without a smile, Come! *Suda!* My Russian education had proceeded to the point that I understood her. She led me off to the back of the house like a sister comrade bent on serious business. We went down a corridor and suddenly she stopped and flung open a door. Here – in what must once have been a servant's room – there was a bed and a mattress that had seen better days. She gestured me in as if she wanted me to paint the place. The door closed and she clamped her mouth on mine. Then she fell on the bed and the embroidered skirt was lifted as an invitation. Which of course I accepted with so much gratitude I would have had trouble uttering it.

In each of the towns the breadlines along the pavements were very long. People told us they stood in line for six hours for a few grams. This was what Kerensky's revolution had brought them.

A supply problem, Artem told his sister and me. And a hoarding one.

I looked at Trofimova's frown. Like her smile it took up her whole face and was as beautiful. But I found it easy to imagine her as a pursuer of hoarders.

Whenever we were served a meal in those days, it was chiefly sawdust bread and thin soup with a piece of gristle in it.

Don't enquire into where the meat in the soup comes from, Artem advised one evening in a canteen in Zaporozhye. Just be grateful there isn't more of it! And he'd laugh.

Hunger pangs would wake me a number of times a night in the rooms Artem and I shared. My rib bones had never hung over my stomach like they did now. Trofimova too was gaunter than she had been but it didn't seem to reduce the size of her soul.

Of course I thought her very beautiful in her second dress – the green she brought out of her bag and put on. Green seemed to me a sign of forgotten widowhood. In any case I loved travelling from town to town with those two great spirits.

From the windows of the trains we caught around the coal towns I would see lean-looking peasant-women staring as we went past. It was like they were ready to derail trains if they thought they were carrying any food.

When we got off the train in Kharkov – which I now thought of as home – it wasn't like the old days. There were no bands to meet us. Things were too grim for that sort of thing. We caught a tram back to the Gubin mansion and my hopes rose when I saw it – all the more so since Trofimova was with us. When we arrived we saw the soldiers huddled around smoky fires in the front garden.

As we went up the stairs Tasha and Olya came out from their office–bedroom onto the landing. Trofimova gave both of them the same formal sisterly kiss and then they all disappeared into their room and left Artem and me standing there in our male lack of consequence.

17

Artem insisted I should now learn how to fire a rifle. I still did not even know how to get the clips of bullets I'd left under my bed into the thing. I might have if I'd grown up on a farm as Australians were supposed to. But it was not only that I was unfamiliar with firearms. I had a strange reluctance besides that. I trusted my body but not this added and unwieldy piece of wood and metal. Yet something was afoot and Artem insisted.

One morning a sergeant named Oleg and I – carrying our rifles – jumped aboard a truck crowded with soldiers, which dropped us off in a clearing on the edge of the city. The sergeant started rumbling at me now and raised his own scarred weapon while I imitated everything he did. He shot first and frightened crows out of the woods with a noise that seemed to crack the sky open. My rifle was heavy when I raised it. It buffeted my shoulder so strongly when I fired that I stumbled backwards and Oleg laughed. My shot had plunged the bullet into the earth less than fifty yards from me. But after firing more shots I got to be more at ease with it. I had refused to take up arms in the name of the British Empire and now – in the name of international fraternity – I was learning to shoot people. I know the cause was different. Even so . . . The smell of my gunpowder hung in the air and the uneasy question of the young men in leather jackets and Artem's knowledge arose again.

By noon I was a certified rifleman of the revolution.

Meanwhile the widow Trofimova worked quietly in Tasha's office and was back to wearing a grey scarf around her head like a peasant woman. But I suppose that's what she was. She sometimes came into Artem's office to look at one of our wall maps and she would smile at me briefly. She had a businesslike air about everything she did. Let's attend to this problem. That was the way she went about love. If she did love me, that is. The word had not been uttered even though I now was far enough along to understand it if it had been.

She would stride downstairs with that same air to go into Federev's office without invitation – even though the place had become a sort of Holy of Holies – and view the more detailed maps there. I could tell she didn't like Federev no matter what her brother said. She obviously thought him haughty. But she liked his maps.

One day when making my way with a bucket to the hand pump in the garden, I met her on the landing of the back stairs. These were the stairs the servants used in the grand old days of the Gubin mansion – away from the gaze of their masters. It was an appropriate place for an accidental meeting.

She was looking out the back window at the soldiers in the yard below. Without a conscious thought I took her shoulders and pressed against her and kissed the back of her neck. I called her Zhenya – the taboo first name. She was entitled to brush my hands away and tell me to go to hell. Instead she turned and pushed me into a seated position on the windowsill and found life where I'd never expected there to be any. Then she lifted her skirts despite the risk of being seen or other people using the stairs. (Hardly anyone did anyhow because the revolution had given them the right to use the front ones.) She placed her body over me and mewled in a way that was divine music. To my surprise she didn't simply adjust her dress once all was done but spent quite a time kissing me. Then she stepped back and smiled and straightened her dress and slowly climbed the stairs. She turned once to smile and speak in a lowered voice – Russian endearments.

From then on I felt an ache that was unfamiliar. Now she would smile at me a great deal and one day over barley soup in the canteen downstairs took my hand in hers and then fiercely stared at some Red Guards at a nearby table who dared to smile. The back stairs remained our favourite meeting place.

One night when it was raining hard – it had rained for four days, and Artem and I now had grey army greatcoats to add to our blankets – Artem murmured, I intend to ask Tasha to marry me. She is a wonderful woman. An intellectual but without pretension.

Straight away I thought what I hadn't had time to think before – that he shouldn't marry Tasha. I did not see her as a wife. Despite her gifts as an orator and despite her beauty – which she spent no time on – there was still something flimsy, something contrary to Artem's character, about her. Federev had once mentioned that prison – even though it gave her a kind of prestige – had been hard on her. The problem was that to me Tasha didn't seem to exist beyond her reputation. She was most alive and was a real presence when she spoke at factories around Kharkov. In the Gubin house she was a bit like a ghost.

She's very young, I said – as diplomatically as I could.

So does that mean you don't approve, Paddy?

I just wondered . . . would it do any harm to let a bit of time pass?

No, no harm in normal circumstances, he said without seeming to resent the question. But it seems Tasha is to have a child.

Oh well, I said. I was amazed. They must have met some other time than the night on which he'd protested his innocence. But pregnancy trumped everything.

You'll be my best man, Paddy, of course.

Of course, I said.

What a shame we can't make it a double celebration. Myself and

Tasha, you and Trofimova. She wouldn't be a good peasant if she didn't want to remarry. But you're probably not ready.

I had a sense he was winkling me out. He certainly knew something about Trofimova and me. For once I didn't mind that.

On a rainy Saturday Artem and Tasha were wed at the Kharkov municipal building. Tasha had come all in white and wore a colourful lace shawl. Artem was in his grey jacket with red armband and pants and military boots. Not for the first time a marriage was made because of the seed already in the mother's womb. Trofimova beamed through the ceremony. She didn't have the doubts I had.

Afterwards we all went to Federev's apartment for an excellent dinner of borscht, potatoes, pig knuckle and veal he'd bought from a black-market butcher.

The marriage of Artem and Tasha was a revolutionary marriage. Our living arrangements were not changed to allow the bride and groom to share a room. It wouldn't have worked anyhow – in the Gubin mansion there was no more privacy anywhere for a married couple. The strange thing was that matters were in fact easier for Trofimova and me.

18

In a town named Gorlovka down in the south-east Donbas a meeting of the miners' soviet was broken up by a Cossack regiment that rode into the mining camp shooting and slashing. No one had decided yet on a figure for the miners killed there. The Cossack officers had not taken too well either the strike by thirty thousand Donbas Menshevik and Bolshevik railway men. At the rail junction of Karuga twelve railway workers were shot. But still very few of the men went back to work. Then a town soviet building was shelled by artillery and as a meeting of Bolsheviks fled the building there was another slaughter with the Cossacks yelling, This is what we'll do to all the other Bolshevik Jewish bastards!

This was the intelligence that made its way to Kharkov. Sometimes it was carried by grey-faced survivors.

The problem is, said Artem, to work out if these are isolated instances – a wild regiment here, another there – or if they are all going to behave that way.

This was a thought that frightened everyone.

But in the end the Cossacks are farmers, he reasoned. The only way to their hearts is to promise them land.

We drove out with Sergeant-Major Brevda to visit our outposts in the fields either side of the road to Chuguyev. In a crowded tent

Artem met the veteran officers – men risen from the ranks in most cases, and some of them hard-faced veterans and others surprisingly fresh-faced and poetic looking. All men who'd proved themselves to their soldiers. Artem suggested to them we send emissaries to meet up with the Cossacks. It wouldn't be without peril of course. (Of course indeed! I thought.) Artem told them he was willing to lead the delegation the following night.

Be a good fellow, Paddy, and don't mention anything to Tasha, he said on the way home.

For once I was left behind when Artem was driven out the following night to collect his team at the outpost and roll on in an armoured car towards Chuguyev and Malonovka to parley with the Cossacks. By now our intelligence was that a majority of the Cossacks had at least formed their own regimental committees which their officers could no longer discipline out of existence. Their overall representatives were the people to speak to. With something of a journalist's selfishness – if I was still a journalist after all – I thought I'd miss out on a good tale of a nighttime encounter but as well as that I was worried. Lately Tasha had shed a lot of tears. Sometimes it was Olya who was the comforter. Other times you heard Artem's rumble from within the office. Artem had mentioned she was frightened for their unborn child. And now – in a meeting of the kind being planned by Artem – some small shift of events could lead to it being born fatherless.

Somewhere out there on the dark road at the edge of some dimly lit village Artem was greeting a number of Cossack deputies at an inn.

Cossacks aren't fools – that was one of Artem's constant sayings. Those he met told him their officers had them properly steamed up with the idea that the Bolsheviks meant to put every Don Cossack to the sword and take their crops and womenfolk. It can be imagined what Artem and our other people said: It's your hetman – your beloved leader – who has his eye on your land, boys. And what's happening to it anyway while you're out here fighting your Russian brothers?

The other thing the Cossack delegates told Artem's group was better news: that the artillery units were on the edge of revolt.

That delighted Artem – the father of an unborn child. Babies and artillery are a terrible mix. Kharkov won't be shelled? he asked.

How can we say for sure? asked one ageless Cossack.

Artem was secretive at first when he arrived back by truck about breakfast time and sat with me downstairs drinking bitter coffee. Tasha was pale as she came in to join us and grabbed Artem's offered hand. Yes, still a tigress in the handbills and articles she wrote but there was a gloss of tiredness on her face.

I could tell it worried Artem. He who sat scanning her fine but harried features.

Meanwhile I'd noticed the way Trofimova chatted a lot with the Red Guards in the garden and the corridor. Somehow I could tell she had a gift for remarks you'd call pungent and I heard the men laughing with her. One evening I saw her in Federev's front office speaking in a pleasant and lively way with the lawyer's young aides. Carrying a sheet of paper in her hands she seemed to be jotting down names as these polished young gents uttered them. After half an hour she emerged into the lobby where I was lounging. She lifted the page she had. It was a series of names. I read one. V. A. Bondarchuk. She no doubt intended to take her own action. Surely not as extreme as Federev's men had been. I wondered would Federev himself be all serene with her intended activities.

But the growl and detonations we began to hear two mornings later seemed to show how unreliable the Cossack delegation Artem met had been. There was a period of brief questioning – men and women looking at each other. Is that thunder or what I know it is?

With a group of Red Guards – some of them looking a little paler than they had when parading the streets – Federev, Artem, Sergeant-Major Brevda, Ismaelovsky and I drove. We were all armed – or nearly so. I'd given my rifle to a soldier in the back of the truck to mind.

Those men in the back were clutching their rifles with intent. Listening to the guns of the anti-revolution, carrying a rifle still seemed more fantastical to me than carrying a cane.

From a headquarters tent near the village on the road to Chuguyev we could hear some of our own light guns returning the fire from hilltops around. The southern forces of General Kornilov were moving on us. Artem and Federev studied a map in an impromptu staff tent. It was marked with the names and numbers of our infantry and mounted regiments spread out north and south of the road behind breastworks of various heights and quality.

The noise from both sides' cannons continued. The officers were discontented because as yet – until we captured bigger ones – our guns were of lighter bore than theirs. Everyone seemed to think this was a considerable problem. But both sets of artillery seemed to rock the earth we stood on and make the canvas of the tent shudder. I had never been so close to the firing of such huge machines before. As the shells left the mouths of our nearby inferior cannon they took my breath streaming out behind them.

After a while one of our intelligence officers came into the tent and shouted to Artem that their artillery was strangely disorganised – no concerted barrages, he said. No damage to human beings on our side. Some damage surely? asked Artem. Some scratches and wounds surely. The expert shrugged.

Within an hour and a half all firing had ceased. From the tent flaps we could see that our soldiers still stood by their barricades of timber.

Artem looked at me and jerked his head towards the tent opening. We went outside and got into the front seat of a lorry and Artem told the driver to drive down the road. We drove for forty minutes and then found ourselves in a crowd of wagons carrying soldiers eastwards. Since the Cossack army wore uniforms of the same colour as us, it took me a while to understand we were among a Cossack rearguard and that they were going back the way they'd come. Their generals had brought them to water but they had refused to drink. We stopped and let them all pass us by. Then we turned and rolled back towards our lines and Kharkov.

It was a most astounding journey and it taught me that all military operations have more in common with the ridiculous than newspapers ever say.

19

Trofimova was soon at work in Kharkov's new season of peace. She came into Artem's office where I was working alone on my piece about the Cossack retreat and urged me towards the corridor. Downstairs – at the door of the mansion – she had gathered a squad of about ten attentive Red Guards who seemed flattered to be her helpers. These days she looked a little like an eccentric Red Guard herself, because over her green dress she wore a grey army jacket.

Beyond the gate of the mansion a truck waited for us and Trofimova's Red Guards hauled themselves into the back while we took the seats beside the driver. When the truck began to roll across the city towards the west, she took from her pocket a sheet of paper. I knew she'd been milking Federev's boys for the names of grain and flour hoarders – they seemed to be always on her mind. Now she had her list of possible targets.

She pointed to one name in particular: I. M. Krakowski. She jabbed the name with her finger as if she were crushing a fly.

We pulled up outside an ordinary-looking warehouse among engineering works. Trofimova and I got out of the front seat and her Red Guards had already clambered out and were waiting with a hound-like eagerness. A watchman carrying an ancient rifle emerged from the building. He quickly judged himself outnumbered and pointed to the door of the warehouse as if he was willing to make a gift of it.

We were then inside a vast room stacked beyond the rafters with flour bags marked with the number of puds – the Russian unit of measurement – in them. Two of the Red Guards minded the rifles while the rest of us carried out the half-pud bags – about sixteen pounds in weight – on our shoulders under Trofimova's loud and cheery orders. So we filled the truck. At least four-fifths of the flour in the place was still there by the time the truck was full. Trofimova left two Red Guards to guard the place and tell Mr Krakowski – if he turned up – the flour was no longer his.

Together we now travelled with the truckload across the city to the soviet warehouse a half-mile from the Gubin mansion. In the truck Trofimova grinned at me. She was tickled pink with herself. She had at last become active.

In days to come she would burst out of the Abrasova sisters' office like a high wind. She was bringing bread to ordinary mouths. She was trampling on the profit desires of a bastard named Krakowski and of other bastards as well. She just needed more trucks and guards in order to finish the job. She charmed Artem into allocating them. And if Artem was missing with Tasha – then she charmed Federev's aides. Later Artem said to me, Have you seen Federev scowling? It's because Trofimova's stolen his thunder.

Federev's jealousy – which we had seen hardly at all in the old days – grew by the day. Every day when Trofimova arrived in the yard a group of Red Guards and soldiers would present themselves to her like a mob of kids looking for an outing with a favourite teacher. They loved the idea of relieving merchants of their secret flour stashes. I thought Trofimova moved among these men like a light. She was like the angel of bread.

Kharkov was safe. But it seemed the revolution wasn't. The week after the Cossack withdrawal Kerensky named a new government made up of people he liked: Cadets and old-fashioned Trudoviks – soft Laborites in the style of T. J. Ryan – and smock-wearing Socialist Revolutionaries from the provinces. Kerensky hoped his new coalition might hold out until – in the style of the French Revolution – a constituent assembly was convened. What might bring it down was General Kornilov on one hand or us on the other.

Vladimir Ilich had by now crept back into Piter again. His presence there was an open secret but he was protected by army units who'd turned Red. Every night he was sheltered in a different supporter's flat. As for Krupskaya – well, at the time I had first met Vladimir Ilich in the little hut near the Baltic she was still hiding in Piter. But she ended up joining her husband for a period in Finland and had now returned with him and was also moving from flat to flat.

A thin ill-dressed emissary arrived at the Gubin mansion with a summons from Vladimir Ilich. Artem was to come to Piter. Vladimir Ilich needed his vote in the Central Committee. Artem took it for granted I would join him and write my version of what happened – whether it was a triumph or a bloody disaster. I was to be witness for the English-speaking world. I was not yet aware there were other and better writers in Piter.

Everything was on a knife-edge in Piter. Kharkov would be a safer place for the womenfolk who in any case had their own work to do. The news of our departure sent Tasha into one of her slumps and I felt genuinely sad for her. A woman carrying a child deserved to give off an air of blame and fear at such a time as this – uncertain and dangerous – but there was no open argument between them and no question at all whether Artem should go or not. They were both obedient revolutionaries. Artem had promised to bring Tasha and Olya and his sister on to Piter anyhow – just as soon as things settled down there.

Trofimova accepted the separation as a matter of course. She had her list of profiteers and her gang of Red Guards to occupy her. Federev was too busy to be jealous these days. He had bought a house three doors from the Gubin mansion and he moved half his people there. This was to be a prison for the party's enemies. I hoped that this meant the end of cordite but I was not so sure. And – given I'd heard the Cossack army's cannon – I found I didn't care that much if it didn't.

Artem reminded me to fetch my rifle as the time came to catch the train. Taking a rifle on a train – from my point of view – was a bit like inviting a stranger to travel with you. But I obeyed him.

I slept through the journey to Piter in our corner of a crowded compartment. But I was wide awake as we came into Vitebsk station. If I'd thought it was a shambles earlier in the year you should have seen it now – crowded to the very edge of platforms by sallow women who looked as if they did not care if someone tipped them onto the track and into the path of a locomotive. Whole families were camped here permanently. Women were folding blankets while grannies sat on chests full of clothing and family treasures. Small girls were skipping and men stretched their necks to dry-shave themselves. Over the crush and stench came the desperate twang of balalaikas. The players knew they weren't going to get much out of this crowd for their trouble. Winter was coming and people didn't have a spare kopek. Kerensky was feeding only his army – dreaming it would take up the war again and end the ceasefire and rout the Germans at last. And – on the way – give him a reputation as a saviour general.

No one met us at Vitebsk station. The days of receptions had ended – and properly so. Outside, we waited for a tram which did not come, and were approached by a man who offered to take us in his coal wagon – he was operating it as a rough hackney cab. It was with him that we travelled across the canal. The boards of the thing were ingrained with coal dust. But we didn't mind that. There was too much else to look at. It seemed like the old Piter but all the activity on the streets was more hectic than it had been. In fact it looked as if three-quarters of the population or more were on the streets. Soldiers and sailors were promenading with girls who carried rifles. Some citizens were hawking family jewellery or furniture. Men and women orators by the hundred harangued small crowds which – if you clumped them together – made up thousands of people. The prostitutes on the corners were advertising themselves by now and then leaning against a wall with one leg thrust in front of another. And they were better dressed than the full-time women of the night who'd been so common last time we were here. In the coal man's cranky old cart it took us nearly an hour to reach the outskirts of the crowd outside the gates of the Smolny Institute.

The Smolny was guarded by even more soldiers and Red Guards than before. Not only was the gate patrolled and the garden full of soldiers but now there was a system of sandbagged redoubts that ringed the building. Machine-gun nests behind sandbags were positioned to cover the approaches to the fine arches of the ground floor. There was still a lot of milling of civilians and soldiers going on outside the gate and inside the garden. Everyone was challenged a number of times before being let inside – first at the gate and then at the steps and the doors. Then – in the lobby – the Red Guards wanted to see a person's papers. Someone in the line told Artem that so many government spies had got into the place early on that they were now starting to be very strict.

We got past the gate through the power of the authorising letter Artem carried. At the door though we were held up and he kept turning around and smiling at me with a frustrated look. He kept telling the soldiers at the door he was a member of the Central Committee.

They can't read my pass, Artem complained in English. To hell with it!

The soldier in front of him wasn't impressed at all by this foreign language and gave Artem back his pass and waved him away. But just then another soldier arrived who seemed to be the commander of the sentries though he wore no badges of rank. Artem presented him with his letter of summons signed by Sverdlov, the secretary of the Central Committee. The chief guardian of the door finally let him past. But then he stood in my way and Artem had to argue further with him – I was an aide from a far country and a friend of Comrade Koba of the Central Committee who called me Tovarich Wah-Wah.

Wah-Wah? asked the officer. Koba?

Then he looked at me and laughed and made room for me to pass. So we were inside the front door but there were further queues.

A clerk at a table was filling in new passes with a date on them. Everyone was talking at the same time and at such a pace that I wondered if my simple vocabulary would ever keep up. Everyone was smoking their filthy tobacco at the same time – even some of the women who had little clay pipes in their mouths. Sweat and sour breath rounded out the awful fug of the place.

Here rumour had reached its boiling point and was bubbling on fantastically. Many of them were like old songs heard before. Kornilov had given up trying to take Piter. But Kerensky was going to send all the Bolshevik troops to the front and replace them with army regiments and Cossacks loyal to his government. Some rumours were absolutely fresh. The priests were going to bring out an old icon – the *Krestny Khot*. It showed Christ on the cross and had been used to bless the Russian armies that defeated Napoleon in 1812. Now – in 1917 – its clients wanted it to crush the revolution and those in the lobby who were still believers were disturbed by its magic power.

We were waiting for the clerk to fix us – or refuse to fix us – with a pass when out of the blue Slatkin appeared at Artem's side. Even he smelled of sweat but he also gave off a scent of cologne. Slatkin kissed us both on the cheek joyously and brought us forward and spoke to the clerk at the table. Soon we were free of the scrum and going up the broad stairs to the upper floor.

Slatkin said to Artem, It'd be a tragedy not to let you in, Artem. Vladimir Ilich wants your vote. There are some lily-livered people around here and one of them is our friend Zinoviev. He'd rather be at the moving pictures than grabbing the moment by its balls.

He took us up to the first floor and along the corridor to a classroom marked by an enamel plate identifying it as No. 36. What a No. 36 it was! Not No. 18 where ordinary delegates had met last time. No. 18 had been absorbed by some other faction. Inside No. 36 were clustered the men and women of the Central Committee – wan-looking people in a lot of cases in need of a fresh shirt. I could see the thin Pole Felix Dzerzhinsky and his staring eyes. From photographs I could recognise Trotsky – his masses of hair and his narrow little glasses – writing calmly at a table in spite of all the noise.

Other members of his Military Revolutionary Committee – the same sort of body we'd had in Kharkov – had the whole end of one table to do their work and make their plans on. The wild-haired and exhausted-looking Antonov-Ovseenko wore an undertaker's black tie – crooked. He had been an engineering officer in the tsarist army but was expelled from the army engineering college for baulking at taking the oath of loyalty to Nicholas the Second. Everyone called him Antonov-O. Then there was big tall Dybenko the sailor. His lover Alexandra Kollontai was in the room too. In a spotless blouse and pleated skirt Kollontai looked as if she came from a different planet to the frazzled men.

Seated at one of the two tables was Vladimir Ilich himself. It turned out that indeed he did work here most days – and often well into the evening. Krupskaya was not in No. 36 as it turned out but attended to Vladimir Ilich's normal work while she herself hid in the city.

As Artem arrived in this company some of those at the tables rose from their seats and briefly greeted him and even me. If it was true that there were backsliders here in the room then Artem must have appeared to Vladimir Ilich like reinforcements at a siege.

20

I didn't stay in that august No. 36 for long but went into the room next door where the task of typing up the Central Committee's paperwork was left to a contingent of white-bloused young women. The typists' fingers flew over the keys – their typewriter carriages clanging like street trolleys at a rate that would have impressed dear old Amelia. There I found an edge of a table where I began to write a few notes covering our arrival in Piter and what was happening at the Smolny. Sometimes through an open door I would see Slatkin pass in the corridor. His broad and florid face reminded me of some bush bookmaker. But he seemed to have access to every office.

A tall man in a good suit came into the office where I was working and borrowed a Roman-script typewriter from a corner table and began typing from notes. When he paused he must have heard me muttering over my work in English.

You American? he asked.

Australian, I said.

What in the name of God are you doing here?

I didn't bother going into it. I knew now from his accent that he was American.

Did you know Kerensky's talking this afternoon? he asked me. At the Marinsky Palace. Two o'clock. Remember the old Supreme

Council of Soviets? Used to meet in the Tauride? Well, now they're at the Marinsky. I mean, you ought to be there if you can, sport. It'll be quite a circus. Kerensky's last chance I'd say. Did you know that his father was a high school headmaster and taught Vladimir Ilich Lenin? In Simbirsk this was. In a huge country like this! Bit of a coincidence . . .

I told him I had heard something about that. And I thanked him for tipping me off. But where's the Marinsky Palace? I asked him.

Come with me if you like. We can catch a tram together.

Now the American introduced himself. His name was Reed. Just in case Artem came out of No. 36 I wrote a note explaining why I wouldn't be in the Smolny for the next few hours and left it with a typist. On the way out of the building Reed suggested we had time to get lunch down in the basement – as long as you called cabbage soup a lunch, he said.

We lined up for the soup and bread and ate it at a soup-spattered table. Reed talked all the time. He was writing for an American newspaper called *The Masses.* He asked me where I was from in Australia and I described Broken Hill and Brisbane.

And I thought Portland was a hick town! he said.

Outside in the fresh afternoon I wore the military tunic I'd got in Kharkov. I was still a little sheepish about it – I knew I wasn't a soldier's bootlace. But at least I'd left my rifle behind in the office. But no one laughed at me as we caught the tram across to St Isaac's Cathedral. It was only when we were rattling along that I realised I didn't have any means of getting back into the Smolny again. I mentioned that to Reed. Don't worry, he said, I can fix it.

The Marinsky Palace was a beautiful building of classical lines across a square from St Isaac's Cathedral. I had seen it before but had not known its name. Napoleon mightn't have captured Russia but all the French architects seemed to have done all right here. There was a crowd on the steps of the palace – thousands trying to get in.

We walked down a street off the square – it took us about five minutes. All the houses around the locality seemed to be palaces too. And then we emerged in the corner of the huge Winter Palace Square with its cobbled surface stretching away. We stood and looked across the square to where there were cannon – twelve of them arranged in front of the building to defend it. Others were visible at the side of the vast building. Soldiers stood by them. Kerensky's cannon and Kerensky's gunners. Behind the cannon the artillery horses were being led away somewhere safe – at the back of the palace.

Those boys are Junkers, said Reed. Officer candidates. Kerensky has *them* guarding the place, poor guys! There's a rumour he's moved his government in there. I don't know if it's true or not but the cannon – they sure seem to imply it.

Now he decided we were late for Kerensky's speech. We sprinted back to the Marinsky Palace and Reed turned out to be a bit of an American athlete. The press of the crowd on the steps soon slowed us down. But I saw in front of us a head on top of narrow shoulders – a combination that looked familiar to me.

Suvarov, I called.

If it was Suvarov his head didn't turn.

I said to Reed, I'll just go ahead. I think I've spotted a friend of mine from Brisbane.

My God, said Reed, there are more of your fellows here than there are Americans.

He joined me in my scrimmaging towards the head I was aimed for. I called Suvarov's name again – *Suvarov . . . Grisha* – and the humorous Reed was kind enough to take up the yell as well. Finally the man I suspected of being Suvarov turned around. And it was Suvarov himself – the corners of his mouth pulled down in that smile I knew.

I reached him and turned into a Russian, hugging him and kissing his not-very-well-shaven cheek.

I knew Artem was back, he said. I read his name in *Rabochii Put*. But I thought he was in Kharkov.

Yes. But he's here now.

If I believed in the saints, Suvarov said, I'd say it was a miracle.

I introduced him to Reed.

And what are you doing here? Suvarov asked me. Have the police chased you out of Brisbane?

I'm trying to learn Russian, I told him. And writing pieces for the *Australian Worker.* No shortage of stuff to write about. What about you?

It turned out he'd been at the Smolny since July, working with the Bureau of Factory Committees in one of the classrooms.

I can't wait to hear what that conceited bugger Kerensky has to say, he told me. And he laughed exactly the same laugh he'd had in Brisbane before the police tried to pin Menschkin's death on him.

You'll both enjoy this, Suvarov guaranteed. It's Kerensky's last throw of the dice. This is the fellow who now lives in apartments in the Winter Palace like some tsar and who plays around with his sister-in-law and eats opium.

That's all true, said Reed, from what I hear.

Inside what must have been a big ballroom once – with its columns and its angels and its painted ceiling still intact – more people were standing than sitting. Suvarov started smoking a cigarette and Reed offered him a Turkish one from his own case. Suvarov took it and stashed it away without apology in a pocket for use in the future. It was peculiar how want made people do things like that without feeling any shame.

Onto the rostrum near the front of the stage – partly screened by a crowd of military officers – rose a man I recognised from postcards and newspapers as Kerensky. He had in the past dressed up in generals' uniforms – and even as an admiral – and had carried his hand inside his jacket like Napoleon. But now he was wearing a plain military uniform and stepped out away from the protection of his military staff to hold his hands out – Moses parting the waters. He was a neat, slim fellow, even smaller than I'd imagined. He looked as harried as Suvarov had predicted he'd be. Even now nearly everyone in the hall kept talking. If anything they raised the volume a bit in defiance of his gesture.

I saw Reed strain his ears and begin taking notes on a pad. It was obvious he could speak and understand Russian. He was certainly the one person listening most closely to what Kerensky had to say.

Vladimir Ilich would have been flattered because Kerensky mentioned him within five seconds of starting. He claimed Vladimir Ilich was a criminal at large and often disguised as a woman.

Horsefeathers, Reed told me.

Together with the president of the Petrograd soviet – Bronstein-Trotsky – Lenin told the people and the Petrograd garrison to begin an immediate armed rising. The result would be ruin and pillage and massacre and the death of free Russia. Russia would then be thrown open not just to anarchy and rapine but also to the kaiser's iron might – because Vladimir Ilich intended to do a lot for the German governing classes by surrendering to Kaiser Wilhelm and his soldiers. Vladimir Ilich and all who followed him were guilty of acts of treason to Russia! said Kerensky.

There was a huge amount of yelling and laughter and mockery in the hall. Suvarov shook his head and laughed and Reed scribbled. Kerensky said he was going to make the arrests needed to stop the uprising. Again booing and catcalls and yells as Kerensky declared that he and others would prefer to be killed rather than betray the independence of Russia and the revolution of last February.

A man suddenly climbed onto the rostrum and put a paper in Kerensky's hand. He read it and then he yelled that he'd just received the proclamation the Bolsheviks were distributing to the regiments. It ordered the soldiers of the army to mobilise as for war and await new orders – not from Kerensky himself but from room No. 36 at the Smolny. Trotsky – with Antonov-Ovseenko and big Dybenko – dared to proclaim that any units that failed to obey their order were guilty of treason to the revolution.

This order Kerensky – in contempt but also with fear – read out to the raucous crowd. It was not clear whether the cheers that followed were for Kerensky or for the Military Revolutionary Committee. I wondered if Kerensky himself knew. He shouted that his provisional government had never stood in the way of the liberty of citizens. Now it was going to come down with a heavy hand against those who wanted to destroy the free will of the people. It is time, he shouted, to liquidate the Bolshevik elements!

Amid the howls of the ordinary people in the chamber I could recognise two words that came up again and again. *Inpravda*: lie. *Estmevadia*: shame.

In the end Kerensky didn't so much finish his speech as give it up and step down looking ill – walking out with his escort of officers on his way to get the Bolshevik criminals! That didn't stop the arguments in the Marinsky. The famous Martov – he'd once been kind to Tasha and Olya in their Swiss exile and his face was almost overgrown with white hair of old age – said there would be civil war if the Bolshevik decree was followed by the army. All would fall apart and the tsar – mark Martov's words! – would be back. And so would the Black Hundreds, the gangs of criminals and insane that the tsar had armed with orders to shoot and hack Jews and socialists. To hang them from lampposts with their testicles and penises rammed in their mouths.

I can't say that I wasn't fascinated to see in the flesh these men who had been names to me until now – Kerensky and Martov. But at the same time I started to feel faint. Kerensky and Martov had taken all the air and now there were only the gases given off by the crowd and by the speechifying. And no one had stopped smoking through it all – we could all have been incinerated if the glowing tip of a cigarette reached the grease in our clothes.

We've got to get back to the Smolny, Suvarov told me just in time. Or at least I have to. There's a meeting.

Another meeting, I thought. To go with all the others! The Russians had a bottomless appetite for bloody meetings. But I was going wherever Suvarov went. We said goodbye to Reed. I did not know then that this amiable fellow was putting together articles that would then be gathered to make a classic book of those days – one far superior to my scratchy account.

21

When we made it through the lobby of the Marinsky and stood outside, the fresh, cold air hit me like a kindly slap on the cheek from a mother. But there were no trams. We marched across to the cathedral into a side street skirting the Winter Palace – guarded by cannon and gunners on the orders of Kerensky – and walked flat-out to the Prospekt. Part of the way down this broad thoroughfare we came to sandbags and barbed wire behind which stood soldiers and sailors in place. Though they wore no red armbands we presumed they belonged to us – none of the sailors were for Kerensky. Antonov-Ovseenko – the calm, grubby, tired-looking fellow back in No. 36 – had placed such barriers and squads all around the city to stop Kerensky ordering more of his troops into the area around the Winter Palace.

Suvarov stopped and talked to them and the sailors told him more of their comrades were coming – there were still thousands of them on the way or waiting to come across from Kronstadt in launches and other vessels.

I noticed a string of cars lined up empty along the pavement between the autumn trees. Another automobile on the way to the river rolled up to the barrier and the soldiers and sailors stopped it. Inside were a driver and a prosperous-looking middle-aged man and his wife. The guards told them that if they wanted to get where they were going they'd have to walk. A soldier took to the wheel of their car and roughly kangarooed it into place among the others. Suvarov asked me did I think we should use one of these to get to the Smolny. But a tram was waiting further down the Prospekt and Suvarov and I hurried towards it.

Did you see? Suvarov asked me once we were aboard and rattling along. Those sailors had on their hats the name of their ship. It was *Aurora* – the name of the cruiser in the river. If it starts firing on Kerensky and his cabinet – well, it'll be the end of all blather.

A barefoot urchin jumped on the tram selling copies of *Rabochii Put*, the newspaper Koba had been editing overnight. Suvarov read headlines which told soldiers, workers and citizens of Piter that the enemies of the people had gone on the offensive by bringing into the capital by dead of night the female Shock Battalions of Death from Oranienbaum – a palace west of the city – to join forces with Junkers from the officer schools. Even so some of the Junkers were refusing to defend Kerensky and the provisional government. I thought it was strange that women's battalions – if you were going to have them in the first place – would put together the two words *Shock* and *Death* in their title. You'd think one of those alone would have done. It was another Russian mystery.

A number of delegates and others joined our tram as it rolled along and it was nearly full by the time we arrived at the Smolny. Suvarov knew the clerk on the desk and got me inside again. Then he went into the main ornate hall where once the noble girls of Smolny had danced with naval cadets to a meeting at which – I would learn later – five delegates from each city ward convened with Trotsky and the other members of his military committee. Suvarov represented Vyborg.

I went back to the room where I'd met Reed and tried to get my thoughts in order. There was no message waiting from Artem. Why would there be? As later reading of the history of those days would show – there was a ferment in No. 36 where Vladimir Ilich and a few allies like Artem were trying to persuade the doubters that they must act before the Congress of Soviets met in less than two days' time. Otherwise the party would be swamped and its plans blunted down to nothing – to some daydream of a future always far off.

Now I wrote a note to Artem telling him that I'd found Suvarov – that he'd been working all the time downstairs in the Bureau of Factory Committees. I gave it to a typist delivering documents to take it in to him and I waited. I wrote about the afternoon but did not work at any speed. I was still a bit edgy about the fact Mr Reed was writing the same story as me but with the extra advantage that he could speak Russian and seemed well educated.

When night fell outside the bare windows the darkness looked cold. Even though I stuck to the Roman calendar printed in one of my little notebooks – which said it was October in the world I'd left – it was already in fact the Russian month of November and nights felt even to me as if the air was getting itself together to produce snow. I sat on the office floor with my back to the wall and fell asleep. I slipped into one of those dreams where the same thing happens over and over but it's totally crazy – in this case that Commissioner Urquhart of the Queensland police would cancel all charges against me if I would marry Trofimova, and though Trofimova stood by smiling I couldn't get her to speak. So I began to feel rage towards her. I harangued her as I climbed with Urquhart over breakneck sandstone rocks. Trofimova stopped to smoke a pipe. I didn't know you smoked a pipe, I growled at her. She told me Krakowski – the man whose warehouse we plundered – had given it to her and she didn't want to waste it.

Suvarov woke me. I was embarrassed to be caught asleep on a day like this – when hardly anyone in the Smolny was sleeping. Behind Suvarov I saw Slatkin. He was wearing his usual knowing grin and his overcoat with fur lapels. But he'd taken off his tie and his collar looked greasy in the Smolny style.

Suvarov was saying to Slatkin as I stirred, This is the same argument we had this afternoon. And it's rolling on and on. Then he saw my eyes were open. Ah, Paddy. Welcome back to the evil waking world, my friend. Do you know Mr Slatkin?

I told him I did.

He wants you to go on an errand with him.

I immediately struggled to my feet. Would he put a Mauser in my hand again? With the Junkers placing their artillery in front of the Winter Palace, why shouldn't I have a bloody Mauser?

Ready to go? Slatkin asked.

I was still dopey from sleep. But I said I was ready.

Bring your rifle – though it's only for window-dressing.

I didn't know what in the hell he was talking about but I went and fetched it from the corner of the room I'd left it in earlier – not even leaned against the plaster but lying still like Moses' rod that might turn into a snake.

Suvarov offered me an overcoat. I found this for you, he said. You'll need it tonight.

It smelled of sour wool but I put it on gratefully and followed the two of them out into the hallway.

Where are we going? I asked.

Slatkin placed his finger at the side of his nose. Something about all this fake secrecy and smart-alecry of his angered me.

Tell me, I insisted. Where in the hell are we going?

Slatkin didn't seem put out by my insistence. He said, We're going to meet some of the sailors.

That makes everything clear, I muttered.

You'll be an example to them, Paddy, Suvarov assured me.

Slatkin was for once sober-faced. It's an order of the military committee, he said.

I shook my head but was willing to serve. We bid Suvarov farewell then went down the stairs and pushed and shoved across the crowded lobby.

Out we went through the front door past the sentries sitting at their Mannlicher machine-guns. The soldiers in the garden stood by their fires with a strange mixture of seriousness and dreaminess. Slatkin fetched a rifle for himself from a stacked stand of them and slung it over his shoulder. He collected four young soldiers who had been waiting by a fire and we marched out the front gate to one of the armoured cars now waiting there.

There were two more soldiers in the car. One was standing up on a platform in the middle – the machine-gunner – and another sat at the steering wheel in the front. As soon as we were seated on the benches – rifles between knees – he drove off. Because we were encased in steel I couldn't see out into the streets. But squinting through the front slit of the armoured car they looked strangely empty to me except for trams. Their drivers stood beside them waiting for something definite to happen or for news about which routes were barricaded and which not.

We cut off a main road and followed narrower ones until we reached the river and turned left along an embankment. The armoured car soon pulled up and the machine-gunner got down from his stand and came and opened the rear door for us. Slatkin and his four soldiers and I jumped out. We were right outside the door of a *tabak* – a sort of tobacco and cigar shop that also sold coffee and liquor. It was locked up. But Slatkin gave his rifle to one of his soldiers and crossed the pavement and hammered on the double doors.

One of the leaves of the door opened a crack and I got a glimpse of a young man in a navy blue overcoat. He and Slatkin seemed to exchange passwords and the door opened fully.

We entered a long bare room. All the tobacco had vanished from the shelves and all the liquor from the counter. The room was bare of the normal furniture too – it had a scrubbed table lit by a kerosene lamp set in the middle, and around the table six or seven sailors were sitting. They were drinking vodka out of pannikins – there were two nearly empty bottles on the table.

The fellow at the head of the table was an older man with a heavy beard. By the air of command I saw when he pointed us to two empty chairs he must have been elected to some level of power by the fleet soviet. Slatkin and I set our rifles aside and sat down. A young sailor along the table offered us each a pannikin of liquor. I said no and the bearded sailor frowned at me.

Then – picking up a mug – he flicked some drops left from a previous drinker onto the floor before half filling it and passing it to Slatkin.

Slatkin began talking to the sailors. When he finished the older sailor at the head of the table spread his hands and argued for a while. Slatkin pointed to me. He made quite a long speech then turned to me.

Paddy, he said, if I declared you were a friend of Kerensky – what would you reply? In Russian, I mean.

Inpravda! I said.

Bravo!

He turned back to the sailors and spread his hands like a reasonable merchant making a sale. Then he turned back to me. I'm telling them that if you could come all the way from Australia for the revolution, they can bring all their men across from Kronstadt and at least open fire on the Winter Palace from their cruiser in the river.

I didn't know why they should be at all unwilling. Maybe they couldn't guarantee the movements of their men.

Then Slatkin and the sailors started talking again. I had served my role – as the sort of statue you saw in churches acting as a spur to the faithful. Except for my one word.

When we were leaving there were handshakes all round. The sailors smiled at me and clapped my back again and again. Then Slatkin and I left through the door to the street where Slatkin's four soldiers guarded us on our way into the armoured car.

Slatkin beamed at me as the engine roared. That went very well, he told me. You impressed them, Paddy.

22

I was taken back to the Smolny and vouched for again. Out of curiosity I went through the lobby into the grand hall which just now was serving as a bivouac for soldiers and Red Guards.

The Smolny stink was still very sharp where tomorrow night – apparently – the All-Russia Soviet Congress was to gather where all the delegates of all the factions would meet and argue on the one great issue – to destroy Kerensky and his government or not.

I climbed the stairs to the office in which I'd been working what seemed like an age ago. Three typists were still typing flat out in there. Reed wasn't around and I felt sorry about that. Because I thought he clearly had a nose for where and what things were happening. I sat down at a table. I had another incident of the would-be revolution to write up but I found it was hard to settle to anything. The building itself seemed restless. A lot of people rushed down to the lobby to hear that a Bolshevik agent had been out to the Twelfth Army on the northern front and its regimental soviets had all voted to follow the orders of the Military Revolutionary Committee. The earth was shifting under the Smolny but none of us knew how far it would slide.

Then I saw Artem amongst the press of people listening to the tidings. He didn't look exhausted at all as I made my way to him. He turned to me with his bright face. I couldn't believe he could still look so fresh – but that was one of Artem's gifts.

Paddy, he yelled. But where's Suvarov? I sent one of our people looking for him.

We looked around the room ourselves but he did not seem to be there.

It was time for the reunion of the two old campaigners – to hell with everything else! We went searching for Suvarov all through the Smolny and in the end found him in the garden smoking a cigarette by a bonfire. Artem was approaching him with arms thrown wide and calling his name before Suvarov even saw him. Suvarov stood, hiccoughed a laugh and brought both his hands up to his forehead under the rim of his cap. They embraced like bears wrestling. Watching the two of them I got a feeling that all the right people were now in place and in touch. And now anything at all could happen. The world could after all turn itself upside down. It could be taken from the men in flash uniforms and frock coats and given to a fellow like Suvarov.

I've told him, Artem yelled at me, he's got to come to Kharkov and work with us. No Don coal, no bloody revolution!

Artem soon had to excuse himself but Suvarov and I stayed by the fire. He kept saying, Imagine *that*, eh? Imagine Artem! Central Committee. Well, blow me down!

Appreciating it all, he stared at the flames and spat into them with utter happiness.

Did you know, he asked me, I nearly got trapped into marriage with a girl in Sydney?

I'd heard something, I admitted.

Imagine that. What would I be doing now? Probably washing up.

He threw his arm up at the dark sky the sparks from the flames disappeared into. Then what would have happened to all this?

We waited there for two hours and Artem at last came back to join us for a while. He told us an anecdote about Vladimir Ilich. In disguise he'd come across to the Smolny that morning on a local train from the flat he'd sheltered in and he'd had a choice of seats – no one else dared travel in case Kerensky's troops or the gendarmes boarded the thing. So there came Lenin – to deliberate on great schemes – all alone on a little neighbourhood rattler.

There'd been a lot of vacillating and even fright in room No. 36. Our old friend the moving-picture enthusiast Grigorii Zinoviev and his comrade Kamenev didn't think things were ready yet. Maybe the stars weren't in alignment. Vladmir Ilich had said to them something like, In two years you'll still be saying that. Artem had voted to go ahead without hesitation – which maybe explained his air of repressed excitement as he talked with Suvarov and me.

So if we actually win – someone at the meeting had asked – what will we call our ministers of state?

Trotsky suggested *commissars* – that was the term the Jacobins used in the French revolution. That's how casually and how fatefully things happened in No. 36 – with the rest of the building and the soldiers in the garden and the people of the city and country and world itself none the wiser.

Artem disappeared again and Suvarov and I remained at the fire – excited innocents. In Room No. 36 Antonov-O – former engineering officer – was working on the plans for the next day and sending out messengers to the barracks around the city. The telegraph office had to be occupied. Then the telephone exchange, the Marinsky and any of the bridges held now by the Junkers. The sailors from Kronstadt were expected to be in place with the soldiers by the middle of the morning. Ready to do all! The Winter Palace and Kerensky inside it would be assaulted in good time for its capture to be proclaimed before the Congress of Soviets met downstairs tomorrow evening. And if not, we'd all be looking for places to hide.

We rattled on at the fire while upstairs Vladmir Ilich was stretched out on the floor resting his back. He was a man who'd settled everything in his mind and the great stone set rolling! Within thirty-six hours he could be dead – but he didn't want to go down with backache.

Artem returned and announced we could go to the Alliluyevs' apartment now. All three of us would have to fit into the sewing room since Suvarov couldn't possibly get back to the Vyborg side because government troops held the two bridges.

Don't worry, Artem assured him with a yawn. We'll clear them out tomorrow.

You'd think he'd just been to another normal small-beer union meeting. Happily he found a car and we were driven across the city to our Piter home where Alliluyev and his wife were still up, fully dressed and very excited. We were offered tea but refused with thanks. As the most junior rebel in the sewing room I insisted I would sleep on my overcoat on the floor. In fact it looked inviting. But Artem said, I must be up early. And over our protests took the floor himself. I saw Suvarov was still asleep when I woke three or four hours later. But Artem was already gone.

23

After drinking a rushed tea with the flushed and excited Alliluyeva women, Suvarov and I took to the street. I was used now to the weight of my rifle and even felt it was comforting on this strange militant morning. On the main avenues there were the usual breadlines and prostitutes but also knots of people standing on the pavements as if they were waiting on some procession.

We hiked all the way to the Smolny. We had this idea that while we'd been gone something crucial that we didn't want to miss was happening there.

But when we got there – into the normal crowd in the lobby – we were uncertain what to do. People there were brimming with even more news than yesterday and every rumour had the power to delay us. The opening bridges over the Neva had been cranked upwards into the air by Junkers working the controls in the gatehouse. No, someone said, the gatehouses had now been captured by the Kronstadt sailors and the bridges opened up again for traffic to and from Vyborg. Workers were milling south over them.

Reed fought his way across the lobby. He called out to me that Kerensky had fled town in a car he'd stolen from the American embassy and was out in the country looking for soldiers who'd fight for him. I wish him well, Reed called and then vanished.

For a while Artem appeared like an apparition on the steps – looking a bit more sallow this morning. We fought our way up to join him. I did not like the particular kind of insomnia in his eyes now. For the first time he looked like a man who could lose.

The railway workers have jumped, he told Suvarov and me. In spite of all the letters and proclamations and so on they're staying with the Mensheviks and Kerensky. Some will come with us. Enough to slow Kerensky's troops I hope. By the way, did you know the mongrels cut off our telephones? We've taken the exchange back again. So now it's no telephones for them.

He was yawning and I saw now he was reeling with tiredness. And the railway men – *his* railway men – had let him down.

Paddy, he said, Grisha. You ought to take a spell. You look buggered. Everyone's tired.

He shook his head. He went on down the stairs to see someone in an office on the ground floor – very likely the delegates of the railway soviet.

Suvarov headed to his office on the off-chance there was something to occupy him. I returned to the typing room where I sat and wrote some notes.

I found a woman typist making transcripts of what had been said and decreed in No. 36. I asked her in broken Russian could she take a note in to Artem? *Artem*, it said, *do you need me this afternoon? I am ready to do whatever you need. Paddy.*

An edgy forty minutes passed and I looked up and saw someone familiar to me from Brisbane. In the corridor – sitting on a suitcase and catching his breath – was Rybukov the engineer. I bounded out to the corridor and there he was – corporeal as buggery, as they say in Broken Hill. His face lit up. He struggled up and we shook hands.

You look in better health than you did in Brisbane, I told him.

The British fed me well, he agreed. But I escaped. On a counterfeit passport too. So I am a criminal again.

We're all criminals, I assured him – proud I'd been party to the stealing of weapons in Kharkov and the incitement of sailors to violence in Piter.

They had me designing tanks, he told me, but I couldn't escape till things were chaos here. Otherwise they would have got the tsar's government to hunt me down and send me back again. I had to wait till anarchy struck. And it has.

It was easy to see he was pleased with himself for managing to get here.

It's just that I can't get to see Artem.

He's been in No. 36 for days, I explained. With just a few breaks. I don't see much of him. I reckon he slept for about twenty minutes last night.

It doesn't matter, Rybukov told me. I'm going to wait. Do you know what he always said? Come the revolution he'd make sure Vladimir Ilich allowed me to build the People's Train. The same one I was going to build for my dear friend Mr Bender. It doesn't matter if I have to wait all afternoon and all night – I'll see him. And then we'll amaze the world.

I think we might be doing that already, I told him. We're on a sort of train right now. We're certainly moving anyhow.

He wouldn't leave his place even to go and eat a meal, so I brought him a pannikin of soup and a lump of black bread from the canteen. He seemed to drink and eat it more out of politeness than because he needed it. The same hollow eyes I had known in Brisbane kept veering towards that door – the one the Central Committee sat behind.

While we were talking a young secretary in a white blouse and a long skirt brought me out a note. It said, *Plenty to do later, Paddy. For the moment the Winter Palace is going to be the place. But make sure you keep out of harm's way.*

I grew restless and after a while I asked Rybukov to excuse me and went downstairs carrying my notebook and my rifle. In the crowded hall I saw Suvarov talking to some soldiers. The first miracle was finding him in that berserk building at all. The second was what he next suggested.

Paddy, I was looking for you. I'm just waiting for a car or something to take me down to the Winter Palace. Want to come?

It was said like a man inviting a friend to the beach.

I'm on for it, I said. Suddenly I was as bright as a schoolboy guaranteed some mischief. Suvarov took a rifle from a stack near the door then we went out into the yard and stood beside a machine-gun crew. Suvarov smoked and they smoked. The fumes of their tobacco reached up to a low steely sky. One of them told Suvarov that the cloud was to hide what we did from the eye of God. It had to be done but God might not be onside yet. So the soldiers weren't atheists, not by any stretch.

We piled into an armoured car bound for Palace Square and were jammed in among the brotherly stench of about a dozen men. Fortunately it was a short journey of barely two or three miles.

We pulled in behind some unlimbered cannon in the corner of the square by St Isaac's Cathedral. They were our guns and were aimed at the massive pile of the Winter Palace. The cannon of the Junkers were arrayed in front of it. A fairly impressive line of Cossacks – maybe brought in to stiffen the Junkers and the Death Battalion – was drawn up at the bottom of the palace steps. If the two sets of cannon started firing at each other . . . it'd be bloody murder here.

Our gunners wore red on their sleeves and caps and all had rifles in their hands. It turned out they'd been shot at from a place high up near the cathedral's dome. It seemed the rifleman had given it up as a bad job, though, for Suvarov and I stood there a time but nothing happened. Still, I couldn't help clenching my brow as if to keep a bullet out. Of course the jovial Suvarov got talking to some of our artillerymen. I noticed on an occasional collar the red insignia of an officer – and on others patches of paler fabric where their tabs had been. These were former tsarist officers who'd been reliable enough to be elected by their regimental soviets and who'd been considered humane enough not to be shot by their soldiers.

They're very confident, Suvarov told me after interviewing one of the gun crews.

Behind us more of our troops were still arriving – a truckload or armoured carload at a time. But not enough sailors yet – as one of the gunners had told Suvarov. From where we stood I could see some of the streets beyond St Isaac's were blocked off with barricades made of timber, barrels, baskets, a wagon with its wheels off, even a disused bathtub. I asked Suvarov if he knew which side put it all there. He confessed he didn't know and grinned at his own ignorance. It's a pretty confused picture all right, he said.

As if to add to the confusion we now saw a black figure come down the stairs from the Winter Palace and cross the open ground between the opposing sets of cannon. We imagined it might be a minister of Kerensky's coming to try to make a deal with us. But when he got close I could see it was Slatkin – all properly shaven. He was wearing a clean shirt and pressed coat and trousers and was as neat as a pin. His face was split as always with that know-all grin.

He and Suvarov greeted each other and Suvarov turned to me. They let him in because he looks like one of Kerensky's ministers.

Again Slatkin smiled his smug smile. I said I was from the Ministry of War, he told us. But anyone can get in there. I mean, in ones or twos. As long as you're not armed.

What did you learn? asked Suvarov.

Well, said Slatkin, they aren't armed so badly. But their hearts and their minds can't be predicted.

Slatkin went to speak to our gunners. I could see his car waiting behind the guns.

Now Suvarov could hardly contain himself. He shook his right hand up and down with excitement. Do you want to try it, Paddy? We could leave our rifles with these boys.

The idea excited me as an individual and a would-be journalist as well – to walk into the palace where the tsar had lived and where the cabinet of the provisional government was hiding. And where the Junkers and the women of the Death Battalions – supposed Amazons – had sworn to die to protect Kerensky and the rest.

We dumped our rifles with the artillerymen and set off across the square. Our boots were noisy on the paving stones but it was a matter of pride that they should be. I wondered if the sniper at St Isaac's was really gone – though that did not worry me half as much as it would have normally. Ahead of us stood that wonderful building – the palace whose architecture on its own made you think that it would bring ordinary people like us to a halt just by its own authority. But not today. I felt very much alive today – a gent entering his inheritance.

Just let me talk to them, said Suvarov who strode in a commanding manner. I certainly wasn't going to try to do the talking in my bits and pieces of Russian. Soon we walked through the line of guns and up to the moustached Cossacks standing behind barrels set at the bottom of the steps. It made me a little awed to face them – their reputation did that to a person. But Suvarov began to talk his way past them, telling an officer that we had an intelligence report from Smolny for the ministers of state. It took a few minutes. Of course he had no formal paperwork on him, he said. If the Bolsheviks at Smolny had found anything like that on him they would have shot him! I could see the officer respected Suvarov's haughty manner enough not to pester me. We were suddenly through the fringe of guards and mounting the vast steps built to make men feel like insects.

You see, hissed Suvarov, they let us in so easily. That wouldn't happen at the Smolny. They're indifferent – that's why. Indifferent.

In the giant's doorway at the head of the steps stood an old official in a blue uniform with gold braid all over it. He held up a hand to stop us going in. Suvarov repeated his story with plenty of gesturing. At last the old man – probably influenced by the fact we'd been let past by the guards below – sighed and gestured that we were free to enter. His visage told me he thought the whole place was going to the dogs.

The entry hall was all veined marble and ran away for acres – or so it seemed. It was designed to make the smallest sound bounce off the walls and belt you about the ears. Above our heads hung chandeliers as big as the house I'd grown up in. Either side of a central door in the furthest wall, two staircases rose to the upper floor. Our boots thundered on the marble as we crossed a space large enough to fit a village in and climbed one of the staircases. At the top we ran into a young officer in the sort of uniform I had only seen either on stage or on the dead boy in Kharkov. The man kneaded the right side of his face and knotted his brows, fiddling with his moustache. On top of that he carried his face to one side as if he had a toothache. Suvarov saluted him and went on with his urgent rigmarole about news from the Smolny – telling him breathlessly that a battalion from the Smolny had been dispatched with orders to capture the Interior Ministry and that the minister must be told.

In return the officer said curtly that the cabinet already knew this. Suvarov had some experience as an actor and really hammed up the urgency. He must be permitted to tell Kerensky. You see, the young officer told us suddenly in French, Monsieur Kerensky wasn't here so we should simply go. Monsieur Kerensky had gone to fetch *une armée de sept divisions* from the northern front.

Thank God! said Suvarov with an air of piety.

The officer waved us away now and told us to leave the building. Suvarov saluted him and he turned away and disappeared up a further staircase without seeing to our departure at all.

Suvarov and I wandered down a corridor and stopped at a panelled doorway.

Listen to the sound in there, he said.

I could hear a gramophone record scratching along and men shouting to each other and – now and then – laughter. An old Winter Palace flunky in his blue uniform came limping along the corridor. Shaking the handle Suvarov asked him why the door was locked. The old man told him that it was locked by order of the officers. Suvarov rose up to his fullest height – so much higher than myself or the old servant of the tsar – and asked him did he mean that unless the men were locked in they wouldn't fight for the home of God's Great Servant the Emperor or for the cabinet?

The old man told Suvarov he knew nothing about that. But Suvarov had impressed him and he began calling him *barin* as if he was a member of the nobility. It made Suvarov adopt a pose even more grand. Open it at once, he told the man.

The old official found a key from his pocket and opened it. Tell me when you leave, *barin*, he pleaded with Suvarov.

How are the Junkers going to get out to fight, Suvarov asked him, if they are locked away?

The old man shrugged reverentially. This question touched on only one of all the stupid orders he had received in a lifetime of bowing to people who barely deserved a nod.

We entered what I would have considered a massive room if I had not seen the hallway downstairs. The lower walls were wainscotted with beautiful wood and further up there was gold paintwork on the mouldings and French chandeliers hanging above us. I had never seen such splendid items as I'd seen in Piter – even though they were built on the misery of ordinary men and women. High up on the walls beyond the wainscotting were paintings of the battles of 1812 when Napoleon invaded Russia. Brave Russians were dead and dying in neat lines up there on the wall for their tsar. But at floor level the whole place was a shambles. Junkers were lying down on palliasses and blankets and further up the room was a group drinking with women in soldiers' uniforms – no doubt part of one of the famous Shock Battalions of Death. Cigarette butts littered the floor and so did copies of nearly every stripe of paper, Bolshevik, Menshevik, Cadet. Those defenders of the Winter Palace who were wearing their jackets carried the patches at their collars that meant they were officers-in-training. But here they were no better than privates. Unwilling ones too. Their rifles weren't stacked – some of them leaned against the wall and some of them just lay around on the polished wood as if they didn't belong to anyone. At one end of the room machine-guns were sited in the tall windows overlooking Palace Square. No one manned them at the moment but they were capable of executing plenty of besiegers.

We weren't far into the room when a number of the men on their blankets spotted us and rose – impressed by Suvarov's air of command. It wasn't something I'd noticed in Brisbane but he certainly had it now. He asked these men who'd stood why their friends were entertaining the women's battalion. The girls were nervous – one Junker said – and had got in by hacking out a panel in the wall with bayonets. Suvarov turned and winked at me before telling a handsome young officer candidate to go and order them back into their section of the building. The young man obeyed. He strode across the room and was booed by the men who had been sharing wine with the girls. We saw the girls get up – heads down in shame. There were whistles and catcalls as they crawled – one at a time – through a sort of mouse hole in the panelling. When the last had gone the conscientious young Junker then blocked the place up with blankets and kitbags.

Where are your officers? Suvarov asked.

On the next floor, they said. It's an officers' mess.

Suvarov relaxed then and introduced me as a journalist from the West who wanted to write about how well and loyally defended the Winter Palace was. A number of the men shook their heads at what they saw as simple-mindedness. A few cried out they'd do their very best. I don't like Kerensky much, said one. But I don't like Bolsheviks at all. Others wanted no part of it – the journalism or dying for the Winter Palace. I felt sorry for them. One of them told Suvarov that he intended to keep a last bullet for himself because there was something so large and so diabolical about the Winter Palace that it turned normal men into savages. Look what it had done to the tsars and to the crazy tsarina who sought God through that devil Rasputin. It would turn the Reds into beasts too.

You may not need your last bullet, Suvarov suggested to them.

But one thing was clear. These were not true tsarist officers – not from the old tsarist officer corps. They were men chosen from the ranks because they could read and because they either hadn't seen battle or hadn't run away during a brief exposure to it. (All those who had long exposure under generals like Brusilov and Kornilov were dead.) Now these young men might need to die for all this holy architecture. How easy it was for men to end up locked in on the wrong side. Here I was – a rough trade unionist from the ends of the earth – but I wasn't locked in – I had strong hopes of getting outside again and crossing the square.

We left the defenders to their waiting and went out the way we'd come. We nodded to the old attendant in the main corridor and he locked the Junkers in again. Downstairs we roughly saluted the Cossack officers drawn up in front of the steps and walked back across the square like princes. We stamped on the stones and were indifferent to the cannon in either corner of the palace. It was a long promenade across to the far side and the Red guns.

Another battery of our guns had come in by now. More sailors were marching up from the direction of the post office. They were massing around the Russian Imperial Staff building – a big red pile near the cathedral that seemed to be empty of all staff officers today.

We stopped and told our gunners what we'd seen. There were arguments in progress. Some men wanted to ease the tension by going in against the palace right now. But Slatkin told them everything was waiting for the sailors. When they heard the guns from the Peter and Paul and from the *Aurora* in the river – then it would be time!

Suvarov and I decided on a brisk walk to get back to the Smolny. My rifle seemed to weigh nothing now. We were full of energy – almost drunk on it – and could have marched thirty times to the Smolny and back and not complained. We were so full of the moment. Along the Nevsky soldiers and sailors were crowding around barefoot newspaper boys to buy the latest edition of whatever they had. We saw Red Guards outside a bank they had taken over. They looked as calm and careful as any board of directors.

We got back to the Smolny gates in the early dark of evening. We had become familiar figures and the sentries didn't ask us to show passes any more as we ran into the building past the sandbagged strong points. From the great hall to one side of the lobby we could hear the shouts and laughter and hooting and foot-stamping of the congress in its opening session – the three main parties all competing to register their delegates. But we were full of mad haste to see Artem or someone else from the Central Committee or Trotsky's Military Council. Upstairs the Central Committee was still installed in No. 36. They would leave it till a little later to invade the congress downstairs. Suvarov demanded that Artem Samsurov be brought out to see us because we were just back with important news from the Winter Palace.

We went to wait in my accustomed haunt – the typing room. There was poor old Rybukov who'd come home to Russia on the one day no one had time to make a fuss of him. He was sitting at a desk and had gone to sleep on his folded arms.

At last Artem came through the connecting door into the office where we stood still fizzing with our afternoon adventure. He seemed full of the same delirious tension as we had and had the air of a man who was enjoying himself again and had forgotten the business of the backsliding railway men.

Did you see Rybukov's here? he asked us first. What an omen!

I said I'd met him that morning – which now seemed to me just minutes before.

He's here with his plans, said Artem. I tried to send him off to the Alliluyevs' for a rest but he's waiting to see Vladimir Ilich and hear some of the speeches downstairs. He's got a long wait ahead of him. But we've got to build that thing for him. It'll be a symbol.

Artem gave full attention to us now. Well, what can you tell me, gentlemen?

Suvarov and I – but mainly Suvarov – then made a report of what we'd seen in the Winter Palace. Suvarov's opinion was that our men should try to take the palace immediately.

I'm certain you're right, Grisha. But it's Antonov-O pulling the strings from here. He and his friends think we need more numbers, and he's supposed to be the expert. I'll pass all you've told me on to them, but I know what they'll say. It's easier to get a party of one or two inside than it will be to storm the place.

Artem lowered his voice. But I think you're right. We should just go ahead with it and take the cabinet prisoner. Then the news could go out to Moscow and all the cities that we control all the organs of government and most of the army. I mean, the congress is starting, and they're messing around with credentials and that sort of thing. But Vladimir Ilich wants to announce the fall of the palace before the first session really starts. He thought he'd have it by three o'clock this afternoon, then by five. But here it is – after six! So there'll be all sorts of speechifying from some of the older gents about how we've failed and should get back into our box. But they can't say that once we get the damned place!

We could take it ourselves if you like, I offered. Suvarov and me. Just waltz in there and make the buggers surrender.

Artem was amused and shook his head. Our journalist has become a warrior, he said. Yes, it's hard to believe sometimes we're not just kids playing games in our heads. Just hold hard for now, boys.

He said goodbye and walked back into No. 36.

24

While Suvarov went downstairs to see how the congress was getting on I took a desk in the typists' room and began writing a feverish account of what I'd seen this afternoon. The thing – as journalists say – wrote itself. I was agog with the adventure and was finished writing in forty minutes. Then I found in a corner the Roman alphabet typewriter Reed had been using and began to tap out my account with four clumsy fingers.

When I was finished I decided to try to visit the congress downstairs in the ballroom.

In the lobby I found Suvarov arguing outside the double doors to the great hall with a grey-bearded man in a worker's ragged suit. It was – I would discover – an old friend of his from the metalworkers' trade union. The argument was the same one that was occurring all over the building. If we destroyed Kerensky's government, said the man, no international revolution would be sparked by what happened in Russia. The fact it happened only in Russia would help the rest of the world destroy Russia – if Russia didn't destroy itself first.

Having been to the palace and seen the possibilities Suvarov found the man an annoyance, and brushed past him to approach me.

He made a fist and knocked his brow with it. They've been waiting all their lives for this day, he said furiously, and when it bites them on the arse they don't want it to be here. The hardest thing about a revolution is persuading the damned revolutionaries.

Then – dragging me by the elbow – he pushed me forward past the man and through the double doors into the ornate hall. I'd thought this room was grand beyond belief when I first saw it. But now that I'd had my architecture lesson from the palace it looked only medium ornate.

The first thing I saw was a young soldier at the front of the hall standing on his seat and pointing to some officers with neat uniforms at the back of the hall, declaring they were not true delegates. Women delegates and soldiers and sailors began jeering at them too. The women wore their shawls and dresses or their bits of army uniform.

On the rostrum above the credentials table – where things were still being hammered out – appeared a young soldier in the uniform of the Latvian division. This division was devoted to Vladimir Ilich's side and – shaking his fist and roaring through the mists of tobacco smoke – the young soldier called for the impostor delegates to be hanged in the garden.

At last the crowd around the credentials tables cleared. The congress began and the secretary at the rostrum called on the first speaker on his list. Suvarov and I stood for a while by a fluted column at the side of the room as a Menshevik in a bad suit spoke – no doubt uttering the usual condemnation of room No. 36 and all its contents. And the predictable cries went up from our people who had done well enough in the credential process but hadn't got as many delegates as the Mensheviks.

None of that mattered now while No. 36 controlled so much of the army. And none of it would matter either if the palace was captured.

Suddenly there was a huge amount of cheering and whistling going on. Trotsky was coming up to the rostrum and the soldiers greeted him like a messiah. With his eyes of mercury and his composer's face and flying hair, Trotsky had a presence that grabbed the room by its lapels. His gestures took on a new scale and huge meaning. He could look amused and ironic and then angry as well as any world-class Hamlet.

He gave a speech often reproduced in years to follow. The Mensheviks and the Socialist Revolutionaries had last February conquered the Cadets, he said. And then when they got to power in the Duma, they gave it all back to the Cadets. Such was their natural taste for serfdom!

Our delegates were laughing in great waves of sound at his jokes and then cheering his political jibes like thunder.

Old Martov – who had for years shared exile and the occasional coffee and pastry with Vladimir Ilich – scrambled up to the rostrum with the same message as a few days earlier at the Marinsky. His faction wasn't opposed to the power of the people and only opposed to the Bolsheviks. But this was *not* the time to seize power.

Noise followed by noise followed by more still. The Winter Palace stands! a number of Menshevik delegates cried. A fortress in the sea. And may it stand long since it is the home of the cabinet to whom the decisions of this congress will be taken and upon which the cabinet could not help but act! Why does there need to be a sudden coup tonight, they asked, when every sign suggests it's wise to wait?

I could not see Artem here and even Trotsky had gone back upstairs after his speech. In their absence an expected motion was offered by the Mensheviks condemning any uprising, and then the debate became apparently endless and – for Suvarov – infuriating. The hot gas given out by the naysayers might kill for him all the fervour and fizz of the day that was now closing. Maybe there was a kind of sickly comfort in always being a righteous persecuted group and if it was so it was turning men into revolutionary eunuchs.

Suvarov and I turned to leave the meeting. But as we reached the lobby we heard the enormous sound of a cannon firing and of a shell that seemed to me to have been fired in the street just near the Smolny. Suvarov stood still staring at me until we heard an explosion from wherever the thing fell.

The *Aurora*, Suvarov told me. The start of things.

We fetched our rifles and left the building straight away – discussing nothing but knowing by some intuition where we were heading. In the garden many Red Guards and soldiers were craning their necks to try to read the dark sky and to see the *Aurora*'s thunder reflected in low clouds. We couldn't find a truck to the palace at first. As we waited a number of civilian congress delegates – a few brave Cadets might even have been among all these Mensheviks – filed out through the door into the garden and on into the street. They were men and some women – I would discover – who'd been members of the former Duma. Some of them carried little parcels or string bags of provisions with them which must have been under their chairs in the hall. They announced to the surrounding troops they meant to march through the firing lines to the Winter Palace and make a human shield for Kerensky's cabinet – as imperfect as it might be – and help supply the garrison with what was in their bags and parcels. Other delegates followed them out to the arched doorways of the Smolny and shouted insults after them.

In the street they formed up and started marching and no one interfered with their progress. Departing in their rescue column they looked braver than they'd sounded inside. But they also seemed a bit theatrical and overblown.

How ridiculous! Suvarov said.

Another furious noise and a cannonade arched over the sky. The column didn't hesitate but kept steadily on.

Artem – in his army overcoat and boots – came out of the building seconds after them. It took Suvarov and me a few seconds to notice him there. Tired out he was still smiling. I'd never seen such a man for smiling – maybe the only one in the whole damn Smolny.

Ah, he said, it's a great thing to be everyone's friend.

It's a gift you've got, said Suvarov. Can you imagine Trotsky being liked all the time? And drinking tea with grubby old Antonov-O?

Trotsky's military council are too busy here, he told us. They asked me to go down and see why the place isn't ours yet.

The place? Suvarov asked.

The place! said Artem.

Now? I asked.

Yes, said Artem. Coming?

But you don't have a rifle, said Suvarov.

Paddy will protect me.

Yeah, I said. Dead-eye Dykes.

I was close to trembling with exhilaration about this excursion with Artem. Back to the palace. The biggest excursion in the world. I didn't give a brass farthing for whether life went beyond that or just closed down around me. As long as I went to the Winter Palace with Artem.

Okay Paddy, said Suvarov, let's show Artem the ropes. Where will we find a truck or something like it?

It was easy to ask but there wasn't one waiting in front of the gates. The armoured cars were all gone too – on errands and taking the city over and maybe assaulting the palace. The result was we had to set out on foot behind the procession of worthy souls. We heard rifle fire – way off and like the noise of meat on a spit. But there was no sound of big guns.

We hadn't gone far when we met a truck coming from a side street and loaded with leaflets printed in the Smolny cellar. Artem and Suvarov and I were permitted to climb aboard.

Our truck honked as we drove past the column. Dignified-looking men in frock coats were determined to be brave. The women seemed to show their courage by buttoning up their capes and hugging them around them. From our truck the soldiers threw out leaflets to the marchers. We clutched at a few ourselves – for history's sake. The leaflets were a bit premature: *Citizens, the provisional government is deposed. State power has passed into the hands of the Petrograd Soviet of Workers' and Soldiers' Deputies.*

Some of the marchers balled the leaflets up in their fists without reading them and threw them back at the truck.

There were a lot of people along the Prospekt – they had come out of their houses and cellars and were peering in the direction of the rifle fire and wondering. As we passed they picked up the thrown leaflets too and read them.

We got as far as the place where the canal flowed under the Nevsky Prospekt and where the roadblock with even more parked and abandoned vehicles was still in place. So we jumped down from the back of the truck. But as it turned out the self-sacrifice squad were turned back by the laughter and mockery of ordinary soldiers and sailors and sailors' girls. One of the gentlemen exhorted his fellow marchers to retreat.

We were let through and arrived trotting beside a Red battery near the old staff building. The guns weren't firing at all. When Artem asked them why, they said it was because our troops had gone in and – the gunners hoped – were doing well enough as it was. We could hear and smell plenty of small-arms fire echoing within the palace. One gunner told Suvarov that the infantry were taking it room by room – an idea that seemed very dramatic. Were the Junkers really fighting to the death after all?

The three of us followed a squad of Red Guards who were suddenly running across the square with their boots clattering. I could see as we got closer that some captured and fearful Junkers and sobbing Death Battalion women were being brought out of the building with their hands up. We went on inside to the entry hall that had taken my breath away that afternoon, and where the noise of rifle fire from the corridors of the building was setting off deafening echoes. We made for the stairs and all at once met soldiers coming down them carrying rolled up tapestries – one soldier to each end. Another man was carrying a big ornamental German vase. While fighting continued somewhere behind them! Artem held up his hand and stopped the looters. Didn't they understand, he asked them, that all this belonged to the people now and they were disgracing the people and themselves?

The soldiers looked both shamefaced and cranky. But they obediently put everything they had down on the stairs. At the top of the stairs and in the corridor beyond Artem had to talk to other men hoisting Meissen vases, ormolu clocks, some pieces of tapestry ripped out by bayonet, a Persian mat, and an ornamental pair of binoculars.

Fresh Red Guards and soldiers came up the stairs behind us and down the corridor. They were rushing past us to get into the fight still going on in the back of the palace. We quickened our step. Part way along the corridor we saw another line of Death Battalion girls being brought down the marble stairs from the second floor under guard. Their escorts were mocking them and threatening of course to root them. But Artem called the soldiers to order. The women soldiers were pathetic to look at – just girls really. Some of them wept like the women we'd seen being led away outside. When they had joined their legion they'd pledged to die for the tsar. But they had properly chosen not to die for that little show-pony Kerensky.

Be of good heart, sisters! Artem told them. Suvarov called, Now you can fight for the people!

Well, said Artem when they were gone down the corridor towards the front steps. Things seem to be moving along.

We heard further footsteps descending the marble stairs. A bunch of Red Guards in bits and pieces of civilian and military clothes were bringing more prisoners down the stairs. The leading guard yelled, *Pazhal'st, tovarichtchi!* Get out of the way, comrades! Behind him came a number of gentlemen who looked tired and pale but well dressed. I recognised at once the frock-coated Doctor Kishkin – a Cadet. I'd seen his picture in magazines. After him came Terestchenko. Terestchenko was a youngish fellow – about five or six years younger than me – and he let his cold eye fall over the three of us. He seemed less scared than the doctor but was the most hated by soldiers because he had tried to bring back execution for disobedience to officers. He had also been one of those they called the Freemasons – they plotted the February revolution inside the lodges the way the French had with theirs. Now he was on his way into oblivion. This was the cabinet of the provisional government – powerless now – being marched downstairs by three working men with rifles. The provisional government really was falling – like the archangels God threw out of heaven.

Terestchenko saw Artem. Monsieur Samsurov, he said coolly.

Artem nodded. Comrade Terestchenko, he said.

He asked Terestchenko where Kerensky was.

Terestchenko cried, At the gates of Petrograd – with a new army!

When these prisoners had passed Artem decided we'd climb to the next floor. From the marble corridor up there we could see an opened door. We walked in and I was surprised to see Reed and an

American woman-friend of his – as young as he was and pretty and full of energy. They were wandering around the cabinet table looking at the ministers' notepads.

Reed called to us. Hello, gentlemen. Hello, Australia. Look, they didn't know what to do next. They were doodling.

He held up a page on which one of the ministers – instead of writing an edict – had drawn a lamppost.

Why not? asked Artem. Kerensky's abandoned them.

A large group of Red Guards flooded into the room and tried to grab Reed and his woman-friend – presuming they were well enough dressed to have something to do with the Provisional Government. Artem ordered the guards to leave them alone. Foreign comrades, he said. He pointed to me. Like Mr Dykes, he told them and grinned at me. A huge joke! After all – soon he'd be back at the Smolny with the best of news.

It was all over on that floor. But there was still firing elsewhere. As we came down the stairs again we had no way of knowing then that that was about the time the Red Guards started looting the wine cellars and drinking up vintages beyond their maddest dreams. We could hear soldiers still exchanging shots at the back of the building. Someone must have been resisting! Surely the shots weren't executions.

Suvarov suggested we head through the room he and I had been in that afternoon. As we reached the corridor we found a number of unarmed Junkers – pale-faced and hatless – under the guard of two sailors. Some looked sullen. A few of them trembled and were tear-streaked. The Red Guards were yelling threats of execution.

It was Suvarov who stepped up this time – taking Artem's cue – and told the Junkers he realised they'd been forced into defending the place. Now they could fight on the side that was naturally theirs. After this same speech Artem had given the women prisoners the Red Guards began escorting the Junkers downstairs. No executions, called Artem.

I thought innocently what a model revolution this was – passion and no slaughter.

We strode into the big room with the paintings of Russian victory set high up on the walls. In the windows the machine-guns we'd seen that afternoon stood still unmanned and still pointing out into the square. We went up to look at them for a second and felt them and found them cool to the touch. These weren't fired much, said Suvarov.

A good thing, said Artem.

Abandoned rifles and rubbish and strewn blankets littered the floor of the big chamber. A door stood open at the far end of the room and we could hear a shot or two coming from somewhere close by. There were some voices and the sound of boots. Then silence. The place *was* being converted. From a place of power to a museum. We crossed the floor littered with dropped rifles and rubbish and were ready to go through into that further corridor but we heard before we were even at the door the sudden screams of a woman. Then the screaming gave way to a howl of pain. We emerged into the corridor to find the bloodied bodies of two Junkers and, a few yards further along, someone in a frock coat with his black and grey striped trousers pulled down, grinding into a wailing girl of the Death Battalion. She wailed and had her hand on his jaw pushing it up. One of her fingers fell into the man's mouth and he bit it and she screamed piercingly.

The man was Slatkin.

25

My first thoughts – if you could call them thoughts – are shameful to admit. They are a confession of what war and conflict can call forth in men who've always fancied they're decent fellows. I hadn't felt any rage about the Death Battalion women on the stairs. But on seeing Slatkin – instead of being shocked – I thought yes, this is a girl who'd chosen to serve the tsar until death. Why shouldn't the bitch be split open and torn apart and punished?

The shock of that idea stained everything. It was one of those things that if you thought them once they could poison a lifetime. But then – the next second – the object of my anger became Slatkin. He went on struggling with the girl. It seemed he hadn't noticed us. A tapestry and a Meissen vase were damn all compared to this. Why would he shame the revolution after all he'd done: the raids on arms depots and the planning with the sailors. The wealth Vladimir Ilich had let him enjoy? And on the rim of a new world. Why would he betray us and the woman by hauling her army pants down around her boots and exposing her to his anger and his punishment like that?

I could see Artem was for once flabbergasted. Suvarov yelled, Slatkin, stop it for Christ's sake!

My reaction was more primitive. I went to Slatkin and kicked him full-force in the ribs. He fell off the girl. One of his arms was folded into his torso like a broken wing and he began cursing me in his mother tongue. Artem and I moved in and hauled him upright with his pants around his knees still.

Slatkin, Slatkin, said Artem as a reproach. Slatkin's prick was still upright but he didn't blush about that and he was telling us he'd kill us. Artem reached down to the girl – her hair was dark and her face an oval of fright and she trembled and thought we were part of her punishment too. Artem reached down and – as she yelped in terror again – began pulling up the army pants she should never have been let wear. If he hadn't been so quick about it I would have said he'd done it tenderly. His face was scarlet as if he was the criminal. Letting go of the girl, he yelled something angry at Slatkin. Slatkin didn't bother fixing his own dress up. I heard Suvarov whistle and turned and saw Slatkin had pulled a Mauser from a holster strapped near his armpit. He swung its elegant black barrel between all three of us.

Artem said, Stop it, Konya.

I'd never known that was Slatkin's pet name. Konya Slatkin was certainly selecting who to shoot and I felt the old anger rising in me at being a target in the first place and knew I'd charge at him soon – regardless. The girl saw the gun and was screaming anew – certain she would be the chief target. But it didn't seem so. It was between me and Suvarov that Slatkin swung the gun. He had decided not to kill his old friend Artem but he hadn't given up the idea of shooting one of us. Suvarov wisely reached out and held the thin girl with the oval face by the wrist – an instinct told us both that if she fled he would then have certainly turned the gun on her.

I was saved from making a mad run at him by feeling on my shoulder the weight of my now-familiar rifle. For the first time I unshouldered it to point it at another human – Slatkin. I moved the safety lever and worked the bolt while I yelled at him. I called him obscene names – a fucker, a rootjockey, a sodding disgrace. Suvarov – while hanging on to the girl with one hand – had his other one out while he pleaded in Russian. Artem said, Slatkin, men and women were killed taking this palace. Will you disgrace them?

Nothing changed. Slatkin's pants still had him hobbled and he still looked like a crime against heaven. I had raised my rifle and had him in my sights even while he had the little black bore of the Mauser pointed at me. Then he simply swung the Mauser to the girl and shot her in the head. The bullet and the sound both flew off the walls of the corridor.

Artem rushed to Slatkin and restrained him. And Suvarov came to restrain me from shooting Slatkin. Then the three of us – me still holding my rifle – knelt beside the girl whose eyes were still half-open. Her lips made a hissing sound – lower than a hiss though – a whisper without words. I started crying like a kid because I could see a light – already dim in her eyes – going dimmer still and dwindling away to the very limits of dimness. Piss stained her pants, poor thing.

I got up again and Artem – who'd once insisted I select one – now reached out to take my rifle from me. But I clung on. Slatkin had dressed again and had a look on his face that showed you he'd already begun to make excuses for what he'd done. I came raging in at him and smashed him in his uninjured side with the butt of the thing. The Mauser flew from his hand and fired when it hit the marble floor. Where the shot went none of us knew. It harmed none of us and it was the last poisonous shot of the capture of the palace.

I retreated from Slatkin and picked the Mauser up and made a gift of it to Suvarov who was still kneeling beside the girl as if he thought she could be revived.

Suvarov pocketed it and stood and went either to hit or help Slatkin. But in his pain Slatkin refused all friendly hands. He glowered over his shoulder at me.

Bugger you! I yelled.

I had probably made an enemy for life. I hoped so. He'd besmirched everything. He had soiled me with all the rest. The bastard! At the highest point of fraternity – when the world had changed – I had found out too much about the beast inside me, the one I had rushed to wall up but had never known was there until now. And the beast in this old campaigner Slatkin.

Artem went to Slatkin who was crouched from my assaults. He spoke almost gently to him.

Get a blanket from in there. He pointed towards the door of the great hall we'd been in. And then cover her, he said.

Slatkin stood crookedly and went on buttoning his jacket. Get one of your lackeys to cover her, he said.

No, Artem roared. No. You! He pointed again to the big ballroom. If not, he said, I'll make you carry her across the square.

Slatkin slunk off in a way I wouldn't have said was possible for the man who raided the Kharkov arms depot – though it was credible in a man whose ribs had been assaulted. Soon he was back with a blanket and threw it slapdash over the girl so Suvarov had to finish the job. I noticed how bony the girl's wrist was and how small her hand – the only bits Suvarov didn't cover. A few tears stung my eyes. I thought that something as vague as what had brought me to Russia had driven her into the Shock Battalions of Death.

When I looked up again Slatkin stood upright in spite of his pain and pointed a finger at me. It was meant to be a threat. Then he began arguing with Artem in Russian. But I could guess what he was saying. We're all men together. These things come over a fellow. The silly bitch provoked me. Artem shook his head but not in the way I would have wanted – not like someone casting Slatkin off forever.

We'll go, Artem said.

It was one o'clock before we came down the steps to the massive entrance hall of the captured Winter Palace. Red Guards sat on the marble drinking the tsar's wine. Other men and women were reeling round and raising the bottles they'd captured so easily. One of them yelled, Rasputin's altar wine! and then poured the stuff half down his jacket and half into his mouth. They knew by now we had the palace and the main blood they were spilling was the blood of the vine.

Out in the square there were lumps of plaster in the square fallen from high above where a shell had dislodged it. Apart from that the building looked the same as it had that afternoon. But now, as Suvarov said, it was under new ownership.

We got a lift back to the Smolny in a truck. This time we were not exhilarated. Slatkin also sat with us. Sometimes he talked in Russian to Suvarov and Artem and sometimes turned hard eyes and hardened mouth at me as if I were the bloody miscreant.

We'll see who comes out of this standing, I wanted to tell him. But it would have been useless. I decided the bastard would have enjoyed robbing banks whether asked to by the party or not.

The sentries at the gate and in the garden of the Smolny wanted to know what the news was. Suvarov told them the Winter Palace had fallen and they cheered and embraced everyone in sight. Inside the Smolny – beyond open doors in the hallway – the congress was still in session despite last night's walkout of some delegates. We could hear the little schoolmasterly Kamenev who a few weeks before had written articles saying revolution was impossible. He was reading a list of arrested ministers and declaring that Kerensky had fled and the provisional government had fallen. All organs of government were in Bolshevik hands. The Bolsheviks in Moscow and other provincial cities would both act and make the reality of revolution apparent to all in every part of Russia.

From the stairs above us appeared Vladimir Ilich free of all disguises and walking into the ballroom to speak. Koba strode behind him – smiling like a cat and winking at us. The Alliluyevs would later tell me admiringly that Koba had been up for five days straight without so much as a doze. Slatkin attached himself smoothly and with an air of revolutionary responsibility to Vladimir Ilich. For that reason Suvarov and I didn't go in to listen to Vladimir Ilich. When you're tired out and disgusted it's easy to miss history. We went upstairs to No. 36 – the door was open now. Artem was already there – reporting to Antonov-O. I could tell somehow – maybe from the pace of his delivery and the evenness of his tone – that he was not making a large issue of Slatkin. But I suppose that was understandable when it came to politics – one Russian girl balanced against the whole Winter Palace and its cabinet and garrison. I saw a dozen other notables in the room – including Madame Kollontai. Artem pointed us out to the others and some came over and embraced us in congratulation.

Suvarov and I then wanly slouched next door and just slumped there. Artem came in where I sat idle at a typewriter and told me that Slatkin had made a complaint against us to Vladimir Ilich.

Of course, Artem acknowledged, he's a barbarian.

The bastard tried to shoot us, I reminded them.

Shades of Menschkin, said Artem, shaking his head. But listen. I spoke to them. Trotsky, Dybenko, Antonov-O. I didn't leave them in any doubt as to what happened.

And what will they do? asked Suvarov.

They're very tired, said Artem.

And . . . ?

They think it's bad to admit Bolsheviks were fighting with each other. So they'll make Slatkin a Hero of the Winter Palace. He can't say anything or do anything to us then. He'll want that on his grave.

I never told Artem how deeply disappointed I was.

But he looked at me and I knew he understood my feelings. Paddy, he said, we can have a revolution. But it will take time to overthrow the squalor of the human soul.

Already soldiers were rushing up the stairs to No. 36 with further weighty news. Telegrams that said yet one more time that Kerensky and Kornilov were sending soldiers against Petrograd. Artem left us and went downstairs to the great hall to call on all soldiers in Russia to refuse to board troop trains and to call on the railway men – Bolshevik and Menshevik – to refuse to drive them.

I went downstairs and out under the archways where the bonfires blazed scarlet against grey. It wasn't a great day for the beginning of history – if that's what today was. A cloudy morning was just starting. Trams went rolling past the Smolny because no one had told them not to. I wondered if we had dreamed it all up – taking the palace. And the chocolate soldiers called Junkers. And even Slatkin shooting that girl. It seemed possible at that fantastic hour that it was all the vapours or hallucination. Because there was an emptiness out there. In the air and the sky.

The girl lay under the blanket. Or had they moved her away? Had they been tender? I wanted to go back and see to it but I also felt a sudden need to write a letter to Trofimova if I could and make contact with her honesty. I could not forget my second of sympathy with Slatkin when I first saw him on the woman who was then murdered. I needed to be civilised by Trofimova.

A brief letter full of the most simple and butchered words I could put together – Dykes's first Russian note – was written. Hunger got to me in the end and I went downstairs for some acorn coffee and bread. There sat Rybukov – wide-eyed with exhaustion – drinking tea from a tuna can. He smiled and I felt consoled. I was the sort of man who would have laughed before now at the idea I needed consolation.

It's all done, I believe, he said.

It's all done.

The People's Train was rolling along in that steamy room and in the streets beyond. But for the first time I knew not just in my mind but in my blood that some travellers were the best of men and women.

While others . . . Artem had said it. Bastardry doesn't die in a night.

Author's Note

My central character, Artem (Tom) Samsurov, is based on an escaped Russian prisoner named Artem Sergeiv (or Sergeiev, Sergeyev or Sergeyeff) who lived in Brisbane with other Russian escapees and exiles, and worked as a labourer, newspaper editor and activist there for between six and seven years in the second decade of the twentieth century. I encountered his story, by accident, in an article by Tom Poole and Eric Fried, *Artem: A Bolshevik in Brisbane* from the *Australian Journal of Politics and History* (see Acknowledgements). Like Samsurov, Sergeiv was in regular trouble with the Queensland police and spent time in Boggo Road jail. Suvarov is his fictional fellow-escapee and friend, and Artem Sergeiv in reality had many such friends. Like my character Samsurov, Sergeiv returned to Russia in mid-1917, in time to be elected to the Central Committee of the Bolsheviks, and participate in the October revolution and the coming Russian Civil War.

He attracted a number of Australian socialists to Russia, but none as early as 1917, so that Paddy Dykes is entirely my creation, though based on a characteristic Australian working-class radical of his time. On the same principle, all the characters we know on an intimate level in the Australian section of the book are fictional, but – I hope – not unlikely for that period of ferment in Brisbane, in Australia, in the world. The Australian politicians mentioned or met occasionally are real politicians.

In the Russian section of the book, most characters are fictional, though again – one hopes – characteristic. But of course the major Bolshevik and other political figures are real, from Kerensky to Lenin to Zinoviev to Kollantai to Trotsky to Antonov-Ovseenko to Koba (Stalin) to Martov, and so on. The remarkable family of the Alliluyevs were also real people of the Bolshevik revolution. The American, Reed, encountered late in the book is obviously John Reed, author of *Ten Days that Shook the World*. Slatkin is fictional but his story is based upon the real case of the Bolsheviks V. K. Taratula and A. M Andrikanis, who were ordered by Lenin to court and marry two heiresses to enlarge his party coffers. Trofimova, the Abrasova sisters, Federev, and other intimate associates are utterly fictional.

Sergeiv was buried beneath the wall of the Kremlin after a hero's death, which occurred some years after the events of this novel, but I would like to keep my narrative powder dry on the details, since I hope that if a handful of people have enjoyed this story, I might continue it with the adventures of Artem, Tasha Abrasova, Suvarov and Paddy Dykes through the Civil War to the tormented Russia beyond, in which Sergeiv perished.

Acknowledgements

Though they are not to be blamed for flaws in the text, I thank in most earnest terms the following enthusiastic collaborators in this book:

Silvie Smetkova, who translated many documents concerning Artem Sergeiev, who was the model for Artem Samsurov;

my agent, Fiona Inglis;

the first reader of this book in manuscript, Judy Keneally;

my publisher, Meredith Curnow;

the editor of first recourse, Jo Jarrah;

the copy-editors, Heather Curdie and Ali Lavau;

Simon Sebag Montefiore, eminent historian of Russia, who read the book for obvious solecisms.

May they all flourish.

Works to which the author owes a debt include:

V. I. Astakova, et al., *Tovarishck Artem, Vospomilia o Fedore Andreeviche Sergeive (Artem)* (Kharkov 1975)

Orlando Figes, *A People's Tragedy: The Russian Revolution 1891–1924* (London 1996)

Maxim Gorky, *My Childhood* (London 1966)

V. I. Lenin, *What is to be Done?* (Moscow 1970)

Stuart Macintyre, *The Reds* (Sydney 1998)

Simon Sebag Montefiore, *Young Stalin* (London 2007)

Vladimir Nasedkin, *Fifteen Years a World Wanderer* (Moscow 1960s)

Tom Poole and Eric Fried, *Artem: A Bolshevik in Brisbane*, including a translation of Artem's *Australia the Lucky Country*, from *Australian Journal of Politics and History*, vol. 31, no. 2 (1985)

Poole and Fried research boxes relating to Australian radicalism at the time of Sergeiev and beyond, Fryer Library, University of Queensland, including the political memoirs of Tom Pikunov, another Tsarist escapee

Christopher Read, *Lenin* (New York 2005)

John Reed, *Ten Days that Shook the World*, e-book but also New York 1962 and other editions

Robert Service, *Lenin* (London 2000)

Robert Service, *Stalin* (London 2005)

Ian Turner, *Industrial Labour and Politics* (Melbourne 1965)